HALO®
THE
THURSDAY
WAR

HALO®
THE THURSDAY WAR

KAREN TRAVISS

TOR®

A TOM DOHERTY ASSOCIATES BOOK
NEW YORK

HALO®: THE THURSDAY WAR

Edited by James Frenkel

A Tor Book
Published by Tom Doherty Associates, LLC
175 Fifth Avenue
New York, NY 10010

www.tor-forge.com

Library of Congress Cataloging-in-Publication Data

Traviss, Karen.
    Halo. The Thursday war / Karen Traviss.—1st ed.
        p. cm.
    "A Tom Doherty Associates book."
    ISBN 978-0-7653-3363-6 (hardcover)
    ISBN 978-0-7653-2394-1 (trade paperback)
    ISBN 978-1-4299-9714-0 (e-book)
    1. Imaginary wars and battles—Fiction.   2. Space warfare—Fiction.
3. Soldiers—Fiction.   4. Halo (Game)—Fiction.   5. War stories.   I. Title.
II. Title: Thursday war.
PR6120.R38H38 2012
823'.92—dc23
                                                                    2012019875

First Edition: October 2012

Printed in the United States of America

0 9 8 7 6 5 4 3 2 1

For Sam,
who always talks good Texan common sense when I need it

ACKNOWLEDGMENTS

My grateful thanks go to Frank O'Connor, franchise development director for Halo, and Kevin Grace, franchise manager for Halo, of 343 Industries; Jeremy Patenaude, franchise writer of Halo, 343 Industries, for being a walking Halo encyclopedia; Jim Gilmer, for moral support; and "Aryss SkaHara" (you know who you are) and the wonderful Russian Halo fans on Twitter for Russian language support. Bless you all.

343 Industries would like to thank Scott Dell'Osso, James Frenkel, Stacy Hill, Bryan Koski, Matt McCloskey, Whitney Ross, Bonnie Ross-Ziegler, Rob Semsey, Matt Skelton, Phil Spencer, Karen Traviss, Carla Woo, and Jennifer Yi.

None of this would have been possible without the amazing efforts of the Microsoft staffers, including: Ben Cammarano, Christine Finch, Kevin Grace, Tyler Jeffers, Carlos Naranjo, Tiffany O'Brien, Frank O'Connor, Jeremy Patenaude, Brian Reed, Corrinne Robinson, Eddie Smith, and Kiki Wolfkill.

HAL☉®
THE
THURSDAY
WAR

PROLOGUE

This job is about trouble.

Seeing trouble coming, neutralizing trouble . . . and causing trouble for others before they cause it for you.

On a day when there's no trouble, something's wrong. There's *always* trouble. You simply haven't noticed it yet, so you have to seek it out before it comes looking for you. But today's a normal day and I don't have to hunt. Captain Serin Osman has just reported in from Venezia. She's calling off the mission for the time being and breaking orbit to return to Sanghelios, because we have *trouble.*

And where's my damn coffee?

Osman's lost contact with her Sangheili language expert, Phillips. One minute he's spying happily under the noses of his Sangheili hosts, and the next there's an explosion. Now we're scrambling to find out what's happened. The Arbiter's no fool. He invited Phillips to visit. He has a reason, and if he's sane, he *has* to be suspicious of us. Yes, perhaps it's all part of genuinely wanting to build bridges with Earth, but I can't afford to assume the best. My job is about planning for the *worst,* and making sure that it happens—to Earth's enemies, anyway. My job isn't about *okay.*

The whole point of this mission, the whole raison d'être of the Kilo-Five mission, is to make things as *un*-okay for the Sangheili as we can, to keep them feuding and fighting while we re-arm and neutralize them once and for all. But we have an operative stranded there with an AI, a civilian academic, not an experienced ONI agent like Osman. So she has to extract him. I'd do the same if I were her. Venezia can wait, after all: it's been a terrorist haven since before the Covenant War, and it's not going anywhere. Besides, Mike Spenser is there. A safe pair of hands, our Mike. In this job, you handpick your people. You need the best. You need the most loyal. You need the most ruthless.

And ruthlessness and loyalty in a single human being is a rare combination to find.

So . . . where's my coffee? Don't make me beg, Dorsey. I hit the intercom. "Flag, are you still alive out there?"

"On its way, ma'am." Lieutenant Dorsey knows my routine. He's never normally this late with my morning mocha. "Sorry. I got stuck on a call."

"I'm not getting any younger, Flag."

He's a good boy. I couldn't wish for a better flag lieutenant. So the coffee is on its way. Let's take a deep breath and assess the situation.

On the plus side, we've managed to arm and foster a Sangheili insurrection, and we have both a live Sangheili prisoner and four Huragok, three of which have unique knowledge from the days of the Forerunners. With their assistance, we're extracting a treasure trove of Forerunner technology from what's left of Onyx. We've also arrested Dr. Catherine God-Almighty Halsey, who's now making herself useful by incorporating that technology into *Infinity*. Oh, I waited a long, *long* time to get her, but it was worth every minute. She will now do my bidding.

I'd call that a very productive three months' work. Wouldn't you? Excellent value for the taxpayer.

On the down side, though, Phillips is potentially in real danger, and by that token so are we. He's not been trained to resist interrogation. The AI fragment he's carrying won't be much use to the Sangheili if he's caught, but the last thing I need is for ONI's destabilization policy to become public knowledge.

And there's another fly paddling around in the ointment. There's no lid on Venezia now that the Covenant's collapsed. The rebels can come and go as they please—not just human rebels, alien malcontents too—and the black market's flooded with hardware and vessels. Everyone's dusting off their old grudges. We shall be *busy*.

But on balance . . . things could be worse. Osman's doing well: she's proving good in the field, although I hope she doesn't get a taste for it. She's my anointed, my heir, my successor. The office of CINCONI will be hers before long, and she has to fill this chair. I have to admit there's a delicious irony in having a failed Spartan head up the agency.

And Kilo-Five is shaping up, too. There's a lot to be said for a mixed bag of oddballs. A few ODSTs, a Spartan, a civilian linguist—and BB. God, I miss Black-Box, but he's where he needs to be right now. It's a strange squad. The best ones always are.

Ruthless and loyal, as I said. I *like* ruthless and loyal.

The door opens and Dorsey trots in, balancing a steaming cup and a small plate. "Here you go, ma'am," he says. "And . . . *ginger nuts.* That was the cookie you wanted, yes?"

He makes it sound like a strange perversion. He's not been in Sydney long enough to understand *biscuits.* It's hard to find ginger nuts these days. "Indeed it was," I tell him. "Perfect for dunking. I insist you try some."

"Okay, ma'am. Thank you."

There. I've metamorphosed fully from Torquemada to a grandmother foisting cookies on the youngsters. It's not just to maintain morale. This is my conscience intervening. The older I get, the more I find myself imposing affection and generosity on those around me, as if that can atone for all I've done and *not* done.

I dunk the cookie in the mocha, hold it in the hot liquid for exactly four seconds, and then remove it. *This* is perfection. Ginger nuts are baked so hard that in a few seconds they absorb just enough coffee to soften the outer layer, but not enough to make them soggy. They yield to the bite, then the interior snaps and gives up its sweet, spicy pungency. A lesser cookie would dissolve and sink to the bottom of the cup in surrender.

Have a cookie. Forget that junior officers call me *organized crime in uniform.*

I regret a great deal. I don't regret much of the dirty work I've done, but I think I do regret the SPARTAN-II program. I regret it not only because it was built on something utterly wrong, but also—mainly—because the likes of Catherine Halsey can only do what they do if the likes of me let them, knowingly or otherwise.

I should have kept a closer eye on her. I knew what she was like.

I know what *everybody's* like. That's my job.

I can remember far too much, so many things that I wish I could unsee and unhear. Life's perverse. Most people in their nineties worry about losing their memory, not about being tormented by its clarity in the small hours each sleepless night. But such is power. You get it, then you do things with it, and then you have to live with it.

I won't apologize for saving my world from terrorists and aliens. I don't owe God any explanations when the time comes. Halsey's an atheist, so she can look forward to it all being over, really *over,* one day. But I'm . . . agnostic.

And the closer to death I get, the more I'd prefer God to exist. I have some questions for him. I'm great with questions.

If he made us in his image, why didn't he make us nicer,

kinder, gentler? Or did he make us like this just to see how vile an organism we could become? What kind of god would make *us*?

Dorsey sticks his head around the door. "Are the ginger nuts okay, ma'am?" he asks.

"Glorious," I say. "*Infinity* had better have a supply of these."

(ADMIRAL MARGARET ORLENDA PARANGOSKY, COMMANDER IN CHIEF,

OFFICE OF NAVAL INTELLIGENCE, UNSC)

CHAPTER
ONE

ARBITER, I HAVE LOST HIM. THE BRUTES ARE REBELLING AND
ONTOM IS IN CHAOS.

(CADAN 'ILMIR, PILOT AND BODYGUARD TO PROFESSOR
EVAN PHILLIPS, GUEST OF THE ARBITER)

TEMPLE OF THE ABIDING TRUTH, ONTOM, SANGHELIOS:
MARCH 2553

Evan Phillips could manage only one thought: Sangheili breath
stank.

It was like waking up face to face with an old dog who'd
sneaked onto the bed, and it wasn't just the terrifying mouthful
of fangs. Avu Med 'Telcam, religious zealot and ONI-sponsored
insurgent, was kneeling right over him, staring into his eyes.
Phillips could hear a tuning fork singing deep inside his head
but the yells and roars around him were muffled, a world away.
He struggled for breath in a fog of brick dust, smoke, and something that smelled horribly like ammonia. How could he smell
all this if he couldn't breathe?

Oh, God. A bomb. I was walking into the temple, and . . .

He was walking into the temple with 'Telcam, and 'Telcam
had asked him a really awkward question about a Sangheili he
wasn't supposed to know.

Jul 'Mdama. Oh . . . shit.

And then there'd been an explosion. But Phillips's biggest
problem right then was getting his breath, followed by checking

that he had all his limbs and wasn't bleeding to death light-years from home on a planet where they wouldn't take kindly to ONI spies.

Because that's what I am now. Aren't I?

He kept trying to suck in air. His lungs felt disconnected from his brain, beyond his control, then they relented and a huge, convulsive wheeze shook him. He started coughing so hard that he almost vomited.

"I thought you were dead," 'Telcam said. He sounded irritated, as if he thought Phillips had been shamming. "Can you speak? Are you injured?"

Phillips's eyes watered painfully. "Am I bleeding?"

"Not much." 'Telcam stood up and started roaring orders, although Phillips couldn't see who he was yelling at. "Is anyone injured? Answer me! Did anyone see what happened?"

Voices called back from the gloom. "A wall has collapsed, Field Master. We're still trying to find all our brothers."

"Be quick about it." 'Telcam drew his pistol and stalked toward the outer gates. "And secure the perimeter until we find out who did this."

Who would attack the temple? It was a sensitive target, sure to cause outrage. Perhaps the Arbiter had worked out where his opposition was coming from and had launched a preemptive strike. *And I walked into the middle of it. Should have stuck with Cadan, shouldn't I? I bet he's panicking now, trying to find me in case the Arbiter shoots him for losing me.* Phillips eased himself up and tried to stand. Razor-edged rubble cut into his palms. He could hear mayhem outside in the plaza, filtered by the thick walls around the temple grounds, and the thud of Sangheili feet echoing in the passage behind him. Now that the smoke and dust were settling, he could work out exactly where he was: about twenty meters inside the temple compound, right in the ancient doorway of the Forerunner building.

Nobody seemed to be taking any notice of him. He got to his feet, tested his balance—not great, but at least he could still hear—and tottered toward the gates.

At least this had killed the conversation about Jul. Phillips hoped 'Telcam would forget he'd even asked the question, but he doubted it.

Damn, I could have died. Really died. This is getting a bit too real.

His legs were shaking. Now that he stopped to think about it, he realized he could have been killed any number of times in the past few months, but it hadn't felt quite this immediate before. How did Mal and Vaz handle it? Now he understood something at a gut level, something he didn't have words for, and suddenly the world looked different. Then he remembered.

Oh God. BB. Where the hell is he?

The AI would usually have been chatting to him in that arch, slightly bitchy way that was somehow incredibly comforting. BB knew all and saw all. He probably spoke Sangheili even better than Phillips. But now he was uncharacteristically silent.

"BB?" Phillips whispered. He peered down at the coin-sized radio with its pinprick camera lens, unable to see any indicator lights. Military comms equipment was designed to withstand all kinds of shocks, and ONI was certain to have the very best kit that money could buy. "BB, are you okay? You can come out now."

But the radio remained lifeless. Phillips took it off his jacket to examine it, and it was only when he held it right up to his eye that he saw the chunks of metal embedded in it like lead shot. It took him a few moments to think that through. The realization made his stomach knot again.

Shrapnel. That would have gone into my chest. Holy shit. So that kind of luck really happens.

He tried to focus on the luck, that a potentially fatal injury had been deflected by that little device, but it didn't keep him going long. All kinds of fears and worries were now flooding back. Cadan, the pilot the Arbiter had assigned to take him on a tour of Ontom's ancient sites, would have heard the explosion and come running to find his charge. And did Osman realize what had happened? Phillips had been transmitting right up to the moment of the blast, so she must have known his last position. But how was he going to contact her now without a radio and without BB to guide him? Damn, he'd have to find Cadan and get him to contact UNSC. Searching the temple for Forerunner clues to the locations of the other Halo rings would have to wait.

It could take me years to wheedle my way back in here. We might not have years.

He made his way through the rubble in the courtyard. Walls that had stood for millennia, built by the Forerunners themselves, had collapsed in places, giving him jagged, chaotic glimpses of the huge plaza outside. It was pandemonium. Troops were stalking around, barking orders at Sangheili who were milling about, inspecting piles of what Phillips thought was more rubble until he realized there was no masonry close enough to fall in heaps. The plaza was an open space like a parade ground.

The piles were bodies.

He stumbled out of the gates, as if the notional line between holy ground and the public space would shield him. A crater about seven or eight meters wide had gouged a scar in the elegant geometric paving. That was where the device had detonated: not in the temple grounds, but out in the plaza. Purple Sangheili blood lay in glossy pools or trickled into gutters. Phillips tried not to focus on the dead and injured. Mal and Vaz might have been used to seeing body parts, but this was all new and sickening for him. He didn't recognize some things. He made himself look away before he did.

It was sobering that even on an alien world, in a city of towering creatures with four jaws, the carnage that followed a bombing looked pretty much like any shattered street on Earth in the aftermath of a terror attack. And people were just as scared and shocked and grief-stricken.

People. Yes. They're people to me. Sorry, Vaz. I can't see them any other way now.

'Telcam stood absolutely still, fists clenched at his sides in an oddly human way. He was seething. Phillips edged up beside him.

"So . . ." Nobody seemed interested in a lone human now. An hour ago, he'd been a sensation, an unlikely little pink creature who could rapidly unlock the *arum* puzzle that left most Sangheili perplexed. "Who did it? This isn't about the temple, is it?"

'Telcam scanned the scene with a slow sweep of his head, taking in the neatly trimmed shrubs and trees that lined the plaza. Phillips thought he'd spotted something suspicious. But he curled his lips back, parting that cloverleaf set of jaws and baring his fangs in anger.

"What do you *not* see, scholar?" he asked.

Phillips wasn't back to his best yet. He tapped his radio again, hoping BB was just keeping his head down and gathering information. It took a while to check the scene and not pay too much attention to the grisly detail. A pair of Sangheili trotted past carrying something on a sheet of fabric, a makeshift stretcher. Phillips looked away.

"Sorry. What am I missing?"

"Where are the Brutes?" 'Telcam demanded. "There were Brutes working out here. They were tending the gardens. Where did they go?"

Phillips's first thought was that they'd been killed or taken away wounded. He was about to suggest that when 'Telcam caught his arm and hauled him into the plaza to inspect the scene for himself. Phillips had no choice now. He found himself looking down at a body, a male in his middle years, minus legs and part of his head. The smell—sweet, metallic, but also tinged with ammonia and sulfur—struck him more than the glistening shreds of flesh. Somehow he managed to switch off. He hadn't realized he could do that. When he looked up, 'Telcam had stalked away and was moving from casualty to casualty, grabbing troops by their shoulders and questioning them.

"Where are the Brutes?" he demanded. "Have you found any Brutes? Where did they go?"

He was right, though: the Jiralhanae had vanished. Not many had stayed with the Sangheili once the Covenant fell, but their absence was suddenly conspicuous. Phillips struggled with the idea that these might have turned on their former superiors.

'Telcam came striding back, jaws working angrily. "Not *one,*" he snarled. "Not one has remained."

"You think this is an uprising?"

"Most of the Brutes turned on us in the Great Schism."

"Yes, but lots of them just took ships and went home, too."

"You seem to have missed the point, *Philliss*." Yes, he really did make it sound like *Phyllis,* just as Vaz Beloi had said. Those extra jaws made explosive consonants hard going. "There is no affection between our species."

"Perhaps they just ran for it," Phillips said. No, he didn't believe that. A Brute had tried to take on Naomi and lost—not that he could share that with 'Telcam. "We'll find them quaking in a cellar somewhere."

"I knew we should never have tolerated them. This is the worst possible timing."

Ah, so that was his problem: not that they'd dared to kill Sangheili, something that he was preparing to do himself, but that they'd messed up his tidy insurrection.

"Yes, but how do you—"

Phillips never got to the end of the sentence. A bolt of energy hit the paving twenty meters from him, spattering him with painfully sharp grit, then another and another, bright as lightning.

He dived instinctively and hit the ground, not that it would have saved him, and another alien sensation overtook him: real fear, the absolute fear that he would die any second. His body ignored his conscious mind completely. It saved itself. He couldn't move. All he could do was listen to the crack and sizzle of energy rounds zipping past his ears. That was how close it felt. He could smell it, too, like paint burning on a hot radiator.

"Brutes!" someone yelled. "It's *Brutes*! Filthy traitors! *Kill them!*"

Boots thudded near his head. "Outrage!" one Sangheili kept shouting. "Ingrates! To think we gave you food and shelter!"

Phillips tried to turn his head, looking for somewhere to take cover. Three Sangheili were still trading shots with somebody up on the walls. Was it a Brute? He couldn't tell. He couldn't raise his head far enough to see. He just wanted the shooting to stop. He was sure he'd crap himself if he had to lie here in the open a moment longer. He was going to die alone without even BB for company. This wasn't how it was supposed to end.

Get a grip. It's seconds. Vaz told me so. You think it's going on forever, but it's only a few seconds.

There was more zip and crack as the shooting continued. Then it stopped and the echo around the walls seemed to go on forever before being swallowed up in roars and murmurs. Phillips didn't know whether to raise his head or stay down, but someone made the decision for him and hauled him upright by his collar.

'Telcam stared down at him, nostrils flaring, looking distinctly unimpressed. "Those shots were nowhere near you."

Phillips had had enough for one day. He'd been bombed and shot at. He'd seen people killed. And he was on his own a long way from home. The novelty of playing spy games was over. It was a lonely way to end up dead.

"I'm going to go and find Cadan," he said, trying to keep his voice steady. More heavily armed city militia were streaming into the plaza, arriving in all kinds of mismatched vehicles that parted the crowd. The mood had now changed from shock to anger, something Phillips was certain he could smell. "My pilot. He went to a tavern. He'll be looking for me. I need to call in to tell everyone I'm okay."

'Telcam still had a tight grip on his collar. "And then what? Go back to the Arbiter's keep?"

"That's the idea."

"That would be an unwise choice of sanctuary, and you're well aware why."

The closest that Phillips had ever been to a riot was a rowdy night in Sydney when the Aussies had won some rugby trophy and the bars had started overcrowding, then overflowing into the streets. There'd been arrests, scuffles, deafening noise, and a few moments when he was sure he was going to get his head kicked in while simply trying to hail a taxi. He'd felt just as confused and alien as he did now. Just like that night, the hundreds— maybe thousands—of Sangheili were a wall of muscle and hostility, not particularly aimed at him but still volatile and potentially lethal.

Then something distracted them. Phillips saw every head turn simultaneously before he heard the shouts of *Jir'a'ul, Jir'a'ul*— Brute, a play on the Brutes' own name for themselves and the Sangheili word for a lump of wood, *a'ul*. It was an ugly term of abuse. He could guess what was coming when a loud, communal hiss like escaping steam swept through the crowd. He'd never heard that before and wasn't even sure what it was, but the meaning was instantly clear, the kind of knowledge he'd never have gleaned in a lifetime's research in the safe comfort of his office at Wheatley University.

The crowd parted. Now Phillips could see a Brute struggling in the grip of two Sangheili troops, snarling and spitting, and the crowd closed again like a wave. The Brute's snarls were drowned by Sangheili roars. Phillips couldn't see what was happening, just the ripples of movement. It was a lynch mob. But Sangheili didn't use ropes. They were carnivores, and they fell on the Brute like a pack of dogs. Phillips let his imagination fill in the gaps. It was time to run.

"I've got to go," Phillips said. He could remember where the tavern was. He had to get out. *Jesus, BB, why pick now to break down?* "My radio's not working. I'll contact you later."

It was hard to see what was happening because he was a lot shorter than the average male Sangheili. He was a child lost in a dark forest, staring at legs and weapon belts. Then the firing started again. But it was coming from the walls: he risked looking around and now he could see a lot more Brutes with rifles. His belief in invincible Elite superiority was waning fast. Bolts of energy sizzled through the air before an explosion sent debris flying. The blast was much farther away on the north side of the plaza, but still deafening, still powerful enough for Phillips to feel it in his chest and ears.

"Oh, shit—"

"There is your answer, scholar." 'Telcam yanked him back toward the temple so hard that his arm hurt. "You'll be safe here."

"Cadan will come looking for me."

"It's too late. It must begin now."

Phillips struggled to match 'Telcam's huge stride. Somewhere at his back, all hell had broken loose. He didn't know if it was a pitched battle or just the crowd erupting in fury, but his legs had made the decision to keep moving away from the noise as fast as they could.

"What does? What's got to begin?"

'Telcam shoved him through the gate into the temple grounds. "What do you *think*? We have to bring the revolt forward, to strike before the Brutes force us to fight on another front." 'Telcam slipped into English. He was fluent, trained as an interpreter for the fleet, and it was hard to tell whether he thought that Phillips didn't understand him or if he'd switched languages for some other reason. "*Cowards.* Utter cowards. Why do they plant bombs? This is a filthy, sly habit they have learned from you humans. *Terrorism.* That is the word, yes?"

That was the whole point of being here: Phillips had known the unspoken deal with ONI from the start. He wasn't here to study the Sangheili or build bridges with them. ONI's mission was to crush them before they regained their military strength, and he was the one man who could talk to them and gain their trust because he was so *harmless.* He felt like a complete bastard. But then he thought of billions of dead humans, and Sydney in flames, and talked himself back into knowing which side he had to be on.

Terrorism. That's the word, 'Telcam. We're all doing it, one way or another. It's just semantics. I'm good at that.

"It works, though," Phillips said, catching his breath. He could still hear the rioting but the walls muffled the sounds, creating an illusion of safety. "Efficient. Cheap. You can keep it up for years. You could learn a lot from us monkeys."

Phillips was only saying what was factually true, and playing the game of planting a suggestion that 'Telcam might follow to the benefit of Earth, but the monk rounded on him as if it was blasphemy.

"No!" For a moment Phillips thought he was going to shake him like a badly behaved child. "That is *not* war! There is a line between catching the enemy off guard and being too cowardly to show yourself. *I will not cross it.* It defiles us. We fight for faith, *Philliss*, we fight to restore what we were, to come close to knowing the gods' intent for us again—not to make them shun us in disgust."

Phillips had never really got used to rules of engagement. He wasn't going to debate about them now. 'Telcam strode back into the temple lobby, pushing Phillips ahead of him. Monk-warriors and former Sangheili soldiers who'd found themselves purposeless in what was to them a sudden, catastrophic peace were already sweeping up the blast damage and fortifying the temple again.

How could he get word back to Osman that he was okay? He had nothing with him except a broken radio—not even a change of underwear. He was sitting in the middle of an unfolding civil war, clueless and alone. He might be back on board *Port Stanley* in a few days, or still hiding in tunnels months from now.

Or he might have been counting down the days to his death.

Suddenly he realized he felt more real, more alive, more *relevant* than he ever had in his life. The thrill of it ambushed him. It wasn't fun, but the adrenaline had ebbed and the paralyzing fear had been replaced with an extreme focus. He *liked* this new feeling. It was sharp, bright, and intense. Everything—sound, color, smell, every sensation in his body—was vivid and minutely detailed.

Maybe this was what kept his UNSC buddies going. He understood them a lot better now. If he played his cards right, he might live to swap this tale with them over a beer.

'Telcam walked up to a table that had just been set upright again and slammed his fist down on it to get attention. Everyone stopped and listened.

"Brothers," he boomed. "This is the work of the Brutes. An irrelevance. An annoyance. Are we all fit to fight?"

"We are, Field Master."

"Are we set on our path? Does anyone wish to step back from the war to come?"

'Telcam was a monk who still believed in the Forerunners as gods, even if the San'Shyuum had been discredited as false prophets. But he also had a pragmatic political streak. Phillips had started to think of him as medieval Pope material, a Borgia of a creature, both ruthless commander and devout bishop. The Sangheili was playing a bit of both now. He looked from face to face as if he was searching out the waverers before devouring them. Nobody twitched.

"Are we ready to launch our assault?"

"Close, Field Master. Very close."

'Telcam hit the table again. Dust jumped. So did Phillips.

"Then that is close enough. Ignore the Brutes. Kill any that get in the way, but focus on the main objective." He turned his head slowly from side to side to take in the whole room, suddenly seeming more like a swaying cobra. "The assault on Vadam must begin *now.*"

UNSC INTELLIGENCE SAFE HOUSE, NEW TYNE, VENEZIA: MARCH 2553

Me and my big mouth.

As soon as Vaz Beloi said the name *Naomi,* he knew he'd regret it. But he couldn't stop himself. He just wasn't expecting to scroll through mug shots of Venezia's resident undesirables and see her father's face looking out from the rogues' gallery.

Staffan Sentzke. Terror suspect. Colonial insurgent. Ready to take a pop at Earth any chance he gets.

Sentzke was the one conspiracy theorist in a million who was actually *right*. His long-lost daughter really was alive and the child the police had brought back to him was an impostor, just like he'd claimed. He didn't know she was a Spartan, though. And Naomi didn't know he hadn't been killed when Sansar was glassed by the Covenant. Vaz sat staring at the datapad, wondering where the hell he'd start explaining this escalating disaster to her—or anybody else, for that matter. He'd thought ONI had finally done the decent thing by letting the Spartans know about the families they'd been snatched from as kids and brainwashed to forget, but now it didn't look decent at all. It looked agonizingly messy. There'd be no happy endings and no healing reunions, not for any of them.

Maybe she's better off never knowing where she came from.

But it was too late for that. Naomi knew, and now he and the two men peering over his shoulder knew a lot more. Vaz craned his neck to look up at Mal Geffen for a reaction. Mal wasn't just his friend. He was his sergeant, too, and—Vaz had to admit it—a lot calmer when it came to these kinds of situations. He didn't get angry. Vaz did.

Mal just let out a long breath, hands still braced on the back of the sofa as he leaned over Vaz. The basement was a scruffy jumble of old furniture and high-tech comms equipment, with the dead, musty, muffled silence of a soundproofed room. It swallowed every breath and creak.

"Well, bugger me," Mal said quietly. "Small world, eh?"

Mike Spenser, the veteran intelligence agent who'd been posted here, frowned in that hang-on-a-minute kind of way that said he'd put two and two together and had come up with an embarrassing answer. Vaz was never sure how much Spenser had been told about anything. He was military intelligence, but he wasn't ONI, and ONI was a law unto itself even in the intelligence world. As far as Vaz knew, Spenser hadn't even been briefed about Kilo-Five's mission to destabilize the Sangheili state. Just because they were all on the same side didn't mean they could share information.

I shouldn't have said Naomi. *Jesus, what was I thinking?*

"You don't mean *Naomi* Naomi, do you?" Spenser asked at last. If anything, he sounded bored, and that had to be an act. "*Spartan* Naomi? The Valkyrie?"

Spenser wasn't the kind of guy to forget a name, and he certainly wouldn't have forgotten Naomi. She was at least two meters tall, so pale that Vaz still wasn't sure if she was platinum blond or silver-gray. She could take down an Elite or a Brute with her bare hands, and Vaz had seen her do both without breaking a sweat. She was what a human could become if you took the smartest and strongest, and pumped them up with gene therapy, ceramic bone implants, and the most intensive military training the UNSC could offer.

Provided you did all that while they were still little kids, of course. That was the heart of the problem as far as Vaz was concerned. It was a recipe for retribution. And he knew that day had come.

"Yes. *Naomi* Naomi. Spartan-Zero-One-Zero." Vaz stood up and handed the datapad to Mal. There was a certain wisdom to stopping digging when you were in a hole, but that would only make Spenser more curious now. "That's her real name. Naomi Sentzke. I've seen her file."

Spenser nodded, still pretty relaxed. "Yeah, I wondered when all that crap would come out." He didn't elaborate on what he meant by *crap* and Vaz didn't know how to ask without revealing anything. The dirty details of the Spartan program had certainly come as a shock to the marines. "I can see the resemblance now. That *boiled* look. You think he knows? It would explain his attitude to Earth."

"He worked out some of it." Mal narrowed his eyes a fraction. "You know how they recruited for the Spartan program?"

"I didn't *need* to know. But I do know some operatives declined to take part in the recruitment. I'm being heavy on the euphemism there."

"What happened to them?"

"What do you think? This is ONI we're talking about, not an animal shelter. ONI really *does* put healthy dogs down."

Vaz tried not to dwell on that. Mal missed a beat, but only one.

"So you know they took kids," he said.

"I do now."

"Oh." Mal blinked a couple of times, finally caught out. "We never learn, do we?"

"Ah, come on. You're ODST. Honest marines. Just stick to low-orbit jumps and shooting things. You'll sleep better." Spenser sloshed the dregs of his coffee around his mug, then took the datapad back from Mal. "The question is whether Sentzke knows. Or whether *she* does."

"She knows who her real family is," Vaz said. *Do we tell her? Do we* not *tell her? Do we tell her before we tell Captain Osman? What the hell's right?* "But this will be news to her."

Spenser shook his head, slowly and ruefully. "We're going to miss the Covenant. Nice simple stuff. One jaw, good. Four jaws, bad."

"Are you going to call this in, Mike?" Mal asked.

"No, because you're going to do it. Aren't you?"

Vaz wasn't sure how to take that. There was another awkward silence. He could feel the vibration of traffic from the main road. Beyond these walls, old enemies were picking up where they'd left off before the Covenant had arrived and interrupted the long-running war between humans. Venezia had always been a haven for criminals and assorted outlaws. Now it was open house for any species with an axe to grind with its government, but that suddenly seemed a much more theoretical problem than facing Naomi.

Naomi *had* to be told, one way or another, and Vaz would do it. She'd make a big show of being completely above all the personal loyalty stuff, maybe even want to arrest her dad to prove she put her duty first, just like the way she'd reacted to Halsey. That didn't mean it wouldn't hurt her. Spenser was right: killing hinge-heads had been a blissfully simple kind of war. It had never left Vaz feeling dirty.

"Devereaux here, guys," said a voice in his earpiece. "I need you both back here pronto. Osman's banging out."

Mal's head jerked around. "What's the problem?"

"We've got an incident on Sanghelios. We've lost contact with Phillips."

"Christ, that's all we need. Is this going to be an extraction?"

"Possibly. Now means now, Mal. Move it."

Spenser watched the exchange with mild interest, unable to hear the other side of the conversation. "Is that Oz?"

"Devereaux," Mal said. "Change of plan. We need to get back to the ship."

"Well, I'd better drop you off, then, hadn't I? Spenser Cabs. We never close." Spenser began switching off the various screens and monitors in the shuttered basement. He didn't ask for details. "When are you coming back?"

"I'll tell you when they tell us."

"Never mind. I'll keep the scumbags warm while you're gone."

Spenser had a hell of a lot of security devices to activate before he finally locked the front door behind him. There was no such thing in New Tyne as neighbors who minded their own business. Vaz slid into the backseat of the pickup and tried to look normal for Venezia, which actually seemed easier than fitting in on Earth. Everybody here looked what Mal called *dodgy*, so Vaz felt that the scar across his jaw came in handy. Nobody would work out that he got it trying to tackle a hinge-head. It looked like the outcome of a bar brawl with a knife. He hoped it would deter the curious.

"Do me a favor, Mike." Mal slid into the passenger seat with his carbine half-hidden under his jacket, finger inside the trigger guard. "Hang fire on Sentzke until we get back."

"Wouldn't dream of shooting him without your permission."

"Seriously. This is going to be awkward."

"I'll bet."

Spenser started the engine and headed for the highway. The ancient Warthog eased into the traffic, weaving slowly around trucks until it pulled up at the stoplight in the city center.

Vaz risked looking at the vehicle idling in the next lane. The driver was a Kig-Yar. The assortment of species living side by side on Venezia was the only sign that this wasn't a regular colony, not that Vaz had ever seen one of those. By the time he got to a colony world, it was usually smoking ruins or a glassy sheet of vitrified soil. The war with the Covenant had started long before he'd enlisted, and he was an Earth boy.

"Ugly bastards," Mal muttered. The Kig-Yar turned its malevolent heron gaze toward him like it had heard him, but it was just checking the traffic. "You know how long it took me to get the smell off my hands the last time I picked up a dead one?"

"You know how long it took me to build up a working relationship with the ones you shot?"

"Sorry about that."

"They've still got a *mev-ut* out on you two for that. You know what that is, I hope."

"Yeah, Phillips did explain. A cash bonus for bringing back our skulls and cervical vertebrae. We're collector's items."

Mal must have been more worried about Phillips than Vaz

thought. Silence meant he was thinking about a bad situation: swaggering humor meant he was trying *not* to think about it. Phillips was a clever guy with plenty of guts, but he wasn't trained for these kinds of situations, and Vaz could only imagine what a hinge-head could beat out of him given enough time and a big stick.

But they don't trust us anyway. You can't suddenly start trusting an enemy after you've been at war for that long. No, it's not about exposing ONI. It's what they'll do to Phillips.

Phillips had a fragment of BB with him, at least, and BB could always think his way out of a tight spot. But the fragment had orders to activate a lethal injection if Phillips found himself with no other way out. Vaz had lost a lot of comrades over the years and had always suspected that one day his last bullet might be best saved for himself, but the thought of having to put a buddy out of his misery was more than he could cope with right then. Maybe BB would find it easier.

"You okay, Vaz?" Spenser asked. "You don't look too happy."

"This is Russian elation," Vaz said. "You should see me when I'm miserable."

Spenser made a noise in his throat that might have been a laugh. There was a trick to driving a 'hog in a don't-mind-me kind of way and he seemed to have it. Vaz noted that the old pickup variant had exactly the same degree of denting and neglect that most of the other vehicles here did, no more and no less, so that it simply merged into the cityscape. Spenser was driving briskly, not breakneck fast but not hanging about either, and clearly watching everything around him without looking as if he was staring at anything at all. He simply moved his gaze, casually scanning from side to side and occasionally checking in the mirrors, making it look perfectly normal. Vaz noted the technique. He decided he might need it one day. Spenser had probably been a spook for thirty years, and a guy didn't get to survive covert operations behind enemy lines for that long without exceptional skills.

Am I ever going to get used to this kind of war?

Spenser had known a time when the only enemy was other humans. Vaz hadn't. Neither had Mal. Vaz wondered how hard it would be to fire on his own species.

The buildings thinned out from offices and stores to houses, and then melted into open land. Less than thirty minutes after receiving the recall they were grinding through scrubland on a dirt road, heading for the RV with Devereaux. The ONI dropship—not just any old Pelican, but a stealth variant—was laid up in a wooded gorge, out of sight of passing ships or vehicles. Stealth didn't mean invisible to the naked eye. Mal fiddled with his radio and Vaz caught a microburst of signal in his earpiece. Not that Devereaux needed a signal to start the engines: Vaz could already hear the faint whine of drives even before Spenser came to a halt.

Spenser stopped under the cover of trees. He had to live here, after all. "I'll wait until you're clear," he said. "Just in case."

Mal slapped him on the shoulder and jumped down from the passenger seat without a word. Vaz hadn't even secured the dropship's door before Devereaux started to lift. She skimmed along the top of the gorge, putting as much distance between herself and New Tyne as possible before she had to hit the throttle and make the final fast climb out of the atmosphere. Vaz watched tops of trees streak past the cockpit windshield, worryingly close.

Mal stuck his head through the cockpit hatch, squeezing Vaz out of the way. "You got a sitrep, Dev? How bad is it?"

"How bad do you want? Phillips ran into 'Telcam, and 'Telcam asked him what he knew about Jul 'Mdama."

"Oh, Christ. So our cover's blown."

"No idea. There was an explosion, and the last thing Osman heard over the radio was 'Telcam telling Phillips that it wasn't them, whatever that means." Devereaux paused and the drop-ship suddenly shot up almost vertically, making Vaz grab for a handrail. He should have buckled in. "Then she lost the signal."

That was what came of playing a double game—a treble game, in fact, smiling at the Arbiter while arming the religious zealots who wanted to overthrow him, as well as kidnapping one of the rebels who happened to get in the way. Well, ONI had certainly succeeded in keeping Sanghelios off balance. That was what Parangosky wanted: to kick the hinge-heads while they were down, to kick them so hard that they could never get up and bother Earth again. Vaz didn't have a problem with that. He was just finding it *tangled*.

The patch of sky framed in the cockpit screen faded from blue to violet to black. They were clear of the planet now. Devereaux turned the shuttle over to the onboard AI with a tap on the console. She didn't look back over her seat.

"He'll be okay, Dev," Mal said.

She sounded a little hoarse. "Yeah."

Her tone was resigned. Vaz realized he hadn't picked up something that Mal already had. So Devereaux was fond of Phillips. It wasn't until Vaz heard that slight crack in her voice that he realized it was more than a comradely concern for his safety.

"I mean it, Lian." Mal's voice dropped to firm, quiet reassurance, the first time Vaz had heard him call Devereaux by her actual name. There was a rock-solid fatherly certainty about him now. "He'll make it. He can talk his way out of anything in three alien languages. Chin up, kid."

Devereaux just nodded. Somewhere in the glittering black void, the ONI corvette *Port Stanley* lurked with an impatient captain, a Spartan who was about to get more bad news after a very bad week, and an AI who'd lost part of himself along with

Phillips. On the console, the navigation plot showed the ship as a delicate green mesh of light.

"So how was your day?" Devereaux seemed to be making an effort to be her chirpy self again. "Track down any bad guys?"

It was hard to answer. As Kilo-Five's commanding officer, Osman should have been told first, but then Naomi had the moral right to know before anyone else. On the other hand, Devereaux was ODST, 10th battalion, one of their own, and Vaz didn't like keeping fellow marines in the dark even for a few hours. He struggled with the news. Mal didn't step in to help him out.

"We did," Vaz said at last. "And it's complicated."

HANGAR DECK, UNSC *PORT STANLEY:* VENEZIA ORBIT

Pain was a strange sensation when you didn't have a body.

BB was an entity of pure thought, beyond the reach of aches and injuries, but now he realized what a traumatic amputation felt like. He'd been integrated with his fragment while it was stored in Phillips's radio cam. Then there'd been an explosion. The link had been cut. And it *hurt.*

That was the only way he could describe it. It was the interruption of his thought processes, unpleasant, disorienting, and lingering. He felt something of him was missing and gone forever.

But I'm used to splitting off fragments and closing contact with them. I've got a fragment wandering around Bravo-6 in Sydney, too, and I'm out of touch with that all the time. I could split off a dozen more, no problem. This feels different.

He'd been inserted into Naomi's neural implant just once, plugged into her nervous system in combat, so he knew what stress and adrenaline felt like to a human. Perhaps that was the cause of this. He was identifying too much with flesh and blood.

His existence, his body, was input and data: suddenly pulling the plug was like having a chunk of him ripped away, leaving him in shock.

And thought is all I am. It's my blood. Data is my existence, like breathing. Without it, I'm dead.

It was also worrying to imagine what might have shut down the radio. Just a blast? Surely not. ONI kit was far more robust than that. Radios even went on functioning when their owner stepped on a mine.

Well, there's only one way to find out . . .

BB was spread around *Port Stanley*'s systems, performing billions of operations a second and monitoring events light-years beyond the ship. Each sensor was his eyes, ears, nose, and fingertips, but he could detect and interpret inputs far beyond a human's senses. He knew more than any individual man ever would. Uncertainty was a new and disturbing experience for him.

Curiosity is wonderful. Ignorance . . . isn't.

"*Tart-Cart* to *Port Stanley*—put the kettle on, BB. ETA four minutes." That was Devereaux, forcing cheerfulness but betrayed by the slight rise in the pitch of her voice. BB knew the dropship's position to ten centimeters and exactly when he'd need to seal the interior bulkheads and activate the hangar doors. He wasn't the only one struggling, then. "Any news?"

"No." BB could hear a conversation going on behind Devereaux, just broken snatches while she was transmitting, and too quiet for human ears to pick up. "Contacting the Arbiter's people requires some diplomacy."

"Oh," Devereaux said.

Mal and Vaz were arguing. BB could detect the changes in frequency that indicated clenched jaw muscles and more rapid breathing. BB caught half a phrase from Vaz, his Russian accent more pronounced, which meant he was angry: *—mi, then I will.* "Okay, then. *Tart-Cart* out."

BB was linked only to the dropship's onboard nav now, talking machine to machine. While he monitored and adjusted its flight path, he speculated on what the rest of that overheard sentence was, and what had preceded it.

Mi. Nao . . . mi. "Then I will" . . . usually preceded by "If you don't."

So if Mal didn't do something regarding Naomi, then Vaz would. Do what? Ask her something, tell her something, give her something? The last crisis before the Venezia mission was unsealing Naomi's personnel file—ghastly stuff, details that would disturb any woman, even one who'd been trained and engineered to cope with traumas that would floor a regular human. It had to be something left over from that. Naomi had asked Vaz to read her file and break the bad news to her, so he was best placed to make the decision on what to tell her and when. Yes, that was what it was all about. BB decided to keep an eye on things and make sure everyone was okay—or as okay as they could be under the circumstances.

It was probably an authority thing. Mal was a staff sergeant; Vaz was a corporal. Vaz also had an inflexible moral streak, the sort that got him into arguments in a political world full of very gray areas.

I wonder if I'll ever regret stopping him from shooting Halsey?

The bulkhead warning lights flashed, the seals engaged, and the aft section of the hangar opened to the vacuum as the dropship maneuvered into position. Voice comms were still disabled. Ah, so they were still arguing. They knew BB heard and saw everything. That was why they'd once resorted to hiding under a cargo crate and communicating in silence. He thought they'd got over that by now and had started to trust him, so this had to be rather more serious.

"Come along, chop chop," BB said. "Osman's waiting to slip.

We don't want poor Phillips to have to sit through the Arbiter's home movies any longer than he has to, do we?"

Tart-Cart powered down. The deck clamps snapped into place on her landing gear and the hangar repressurized as the doors sealed shut. The starboard side hatch opened. BB caught the tail end of the argument before the ODSTs jumped out.

"It's got to be *her* first," Mal said.

"And what if *she* finds out? This is about trust."

"And what if she goes mental about it? Did you consider that?"

"Then let her go *mental.*"

"This is what OPs are for."

Devereaux interrupted. "Hey, how about buttoning it?"

The three ODSTs walked away from *Tart-Cart* with their jaws set. BB projected his blue-lit hologram right in front of them as they jogged up to the metal steps leading to the gantry. He manifested as a box, plain and unadorned, because that was how he thought of himself: not a surrogate human, but a black box, a complex and unknowable machine behind a featureless facade.

"Everything all right?" he asked. *Because it's not all right with me.* He wasn't used to being cut out of the comms loops on missions, and now there were *two* blank spots in a memory that was built to know and retain everything. "You need a shave."

Mal glanced at Devereaux. "Yeah, Dev, ditch the mustache. Come on, BB. Out of the way."

"I've missed you, too."

Mal seemed anxious to change the subject. Vaz went silent, jaw twitching with unspoken objections. BB drifted ahead of them as they clattered along the passages to the bridge.

"What happened to your fragment?" Mal asked.

"I don't know. I went down at the same time Phillips did."

"You don't sound right, BB."

"It's not a pleasant sensation."

Mal slowed down and looked at him as he might have looked at Vaz. Organics needed to make eye contact. There were times when BB had considered relenting and projecting some kind of basic face, eyes and a mouth at least, to make humans more comfortable. But that wasn't who he was, and right now he felt a desperate urge to cling to his own sense of self. The squad had managed to cope with his box facade so far.

"Did it hurt?" Mal asked.

That was perceptive of him. "Yes."

"You're an honorary ODST, then. You've got a scar—you're in. Vaz has got one, Dev's got one, I've got one . . ."

"Yeah, he was shot in his ass while he was talking through it," Devereaux said. "Come on, we should be worrying about Phillips."

That was exactly what they all seemed to be doing in that mock-aggressive ODST sort of way. Osman was on the bridge with Naomi, leaning back in her seat with her fingers digging into the armrests in anticipation of the jump into slipspace. She hated it. Naomi sat at the nav console in her UNSC fatigues, a monument to stoic indifference. It didn't fool anyone and BB suspected she knew that all too well.

Osman glanced over her shoulder. "Okay, time to burn and turn. BB, spin us up. How did it go, Staff?"

"We'll brief you when you've got five minutes, ma'am," Mal said, settling into his seat for the jump. Vaz shot him a slow I'll-get-you-for-that look. "So what's the plan?"

"Well, by the time we reach Sanghelios, Phillips might have surfaced again. But let's assume he hasn't. It might not be easy to get down to the surface and find him, but I'd rather be there than here."

"We're up for anything, ma'am."

"I know. I've asked the Admiral to enlist Hood's help, too." Osman shut her eyes for a moment. It was probably more about steeling her stomach for the jump than despairing about things going wrong. "We're giving them enough time to realize he's in trouble before we tell them we've noticed. Not that the Arbiter won't assume we've got our ways and means to stay in touch with him."

BB was reaching the end of the countdown. He ran a last-minute comms scan to make sure there were no messages waiting before the jump put *Stanley* out of comms contact, and took a sitrep from his fragment in Bravo-6, UNSC's Sydney headquarters. It was keeping an eye on the other ONI officers and AIs at HQ. Everyone knew by now that Osman was Parangosky's choice to succeed her when she finally retired as CINCONI, but that didn't stop rivals jockeying pointlessly for position while her back was turned. BB kept watch.

All seemed quiet: everything was under control, even Captain Hogarth and his irritating AI, Harriet. There was also an interesting update from Parangosky on the initial findings from the Forerunner technology discovered in the Dyson sphere. He'd pass that to Osman for leisurely reading later.

"Eight seconds, boys and girls." BB read the report while he timed the jump. The Huragok were already adapting Forerunner tech for *Infinity.* The nav systems that Halsey had discovered on Onyx could control a ship's exit from slipspace so accurately that they could predict exactly where and when it would emerge—no more jumping and hoping, then. Perhaps *Stanley* would get that retrofit next. "We're going to test the drives' theoretical maximum. Enjoy."

Osman let go of the armrests and clasped her hands in her lap. BB released the drive inhibitor. The corvette punched instantly into slipspace and the stars in *Stanley*'s forward viewscreen streaked into white lines, then vanished, leaving a truly black and featureless void. Osman sat staring at the absence of a view for a few moments.

"Okay," she said. "We know where Phillips was, and we've got enough positioning data from him to map the immediate area. BB, I want a projection we can start planning with if we have to insert and go looking for him."

"It's going to be hard to do that covertly in a city, ma'am," Vaz said.

"We might not need to do it." She stood up, but BB noticed her put a carefully casual hand on the back of the seat to steady herself. She took a few minutes to recover from a jump. "So what's happening on Venezia, Staff?"

Mal's heart rate jumped, and so did Vaz's. BB could detect that simply by micro-measuring the visible pulse in their necks. These were men who didn't even sweat when they jumped from orbit straight onto the battlefield with just a coffin-sized pod between them and hard vacuum. He couldn't imagine what Venezia could do to rattle that composure.

"Ma'am," Mal said, "we've got a unique problem."

"That's an unusual word for you, Staff."

"It's an unusual situation."

"Just tell me they've not acquired orbital nukes."

"I think Spenser would have mentioned that, but we've got a complication that . . . well, it's something I think Naomi needs to hear as well."

Osman didn't even blink. "Is it something *I* need to hear?"

"Oh yes."

"Like I've said before—we've got no secrets in Kilo-Five. We've got to trust each other to do this kind of job."

Mal half-turned to Naomi and hesitated, one of those short human pauses that was an eternity for an AI. BB was used to knowing what was coming next: he thought far faster than a human and his awareness was literally everywhere at once. But he had no idea where this was leading, and it both scared and thrilled him. *Information.* It was an AI's addiction.

But Vaz got there first. He didn't seem to relish that.

"Naomi," he said. "Your father's still alive. He's on Venezia."

BB wasn't expecting that at all. It shocked him, not because her home planet had been glassed long ago, but because he didn't know already. How had he missed that? He knew her real background, the backgrounds of all the Spartan-IIs. Somehow he'd overlooked something. He took five nanoseconds to trawl through all his databases again, every casualty list, every criminal record, every census, and still came up blank on Sentzke. Now all he could do was observe Naomi and study her reaction.

She was getting better at dealing with bad news. Like the ODSTs, she didn't turn a hair at operational surprises, but personal matters caught her off balance. She'd hold her breath and almost freeze for a second, then gather herself and look impassive again. She was doing that now.

"I don't know if I even remember him," she said at last. "How come he survived? And why is he on Venezia?"

So *this* was what Vaz insisted he'd do if Mal didn't. He was going to tell her about her father. BB could see from the muscles twitching in Vaz's temples that the worst was still to come.

"He's part of the anti-Earth rebellion," Vaz said. "He's on the terrorist watch list, Naomi."

CHAPTER

TWO

I SHOULD HAVE THOUGHT OF THIS BEFORE, BUT WHAT DO SANGHEILI EAT? I DON'T MEAN NUTRITION. WE KNOW THEIR PHYSIOLOGY WELL ENOUGH NOW TO KNOW HOW TO KEEP THEM ALIVE. I MEAN THE CULTURAL ELEMENT IN THIS— WHICH DISHES COMFORT THEM? WHAT REMINDS THEM OF HOME AND CHILDHOOD? DON'T THINK I'M GOING SOFT. I HAVE MY REASONS FOR ASKING.

(DR. IRENA MAGNUSSON, ONI RESEARCH FACILITY TREVELYAN, TO COLLATION SERVICES, OFFICE OF NAVAL INTELLIGENCE)

ADMIRALS' INSPECTION, UNSC *INFINITY:*
SOMEWHERE IN THE OORT CLOUD

Parangosky could tell everything about a warship from those first few unplanned, unguarded moments when she deviated from the inspection plan and wandered off on her own.

"Ma'am? The command bridge is *this* way." The young petty officer came trotting after her as she peeled off down an unlit passage in the opposite direction. "It's easy to get lost in *Infinity.* She's nearly six kilometers long, and—"

Parangosky carried on walking and held up her datapad like a security pass. "I know, Richardson, I've got the blueprints. I'll be fine. Worry about Admiral Hood."

"You're going to want to take a supply trolley, then, ma'am. The deck transit system's going to be down for a few hours and it takes forever to walk around. Hang on."

He had a point. She stopped, leaning on her cane until she heard a small vehicle whir up the passage and stop just behind her. It looked like a narrower version of a golf buggy. Richardson jumped down from the seat and held out his hand to help her climb on, a perfect little gentleman.

"Thank you, Petty Officer," she said, giving him a wink. "Now go and put a collar and lead on Admiral Hood. We don't want him getting into mischief, do we?"

Richardson took the hint. She heard his boots fading behind her, listened to make sure he wasn't warning the engineering crew that she was heading their way, and started the buggy. If she'd read the deck plan correctly, she was heading for the engineering section at the stern, in the opposite direction to the command bridge located amidships. The Huragok would be there and nobody was expecting her. *Least of all Catherine Halsey.* A scientist who didn't exist on a ship that didn't exist: Parangosky could keep Halsey declared dead and out of contact with all but *Infinity*'s handpicked crew for as long as she liked.

Infinity had swallowed so much of the UNSC budget that Parangosky had to cooperate with Fleet and accept joint control. No wonder this ship cost so much. She could see it all around her. Every scrap of Forerunner technology that they'd recovered over the years had gone into *Infinity.* The ship should have been ready to deploy by now, but then something akin to a miracle had happened: Onyx had yielded a treasure trove of even more advanced Forerunner technology that the artificial world had held hidden.

It made tolerating Halsey a few years longer worth the pain. No hijack and escape to Onyx—no game-changing refinements for *Infinity,* or the Huragok to install and maintain them. The greatly improved drive speed and accuracy of slipspace navigation were just the first things plucked from the Dyson sphere's cache. There was no telling what other tactical advantages were still waiting for the Trevelyan crew to unearth.

An excellent result. Just what we needed. But you're still in permanent detention, Catherine. Because I say so.

The buggy gave Parangosky her own unexpected tactical advantage. Nobody would hear her distinctive gait and the tap of her cane. She rode down the passage toward a faint glow of light, a little too much like a vision of fading, tunneled consciousness for her liking. She shook it off, daring death to interfere with her plans, then checked her datapad for the latest on Phillips. Osman was on her way to Sanghelios; there was no official word from the Arbiter yet. Parangosky couldn't simply call him and ask if there was anything he wanted to tell her—not yet, anyway.

My responsibility. My idea to co-opt Phillips for the mission. So now's the time to see if it can actually present us with an opportunity.

She drove past sealed doors and hatches bearing temporary warning signs like CABLING OUT and SAFETY GEAR MUST BE WORN. A ship in refit was a dangerous environment. The lights at the end of the passage gradually resolved into detail, picking out long horizontal runs of titanium conduit. Then she caught a glimpse of something delicate, translucent, shimmering with points of soft lilac and rose lights, floating away in an instant like an apparition.

As hard-hats went, Huragok were extraordinarily pretty.

Parangosky slowed down. As she reached the next deck flat, a square-shouldered figure appeared silhouetted in the brightly lit doorway ahead. A couple of crewmen walked across from an adjacent compartment and squeezed past him with a cursory glance. He wasn't their focus.

And that tells me everything. Not that I didn't already know.

"Ma'am, you should have called ahead." It was Andrew Del Rio, wearing his captain's best blues. He wasn't a sleeves-up kind of CO. "I've got coffee and cakes laid on for you on the command bridge."

Del Rio wasn't her choice of captain for *Infinity*. She'd learned to pick her battles and had conceded that one, but she felt vindicated by observing his crew's body language. He was just something filling the uniform, a manager rather than a leader. They weren't in awe of him and they weren't devoted to him. She could tell. She'd seen the way crews looked at charismatic commanders, a real snap-to-it kind of willingness to please, very aware of the man—or woman—when they were around. Del Rio would be obeyed, and perhaps even respected for his fairness, but he would never be loved or gladly died for. He didn't have the Nelson touch.

But that was fine by her. His first officer was Lasky. Tom Lasky deserved better than to play bagman to Del Rio, but this was where Parangosky needed him to be, and XOs had control over the things that most concerned her. She'd see that Lasky got a reward for his quiet patience later.

"I know I'm not where I should be," Parangosky said, easing herself off the buggy. Del Rio didn't rush to help her. She wondered if it hadn't even crossed his mind or if he was too scared of her to remind her she was old and finally wearing out. "I've come to see our little friends. How are they doing?"

"Breeding, ma'am." Del Rio stood back and ushered her into one of the engine management compartments. "We've got three more. Yes, I know they don't breed in the technical sense, but they certainly replicate and teach the offspring."

"Well, it's definitely a happy event." Huragok shared all their information, whether by contact or by creating progeny. "A synthesis of all the technical expertise of the Covenant *and* the Forerunners. I'd call that an edge and a half."

Parangosky counted seven Huragok drifting around the compartment, all utterly absorbed with modifying the controls. Their tentacles fascinated her. The tiny cilia on the tips were a blur as they worked, like flagella on microscopic protozoa. The panel they were working on changed right before her eyes, rebuilt molecule by molecule at astonishing speed. *Infinity* might have been the most advanced warship since the Forerunner fleet, but these oddly endearing organic computers were ONI's real prize. One of them—Requires Adjustment, nicknamed Adj by BB— had been snatched from Covenant service. The others were straight from the Dyson sphere, repositories of the original Forerunner technology and cut off from all external contact for millennia, and the Covenant certainly didn't have anything like *that*.

Now we can crush the Sangheili. And they'll stay crushed.

It was hard to tell one Huragok from another. Parangosky approached the creature closest to her, unsure whether to reach out and touch it to get its attention. In some ways they were like autistic children fixated on their task, but she'd had glimpses into their personalities. They could be gently but stubbornly assertive. Gossip originating from the Spartan-IIIs said that back in the Dyson sphere, one had actually smacked Halsey for interfering with his work. Parangosky knew that urge only too well.

She held up her datapad so that the Huragok nearest to her could see the screen. The creatures used sign language. So she would, too. Courtesy cost nothing but bought a great deal.

"Are you Perfect Density?" she asked.

Her screen translated the words into a flurry of tentacle gestures, courtesy of custom-made software from BB. The Huragok turned its little multi-eyed armadillo head to peer at her, then gestured back.

<*I am Adj,*> he signed. The words were relayed to her as audio. <*And I hear and understand your language, even if you cannot speak mine.*>

Parangosky lowered her datapad. So he thought of himself as Adj now. Del Rio watched, arms folded, then seemed distracted by something at the other end of the compartment. Parangosky kept one eye on him as he walked over to a hatch in the deck and peered down.

"My apologies, Adj," she said. In her peripheral vision, she watched Lasky climb up from the hatch on the far side of the compartment to join Del Rio. "How are you?"

<*I am very content,*> Adj signed. <*I have new knowledge and great purpose. Where is BB? Where are the marines?*>

It was an interesting question. "They're all on a mission. Do you miss them?"

<*There was much I could have done for their ship. All left undone.*>

Yes, in his obsessive Huragok way, he missed them. Adj would have been a useful resource for Osman. *One day, we'll have Huragok in every ship. And then we'll end up putting explosive collars on them just like the Brutes did, in case they fall into enemy hands. They still lose.* Del Rio could probably spare a couple of his Huragok for Osman in due course. Parangosky would see to it.

"Perhaps we can arrange for you to finish that one day, Adj," she said.

<*I would like that.*>

"So what have you done with our lovely new ship?"

<*Improved her slipspace capability. Much faster. Much more accurate insertion into normal space. Next we shall work on communications, so that you can maintain contact from slip-space.*>

"No need to drop out of slip to send signals? How do you do that?"

<*By using the—of the—field to bypass—and make—.*>

Some of the words had defeated the translation software, leaving gaps as if profanities were being bleeped out. Parangosky found the idea of a Huragok swearing a blue streak wonderfully appealing.

Lasky caught her eye. "They have physics concepts we don't yet have language for, ma'am. We're the dim kids at the back of the class."

"Does Halsey understand what they're doing?"

"No, and it's really getting to her."

Parangosky was equally wary of anything she couldn't see for herself, but she'd taken far more than that on faith before. At least Huragok had transparent motives. The Forerunners had created them with one overwhelming passion: to make things that worked and to constantly improve them. That was good enough for Parangosky. They weren't going to misuse the budget, break the law, and be a constant pain in the ass like Halsey.

"I'm very pleased with your progress. Thank you, Adj." Parangosky gave Del Rio a pointed look. "And Andrew's very pleased, too. Aren't you, Andrew?"

Del Rio's expression was unreadable for a moment. He seemed to have noted the eye contact between her and Lasky. "They're doing a fine job, ma'am. And we take very good care of them."

Parangosky risked patting Adj on one of his arms, found it smooth and cool, and walked over to Lasky with her hand held out for shaking. *You're my anointed on this tub, Tom. Remember that.* Lasky took it with a smile—a wholesomely good-looking man, easy to like, easier still to trust—and nodded in the direction of the other Huragok, drifting around a terminal with their tentacles working like crazed concert pianists.

"So the civvie contractors end up playing cards a lot, ma'am," he said. "Or relaying the carpet. I'm expecting union objections about aliens taking their jobs any day now."

"Ah, they're getting paid hard-lying allowance and extra overtime. Just remind them they can be replaced by gas bags that work for yeast extract. Speaking of which, how's Halsey behaving?"

"You've not received the updates?"

"I have, but I want to hear it from you."

Lasky glanced at Del Rio for a moment, as if asking permission to divulge the unvarnished truth. He got the faintest shrug in response.

"Well, she got the idea eventually," Lasky said. "But she's still griping about not having access to the Spartan-Fours."

"She'd better not have access to *anybody* except crew authorized to know she's still alive."

"No, we've nailed it down tightly, ma'am. I had to give her back her computer to extract some Huragok translation software, but I've removed it again. I got Perfect Density to check it out for any program she could possibly use to bypass security."

"And you monitor every system for breaches, whether she has official access or not."

"Constant surveillance. If she can hijack a ship and kidnap a Spartan, I treat her as an enemy prisoner who's making herself useful. Sewing mailbags, so to speak."

Del Rio said nothing and beckoned to Parangosky and Lasky to follow him to another hatch in the deck, a much larger square one with black and yellow warning tape adorning the removable grab rail around it. Del Rio pointed down. Parangosky peered over the coaming to see the top of someone's head four or five meters directly below, gray hair pulled back taut in a pony tail.

Catherine Halsey was working at a screen with a notebook and old-fashioned pencil to one side of her workstation. She didn't look up. Waving and calling *coo-ee Catherine* seemed out of the question. Perhaps she couldn't hear what was happening above her: the hum of the aircon and the assorted noises from adjacent compartments might have left her in her own little world. She certainly didn't look up.

"She's security chipped," Del Rio said, stepping back from the hatch. "If she tries to enter areas off limits to her, the doors won't open."

"And if she wants to remove the chip," Lasky said, "she'll have to gnaw her own leg off."

Parangosky wondered how long it would be before she tried to persuade a Huragok to remove it. "I wouldn't put that past her. How does she get on with Glassman?" Parangosky didn't like the choice of chief engineer either, but he was the best technical man for the job. "Any pissing contests?"

"Yes, ma'am, and they're pretty well matched," Lasky said. "She doesn't like being tasked by anyone below admiral. She's obviously used to a lot more gold braid at her beck and call."

"So . . . she's secured, everyone including the Huragok have been warned not to let her con them, and she's getting results."

Lasky looked pained. "Yes, ma'am."

"Good. I don't want her here any longer than she needs to be. The moment she's done, ship her back to Ivanoff." Halsey was less of a risk locked up on an ONI research station. The more people who knew, even those with top security clearance, the greater the chance of the news leaking. There was never a monopoly of information, not even for ONI. "Still no dedicated AI?"

Del Rio started to shake his head but seemed to think better of it. Someone had obviously told him never to actually say no to her. "I'm going to keep Aine until I find the right one. She's used to ships in refit and she does things by the book. That's all I need right now until we start working-up."

"Well, you'd better choose a permanent one soon, Andrew, or you'll get one assigned," Parangosky said. "Top-level AIs are my part of ship. And they don't grow on trees."

Del Rio nodded but he didn't look her in the eye. He was probably thinking it was time she retired or had the grace to die, but even that wasn't going to save him from her scrutiny.

Or Serin Osman's, when the day comes.

"So where's this coffee?" she said. "Let's see how the

command bridge is shaping up before Terrence wolfs all the pastries. Lead on, Captain."

Del Rio forced a smile and led her to the elevator, flanked by Lasky. Parangosky caught the XO's eye and just did a slow blink. *You've got it all under control, Tom.* This ship was all power, all refinements, her capability now far beyond the Covenant's even before its fall.

They had nothing left to throw at Earth now, not unless the Forerunners decided to rise from the dead.

She was going to enjoy that coffee.

ONIRF TREVELYAN, FORMERLY THE FORERUNNER WORLD KNOWN AS ONYX

The perfect blue sky that Jul 'Mdama could see from his cell was as big a lie as any the humans had told him.

Humans deceived. It was their defining feature, their strategy of choice, and it had brought him to this forsaken place. But it was also the key to how he would escape. He simply didn't know exactly how yet.

His life was now lived in a room twenty paces wide by twenty-five paces long, with one large window that he was still evaluating to see how easily it might break. This was no Forerunner building. It was a prefabricated box of steel-framed composite panels, created by humans, whose flimsy artifacts could usually be smashed. But where would he go once he escaped this room? How would he find a ship to leave the planet? These things were possible, he was sure, but there was one fact he had gleaned by accident: this world wasn't a planet at all. It was yet another Forerunner construct, an artificial world the humans called a Dyson sphere.

One of the guards had told him that there was no point trying to escape because the sky he was looking at was a solid roof, its blue perfection and occasional clouds just an illusion. Jul recognized the word *sphere* because the guard had drawn a circle in the air with his fingers as he said it, and the translation device had provided the Sangheili word for globe.

Sphere. Jul practiced the *sffff* sound. It was easier to say than the *ipsss* he tried to make when pronouncing *Phillips.* Where was that little maggot now, and that arrogant AI that floated around looking like a box?

It didn't matter. If Phillips ever crossed his path again, he would kill him. He wasn't even a soldier. And the AI—that was a device, a tool, of no more consequence than a hammer or a blade. It was beneath Jul's dignity to even think of its destruction.

The humans got into this sphere. They must be able to get out again.

So I can, too.

Jul stood at the window, trying out that *ipsss* sound again while he stared up at the sky trying to picture a rust-red planet—home. If he shifted his focus a little, he could only see flecks of saliva on the glass. Then somebody rapped on the door. And that act was yet another lie: he wasn't a guest whose privacy was respected, but a prisoner of the Office of Naval Intelligence, with no choice over who was admitted to his cell and who was not.

He concentrated on Raia. His wife would be frantic with worry by now. Would she talk to Forze, retrace his steps, make the link with 'Telcam and his human associates? She was ferociously intelligent. She could do all this. But how would she know where he was now, if he didn't even know himself?

All he knew was that it was called Trevelyan, and it was lies, lies, *lies*.

"Jul, it's Dr. Magnusson." The woman's two voices were muffled by the reinforced steel door. He knew it was reinforced because he'd rammed it with his shoulder a few times. "Are you going to behave today?"

He paused. Magnusson would not be alone or defenseless. Jul understood her not because she spoke Sangheili, like Phillips, but because she wore a translation device. She tended to whisper in her own language so that the synthesized Sangheili voice was more audible. Jul decided to humor her.

Thank you, Phillips. You taught me that there was no shame in submission if it served the longer game, the wider strategy. See how fast we learn? This is how you make us an even more dangerous enemy.

"I shall behave," Jul conceded. He cocked his head and listened for the click of the lock as she deactivated it. "If you tell me why the sky's blue."

The door opened. Irena Magnusson, light haired and wearing a gray one-piece suit, was small even by human standards. Their females were usually markedly smaller than the males, but they still took up arms and served on the front line. Jul had killed quite a few in his time and it had never troubled him, although he was aware of the human taboo against killing women and children. Throughout their history they seemed to have taken very little notice of that themselves, though. And both women and children were capable of killing, so they could never be ruled out as a threat. Jul decided that trying to understand human morality was a waste of time better spent on planning an escape.

"Rayleigh scattering." Magnusson carried a pile of papers, a folio, and a datapad. She also had what looked like a small walking stick tucked under her left arm—a weapon that would give Jul a powerful electric shock if he got too near her, exactly like the one the Spartan called Naomi had used on him. "Perhaps you credit a Sangheili scientist for discovering the phenomenon, but we name it for John Rayleigh."

An armed guard followed her into the room and stood barring the door, hands clasped behind his back. Jul was beginning to filter out the human language and listen only to the Sangheili translation generated in a good approximation of Magnusson's own voice, but he forced himself to pay attention to this *English*. There would come a time when he'd need to understand as much of it as he could.

"I meant *this* sky," he said. "This isn't a real world. It's a hollow ball."

Magnusson laid out her papers on the Sangheili-sized desk. They seemed to have gone to some trouble to make him feel less uncomfortable. "It's a very *big* hollow ball built around a star, and it has an artificial climate, so it's still caused by scattered light in the blue wavelength."

"And the Forerunners made this."

"Sit down, Jul."

"They made *stars*." He sat, but not because she'd commanded it. He still towered over her. He could reach out and snap her neck without even rising from the chair, although he knew the guard would cut him down a heartbeat later. "Are there not enough stars already? Billions upon billions. Why build another?"

"We're still exploring," she said. "Maybe the star was already there. It's hard to be sure. But the sphere's main purpose was as a shelter from the Flood or the Halo Array. It's well sealed."

"And no sign of the Forerunners."

"What makes you say that?"

"They're long gone."

Magnusson seemed more interested. Humans had these little gestures that gave everything away. She leaned forward a little, pupils dilated, and she blinked more frequently.

"They're your gods."

"Not mine," Jul said. He'd lose nothing by telling her some truths. He wanted her to tell him some in return. That deal usually worked on Raia. "Gods don't die or forget to return. Gods choose better prophets than the San'Shyuum, too."

"Do you believe in *any* gods?"

"No, but I'm prepared to be persuaded if one should appear."

Magnusson gave him that odd look, wrinkling her nose and pulling her brows together, something that Jul associated with human disapproval. But this was something different. Her lips curled. Then her teeth glinted.

Jul didn't like human smiles. They were yet another lie, an expression of happy harmlessness that was actually the baring of fangs.

"Very wise," she said. "I'd ask for proof as well."

"What do you want from me? The Covenant has been destroyed. You hold peace talks with the Arbiter. What use am I to you?"

"Ah, you're unique, Jul. A live Sangheili, off his home territory. I don't think we've ever had one before. Who knows what we can discover about one another?"

"The last time humans sought information from me," he said, "one of your Spartan demons used electric shocks to do it."

"Yes, I'm sorry about that. Spartans aren't known for their diplomacy."

"You still require something from me, or else you would simply have killed me to silence me. It's usually information. You tell me what will happen to me if I don't comply, or offer me some incentive if I do. That's how you work, yes?"

"What intelligence would we need from you? We know where your homeworld is. The Arbiter's hosting human guests in his keep. You no longer have a fleet. And we've acquired Huragok. *Engineers.*" Magnusson sat back in her seat. "They're living blueprints. Everything they've ever built or modified, every ship or weapon—we ask nicely and they give us every detail we need."

Jul simply sat and stared at her. It wasn't his job to beg for answers. She'd grow tired of the game and get to the point sooner or later. He used to think that he despised humans, but he'd come to realize that he was afraid of them: not because they were stronger, but because they were like bacteria, persistent and adaptable, breeding and multiplying and spreading until they overwhelmed by sheer numbers and infected everything. He dreaded them like a plague.

And the Forerunners feared the Flood would overwhelm the galaxy? They should have worried about the humans, too. Did they encounter humans on Earth when they landed and built their artifacts? They should have seen the warning signs.

Gods didn't make that kind of mistake.

"Thel 'Vadam is not entitled to call himself the Arbiter," Jul said at last. "He's a traitor. He'll be overthrown. And then we'll come for you, and finish the job we started, because you'll spread across every planet just like the Flood if we don't stop you."

Jul had almost forgotten about the guard standing in front of the door. For a moment he glanced at the man and noted that he seemed oblivious of the conversation going on at the table, just staring at a point somewhere on the wall facing him. Then he touched his finger to his ear. Jul realized he was listening to something on his radio receiver. The guard moved up behind Magnusson, tapped her on the shoulder, and motioned to her to switch off her translation device.

She nodded, and spoke with him in quiet English words that Jul couldn't follow, except for two: *Sanghelios,* whose meaning was clear, and *hinge-heads,* which he recognized but still didn't understand. Whatever the guard had told her had made her smile. For a few moments, she twiddled a stylus between her fingers, reading the papers laid out on the table in front of her, and then touched the translation device again.

"Things are getting quite tense on Sanghelios," she said.

"There's been a bomb attack in one of your cities and reports of Jiralhanae attacking Sangheili. I thought that might cheer you up, seeing as you've been planning a revolt."

So 'Telcam had made his move. Jul's first thought was worry for Raia, and his second was frustration that he wasn't there to fight. "As I said, 'Vadam will be overthrown."

"I should hope so," Magnusson said. "It's costing us a fortune to arm your insurrection. Yes, your friend 'Telcam knows he's being bankrolled by ONI. Still, we did get a Huragok out of it."

So I was right—at least partly.

Jul had seen the female shipmaster, the one they called Osman, delivering arms to 'Telcam. But he hadn't realized the monk had known exactly who he was dealing with. Jul had been so sure that 'Telcam was being duped. How could a fanatical member of the Abiding Truth strike a deal with the enemy? Everybody seemed to be abandoning their senses.

"What did he offer you in exchange?" Jul asked.

"We agreed to stay out of each other's keeps, so to speak. We help 'Telcam remove the Arbiter and set up a religious state—you agree to stay away from human territory." Magnusson was still fidgeting with that stylus, twirling it slowly between her thin, wormlike little human fingers. "But it's capability that counts, not intent. I'm afraid we have to make sure you can never threaten us again, no matter how many assurances you give us. We're rather unforgiving when it comes to attempted genocide."

Jul should have known better than to expect anything else from humans. They were incapable of giving up their expansionist habits. The Arbiter was a fool, as Jul suspected, and thought he could trust them when they said things would be different. This was exactly what had made Jul join the coup against him.

"We should have wiped you out," Jul said. "We could never coexist in one galaxy."

"But you never got the chance." Magnusson did one of those

tight smiles, the one that showed no fangs but oozed contempt. "Nor will you ever get one again. I agree with you—one of us has got to go, and my job is to make sure it's not us."

"You've lost hundreds of warships. You can't possibly threaten Sanghelios."

"Oh, come now, Jul. You know it won't be that old-fashioned. You're already sliding into civil war for the second time in a year. And we're ONI. We do things differently to Admiral Hood. None of that *Nelsonian square-jawed stuff.*"

The translation software didn't manage to interpret the last few words. Jul heard only the English. Magnusson pushed back from the table and got up to wander around the room. What could he possibly do for her that was of any use? Unless this was all a bluff, unless the humans had no intelligence or functioning warships, then all Jul knew was what ONI seemed to know already. In fact, they knew more than he did.

For a moment he found himself distracted by the idea that the Forerunners could have built *stars*. That dwarfed the technology of the Halo Array. Millennia later, no civilization had even come close to that. What else had these not-gods been able to do?

"I don't like the food here," he said, changing the subject. "It upsets my digestion."

"The more you tell us about your native foods, the more I'll be able to get supplies that suit you. I thought you were satisfied with the meat."

"I am. But the grain gives me gas."

"Wheat, you mean."

"Yes. The grain the Kig-Yar grow—that's a Sangheili crop. Can you not acquire some of that?"

Magnusson smiled again and sat down. "I never saw you people as farmers."

"We're not. The San'Shyuum kept us supplied, and what farms we still had were maintained by alien labor."

"So you're having to learn to take care of yourselves again. No hired help in the fields. No Huragok to build and repair machines for you."

Jul felt a little mocked. "We are, and we are succeeding," he said, indignant. Could this creature survive without the trappings of technology she didn't understand? "And my wife believes self-reliance is the key to regaining our military greatness."

Magnusson just nodded. "We'll find some of that grain for you. What's it called?"

"The Kig-Yar name is *irukan*."

She pressed the end of her stylus, making it click, and pushed it across the table to him with a sheet of paper. "Give me a *shopping list*." Again the translation failed. "Write down a list of common foods. I'll do what I can."

Jul fumbled with the stylus. It was short and slender, far too small for Sangheili hands. Eventually he managed to grip it like a dagger and held the paper steady with his free hand while he scrawled unsteady ideograms. It looked like a child's first efforts, and he was embarrassed. Perhaps Magnusson didn't know what passed for neat handwriting in an alien system. He pushed the paper back across the desk to her and watched her frowning at the shapes, eyes scanning.

"These are all staples, are they?" she asked. "Anything exotic?"

"No. Just basic grains and fruits."

"What do you feed your livestock?"

She was trying to be sociable by chatting about irrelevant nonsense to him. Humans always assumed other species shared their social conventions. "The same grain," Jul said, wishing she would get to the point and simply threaten him. "I'm trying to keep this simple for you."

Magnusson folded the paper and put it in her pocket. "Do you have children?"

"Of course."

"They'll be missing you."

"No. They won't. No Sangheili is allowed to know who his father is."

"I'd heard that. So it's true."

"Yes."

"But you miss them. You know who *they* are, I assume. If someone didn't manage the bloodlines, you'd be very inbred."

"I have not spent enough time with them to miss them. Nor been parted from them long enough." If she thought she could put pressure on him that way, then she had more to learn about Sangheili than he'd thought. "Now, either tell me what you want from me, or leave me in peace."

Magnusson didn't appear offended. Jul knew what to watch for in human faces now. They were a mass of signals, and all could be learned. She looked over her shoulder at the guard, then stood up, collecting the files and sheets of paper again, and Jul wondered why she'd brought them with her if she'd decided not to make use of them.

I must learn to read their language. That's essential if I'm to get out of here.

Escape had to be his sole focus now. He'd take everything else as it came. His next step would be to work out the geography— to understand where he was and what other facilities were here. He got up and went over to the window again, watching for signs of activity. The land outside was rolling grassland, but new low-rise prefabricated buildings were springing up, and he could hear the occasional hum of vehicles. The humans were making Trevelyan their own.

He heard the door open behind him. He didn't turn.

"Actually, Jul, the most useful thing you can do for me right now is just to be yourself," Magnusson said. "You don't have to tell me anything, although it would be great if you had jamming frequencies for Sangheili air defenses and the command codes. But we've got Huragok who can deal with all that. We've even got some that the Forerunners left here to look after the place. Imagine it, knowledge from the time of the gods."

The door closed again and Jul tried to make sense of the encounter. Magnusson was working up to something, or perhaps she was simply not very good at her job. Humans didn't kill incompetent inferiors, so they multiplied. It was a miracle that they could achieve so much.

But they had Huragok now. They could be as stupid and lazy as they wished, and still have the military advantage over Sanghelios.

Huragok left here by the Forerunners. A race that could build stars. That kind of knowledge is too dangerous to fall into human hands.

Jul didn't believe in divine plans, but he did believe in seizing advantages. Who was best placed to stop humans exploiting the Huragok to wipe out the Sangheili? It was him. He was here. He was in the heart of the enemy camp, breathing their air, knowing their intent—and their capability.

In fact, he was in the very best place that a warrior could be to save his people.

His plans needed to change a little. He would start with the Huragok.

ADMIRALS' INSPECTION, UNSC *INFINITY:* COMMAND BRIDGE

There were already three hundred personnel working in *Infinity,* and still she felt like a ghost ship.

Parangosky thought of all the families back home who never asked where their loved ones had been for the past six months. They'd learned not to. Many of the crew didn't have families, of course. They were from colony worlds now wiped off the charts, reduced to glass.

And we'll never let that happen again. We'll reclaim those worlds. And we'll hold them.

She reached for a pastry, watching Hood having one of those very quiet, nose-to-nose boys' chats with Del Rio. She kept an eye on the officers coming and going, too. It was a very junior staff considering that this was the UNSC's flagship. Parangosky racked her brains to think of any of Del Rio's key officers other than Lasky who were above the rank of lieutenant, and came up empty. Rank wasn't any gauge of effectiveness or combat experience, though. It told her more about bottlenecks in the rank structure and the lack of ships to promote people to than the caliber of the crews.

That, and the sheer number of people we lost.

Parangosky felt bullish rather than defiant for the first time in years. The scent of new upholstery, adhesive, and that hot radiator smell of components being run up to operating temperature for the first time was a fragrance she wished she could bottle. It had been a very long time indeed since she'd served in a warship. She recalled her first ship as if it was last week.

UNSC Lutyens. *Broke my heart when she went for scrap.*

You could truly love a ship. She was glad she hadn't forgotten how that felt. But she was here to work, to evaluate, to spot the cracks, and she was letting nostalgia and sugar get the better of her. Her datapad vibrated gently in her pocket. There was only one caller it could be.

"What have you got for me, BB?"

It was the AI's fragment in the Bravo-6 system, not his matrix.

"We've now had contact from the Arbiter—he's sent a message to Hood's office that the official escort has misplaced Phillips. I just happened to fall over it before it was read."

"Well done. Still no sign of him or your other fragment, then."

"No, and the explosion was linked to an attack in Ontom by Jiralhanae still working on Sanghelios. We didn't see that one coming."

"Thank you for the heads-up, BB. I may have to get things moving myself. Stand by."

Parangosky realized this was rapidly adding up to a dead operative. Much as she liked Phillips, his death would be marginally easier to handle from a political perspective than his capture. But she had to be sure. She needed confirmation, and not from the Sangheili.

I'm betting Kilo-Five could infiltrate Sanghelios. I'd lose some of them, though, and it'd be politically messy for everyone. On the other hand . . . I could play this straight, and use the leverage I've already got.

The mission—destabilizing Sanghelios—came first. There were many ways to skin that proverbial cat. Hood could do what he seemed to do best: dealing man to man, handshake to handshake, with Thel 'Vadam, the Arbiter. She drained her coffee and made a beeline for Hood. Del Rio saw her coming and melted away.

"I think I'm finally enjoying my Medusa reputation," she said, forcing a laugh out of Hood. "Women normally become invisible to men at the age of forty. But he can obviously still see me."

"Yes, I warned him not to look directly at you, merely to gaze on your reflection for his own safety." Even Hood's sarcasm was gracious. Parangosky still liked him, for all his excessive optimism. "You really don't care for the cut of his jib, do you, Margaret?"

"No, I do *not.*"

"He's a safe pair of hands. We won't get any surprises from him. And he's Halsey-proof. She won't be able to manipulate him."

Parangosky kept walking. "You don't have to sell him to me any longer. He already has the ship."

"And you have Lasky."

"And you'll *need* Lasky one day when Del Rio can't politic his way out of a tight spot."

"Why do you always go for the straight-as-a-die, man-of-the-people types?"

"Because they're so unlike me, my dear. My morbid fascination with the exotic."

"So you feel you have your budget's worth."

"I'm satisfied we've got a vessel that'll not only loosen Sangheili bowels, but that can also vaporize them."

"I'm hoping it won't come to that again."

"Do you have a few minutes to walk with me, Terrence? I promise it'll be leisurely. It's my only speed setting these days."

Hood followed her out into the passage, hands clasped behind his back. The long, dimly lit, half-finished passage echoed with their footsteps. Somewhere on a deck below, someone was hammering metal, a strangely old-fashioned noise in a state-of-the-art warship.

"Is this about Phillips?" Hood asked.

"He's still missing. If he's been killed, I'm going to take a very dim view of that."

"How dim? Remember that we have a peace treaty with the Arbiter, Margaret."

"But the Arbiter's not immortal, and he's facing another civil war. I need to find Phillips."

"I'm sure the Arbiter's searching for him."

Parangosky trod carefully. Hood knew she'd be monitoring everyone's comms, but there was no point in ramming it down his throat. "I think I'd rather have our own people involved in that. If only to make it clear that we're not the underdogs any longer."

Hood didn't say a word for a while and carried on walking, matching his pace to hers.

"That's what they used to call a very big ask," he said.

"Yes, I'm asking. But I think you would be best placed to actually raise it with him."

"So you want to insert . . . who, exactly?"

"Kilo-Five."

"This ask is getting rather large. What if he refuses?"

"I'm damned if I'm leaving a man behind. I need a body, dead or alive."

"So you're telling me you'll insert an extraction team whether he agrees to it or not."

"Yes."

"Quite apart from the size of the task, we can't trample on their sovereignty like that."

"Then why are you allocating more than half the Fleet budget to *Infinity*? We don't need her to handle human insurgents."

Hood almost smiled. "Perhaps I want to stop you owning her outright."

"You don't trust the Sangheili any more than I do."

"No, but that doesn't mean I want to restart the war."

Any politically aware man would have expected ONI to try to destabilize the Sangheili. Dirty tricks had long been the textbook method for neutralizing threats. *He doesn't want to know. He'd rather be able to look the Arbiter in the eye and feel he was technically telling him the truth.* Hood was a gentleman, but not an idealist. That was a relief.

Parangosky had covered a lot of deck today and her knees were killing her. She ground to a halt at the doors to the atrium, a vast transparent dome over a space the size of a park. When she held up her datapad and checked it against the schematic, oxygen-generating plants and ergonomic seating snapped into place to give her a three-dimensional impression of what a pleasant—and huge—area it would be. There were already some specimens basking in artificial sunlight, a few gingko trees and a Parana pine.

"Lavish," she said, looking for a raw nerve she could twang. It was hard to find one in a seasoned horse-trader like Hood. "I realize habitability is important, but I hope none of our hard-pressed ODSTs or green-jobs see this."

"The ship's complement is more than seventeen thousand. Long deployments. Half the crew never even meet one another. We have to think in terms of the human dynamics of a small city."

"Of course we do." They'd played this fencing game far too often and for too many years to fool each other, but Parangosky detected just a little defensiveness creeping in, a whiff of guilt. Hood didn't like the suggestion that he gave some personnel privileges that ground troops didn't get. *Good.* That was the idea. "When do you want the Sangheili to know we have her?"

Hood ambled across an empty deck that reminded Parangosky more of the Coliseum than a plaza. "When we have those new drives online. So what are we going to do about Phillips?"

"Osman's on her way to Sanghelios. But if we don't find him fairly quickly, I think that the presence of a very large warship might be helpful in a number of ways."

"It's far too soon. And it's not as if the Sangheili are holding him."

"Think of it as a work-up exercise. A Thursday War."

"We've still got contractors crawling all over the ship."

"Just cosmetic stuff. Come on, Terrence. She can deploy."

"She's not ready. Or perhaps *I'm* not ready."

Or Del Rio isn't, you mean. Parangosky put on her it's-all-your-fault-anyway face, a studied, sad regret with a hint of disappointment, and said nothing. Subconsciously or otherwise, most men were scared of upsetting their mothers. Parangosky pressed that primal button and Hood blinked first.

"Just tell me this wasn't part of your plan," he said.

"I know I'm good, Terrence, but even I can't set up something that convoluted. I genuinely fear for his life. And we do need his unique rapport with the Sangheili."

"So what are our options?"

"Call the Arbiter. Ask him a personal favor. If he refuses, then you know where you stand. We don't even have to involve *Infinity* unless things really deteriorate. But this is exactly why we commissioned her—to dominate space."

Hood looked around the atrium as if he was lost, then indicated an exit on the port side.

"Very well," he said. "I'll call him. But we don't push our luck on Sanghelios until we're sure we can win. I will *not* go to war again unless they come after us."

"You won't need to," she said.

It wouldn't be his decision, though. She knew it, and so did he.

CHAPTER
THREE

ARBITER, I WOULD CONSIDER IT A PERSONAL FAVOR IF YOU WOULD ALLOW MY SEARCH AND RESCUE EXPERTS TO LAND AND HELP LOOK FOR PROFESSOR PHILLIPS. IN FACT, IF THEY ASSUME RESPONSIBILITY FOR HIS SAFETY, THEN YOU AND THE SANGHEILI WILL NOT BE MORALLY ACCOUNTABLE SHOULD ANYTHING HAPPEN TO HIM. I REALIZE THAT IT'S A MATTER OF HONOR FOR SANGHEILI WHEN THEY PROMISE SAFE PAS-SAGE TO A GUEST, BUT I FULLY UNDERSTAND THAT THERE ARE EVENTS OVER WHICH YOU HAVE NO CONTROL.

(ADMIRAL LORD TERRENCE HOOD, CINCFLEET,
TO THE ARBITER, THEL 'VADAM)

CURO KEEP, MDAMA, SANGHELIOS

"You." Raia 'Mdama swept into the keep, shoving aside some insignificant adolescent who tried to bar her way. "Fetch your lord. Tell him I demand to see him."

The youth stumbled a few paces as he walked backward, still trying to slow her down. He should have known better. She was the wife of a clan elder, and in his absence—*temporary* absence—she wielded his authority outside the keep.

And he's my husband. Hang the conventions of society. I have a right to know where he is. I have a right to do whatever it takes to find him.

"Who *are* you?" The young male was slow on the uptake,

and wives and daughters were seldom seen outside their keeps. "I have to tell my Lord Forze who wants to see him."

"Child, I am Raia 'Mdama, wife of Jul 'Mdama, elder of Bekan keep." She loomed over him, jaws parted and fangs bared. "Forze knows me. He uses my keep as a storage facility for his vessels. Find him and bring him to me."

The youth finally realized she wasn't going to back down and that he'd avoid a good cuff around the head if he simply did as he was told. "Yes, my lady."

Raia stood in the courtyard trying to hold down a strange mix of anger and fear. Jul often disappeared for days now that he'd decided to overthrow Thel 'Vadam, but this was exceptional. He'd been gone for weeks. Did he really think that not disclosing details of his planned coup would save her from being implicated? The Arbiter wouldn't look at those subtle details. She would be the wife of a traitor if Jul was caught, whether she agreed with his politics or not, and the whole clan would pay the price.

But I do agree with him. There can never be peace with the humans. They'll always expand, encroach, colonize.

She could see faces at the small windows set high in the walls. The children of Forze's clan were trying to catch a glimpse of this roaring, angry female who'd burst into their keep.

What about my children? I know who their fathers are even if they don't. Dural and Asum don't ask where Jul is. But he should be there for them.

Forze finally appeared in the doorway, arms held out in apology. "Raia, my dear respected friend. There's no need to wait out here. Come in. Please, come inside."

"I still have no answer from you, Forze." She strode through the door, head thrust forward in a don't-you-dare gesture, ready to barge him with her shoulder if he didn't give her the right response. "I want to know where my husband is. You must have *some* idea."

Forze ushered her into a room that looked as if someone had rushed out of it in a hurry, leaving chairs at odd angles and data-pads on the table. She heard the clattering of feet in the passage beyond. He'd obviously told his family to leave and give him some peace to talk sense to this enraged female. Did they even know what he was doing? Did they know he was part of the uprising? Well, that was his problem to address, not hers.

She decided to remain standing. It was much harder somehow to keep her anger fed and functioning when she sat down.

"I'm telling you all I know, Raia," Forze said. "I haven't heard from him. I spoke with 'Telcam, and he's had no word from him either."

"Do *not* tell me that everything's all right."

"I can assure you I won't. I'm concerned, too."

"He left to follow 'Telcam, to find out where his rendezvous point with his arms supplier was. Yes?"

"Yes. But I didn't dare mention that to 'Telcam, in case Jul was right to be suspicious."

"So you think 'Telcam has silenced him?"

"If he has, he's very convincing about being outraged by his absence."

"This monk is an adherent of the Abiding Truth. Reason and rationality are hardly their watchwords. Look what they did to Relon and his brother. Veteran warriors, honorable men, slaughtered for some imagined blasphemy against so-called gods who never existed anyway."

Forze looked pained. It was still hard for many to abandon their beliefs, and the fact that the Prophets had been exposed as frauds didn't convince them that the Forerunners weren't divine and capable of noting the names of heretics and unbelievers.

Raia didn't care. If the gods wanted her to abandon her husband to appease them, they weren't worth her devotion. She would spit on them—if there were anything to spit on.

"You might not trust my judgment," Forze said at last, head lowered a little. "But I've spoken at length with 'Telcam, and I think I would know if he was behind this. He's angry. He's *always* angry, but I do think it's genuine, that he feels Jul has gone off on some jaunt and isn't pulling his weight."

Raia had to ask the obvious. "And you're certain that you never mentioned Jul's unease about him."

"I swear I never mentioned it, but Jul made his concerns fairly obvious."

"Very well." There was only one lead she could follow: 'Telcam himself. "You fools still have ships laid up on my land. At some point, 'Telcam will need them. And he'll answer to me, or I'll have them destroyed. Where can I find him?"

"Don't go looking for him."

"I'll do as I please. Where is his keep?"

Forze might have been a courageous shipmaster, but he caved in fairly quickly when faced with her anger. There was probably some guilt at work, she thought, some feeling that he should have stopped Jul chasing after 'Telcam.

"Ontom," he said at last. "Which is why it's a bad idea to go there. You must have heard about the Brutes detonating devices in the city today."

"You're better informed than I am."

"That's because . . . we've been told to be ready to attack Vadam."

"Do *not* keep things from me, Forze."

"What do you expect of me? I'm doing all I can to find Jul. He's my friend. And he wouldn't want you to be involved in this and put at risk."

Raia couldn't help herself. She hissed at him. It was vulgar and unladylike to hiss at someone outside her clan, a shameful loss of control, but she was at breaking point.

"Risk?" she said, feeling the saliva draining down her throat and feeling a little embarrassed by her outburst. "I'm without my husband, and I don't know why. Our keep has no elder. What greater hazard can I face than being left alone?" Her mind was made up. She'd already started listing whose help she might call upon to go with her. "I'm going to Ontom to confront 'Telcam. I expect you to come with me, but if you don't, that won't stop me."

"What if he's not there?"

"It's the only information I have, and the alternative to pursuing it is to stay at home and wait to be told I'm a widow."

Forze had a wife, too. He might have had several for all Raia knew, but a keep elder always had a family to look after, a large one, children he was collectively responsible for whether he sired them or not. He looked defeated for a moment. Then he dipped his head, giving in.

"It's dangerous, and we might well be turned back if the Ontom keeps have locked down the area, but we'll go together. I've been told to stand by—the uprising has begun. They'll be coming to collect the vessels laid up on your land."

"Then I'll be ready to go with one of those vessels."

"You can't."

"I can. Females have served in ships and even been weapons masters."

"Very, very *rarely.*"

"There's no law preventing me, and I *shall* come with you." The ships were on her land. If 'Telcam wanted them, he'd get her as well, or he'd get nothing. "Or else I'll order my brothers and sisters to destroy those ships right now."

"You can't do that."

"I can. I'm returning home now to leave instructions for my sisters in my absence, and I'll be waiting with the ships."

Raia turned and left as fast as she could, mainly to stop herself from changing her mind. If anything happened to her, the keep might fall into chaos. She had to leave someone with clear orders. Uncle Naxan could have the elder's authority. Umira was the most sensible of her sisters, and she could manage the farm and the accounts until Raia got back. Under the Covenant, they'd never had to worry about food supplies. Now, without San'Shyuum support and alien labor, they had to fend for themselves and learn to run their own lives again.

And we will.

Back at Bekan keep, she packed a bag. She couldn't recall the last time she'd done that. She'd never needed to travel, to be away from home, and it felt strange and unsettling. Dural watched her from the door, clutching his practice weapon—a wooden staff—as if he were on sentry duty.

"What are you doing, Mother?"

"I'm going to look for Uncle Jul," she said. Lying to children made them weak and confused. They had to know that the world was a dangerous place, and preparing them for it meant withholding nothing that might distress them. By watching her deal with difficult things, Dural would learn to be decisive and unafraid. "He should have come home by now."

"Is he dead?"

It was a perfectly normal question in a society where almost every male who was physically capable expected to be a warrior and where so many had died in battle. But this was Jul's son, not that the youngster realized that, and Raia was far more fragile about the prospect of losing her husband than she'd realized. The word *dead* wounded her. She tried to look calm.

"Jul's a survivor," she said. "Wherever he is, he'll return to us. But I want to know why he's been delayed, and by whom. Now, be obedient while I'm away. Do as Naxan and Umira tell you. I'll know if you don't."

Dural watched her in silence for a little longer. It was only when she put on her belt with its unfamiliar holster that he parted his jaws, pleased. She was armed. He knew that was a good thing, a sensible thing, and that his mother would be all right. It seemed to satisfy him and he walked off.

Carrying a pistol felt odd, but Raia was fully trained to use it well. All children were taught to fight and defend themselves; adult females rarely served on the front line, but they were expected to fight to defend their keep if it came under attack. And that was how she felt right then. Her husband was in danger, she was sure of it, and her duty was to go to his aid. Some would tut and disapprove of her leaving the keep and the family in the hands of others, but she didn't care.

'Telcam was the one who needed to worry. If he'd harmed Jul, she would kill him. That, too, was her duty.

As she headed for the field where the vessels were laid up, wading through long grass that plucked at her legs, a little nervous voice at the back of her mind asked her if she was mad, and if she even understood what she was doing. She slapped it down—yes, she understood, *of course* she understood. When she reached the warship called *Unflinching Resolve* and gazed up at the massive curve of its hull, she admitted to herself that she was terrified, but that was irrelevant. It was far more frightening to sit and wait in the keep, weak and dependent.

I bore warriors. Therefore I can become one, too.

She could hear a Revenant approaching. She waited with one hand on her holster until it came into view, flattening the grass with its thrust, and as it slowed to a halt she fixed the pilot with her best do-not-toy-with-me stare.

Forze got out of the Revenant and looked at her with his head on one side, eyes on the weapon.

"Now you *really* frighten me," he said. "I hope you don't expect to pilot a ship, too."

"No," she said. "Not yet."

TEMPLE OF THE ABIDING TRUTH, ONTOM: TWO HOURS AFTER THE INITIAL EXPLOSION

Phillips held his breath, listening for the noise of energy bolts and trying to work out how long it would take him to sprint to the temple gates when the shooting stopped.

He glanced at 'Telcam. From the length of his stride, Phillips calculated that the Sangheili would outrun him as fast as a dad chasing after a willful toddler. He'd never make it to the end of the passage. Damn, all he had to do was get outside and grab the first Sangheili he saw—anyone at all—to ask them to make contact with Cadan or the Arbiter's office. Then he could get a message to Osman and be out of here.

"Hey, 'Telcam," he said. He found himself switching between English and Sangheili in the same sentence now, just as 'Telcam did. "Let's be clear about this. While I appreciate your concern for my safety, are you holding me prisoner? Can I leave if I'm willing to take the risk?"

'Telcam was poring over a chart with the others. There were about thirty Sangheili in full armor crammed into the chamber fifty meters inside the doors, trying to find space between the crates of munitions and muttering about a ship called *Unflinching Resolve*. Then he heard the name 'Mdama.

They were discussing Jul, speculating about his disappearance. He had vessels laid up at his keep, and they were going to have to move them in a matter of hours. It alarmed them.

"Do you think he was always 'Vadam's agent?" one of them asked. "Has he maneuvered us into a trap?"

"His friend keeps calling to ask if he's with us. There's something very wrong."

Perhaps 'Telcam had just been asking Phillips what he knew of Jul simply because he was asking everyone, and ONI were as likely as anyone else to have heard if he'd run into trouble.

From the conversations Phillips could overhear, some of the rebels were religious types like 'Telcam, and some were just regular hinge-heads who'd never known anything else but serving as San'Shyuum cannon fodder and hadn't yet found a civilian role to keep them busy. It was all in the language. The monkish ones used archaic tenses and weird Dickensian phrases—if Dickens had been Sangheili—like *ere we presume to know the mind of our betters*. The ones who'd been soldiers had a much less frilly and more immediate turn of phrase. In translation, a couple of them reminded him of Mal.

But none of them seemed to share the Arbiter's vision of a galaxy where human and Sangheili could one day cooperate, once both sides had forgotten they'd been trying to out-genocide each other for thirty years. None of this bunch liked or trusted humans. He could hear what they called him.

"I know what *nishum* means, by the way," he said, in his most colloquial Sangheili. 'Telcam still hadn't answered him, but he must have heard the question. "You stop calling me *nishum*, and I won't call you *hinge-heads*."

He could tell which of them spoke some English from the number who turned to glare at him. *Intestinal parasite. Tapeworm.* It wasn't friendly military abuse of the kind Mal called *slagging,* either.

'Telcam was the last to straighten up and look around.

"The first that many Sangheili saw of humans were men in armor," he said. "On first glance they thought you were arthropods with exoskeletons. Instead they found there were small, soft, vulnerable, pink creatures inside. Or brown ones.

I hope you can understand the analogy, even if it's not flattering."

"That's okay," Phillips said. He was happy to play the harmlessly clever child for most Sangheili, dazzling them with his skills at unlocking an *arum*, but he felt he'd survive better with these ones by showing a bit of fight. "I expect you've worked out *hinge-heads*. I've heard *chuck-heads*, too. You know what a chuck is? It's a little gripping piece on a drill that holds the bit. It opens up just like your damned mouths."

Maybe it offended them and maybe it didn't. Phillips realized he was starting to *feel* like a Sangheili when he spoke the language now, not just consciously switching into trying to think like them. There was always an undercurrent of defensive aggression about them. Their anatomy didn't help, because the way their heads were permanently thrust forward automatically triggered a subconscious reaction in humans that they were spoiling for a fight, but it was more than just bad luck in the skeletal lottery. They really did throw down challenges and tell you where their boundaries were. Phillips had mulled over all kinds of stuff about the origin of their species and their territorial approach to life, but now he found he'd stopped rationalizing and was just snarling back like any other Sangheili marking his personal space among the boys.

'Telcam gave him a long, cold look. So did the others, even the ones who Phillips knew didn't understand more than two words of English.

"Fascinating," 'Telcam said. "And to answer your original question, no, you may *not* leave. You'll be questioned by the Arbiter about where you've been. I have little confidence in your ability to withstand that if he were to ask awkward questions now that the coup has begun. Apart from which—I want to be sure that your shipmaster honors her agreements. Having you here reassures me of that."

You bastard. So I'm a hostage. I should have seen that coming.

Phillips felt his pulse speeding up but he wasn't actually scared any longer. It was a strange feeling. "She doesn't even know I'm still alive. *I can't call her.* You think that's going to guarantee your arms supplies?"

That seemed to focus 'Telcam. "You came here with no communications?"

"No. I've got a radio, but it's been damaged." He pulled the device off his jacket and held it up, suddenly remembering that there was a needle mounted inside that was prepped to give him a fatal dose of fast-acting nerve agent if BB judged he was in too tight a spot for everyone's safety. *Jesus, what'll set this thing off now?* He wasn't sure if he should wear it in case it malfunctioned. "You could always contact Osman. Why not give it a try now?"

'Telcam wandered over to him and peered at the radio. Phillips held on to it, trying to look casual and pissed off. He didn't dare let go of it. He didn't know if BB's fragment was still recoverable and could fall into the wrong hands, and if the nerve agent was ejected, a dead 'Telcam wouldn't help matters. He wasn't sure if Sangheili were susceptible to the same toxins as humans, but he wasn't taking the risk.

"Look," he said. "Damn shrapnel or something. I suppose it saved me from worse, though."

'Telcam stared at it. Another Sangheili, the shipmaster they called Buran, ambled across and took a close look at it, too. It seemed to fascinate them.

"You're very lucky, worm-boy," Buran said. "What were the chances of *that* saving you?"

'Telcam looked riveted. "*Philliss,* I believe the gods particularly want you to live. All the more reason for keeping you at my side."

Phillips took it as another smartass remark, but then he looked 'Telcam in the eye and saw that light, that weird *otherness*. Damn, he really meant it. It was all too easy to see him as the pragmatic field master and forget that he had only one motive for overthrowing the Arbiter: religion. He wasn't too fussy about who ran things as long as they did it for the gods. This was a holy war. Phillips bit back his automatic retort that the gods probably wanted him to call home, too, and looked for a way to work this to his advantage.

"I have to let Osman know where I am," he said.

"Very well." 'Telcam reached into his belt and took out a device designed for huge four-fingered hands. That was one of the things that still came as a daily surprise for Phillips, that Sangheili could manipulate anything sophisticated with hands like that. "I shall call the ship and let you talk with her."

'Telcam tapped a complicated sequence of symbols on the comms unit and waited. Phillips had often been on the receiving end of those signals, but he'd never heard what it sounded like when the call didn't connect. Now he knew. It was a quiet continuous stream of random clicks like hot metal cooling down.

"The ship must be in slipspace," 'Telcam said. "We will attempt to call Osman later."

Please let her be on her way. She has to know I'm here. I was transmitting.

"Okay." Phillips made a conscious effort to relax and look irritated rather than concerned. "So what happens now? How long are you going to keep me here? I haven't even got a change of clothes."

"Is that your most pressing concern?"

"Unless you've got something else to keep me busy."

"By nightfall, our brothers in cities across Sanghelios will be taking arms against kaidons who support the Arbiter, and I shall lead the direct assault on Vadam. We have ships and we have sufficient arms. We may not prevail immediately, but we shall take control within the month. How do you see yourself fitting into that battle plan?"

"Okay," Phillips said. "I'll make the coffee. Maybe play with an *arum.*"

'Telcam snorted like a horse and stalked back to the table. Everyone seemed to be using one of those communicators now, having the same conversation with their opposite numbers in other keeps. They seemed to have a number of ships, but it just didn't seem enough to take over a whole world, not even with the hardware that ONI had supplied.

But they're still floundering. It's been less than a year—a few months, that's all—since the Covenant fell apart. They're still relearning how to organize themselves without the San'Shyuum calling the shots.

And that was all the edge that 'Telcam needed. He was organized. The Arbiter wasn't, not yet.

Phillips realized that he was hoping for a draw, just like ONI. So he didn't trust 'Telcam to keep his side of the deal after all, to leave Earth colonies alone if humans kept out of his way. Well, if he survived this, he'd have one hell of a lecture tour ahead of him, let alone the chat shows and books.

Funnily enough, the last place he wanted to be right now was back in Sydney at the university, safe and planned out to retirement. He started wandering around the chamber, remembering what he'd come here for. He was going to check out ancient Forerunner inscriptions to see if there were clues to the locations of the remaining Halos.

"'Telcam," he said, "do you mind if I look around the temple?"

The Sangheili didn't look up from his charts. "You won't find a way out."

"I meant that I'd like to take a look at the carvings and relics. Is that all right? I promise I'll treat it with respect."

"Very well. You'll know when you've reached an unsafe area."

"Oh." *Booby traps?* "What's unsafe?"

"Some passages have been walled off," 'Telcam said. "That was carried out at the time the Forerunners built this temple, and there must have been good reason. The Servants of the Abiding Truth have never breached those walls, nor shall we."

Phillips had no taboos in his life and found it bizarre that a commander used to making hard decisions on a battlefield would accept that kind of mystical keep-out sign without question. But then Phillips didn't fear the hand of some god reaching out and smacking him around the ear. BB had mentioned the slipspace bubbles in the Onyx Dyson sphere. The Forerunners had contained them in some kind of field and had been able to control the passage of time inside them, so Phillips wondered if they'd built that into other facilities. He didn't want to push his luck and end up in one. He'd heard about the Spartan-III who got lost in one and was lucky there were Huragok around to get her out.

I wonder where Adj is now? I hope ONI aren't vivisecting him or anything. Cute little guy. Amazingly useful.

Phillips could have done with Adj right then, and BB, too. He was really on his own now. He walked slowly through the maze of passages, writing each turn that he took on his datapad so that he could find his way out again, and was struck by the precision of the stone blocks. The temple was thousands of years old but the stonework was crisp and immaculate, the joints perfectly square and almost invisible. He ran his palm along the right-hand side of the wall as he walked. The stone was peach-smooth and warmer to the touch than he expected. A string of dim lights ran the length of the ceiling, but that looked to be a Sangheili addition, not the work of aliens who could bend time and space to create a bomb shelter. Grimy lightbulbs spattered with dead insects just didn't seem to be their style.

And then he saw the panels on the wall, the shadows cast by inscriptions, and the anthropologist core of his being went into a feeding frenzy. He speeded up to a trot and stood gazing at the first panel in academic ecstasy.

He would have described it as a cartouche, but that made it sound quaint and primitive. The symbols engraved on it were what he'd come to recognize as Forerunner glyphs. *Suck on this, Howard Carter. I've just become the first human to read an actual message from the gods.* He decided to risk a thunderbolt and put his hand out to touch the symbols, but his fingertips brushed against something that felt solid, a barrier that he could feel but not see. He flattened his cheek against the wall in case he could see an actual sheet of transparent material, but there was nothing. It was one of their protective fields.

Wow. How the hell did they build that into stone and keep it powered all this time? Damn, BB, you're missing all the good stuff. Come to that . . . why did they put that barrier there? To keep it clean?

The symbols were laid out in rows with lines leading from them to other symbols around the margin of the panel. It reminded him of a touch panel on a kitchen appliance.

Maybe those aren't engravings. Maybe they're buttons. Switches.

Pressing them was a risk, but he couldn't work out how to get past that protective screen anyway. Human logic told him that it might have been the whole point—to stop people pressing them by accident. He was so pumped up with adrenaline now that the sheer ravenous greed to *know* about this thing, to understand it, had made the fact he was a hostage of a heavily armed religious lunatic fade into the background.

Oh, BB, you should see this.

Phillips took a few images with his datapad, noting the charge was low. He didn't know when he'd get out of here to top it up again so he'd have to conserve power. Damn, he really needed BB to see this. Should he risk trying to repair the radio cam? He didn't know the first thing about how to fix it other than digging out the fragment of shrapnel, and he didn't know if he'd end up triggering the needle and killing himself. He stood there in the dimly lit tunnel for minutes, just daring himself to take out that lump of metal.

The needle would eject from the back plate. That was why he had to wear it clipped to his jacket. *Shit, lucky? You said it. What if the impact had triggered it?* He held the radio against the stone wall so that he couldn't fumble with it and accidentally stab himself, then began prying the metal out with his stylus. It started to bend the front cover out as well. The shrapnel suddenly flew out and pinged on the floor.

Phillips kept the radio flat against the wall, just in case, and pressed the switch on and off a few times. The pinpoint of green light came on but died again.

Ah well. I tried. No point wasting time. Better start cataloguing all these inscriptions. I've got Halos to find.

He twisted the clip around on the radio and attached it to his top pocket with surgical care, making sure the back plate was facing out. Then he carried on looking along the walls for inscriptions, searching for repeating symbols that might give him a way in to the Forerunner language.

This one was interesting. It was an oval with what looked like a section through a vertebra in the middle of it, and it appeared in every cartouche several times. He was trying to think like aliens who could bend time when he put his hand on the invisible barrier and a voice suddenly spoke to him out of nowhere.

He almost crapped himself, but it wasn't the voice of God, *anybody's* god.

"Please activate the video input," BB said. "Continue when ready."

UNSC *PORT STANLEY*, EN ROUTE TO SANGHELIOS

"Bloody hell, BB," Mal said, leaning on the chart table. "There's a lot of gaps in this schematic."

"In case you hadn't noticed, *Malcolm*," BB said acidly, "I was put out of action while I was doing the survey. And since when did you ever have perfect recon data before insertion?"

"Just making an observation, mate."

Everyone was a bit sensitive right now. Mal prided himself on being able to focus on the job at hand no matter what else was going on, but part of him had disconnected from Phillips's plight to worry about Naomi's reaction to the bombshell about her father. Perhaps it didn't hurt as much as he'd thought: she said she couldn't even remember her childhood before she'd been taken for Spartan training, so maybe this seemed just as unreal to her. Mal had grown up without a father as well. He tried out the idea of being told that his dad had finally shown up and had a steady career as a serial killer. How did he feel about that? Nothing, nothing at all. It wasn't real and he couldn't make it feel that way. Staffan Sentzke was definitely real, though. And Mal didn't have a mess of buried traumas like Naomi did.

Nobody in Kilo-Five had any family ties. That was part of the selection criteria, BB had told them, no complications if they needed to vanish for years at a time. But now one of them had a real live relative they'd never bargained for, and a really embarrassing one at that.

"Are you listening, Staff?" Osman asked.

Mal wondered what he'd missed. The captain could make him flinch, informal and easygoing or not. "Sorry, ma'am."

"I was saying that as Ontom's coastal, we *could* insert by sea."

"It's going to have to be at night, either way. But we're not equipped for going in by sea. You can't adapt the jump pods to make them into boats."

"I can get in there and drop you without them," Devereaux said. "Swim in, like the good old days."

"We'd be putting a lot of faith in *Tart-Cart*'s stealth," Vaz said.

Naomi had been staring at the 3-D projection suspended above the chart table in absolute silence. She started shaking her head very slowly. "Armor. You need it. And I'm carrying three hundred kilos of it. It's got to be a land insertion, and that means coming in from the north."

"I don't plan to deploy you, Naomi," Osman said.

"Why not, ma'am? This is exactly what I'm designed for."

The *designed* bit stung. Osman looked as if she'd taken a deep breath. She could easily have been where Naomi was now. It was almost the first thing she'd told them about herself, like she'd needed to get it off her chest: that she'd been a Spartan kid, but the surgical enhancements had crippled her, and Parangosky had picked her up and put her back together again.

And I don't have to be Freud to work out that *relationship.*

"I don't want to lose the entire squad," Osman said at last. "If this goes pear-shaped, I'd lose one of the last Spartan-Twos. No offense, marines."

"It's okay, ma'am," Vaz said. "We know she's a bigger budget item than us."

Naomi just looked at Osman as if she was shaping up to argue, but she let it go. They went back to the holographic fly-through of the approach to Sanghelios and Ontom, trying to work out which features from the mapping run were some kind of radar and where the sensors might be. The 3-D projection suspended over the chart table was finely detailed in places, but it stopped dead at the temple doorway. That would have to be enough. Considering how long Earth had been at war with the Covenant, it still didn't have much reconnaissance imaging of Sanghelios. Pretty well everything they were looking at had come from one mission, Admiral Hood's trip to meet the Arbiter. One orbit of Sanghelios had enabled UNSC *Iceni* to map the planet's topography, and the shuttle had surveyed a narrow corridor across the Arbiter's home city of Vadam in some detail, but Sanghelios was still mostly unknown territory. And BB was right. Mal and Vaz had done orbital jumps onto planets with almost no information about where the pods would land.

"I think we're going to have to make orbit and remap all this before we commit to landing anybody," BB said. "It'll be time well spent. Just remember that the last fix we have on Phillips suggests he's in the temple complex, though."

"So we go in," Mal said.

"Forerunner ruins. As Halsey found on Onyx, they can be a tad irregular."

"So we still go in." Mal carried on because not even Osman was filling the gaps, and he needed to kill the silence. "Because we want to recover your fragment as well, don't we? Or can you just throw it away like a duplicate file?"

For an entity determined not to have even a holographic body, BB had quite a repertoire of body language. He could express a hell of a lot with just six plain, flat surfaces that weren't even there. Mal could have sworn that the watery blue light dimmed for a moment. He got the sense that BB had glanced down at the deck, troubled.

He's based on a human brain's structure. Whatever he says about meatbags, that's got to influence how he behaves.

"I've never lost a fragment before," BB said. "I've generated and shut down many, but this one wasn't closed. It was *interrupted*."

Devereaux looked up. "Like pulling out a chip too fast and corrupting the data?"

"That's a fair approximation. Except . . . I *am* data. That's me. I think it's more like brain damage caused by anoxia."

"Wow. So you can't load it all back in again."

"I don't like gaps in my memory, Lian. They're painful and distressing."

"But it's only a duplicate of you, in a way. You can work without it."

"No, it's not, because that fragment is what you'd call BB Lite. It had limited functions in case it fell into enemy hands. And its experiences and memories won't be the same as mine, either, so I need to reintegrate them, to put them back in my timeline, or else . . . I'm sorry, it's hard to explain, but it'll leave me with gaps in my mind."

"I used to get those a lot," Mal said, trying to reassure the AI. "It's called beer."

"I appreciate the laddish chumminess, but when a mind is all you are, that's rather disturbing."

Like the rest of the squad, Devereaux always looked straight at the holographic box as if she was making eye contact. BB was supposed to be omnipotent and omniscient, at least for his seven-year lifespan. Mal thought of all the survivable things that went wrong with human brains—strokes, dementia, hallucinations, memory loss, injury that changed your entire personality—and realized that if those scared him, then it was probably like the threat of terminal illness for BB. The AI thought, or he didn't exist. It was that stark.

"I bet we find your fragment and it's fine," Vaz said. "The first thing it'll do is bitch at us for taking so long to recover it."

Everyone stopped talking again. Mal thought this was the

worst thing about slipspace: not the uncertainty of where you'd drop back into normal space, or if the trip had taken longer than you'd planned, but that you were cut off from comms, left to stew in your own juice until you decelerated and could talk to the world again. And the one thing *Port Stanley* needed now was information from outside.

Osman had her arms folded on the edge of the chart table, bent right over like someone leaning on their shopping cart to relieve the supermarket tedium. The silence was begging someone to break it again.

"Okay." Osman straightened up. "Seeing as we've tossed and gored this as much as we can for the time being, let's discuss what's really on everyone's mind. Naomi, I'm going to want absolute proof that this suspect's your father before I do *anything*. What did you tell Spenser, Mal?"

Sometimes Naomi could look like a wax model. She was so pale that she was almost translucent at the best of times, but when she was doing her I'm-not-reacting thing, Mal couldn't even tell if she was breathing.

Vaz chipped in. "I told Spenser who he was, ma'am. I shouldn't have. I wasn't thinking."

"But Spenser agreed to sit on his hands until we got back," Mal said. "It's not like there's anything big going down at the moment. He's just keeping tabs on them."

"Did he call it in to Parangosky?"

"Not while we were there."

"I would have expected the Admiral to have sent a message before we slipped if she'd been informed," BB said.

If she's totally open with Osman, that is. ONI couldn't move in a straight line if you put it on rails. Maybe she's waiting to see when Osman decides to tell her. I mean, they're buddy-buddy, and Oz is the old girl's favorite, but . . . she's Parangosky. She didn't get to be top spook by going soft on people.

"I'll talk to her when we leave slip," Osman said. "In the meantime, let's agree to some ground rules on this. It's not going to be tidy. Whatever happens, it's going to hurt someone somewhere down the line. Our priority is to protect Earth by any means necessary, but we have to trust each other to do that."

"Ma'am, he's a stranger," Naomi said. "Don't change procedure because of me. Handle him like any other suspect."

"He's probably a terrorist because he lost *you*." Osman paused as if she thought she'd spoken out of turn. It was probably the worst thing she could point out to Naomi. "You do know that, don't you? That he never believed the cloned child Halsey swapped you for was his real daughter? He always claimed it was a government conspiracy."

"Vaz told me," Naomi said, apparently unmoved. "One day I'll read it for myself."

"Okay, then we all level with one another about everything. Understood?"

"Yes, ma'am."

Osman was still learning how to end a conversation like that. Mal could see it on her face, all that doubt about the stuff she now had to do. He pitched in to rescue her.

"Well, seeing as we don't have our little Huragok chum to mod our kit, we'd better go and see what we can put together for a landing," he said. "My money's still on the drop pods, but it's going to be a bugger to exfil, no matter how we insert."

"Fingers crossed that Hood comes through for us, then," Osman said. "And now that I've embarrassed you all, I'm going to execute a tactical withdrawal and catch up on the signal traffic in my day cabin."

There was no bullshit with Osman. Mal now ranked eye-watering honesty equally with competence in his top five list of officer must-haves. BB's avatar zipped off the bridge in a blur of

blue light—not that he had to do the effects to make a point—
and the three ODSTs stood in an awkward circle around Naomi.

"Sorry, mate," Mal said to her. "I'm really, really sorry."

"You're sure it's him?"

Vaz squirmed visibly. "I should have taken a copy of the file,
but we were in a hurry to get back."

"Was there a picture?"

"Yes."

Naomi paused. Mal knew what was coming.

"What does he look like?" she asked.

"He looks like you," Vaz said innocently. Mal felt the knife
turn, even though that was the last thing Vaz would have dreamed
of doing to Naomi. "You're the image of your dad."

CHAPTER

FOUR

I WANT A HURAGOK TEAM ROUTINELY EMBARKED IN EVERY
WARSHIP BY 2557. THIS IS WHAT GAVE THE COVENANT THEIR
TECHNICAL SUPERIORITY. NOW IT'S OURS, AND WHEREVER
THE REST OF THEIR HURAGOK WENT, EVEN IF THE SANGHEILI
REACQUIRE THEM—OURS STILL HAVE THEIR UNIQUE ONYX
LEGACY, AND THAT PUTS US WAY AHEAD.
(REAR ADMIRAL SAEED SHAFIQ, UNSC PROCUREMENT)

UNSC *PORT STANLEY*, APPROACHING SANGHEILI SPACE

"Place your bets, *mesdames et messieurs*," BB said. "*Faites vos
jeux* . . . five, four, three, two . . ."

Osman tried to ignore her cartwheeling stomach as the ship
dropped out of slipspace and the black void in the forward
viewscreen was suddenly peppered with stars that hadn't been
there a second before. The status panels on the console showed
Port Stanley's drives and associated systems dropping back from
well into the red zone. BB hadn't been joking when he said he
was going to push the ship past her tested limits.

"There. We're back." BB placed himself on Phillips's empty
seat. "Only two million klicks adrift and five hours *earlier* than
projected. I win. Making OPSNORMAL and running comms
checks. Lots of messages waiting, Captain."

"Wow, BB, did we blow many gaskets?" Devereaux asked,
leaning over the control panel. "That was *brisk.*"

"Nothing we can't fix with some self-amalgamating titanium strip and lots of genius."

"Let me know if you need a hand. Because I'd like to live to see thirty-two."

Osman pushed herself out of her chair and found that she'd now learned to allow for the twenty or thirty seconds of disorientation on slipspace jumps. *I can make myself do anything if I have to. Just tell myself that the whirling isn't real. I believe me. I do.* The ODSTs never seemed to turn a hair, but then anyone who reacted to jumps like she did would never have lasted five minutes as either a pilot or a Helljumper. A few confused seconds was all it took to crash and burn. Sometimes she felt inadequate beside them.

Naomi never blinked either. But then she was a proper Spartan, not an abandoned project like herself, and she had other distractions that had to be weighing heavily on her mind.

"Anything from Phillips?" Osman asked.

BB lifted off the seat like a dropship and banked away to the comms console. Now she *knew* he was uneasy. That was almost an AI equivalent of whistling in the dark.

"I'm afraid not, but there's one from Hood via Parangosky," he said. "He's asked the Arbiter to allow us to land a search party."

"And?"

"They're still talking. I must say it's real emotional blackmail stuff. All about absolving him of moral responsibility if he lets the *experts* do it."

Vaz made his disbelief noise, a little hiss of breath. "How to win hinge-head friends. That'll really piss them off."

The message flashed onto the main bridge monitor. Osman read the transcript and winced. *"I fully understand that there are events over which you have no control."* Jesus, did Hood know what he was doing? Vaz was right. Sangheili wouldn't take kindly to a human hinting that they were incompetent and chaotic. On the other hand, Hood did seem to have a way with the Arbiter, and perhaps he'd gambled that letting him off the hook might achieve something.

"He's just living up to their stereotype of us," Devereaux said. "They think we're too cocky so they might as well let us in just to see us screw it up and then show us how it's done."

Naomi perked up. She really didn't like being idle. It was still a massive risk entrusting a squad to Sangheili hospitality, though, and everyone would stand a better chance with a Spartan on board. If there was one thing that freaked out a hinge-head, it was a Spartan. Osman jerked herself out of second-guessing Sangheili motives. She couldn't, and it was too late anyway. Hood had interceded.

"Okay. I'm going to talk to the Admiral. What time is it for her, BB?"

"Just after three, Captain. She's still on her *Infinity* inspection. Zulu time."

"Flash her for me, would you?"

"I already took the liberty. She's standing by for a call."

"Try to get hold of 'Telcam, too."

"Do we let him know we're aware that he made contact with Phillips?"

"I'll decide when I hear what he's got to say for himself."

Phillips, 'Telcam, and the whole shebang could easily have been a pile of hamburger by now, of course. But Osman still had to confirm that.

I should be more upset about Phillips. I'm going to tell myself that the reason I'm not is because I believe he's alive. I'd hate to think I was that relaxed about losing a crew member.

"Patch the Admiral through to my day cabin," she said. "And take us in close enough to monitor Sanghelios."

So much for transparency: she could have had the conversation on the bridge, but old habits took awhile to die. With just five people and an AI rattling around a warship designed for a hundred, she didn't have an excuse. As she sat down at her desk and positioned herself in front of the screen, she found her mind suddenly full of all the things she chose not to know, and those she was happy not to be told, and wondered again if she'd be up to Parangosky's job when the day finally came.

Her own personal file was sitting in the system, ready to tell her as much unhappy stuff about herself as Naomi had discovered about her own background. It wasn't so much gnawing at her as starting to nibble around the edges.

Phillips. Don't forget this is about Phillips. Poor bastard. He didn't sign up for this. We've got to retrieve him.

"Ready, BB," she said. The screen came to life, a narrow frame showing a dimly lit corner of a warship that could have been any in the fleet. Parangosky was hunched over folded arms, frowning.

"Hello, ma'am," Osman said. "I see Admiral Hood's been exerting the proverbial diplomatic pressure."

"He still is. 'Vadam didn't dismiss him out of hand, either. You're standing off Sanghelios now, yes?"

"We're going to five hundred thousand klicks to do a survey orbit. In case we need to insert without permission."

Parangosky didn't blink. "I've sent you all the intel we've collated since you lost contact with Phillips. We're pretty blind out there now—no Spenser, and no Covenant relays left to intercept. Almost makes you miss the war, doesn't it?"

"That's top of the shopping list, then." Osman was getting a better picture day by day of the way ONI would have to adapt to the new galactic order. "The more fragmented things get, the more we need to expand our network of sources."

"Our only window on Sanghelios at the moment is the Arbiter, and he says fighting's broken out in a number of cities."

"Perhaps it's best to suggest he's too busy to look for Phillips. Fine by me."

"I'm not being callous, but it would be very useful to monitor the situation as well as finding the professor. If this is the revolution, we don't want anyone winning outright, after all."

"When you say *monitor* . . . you mean hands-on assistance."

"I mean a route into both sides of the argument, but it might require more than just supplying hardware."

"Well, BB's trying to track down 'Telcam, so when that happens I'll have a much clearer picture."

"Probably best to hold your position until Hood's satisfied that he's done all he can with the Arbiter." Parangosky glanced over her shoulder at something Osman couldn't see. "On a slightly different tack, the first opportunity I get, I'll be sending *you* some help. Would you like your Huragok back?"

"Adj? Oh, he'll be very handy. Thank you."

"Adj and a friend, Forerunner-enriched. It's more than handy, Captain—I'm sending them to retrofit *Stanley* with completely accurate slipspace navigation and instant comms."

Osman knew about the navigation refinements, but being able to communicate from slipspace was even better as far as she was concerned. "No more lobbing bottles over the side?"

"Just for the lucky few at the moment. All this is going to transform the battlefield."

Damn right it would. Warships would not only know exactly where they'd emerge and when, but they'd also arrive with the benefit of real-time information. It was like the invention of steam power and the radio all at once. Working with Huragok was something of a mystery tour, but it was worth the uncertainty, rather like a birthday.

I've never had one of those. Not a real one.

"When the dust settles on the current task, I'll look forward to that."

"Is everything all right, Serin?"

There was no hiding anything from Parangosky. She was more than sharp: she was just like a mother, or what Osman imagined a mother would be. "We have a few issues, ma'am," Osman said. "The first of Halsey's chickens have come home to roost."

"I had a feeling that would happen before too long."

"You know what's in Naomi's file."

"Of course."

"Has Mike briefed you?"

"No."

Well, that was something. "Her father's alive, living on Venezia, and Mike's keeping tabs on him—"

Parangosky interrupted her before she had the chance to explain, as if she didn't want to be told the details. "Is this something you're happy to deal with on your own, or do you want me to get involved?"

"I'd like to be all grown up and try to resolve it myself."

"Very well. I'm here when you need me. But it's not causing operational problems, is it?"

"No. Not at all."

"That's all I need to know. Unless there's anything else, stand by for an update on Hood."

"Will do, ma'am. *Stanley* out."

Osman sat back in the chair and rubbed her face slowly. Well, that hadn't been as painful as she'd expected. She trusted Parangosky, but she found herself still looking for the angle, looking for the right answer to a challenge she felt she'd just been set. Should she send a report? She only had a name at the moment, and Spenser had the situation under control for the time being.

I've been at this game too long for Parangosky to be testing me. She's just giving me space. Letting me make my choices, because very soon I'm going to have to make them for ONI.

Oh . . . God.

BB appeared on her desk. "Not all bad news, then."

"*Great* news."

"The boys will enjoy having Adj back. Mal needs a pet."

"Any luck with 'Telcam?"

"I would have bragged about that right away. Still trying."

For the first time on this mission, Osman now had a clear order from above: to wait until Hood had exhausted all avenues with the Arbiter. The sublight drive sent a steady tremor through the deck as *Stanley* edged closer to Sanghelios. The waiting wouldn't be wasted.

Hang in there, Evan. We're coming.

And while you're at it . . . keep your mouth shut.

The radio cam was down, and BB might have been too damaged to use that nerve agent if the worst happened. This was Parangosky's world, the call on who to save and who to sacrifice for the greater good. Maybe this really was a test, then, or perhaps a blooding to initiate Osman in the messy decisions involving personnel she knew and liked, not the distant strategic stuff where the dead would be strangers.

Osman took a slow walk around the ship's deserted passages to give Naomi and the ODSTs some space. When she checked her datapad to see where everyone was, Devereaux's trace showed up on the hangar deck with *Tart-Cart* and Naomi was in the armor bay, the automated system that she needed to suit up in her Mjolnir rig. Vaz and Mal were in the wardroom.

"BB," Osman said, "I'm not asking you to snoop on them, but are the lads all right?"

The AI's voice came out of the ship's broadcast system. "They had a little tiff over who to tell first about Naomi's dad, you or her. I think they're shaking hands and making up now."

"Good." She wasn't alone in finding some decisions too close to home to be done by the book, then. "I ought to be giving that some attention."

"First things first. I'm just starting a survey run, by the way. We'll swing around Sanghelios, map the surface down to a two-meter scale, and see what else I can pick up. If this is small-scale fighting, it might take us a day or two to scan the whole surface, so I'm starting with the Ontom region."

"Agreed."

Osman headed back to the bridge and sat with her boots up on a chair, watching the three-dimensional plot of Sanghelios on the chart table growing a line at a time like a garment being knitted. There were more islands than she'd realized, and far less land mass.

"Ontom," BB said, not appearing anywhere. Osman still looked up to the nearest deckhead speaker. "I'm doing a detailed job on it, but even extended frequency mapping isn't penetrating the temple."

"Does that mean it's a hardened target?"

"With the Forerunners, who knows?"

It must have been two hours before Mal came up to the bridge, put a cup of coffee on the console in front of her without saying a word, and stood staring at the plot.

"Thanks, Staff," she said, sipping the coffee.

"Your turn next, ma'am."

He didn't take his eyes off the plot, gaze flicking from detail to detail. He was probably modifying the insertion on the fly. Maybe Phillips would just pop up again with a story to tell about just losing radio contact, as people sometimes did, and it would all be sorted.

But he's had plenty of time to do that.

"Captain." BB appeared in front of her. "Life just got a little easier. The Arbiter says yes. We can land a squad. Usual drill—an escort will pick up the dropship and take us in."

"Alle-bleedin'-luia," Mal muttered. "Let's get this over with."

TEMPLE OF THE ABIDING TRUTH, ONTOM, SANGHELIOS

Phillips shook the radio cam like a cheap watch. "BB, I'm on my own, so you can drop the sorry-Dave-I-can't-do-that crap. But keep the volume down, okay?"

He kept his voice at a whisper and waited for BB to snap back with something suitably withering. But there was just a long pause. The BB who responded wasn't the one he knew.

"Can I help you, Professor Phillips?"

"Are you trying to be funny, or is something wrong?"

"Owing to tampering and damage, some of my functions have been disabled or deleted."

"Oh *shit*." Just as BB was standing by to shove a needle into Phillips in case the mission went badly wrong, he must have had fail-safes of his own to stop his programming falling into enemy hands. *I should have realized that. I should have asked more questions. But I was too pumped up on adrenaline.* Phillips's attempt at repair had been interpreted as trying to dismantle the radio cam's case. "I'm sorry. I was only digging shrapnel out of the radio. I didn't think. Look, BB, I'm in a tight spot. Do you remember the explosion?"

"I shut down after damage to my host device."

"Well, right now I'm screwed. *Really* screwed." *Stay calm. Just think.* "'Telcam's started the coup early and he's effectively holding me hostage."

"I understand. I remember who 'Telcam is, but not why you're in touch with him."

"Just tell me what you can still do. Can you send a signal?"

"My encryption's been deleted for security. My positioning data tells me we're on Sanghelios, which is still classed as potentially hostile by the Office of Naval Intelligence."

"Try calling *Port Stanley.* Please."

"ONI-PS Three-Nine accepts only encrypted communication. I can transmit in open protocol on domestic frequencies compatible with this device, though."

Great. Just terrific. "So you're just a damn phone now. How about getting into other systems? Can you still hack?"

"I can assist you with productivity management, nonclassified information, and data processing. What would you like me to do? And can you make sure the lens is facing out, please? Otherwise I can't see."

"Okay. Can you also do me a favor and disable that nerve agent thing?"

"Already done. I don't have information on why that was installed."

"It doesn't matter. Just keep it battened down, okay?"

Phillips clipped the radio cam to his jacket pocket again, not entirely confident that BB wasn't going to malfunction and shoot him full of instant death. Now he realized how little he knew about how BB worked, and how much the AI was limited by whatever hardware he found himself stored in. Could he repair himself? No, that would have been another risky function. As far as BB was concerned, he was behind enemy lines—Phillips had even confirmed it for him—and someone had tried to tamper with him, so he'd pulled the plug and reduced himself to a datapad. The last thing he'd be designed to do would be to restore himself to a windfall of secret information for an enemy. Poor old BB had stripped himself down to name, rank, and serial number.

But I can't do that. Can I? They can always beat it out of me.

"Okay," Phillips whispered. "Have you got any databases that can translate Forerunner glyphs?"

"I have notes from a number of Forerunner sites."

"Well, that's good, BB." Damn, this was painful. It was like dealing with a dementia patient, someone you'd once loved or admired but who was now barely the same person and didn't even recognize you. He hadn't realized how deep a bond he'd forged with BB. He found himself making reassuring noises in his mind that the real BB, the matrix, the core of him, was still safe in *Port Stanley,* and this damaged persona was just a temporary glitch that was no more serious than a bad dream. But the decline still disturbed him. "I want you to record some symbols and try to translate them for me."

"Certainly, Professor."

Phillips decided to look on the positive side. He didn't have a fully functioning BB to rescue him, but at least he could complete his original mission—gathering and interpreting Forerunner data. He tracked slowly up and down the passage so the AI could capture the engravings.

"What do you think the cartouches are, BB?" There was no echo. Beyond the big vaulted chamber at the entrance, the temple became a network of stone passages, but it didn't *sound* like one. If he hadn't been standing on flagstones he would have thought the place was carpeted and soundproofed. The air was muffled, heavy, *syrupy.* "Why did the Forerunners build this place?"

"I might be able to suggest theories when I complete the survey."

"Okay. Tell me when you're ready to move on."

"Keep walking, Professor."

Now that Phillips was gathering the data, he had to find a way to get it to ONI, and transmitting it seemed out of the question for the time being. People would be looking for him by now. The Arbiter wouldn't just shrug and chalk it up to experience. He had a foreigner missing in his territory, and even if he didn't care what happened to a useless human *nishum,* he'd certainly worry about what damage he could do on his own. Sanghelios didn't welcome tourists.

He'll find me. Someone's searching for me, whatever happens.

Or I'll find a way out myself.

"You can increase your pace, Professor," BB said. "I can record this easily."

"Okay, BB. Sorry." Phillips hadn't made a note of how far he'd walked. When he checked his watch, he found he'd been exploring for nearly an hour. "Are you mapping the complex?"

"I can if you want me to."

Right. The real BB would have this all catalogued by now and come up with a million suggestions about how I could do my job better. That makes sense, I suppose. You don't want a compromised AI volunteering to do stuff for the enemy.

"Yes, that would be handy," Phillips said. "Thanks. I want a scale plan of the temple. Measure everything and mark the positions of all features."

"You'll need to take me back to the entrance if you want a complete schematic."

"Good idea. I need to visit the bathroom and get something to eat. Let's take a break."

He trudged back up the passage, checking the directions he'd scribbled on his datapad. *Bathroom. Hah.* He was being generous. Sangheili plumbing was depressingly basic and they certainly didn't do fluffy towels. It was more the tepid water from a single spigot and a hole in the ground kind of bathroom. These were the small but morale-crushing things that no adventure movie had ever warned him about: if you were trapped, how did you do your laundry or recharge your datapad or even find bathroom tissue? That was the stuff of which real human drama was made. *Food. Oh, not the dog food again. Not that damn meat.* When he got out of here, he was going to gorge on paella and mango and salmon and snack noodles and licorice and every damn thing he could lay his hands on. He rummaged in his shoulder bag, hoping to find some fluff-covered, sticky piece of candy that might have escaped him previously.

Zip. Nothing. Next time . . . I'll carry at least one twenty-four-hour ration pack. Like the ODSTs.

He opened his jacket as he walked, lifting it by the collar to sniff under his arms, first right, then left. *Ewww. I want a shower.* The Sangheili probably didn't care if he was in need of a change of clothes, but he did. *Morale. It's all about morale.* Now he wished he'd spent more time talking to Mal, Vaz, and Devereaux about the domestic routine of their deployments rather than getting them to tell him warry stories. He'd never laugh at their obsession with washing their undies ever again. They were incredibly disciplined about keeping their kit clean, and now he knew why. They had to stay clean in the field no matter what crap the war threw at them.

I'll listen, Mal. I promise. You can teach me. You can turn me into an ODST anytime you want. Really.

"BB, we're coming up to the main chamber," he whispered. "Better stay quiet. I don't want them to start dismantling you."

"Understood, Professor."

Phillips waited for the punch line, but of course none came. This was a basic AI with just enough personality to react to him sensibly. He was already missing the real, annoying, funny, bitchy, nosey BB as badly as a best friend.

"Did you find what you were looking for?" 'Telcam asked, looking up as Phillips wandered in. Most of the Sangheili who'd been clustered around the chart had disappeared. "I was about to send someone to find you."

"I don't know." Phillips gestured with his datapad. If they'd heard him talking, he'd give them a plausible explanation before they asked too many questions. "I've been looking at the cartouches and recording my thoughts. I don't understand any of it, but it's beautiful."

'Telcam cocked his head on one side. "My brothers were always convinced that humans had no souls, but I think some of you are instinctively capable of being touched by the truth of the divine."

And that, Your Honor, is the case for the defense. "Where did everyone go?"

"To join their ships. I must go, too. Buran's ship won't fly itself." 'Telcam seemed to be in a rare good mood. Either the coup was shaping up or he was feeling sorry for the tapeworm that had a soul. "There will be guards remaining here, so you'll be safe." His voice dropped to a murmur. "If you find meaning in the cartouches, I expect you to share it with me. You have . . . an unusual insight. You chose to learn the culture of your enemy, but you respect it, which makes you *different* from the others."

"Of course." *So I'm reading his bible and even he can't understand bits of it. Right. That'll come in handy sooner or later. Bargaining chip.* "Do you have any spare clothing? I need to wash mine."

'Telcam did the Sangheili equivalent of snapping his fingers and summoned a minion by rapping his knuckles on the table. "Olar, see that our guest gets what he needs."

"He'll need *children's* clothing," Olar said.

"Then get it. I hold you responsible for his well-being. Find him some food, too."

Well, that was one problem solved: nobody was going to kill him, not yet. And he could live on dog food and water indefinitely if he had to. 'Telcam swept out and Olar stared at him balefully for a few moments.

"I hear you can solve any *arum* you're given," he said.

"For some reason, I can." Phillips could feel an opportunity for psychological one-upmanship presenting itself. "I seem to have been born with a lot of Sangheili skills."

Olar chewed that over for a moment and stalked off. The real BB would have had something cutting to say about that, but this one remained silent as he'd been told. Olar returned with a couple of long, plain tunics—knee length when Phillips held one up to himself—and what looked like field dressings. It took Phillips a few moments to work that out.

Ah. Like a sling bandage. I think I know where that goes . . .

"Thank you," he said. "Excuse me."

The temple had a long, narrow bathroom lined with stalls that reminded Phillips of a boarding school. He looked around for their equivalent of soap, a dull gray powder that he'd discovered was a mix of a kind of clay and a plant similar to soapwort, and worked it into a paste in water so cold that it hurt his hands.

I can do this. Think of the lectures I can give on this alone.

He hung his jacket on a nail, took a painfully cold shower that felt like being hit by a water cannon, and tried on his new clothes. It took a bit of ingenuity to tie on the underwear and tuck all the spare fabric from the tunic into his pants, but it would have to do. His shirt and smalls would dry inside the hour, and then he could stick to a routine of doing this every day. Damn it, he was starting to feel *pleased* with himself. He felt so confident now that he swaggered out into the main chamber and helped himself to some of the rations still stacked in one of the side rooms.

"Is there anything else you need?" Olar asked.

"I'm fine, thanks." Phillips was already working out how he'd make a bigger bag from one of the tunics and pack it with a few extra meals, clay powder, and a water bottle so he'd be ready to escape when the chance presented itself. "I'm going to head back into the tunnels later. I've got plenty of things to study."

If there was a way in, there would also be a way out. The Forerunners were too smart not to have a fire exit.

"Okay, BB, shall we get back to work?" he said, taking out his datapad. "What have you analyzed so far?"

"There's a recurring symbol," BB said. "Using Dr. Halsey's notes, I believe it means a powered door, or a door to a power source, or even an instruction for accessing power. But there are a few that I can't interpret yet because there's no sentence structure."

"Is that a linguistic issue, or are we talking about this being lists of isolated words?" For all Phillips knew, they might have been trying to translate the Forerunner language using a department store directory. Context was everything. "Describe them to me."

"I'm unable to interface with your datapad to show you what I mean. But if Halsey's notes are correct, then one word either means someone who lays down absolute rules, or the regulations themselves." BB sounded as if he was going to lapse into being his old self. Phillips could have sworn he was going to sigh in exasperation, but he kept on going in an uncharacteristically unemotional tone. "The recurring symbol next to it contains the negative phoneme. I believe it's an instruction not to do something."

"What is it, then? A warning, a keep-out sign, or the Ten Commandments?"

"Eleven," BB said. "One cartouche has eleven items."

"Thou shalt not . . . what?"

Phillips didn't know. He looked at the cartouche detail he'd recorded for himself. He was hunting for Halos. He was sure the Forerunners would have left records of where they'd located the remaining devices, as well as the locations of bunker worlds like Onyx. It wasn't the kind of thing they'd have kept secret. Everyone would have needed to know where they were, to get to safety before the Halos activated to scour the galaxy clean of sentient life.

"Look for references to rings, Halos, circles, shield worlds, and contamination, BB," he said. "That's what I came here to find."

SANDSTONE QUARRY, BEKAN KEEP, MDAMA, SANGHELIOS

Raia 'Mdama stood at the ramp to the main hatch of *Unflinching Resolve* with her pistol drawn, watching the shuttle approaching low over the hill. If 'Telcam wanted his precious warship then he would have to come through her to take it.

"You think that's going to stop him?" Forze stood beside her, one hand on his holster, showing partial solidarity. "He believes his authority comes from the gods."

"He wouldn't dare shoot a female," she said. "And he wouldn't dare shoot an elder's wife in her own keep."

"His brothers butchered the Relon elders . . . in their own keep."

"I will *not* stand down."

"You and Jul, you're very alike. Do you realize that?"

"You mean that we can only be pushed so far."

Movement caught her eye. She turned her head to see Naxan, one of Jul's uncles, charging down the slope with a couple of the juvenile males behind him, pistols drawn.

"Raia, you can't do this!" He was beginning to show his age, but his willingness to plunge into a fight hadn't diminished. He stopped to stand between her and the shuttle that had now landed on the far side of the quarry. "If this monk knows anything about Jul's disappearance, let *me* deal with him."

"No, Uncle, I'm the keep elder while my husband is absent." Raia tried to wave him away. "I'll deal with this."

"They're *lunatics,*" he snapped. "I won't let you put yourself at risk."

"Stand back, Naxan. I mean to do this. You and the boys, you leave this to me and Forze. Do you understand?"

"This won't end well." Naxan stood his ground for a few more seconds, then backed off. He didn't leave, though. "Revolution or no revolution, I'll take his head off if he harms this clan in any way."

"It might not come to that."

Raia could now see 'Telcam loping down the hill with the shipmaster called Buran. And he'd seen her. She watched his head jerk back but he didn't break his stride. He probably saw a female, an old man, and some juveniles, and decided he only had to deal with Forze.

"Avu Med 'Telcam," she said. "Where's my husband? What have you done with him?"

'Telcam bowed his head politely. "My lady, I too would like to know where your husband is. Ask Forze. I've looked for him. I wouldn't want to think he's defected to the Arbiter."

"You *believe* that?" Raia raised her pistol, a furious reflex, but now that she'd done it she had to follow through. Naxan spat in contempt. Nobody moved. "If Jul had changed his position, he'd have sought you out and told you to your face. No, more than that—he'd come after you and kill you. But he went looking for you, monk, because you never revealed where your arms came from. If anyone's playing both games, it's *you.*"

She waited for him to erupt. She was ready. She'd have a moment's advantage, the moment when he hesitated to lash out because she was a female, and that was when she'd get one shot in. He certainly hesitated. But then he shook his head slowly from side to side, puzzled.

"But where did he follow?" he asked. "Where did he go?

Damn the fool, if he's been taken by Brutes, then he could betray the whole liberation."

Forze stepped in. "The day you declined to let him know where you were meeting your supplier."

That got 'Telcam's attention. He shut his eyes for a few moments as if he was racking his brains to recall the detail of that day. "He was safer *not* knowing," he said. "But if he did follow me, then I suspect he went straight to the Arbiter afterward."

"Why?"

"You're really much safer not knowing the answer."

"If Jul had switched sides, he would have contacted me. He hasn't. So he must have been captured or killed."

'Telcam went to walk past her up the ramp, but she aimed the pistol squarely at his chest. "You do *not* walk away from me until you give me an answer, Field Master."

"I don't have one." He turned to Buran. "If he's been taken by the Arbiter's agents, we'd better find somewhere else for these ships."

Buran was keeping a wary eye on Naxan. "'Vadam would have shown up here and razed this keep to the ground by now."

"Not if Jul's refusing to talk." He made another attempt to walk up the ramp but now Forze blocked him as well. "I understand your distress, but the coup has begun. We *have* to move on Vadam right now. Please, stand aside."

"You want your ship? Then you take me too, and you help me find my husband."

"This isn't the time, my lady."

Raia put the pistol to his head. "I insist."

She was worried that the shaking in her gut would show in her hands. Would she fire? *Yes.* She would. She had nothing to lose. 'Telcam didn't so much look scared as bewildered. Perhaps monks' wives did as they were told. Perhaps he didn't have a wife at all.

He could knock me to the ground. He's not afraid of me. Does he pity me? Does he think I'm mad?

"Very well," 'Telcam said. He seemed more weary than afraid. "There's no time to debate about this. But understand one thing— if Jul is being held by the Arbiter, we might not find him. We might attack a building where he's being held prisoner. I can do nothing about that."

"It's better than sitting here doing nothing." Now she'd won. She tucked her pistol back in its holster, realizing she was now being swept along on a tide of her own making and that there was no way to escape it. "So you're going to Vadam."

"You get the idea," 'Telcam said.

Raia had never been inside a warship before. The scale of it, the strange smells, the confusing passages, and decks that all looked the same made her ask a question she knew she should have asked herself earlier: what was she going to actually *do*? Forze beckoned to her and sat her down at the back of the bridge.

"We have to embark troops first," he said. "Then we head for Vadam. Stay here. And if you see any of the Brutes and you have the slightest concern, shoot them."

"Why?"

"We have no guarantees of their loyalty. Not even the ones who serve in this vessel. This may be the time to cleanse our decks."

The ship lurched and lifted clear of the quarry, and she caught a glimpse of her keep—her world—vanishing in the viewscreen. Now all she could do was wait. She was still at the mercy of the whims and timetables of males. She watched the time crawl by, trying to understand what Buran was doing at the controls, and clutched her pistol's grip with one hand. When the ship landed again, she had no idea where they were, but caught sight of a couple of shuttles sweeping past the viewscreen, and minutes later troops clattered onto the bridge. There were no Brutes among them, just Sangheili.

"We have as near a full crew as we need," Buran said to 'Telcam. He'd started to pace, either spoiling for a fight or having second thoughts about the size of the task. "I say we go now. There's no point waiting for the rest. We need to assess the situation in Vadam."

"We have nine vessels and the forces from Nuan and Rtova keeps—so far."

"It'll be enough. If we delay, the Arbiter's allies will reach Vadam. This buys us time."

'Telcam hesitated for just a moment. "They disappoint me, but you're right. Momentum will work in our favor."

If this had been Jul in command, Raia would have had no qualms about lecturing him on gambling with lives. But she had no authority here, and she didn't fully understand what was happening, other than working out that 'Telcam was starting the coup with fewer supporters than he'd been counting on.

And I can't turn back any more than 'Telcam can.

Forze sat down beside her. "Don't worry," he said. "Once we make inroads into Vadam's defenses, others will find their courage and show up."

"Where are we?"

"We'll be on the Vadam border very soon. You really shouldn't have done this, Raia. Jul will kill me when he finds out that I went along with this insanity."

They were still talking as if his return was imminent. She didn't dare think anything else. "I want to see what's happening."

"Stand to the side of the bridge and don't get in 'Telcam's way." Forze pointed. "You won't be able to see a great deal. The more successful we are, the thicker the layer of smoke."

"I'll use my imagination," she said.

When she stood up and walked to the viewscreen, heads turned. The troops who'd just boarded the ship obviously hadn't realized there was a female on board, and an armed one at that. One or two gave her polite nods. Others stared as if she was an abomination. She considered telling them that she'd come to find her husband, but then thought better of it. She had no duty to explain herself to strangers.

But she could see the skyline of Vadam now, and there was smoke. The assault seemed to have started in earnest.

'Telcam took a call on the bridge and listened carefully. Raia caught snatches of the conversation and could only guess what might be happening at the other end.

"Can you understand me?" He paused and nodded. "Yes, I can hear you. He's safe and I've secured him in the temple, under guard . . . I see, but why was that necessary?" He paused again, looking irritated. "Let us both hope the Arbiter knows nothing of our arrangement. Can I count on you?" Whatever answer he received seemed to reassure him. "Very well." He looked irritated for a moment, then picked up another communications handset and barked at someone. "Olar? The scholar's escorts have come for him. Let them take him so that we avoid inconvenient retaliation from Earth if anything goes wrong. Do you understand? Try to show restraint."

That meant nothing to Raia. Earth? How could humans retaliate? What had this war to do with them anyway? She was trying to work that out when a brilliant flash of white light blinded her for a few moments. A huge roar of approval went up on the bridge. When her vision cleared, she could see what had raised everyone's spirits. Two ships were flying slowly across the city, firing blue-white bolts on the buildings below. Whoever was down there returned fire, spitting burning arcs into the sky, but the ships continued their barrage.

A slim spire next to the river took a direct hit and crumbled in slow motion, collapsing a layer at a time into the water below. More smoke had appeared on the skyline, reaching up to the clouds as if someone had thrown down a coil of dirty rope from the heavens. The Arbiter was under attack.

This was what Jul had wanted. Raia hoped that wherever he was, he would think it was worth the price.

"Take us in closer, Buran, and target Vadam keep," 'Telcam said. "But nobody is to cause damage to Forerunner relics, even indirectly."

Buran and a few of the other males turned to look at the monk in badly disguised disbelief.

"That might not be possible, brother," Buran said. "And what if 'Vadam's forces shelter in them?"

"Then we must find another way," 'Telcam said. "Because the gods are our reason for fighting."

CHAPTER

FIVE

YOU CAN WIN WARS ANY NUMBER OF WAYS. YOU CAN CAR-
PET BOMB, OR SEND IN GROUND TROOPS, OR SHELL A CITY,
OR DETONATE A NUKE. YOU CAN LAY SIEGE, CUT OFF WATER
AND POWER, OR BLOCKADE THEIR PORTS. BUT THERE'S ONE
UNIVERSAL ACHILLES' HEEL THAT EVERY ORGANISM HAS. IF
THEY CAN'T GROW FOOD, OR CAN'T EAT WHAT THEY'VE GOT,
THEY DIE. IT BEATS A SHOOTING WAR.

(DR. IRENA MAGNUSSON, ONI RESEARCH FACILITY TREVELYAN)

TEMPLE OF THE ABIDING TRUTH, ONTOM

"I'll be gone for a few hours," Phillips said to Olar. He'd stuffed
what he could into a bundle made from a knotted tunic and
half-draped his jacket over it in case the Sangheili started asking awkward questions. "I've helped myself to some rations. I
won't get lost."

Olar seemed more interested in what was happening outside.
A couple of his comrades came running back shouting that
more armed Brutes had landed and that there was a stand-off in
the plaza.

"Those tunnels run for many, *many* spans, right across the island," he said, not paying attention. "It's a labyrinth. Don't expect
me to come and rescue you. And don't go down the walled-off
tunnels. It's dangerous."

Dangerous. Right. There was a firefight going on outside and
the coup had started. Phillips thought an unstable tunnel was

probably the least of his problems. "I'll be careful," he said. He headed into the network of passages again, confident that he knew the route to the farthest point he'd mapped and that he could find his way back here. "Don't worry about me."

So the passages run for kilometers, do they? Well, there's definitely got to be a back door or two, then.

He ran his fingertips along the wall as he walked, feeling for the weird barrier that covered some of the cartouches. Perhaps they weren't safety covers at all. Maybe this was a museum and always had been, and the barriers were there to stop sticky fingers from messing up the ancient exhibits. But that didn't mean they were useless. There was information on them, and all information was valuable sooner or later.

He kept walking and sniffed the air from time to time. There was no mustiness, no dampness, nothing at all to indicate that he was a long way underground and getting farther from the entrance with every step. Now he'd been walking for about thirty minutes, and he couldn't hear a damn thing other than his own breathing. He would have kept on walking but BB stopped him.

"This is an area we haven't catalogued, Professor," the not-quite-BB said. "I'll start recording."

Phillips cast around. It was all starting to look the same to him, a monotonous perfection of cream and taupe stonework, punctuated by crisply carved symbols every few meters and the string of scruffy lights. He looked at his datapad again: *left, left, right, straight ahead, left.* He made sure he was recording everything by hand, not just relying on BB, if this husk of the AI could be relied upon at all. He found himself starting to treat BB like a senile relative.

"Adj would probably be able to read all this," Phillips said, just by way of conversation.

"Who's Adj?"

Oh, damn. He's erased data that could compromise us.

Yeah, we didn't want the Sangheili to know we hijacked their Engineer. "Never mind. Just someone I knew."

"Dr. Halsey has made some errors in her translations, I believe, but I'm correcting them."

"Can't wait to see you tell her that."

"I'll have difficulty doing that, Professor, because she died in the assault on Reach."

Phillips marveled at the programming that decided which parts of BB's memory to wipe and which to keep. His selective amnesia was both impressive and confusing.

"Yeah, so she did," Phillips said. "You were saying something about errors."

"The elements of the symbols that she interpreted as nouns. Some of them are actually adjectives, and that changes the meaning somewhat."

"Show me."

"You're a linguist, aren't you, Professor?"

There was no sarcasm. BB didn't remember anything that was classified. Maybe that meant he didn't know they'd been buddies. *So? I'm chummy with a computer. What's wrong with that? He really* does *have a personality. He's real.* When BB got himself back together again and did that reintegration thing, perhaps they'd have something to laugh about. Phillips hoped so.

"I'm a xenoanthropologist specializing in languages," he said. "I hold the Arkell Chair at Wheatley University, Sydney."

"Then you'll understand this. This language is a blend of phonetics and ideographs. It also appears to have pointing to indicate vowels, like Semitic languages. The trick is working out which elements are phonetic and which are ideographic. I'm using the pointing to differentiate, although that might be wholly misleading."

This was Phillips's bread and butter, his life's work. However fond as he was of the old BB, however sorry he felt for him right now, he was damned if he'd be beaten at his specialty by a glorified personal organizer. He rested his arm on the wall and held the datapad's light at an angle to throw a stronger shadow, scrutinizing the symbols. There was no sign of a barrier. That didn't mean it wasn't there.

"So what do you think this one says?"

BB didn't respond for a few seconds. Given the processing speed of an AI, even one in this state, that was the equivalent of putting Phillips on hold and going away for the weekend.

"If I went by Halsey's lexicon, then this symbol here refers to *shield world zero zero six.* I think the symbol on the end is *sarcophagus.*"

"Wow." Phillips scanned the panel, running his forefinger down the surface. Yes, there was something preventing him from touching the stone itself. "Zero zero six is called Onyx. Well, there had to be more than one bomb shelter, right? Which symbol?"

"Down . . . down . . . *stop.* That one."

Phillips studied it, searching for some resonance. He really had to get up to speed with this alphabet. He thought he could see a recurring element in each symbol below the one that BB had identified as Onyx.

"Does that mean these are all shield worlds?"

"I believe so. We know of many, and different kinds."

"So . . . what is this? A commemorative plaque? A map?"

"I can't translate the symbol at the start of each line."

"Okay, if that bit is shield or shield world, and that element is the number, is the thing here just decorative?"

"The Onyx one repeats three lines down."

Now that was interesting: there were eight lines with three smaller symbols next to each—the shield element, a symbol unique to the line, and a third symbol. Five bore one design and two another, and Onyx appeared to be one of those two.

"It might indicate a general location, because I can't see any numerical coordinates," BB said. "But we don't know if the Forerunners thought in terms of star systems, quadrants, or even separate galaxies."

Phillips sketched the cartouche even though he didn't need to with his datapad and BB recording. This was *fascinating*. He wanted to feel the language, to understand how the shapes were formed, to know how Forerunners had felt when they were writing. The sense of connection was exhilarating. He realized he was breathing faster and his back itched with sweat.

"Okay, let's see what else we can find." He was in deep shit but it almost didn't matter while he was having this extraordinary cultural adventure. "Onward and upward."

BB had no choice about moving on. Phillips walked and he was dragged along with him. The next section of wall turned a corner to the right and there were no more inscriptions for another five minutes. How far had they come now? Phillips started calculating his pace and working it out, but it just didn't matter now. He was following a trail, excited as a kid.

I could be dead tomorrow. And all I care about is this.

"This is fun, BB," he said. "Knowledge. You like finding things out, don't you? That's what drives you. Me too."

"May I ask you something?"

"Go ahead."

"We know one another better than I recall, don't we?"

"Actually, yes." Phillips dithered on the edge of explaining in case it triggered memories that BB wasn't supposed to retrieve now. He felt along the wall like a blind man, willing his fingertips to hit that slightly raised edge that wasn't there but felt like . . . fur. That was it: *fur.* "You're a fragment of yourself, and back where we came from, we're pretty good buddies. You'll see."

"Ah."

"Ohhh . . ." Phillips touched that velvet-pile fur again, but he couldn't see anything on the wall. "Here we go."

This time it seemed to go on for a good couple of meters and he thought he was walking into a dead end, but when he reached it, it was just another corner. Then something touched his face and he batted it away instinctively. His brain said *cobwebs, spiders.* But there was nothing he could see, nothing at all. That was the weirdest thing about this place: the passages were as clean as if they were swept daily. He couldn't imagine the Sangheili doing that. He'd been here a couple of days and he'd never seen them doing any housework beyond keeping the main chamber and living areas clean and tidy.

"I keep picking up interference," BB said. "But it's stopped now."

To Phillips, interference meant comms. For a second he thought the link with *Port Stanley* had started working again, and he pressed the radio. But there was nothing. He glanced behind him. The passage was lit, but he couldn't see the jury-rigged lights. He checked his watch. They'd been gone an hour and a half.

"You want to press on, BB?"

"Yes, Professor."

"You know you're not normally this deferential to me."

"I have to take your word for that. Tell me, do I have more functions than this?"

"Functions?" It was upsetting, even pitiful. "Jesus H. Christ, BB, you're probably the most intelligent entity in UNSC, you perform a zillion processes a second, and you can run entire warships single-handed. Yes, I'd say you have a *lot* more functions. Just relax and you'll be your old self before too long."

"Thank you," BB said. "That's comforting. Something about the gaps in my mind is becoming very distressing."

Phillips knew he had to knock that on the head before it turned into the only thing that BB could think about. *Rampancy. AIs can think themselves to death. Literally.* Phillips needed him working, however limited, but his instinct said to take care of a buddy. "BB, you're an intelligence agent. A spy. Whatever's been turned off in your brain is just temporary, to protect both of us."

"Are you telling me the truth?"

"Yes. Trust me."

"Why?"

"Because I'm your friend."

BB didn't respond. Phillips carried on walking and let him think it over a few million times. The floor felt different beneath the soles of his boots, almost carpeted, but it was still a continuous run of immaculately faced, precisely laid flagstones, and he moved on methodically looking from side to side for more cartouches.

"Jackpot," he said. There it was, the first panel he'd seen for ages. "I hope it's a sign for the bathrooms. I need to *pump ship,* as Mal would say."

And the old BB would have said *how very nautical,* but this one didn't even pass comment. Phillips compared this cartouche with his hand-drawn notes. It was much starker than the previous one—six symbols of one design, one of another, with a smaller nonrepeating symbol beside each and two separate lines that could have been headers. He was certain he'd seen these before, or at least part of them. He was still looking through his notes when BB spoke.

"The top line says access, or pathway, or connection," he said. "The row beneath that—I'm uncertain. But the lines below that all contain the word for circle. Loop. Ring."

"*Halos.* Please tell me it's Halos." Everyone thought there were more out there, on standby to be activated and wipe out all life, but finding and decommissioning them was another matter. "With locations."

"It could well be, but I can't see any coordinates. Just ordinal numbers. And something that *might* be relative bearings."

"So . . . one through seven, yes?"

"Correct."

"Why the symbols? Why are there two sets of symbols?"

"Location, perhaps, and the assumption of the person who created this was that others knew what that symbol was shorthand for. Or status."

"You mean *status* status, or black, red, amber status? Like the security alert escalation?"

"I mean on or off, locked or unlocked, up or down—"

And then it hit Phillips right between the eyes. *Status.* One of the Halo rings had been destroyed.

He counted again, comparing the shapes. *No, there are six like* this, *one like* that. *Did I remember right?*

But these symbols must have been here for thousands of years. They were carved into the stone. How could they mean what he thought they did? How could they be indicators of functioning and nonfunctioning Halos when one of them had only been deactivated in the last year?

"Sorry, I was getting too excited," Phillips said. "I really thought this might be a status panel, but it's just stone."

He reached out to touch the symbols, the ones he now thought of as on-off switches. The layer that he could feel and but not see yielded and he found his fingertips against the intricately detailed shape. He could *feel* it.

"I wouldn't touch that if I were you, Professor," BB said.

Phillips stepped back. "Yeah, if that was a big red button, I might have wiped out half of the galactic core."

"Well, you've activated *something.* Look."

Phillips felt his stomach knot. He looked, but he couldn't see a damn thing except the cartouche. "What?"

"Look at the symbols at the top. They've changed."

"They haven't. It's just stone." Phillips looked up at the ceiling and scanned 360 degrees in case he was missing something that BB had detected. "Nothing's changed."

"It has. I can compare every microframe I've recorded." BB was persistent but polite. "I don't know what the words meant before, but they've changed, and now they say to find someone or seek something beyond, or higher, or better. I'm sorry that this is rather vague. Halsey left copious notes and some of them are a little too fulsome and extrapolative."

It sounded like a religious text, some self-improving stuff. But this was *stone,* moving stone, stone that *changed while he was standing right in front of it.* No, that was impossible. But the Forerunners—if they could bend time and build artificial planets, a bit of conjuring with stone was probably easy-peasy for them.

What had he triggered? What did he have to strive for or aspire to? He was thinking in puzzle terms and juggling the language when an idea struck him, one that came straight out of the initial question he'd put to BB.

Black, red, amber status? Like the security alert escalation?

He was an academic learning to be military intelligence the hard way, and the way he thought was changing from anthropologist to marine. The cartouche wasn't telling him to do something spiritually uplifting. It was telling him he had to find someone *senior* to him.

Maybe it was like any weapon of mass destruction on Earth. They usually needed more than one person to validate the launch and activate it, just to be on the safe side. Maybe the garrison here hadn't been trusted to fire Halos on their own. How he'd been able to get the stone to react—and why the Sangheili hadn't already tried this—wasn't half as important right then as working out what the hell he'd done.

"Oh, bugger it, BB," he said. "I think I might have just primed a Halo."

UNSC *TART-CART*, PREPARING TO ENTER
SANGHEILI SPACE

"So how many fragments have you split off now, BB?" Mal asked. "You're not going to have a dissociative episode, are you?"

"Three," BB said. Vaz thought he sounded irritable. "And no. And stop making Naomi nervous. She hates me being in her neural implant at the best of times."

Naomi interrupted on the radio. She sounded as if she was heading their way at a brisk pace. "You know the rules, BB. Do the translating, but don't mess with my nervous system unless I'm in trouble."

"I behaved impeccably last time."

"Tourist."

"Oh, it's all bitch, bitch, *bitch*. You love me really."

Vaz looked at Mal and said nothing. Mal just raised his eyebrows. The ODSTs put on their helmets as Naomi thudded into the crew bay like a truck being dropped on the deck, transformed by her Mjolnir armor into an icon of lethal inscrutability. Behind that gold mirrored visor she was probably a long way from inscrutable, but that was one of the comforts of full-face helmets. Nobody could really tell if you were scared, worried, or just checking your pay-slip.

She settled down in one of the reinforced seats and folded her arms across her chest. "Don't worry, Vasya, I'm okay," she said, reading him like a book. Vaz wasn't sure if she was talking about her father or the fact that she now had a piece of BB on the loose in her brain, ready to enhance her reactions. "Worry about Phillips."

"I already did that."

She didn't take the conversational bait and Vaz found himself wondering if he could pull the trigger on Staffan Sentzke. Staffan needed to know he'd been right, and that his kid had survived.

He had to be told how she'd spent her life and what she did now, because he'd paid a hell of a price for it. But Vaz didn't know if that would give him closure. It might just make him worse.

I'd go crazy. I know I would. No wonder the colonies hated us. If all this ever goes public, the ones that are still left are going to hate us even more.

Osman stuck her head into the crew bay. "Just follow the Elite escort and don't let the bastards provoke you, okay? Vaz, Devereaux—you've been there before. Relax. And remember to launch those comms drones, because that's our only chance to monitor voice traffic down there."

"We're *very* relaxed, ma'am," Mal said. "But I hope you declined the civic reception and parade."

"I'll keep trying 'Telcam. Remember what I said about cultural sensitivity and don't go crashing around the temple."

Just seeing UNSC troops on their patch would offend most Elites. Vaz recalled the reaction to the Arbiter showing up in Kenya for the dedication of the Voi memorial, not exactly a forgive-and-forget moment. Nobody lobbed bricks at him, but the expressions on their faces said they'd have really liked to, given half a chance.

The hatch closed with a hiss and Devereaux started the launch sequence.

Head down, find Phillips, bang out. As Mal would say.

"Head down, find Phillips, bang out," Mal said.

"I *knew* you'd say that."

"Well, I always try not to surprise you, Vaz." Mal jogged him with his elbow. "You think Osman's going to be all right on her own? It's a big ship."

"*I'm* still there," BB said. "Actually, I can deploy *Stanley* without carbon-based help, thank you."

"But who'd keep you entertained?"

"True. And who'd clean the heads?"

Vaz ignored the relentless cheeriness. He found himself ignoring the head-up display on his visor and thinking things that he hadn't realized had ever been in his head. The first was his father, who was a hazy memory anyway. Then it was Huragok. He tried to reconcile the idea of Adj, harmless and friendly as a puppy, and the Covenant doing glassing runs in the colonies. Ah, that was the subconscious connection: *glassing*. His father had gone to do construction work on a new colony, leaving four-year-old Vaz with Grandmother Beloi, but he never came home. *Glassing*. And maybe it wasn't Adj's handiwork—how long did Huragok live, anyway?—but somewhere down the line, teams of Engineers just like him maintained and upgraded those plasma weapons.

Guilt. Vaz had always agonized over the boundaries of guilt and responsibility. Cute or not, Huragok were machines designed to do the job, just like BB. Vaz spent a few more minutes trying to work out if hard-wired reactions got humans and hinge-heads off the hook, too, but decided that anything that was aware of its actions was capable of making choices about them.

I think too much.

I should have shot Halsey. Shoved her out of an airlock.

Do we really want to solve our problems, or just go through the motions? Spenser's worried about Venezia getting hold of Covenant ships. How about us?

"If we really want to stop the Elites," he said to nobody in particular, "why don't we concentrate on acquiring a hinge-head ship and just glass Sanghelios? Finish them once and for all."

The silence around him made him wonder why he'd said it. He really was thinking aloud.

"Rules of engagement," Naomi said. "Peace treaties."

"Is there a law against it? A proper law, not UNSC regulations."

"Genocide. Killing civilians."

"Okay, but where did all the capital ships go? Who's got those plasma weapons now?"

The silence descended again. BB was unusually quiet. Vaz didn't think he'd said anything shocking. Hinge-heads were perfectly okay with their own ethnic cleansing, and he couldn't recall any war where one side had been shamed into behaving nicely because the other side was more civilized.

"I believe there's an ongoing plan to find and decommission those vessels," BB said at last. "One of *Infinity*'s planned tasks."

But save one for us, though. Vaz was damn sure that Parangosky was thinking that way as well. Even if everybody else had been too worried about losing the war to think ahead, Parangosky would have had a plan for every outcome. It was early days yet, just months into the ceasefire.

Mal leaned close to him like he was about to whisper, even though everyone could hear perfectly well on the helmet comms.

"See, this is nature's way of protecting us from brain strain," he said. "Just when you start to overheat about the stupid politics that got you here, some bastard shoots at you, and then your brain's fully occupied with shooting back, saving your own arse, and saving your mate's. Simple."

Devereaux cut in on the circuit. "I'm all for glassing, Vaz. I don't want to be the most ethical corpse in the morgue."

Tart-Cart's deck vibrated gently under Vaz's boots. He shifted his focus back to his helmet display to watch the icons moving around as the dropship closed on the rendezvous coordinates where the Arbiter's escort was already waiting, a small red dot that normally meant *be my guest, blow it up.* Most Sangheili ships still showed up as hostiles on the system. Judging by the fact that they hadn't given Devereaux a map of the landing pad and left her to it, the suspicion was mutual.

"Hey, folks, it's *him*," Devereaux said. "He's speaking English. Switching to voice."

"*Human vessel, this is your escort. Respond.*"

"I hear you, Sanghelios. Give me your instructions."

"Proceed to the coordinates I am transmitting *now*. Do not deviate."

"Understood. We're just going to look for our comrade and stay out of your way."

"I meant do not deviate because we are under attack from traitors."

"We'll be careful. Thank you."

So the rebellion was escalating. Well, the more the Arbiter had on his plate, the more leeway that gave the squad. Vaz shut his eyes and tried to picture the pilot, but got a flashback of Jul 'Mdama a fraction before the hinge-head knocked him across *Stanley*'s holding cell and nearly broke his neck.

Devereaux switched the comms back to cockpit-only. Vaz watched the pinpoint blue light wink out in his HUD. *Bastards, all of them.* One of his chrono displays was counting down, minutes and seconds: in twenty minutes, they'd be entering the atmosphere.

"Do you mind if I wander around your sensors, Devereaux?" BB asked. "I've sent a monitoring package over the comms. But I like to ask."

"You're a gentleman. Knock yourself out."

Naomi didn't move a muscle. Vaz wondered what it felt like to have BB plugged in to your brain and also doing that stuff, all this piggybacking and splitting and infiltration. Whatever it was, the Spartan wasn't reacting.

"Oh, very sloppy . . . ," BB murmured. "You can tell they left the technical work to the hired help."

"What is it, BB?" Vaz asked.

"I'll show you. *Brace brace brace.* Hah."

"Come on, don't—" But that was as far as Vaz got. An explosion filled his HUD, white-hot, dying instantly into orange flame and black smoke. He flinched. If he hadn't been strapped in, he'd have lifted clear off the seat. Then the lack of sound registered on him and the smoke began to clear from the image projected inside his visor. He was looking down on a Sangheili city from what would have been a traffic cam on Earth, and there were palls of smoke rising in the distance. The image then swung around and focused somewhere else. So, not a static surveillance device, then. "What the hell's *that*? Ontom?"

"Whoa," Mal said. "Don't bugger about with the HUD feeds, BB. Now I've got to change my chuddies."

"Live from glorious downtown Vadam," BB said. The image shrank to a tiny icon and minimized to the right-hand margin of Vaz's display. He tried to follow it. "I think that's a feed from an artillery position. Sorry about loosening the old sphincters, Staff. Exciting, isn't it?"

"Not if you're the Arbiter."

"Okay, I'm going to try jumping to Ontom air traffic control as soon as you make contact, so I can find *me*. Then I can trace Phillips."

Vaz couldn't see any of the viewscreens from where he was sitting even if he'd had his eyes open. Mentally, he was now back in his drop pod, a powered coffin of a machine that would dump him on a planet with the minimum of ceremony and spit him out at the feet of the enemy. The ODST life wasn't for the claustrophobic. But this was how he prepped for landing and it was a hard habit to break. He could convince himself that he *didn't* have a few inches of clearance in front of his face. He could tell himself that it was just his eyelids, and he had all the space in the world. His body was telling him to fight, coiling his spring more tightly.

No. Calm. Nonconfrontational. Don't stare them out. Hide the hate.

The vibration changed to a faint shudder. *Tart-Cart* had

entered the atmosphere. They would land in a civilized fashion, and everyone would leave the diplomacy to Mal, backed up by BB's linguistic support. Vaz was dying to see how the hinge-heads reacted when Naomi stepped out and looked them in the eye, though.

"We're coming in very high," Devereaux said. "He's worried about ground fire."

"What, specifically at us, or general anti-Arbiter mayhem?" Mal asked.

"I'll assume both."

"Has he told you where you're parking?"

"No—wait, here we go. I'm turning for Ontom."

Vaz activated the chart display in his HUD before opening his eyes. Now he was looking through the delicate blue mesh of BB's fly-through, following the contours as *Tart-Cart* nearly nose-dived down through clouds to pull up in a shallow but very short approach to the shoreline.

"Never thought I'd be landing here with permission," Naomi murmured.

It took Devereaux several minutes to crack the airlock seals once the dropship settled on its dampers. It was only then that Vaz heard sporadic cracking sounds, all too familiar. It was a firefight.

"Probably just a little local misunderstanding," BB said. "The good news is that my chart's spot on."

Naomi shouldered her way through the hatch first and Mal scrambled out behind her. *Tart-Cart* had landed in what looked to Vaz like a factory parking lot on a Sunday, a big expanse of nothing scattered with an odd assortment of Phantoms, Spirits, Revenants, and small, scruffy Spectres and Wraiths. The Arbiter's pilot was walking toward them and the cracking noise continued, but he didn't seem bothered by it. He looked much more interested in Naomi.

She stopped almost nose to nose with him. She was nearly tall enough to do that. The chances of him ever seeing a Spartan before must have been zero, but it was clear he'd heard all about them.

"You must make your own way now, demon," he said. It was an oddly quaint thing to call her, and if he meant it as an insult he was going to have to try a lot harder than that. "The temple is through that archway."

"I can hear energy weapons," Mal said. "You want to brief us on anything?"

"Still some skirmishing," the pilot said, matter-of-fact, and began walking back to his vessel. "Brutes. Feel free to shoot the traitors. We would have wiped them out sooner, but Ontom is sentimental about its precious *buildings*."

"Wait, are you leaving us here?"

The pilot shrugged without turning around. "I must return to defend Vadam."

Mal watched him go, checked his MA5C, and called Devereaux on the radio. "Dev, did you hear that? You stand by and make bloody sure we can bang out fast."

The radio clicked. "I heard, Staff. Good luck."

"Call us if you get any trouble."

Vaz headed for the archway. Hinge-heads couldn't make up their minds. One minute they didn't want humans going anywhere on their own, and the next they didn't seem remotely interested, not even with a Spartan present. He couldn't tell whether the Arbiter trusted the squad, thought they were too puny to be trouble, or hadn't actually been told about Naomi.

The view through the archway was a big, open space that might have been a plaza or an Elite-sized boulevard. It was definitely a mess, though. Short bolts of light spat one way across the plaza and then the other. Mal knelt slowly on one knee in the opening and sighted up.

"Well, if this is Florence," he said, "someone's trashed the Uffizi gallery."

Vaz stared across the big, open plaza. It was a bomb site. Rubble was scattered everywhere. Then something hit the stonework about fifty meters from him and a small cloud of dust plumed in the air. Energy bolts shot out again from a position opposite.

This was what Vaz was used to. No smiling, no politics, no diplomacy. He hefted his rifle, much happier now. "They never said we'd have to fight our way in."

Mal looked around, shrugged, and pointed to the first wall that would give them cover.

"Details, mate," he said. Then he sprinted. "Just poxy details."

ONIRF TREVELYAN

Dr. Magnusson kept her word, an unusual thing for a human.

Jul let the guard unlock the hatch and slide the tray into the opening. He made a point of standing at the other side of the room or sitting on his bunk at mealtimes so that he didn't appear to be waiting to be fed like some anxious animal. When the outer door of the hatch snapped shut, he counted to ten before wandering slowly across the cell and sliding the inner hatch open.

On the ledge, two bowls on a metal tray smelled of home.

Rather than distressing him with the memories it brought back, it simply made him more determined to escape. He took the tray and carried it over to the table. One bowl contained *irukan* grain and the other stewed meat, probably the one named mutton; unlike the anemic, stringy, white flesh they called chicken, it was closer in flavor to the meat he ate at home, he could digest it without problems, and—so Magnusson had said—it had more of the specific fats that Sangheili appeared to need. But when he scooped a spoonful into his mouth, his life was transformed.

It was *colo* meat. It was farmed across Sanghelios. It was delicious.

And it had to be a trick. Why else would the humans go to so much trouble to keep a prisoner happy?

Jul hadn't found a surveillance device in his cell yet, but there had to be one.

"I am impressed," he said aloud to whoever might be monitoring him. "The Kig-Yar really will trade anything, won't they?" He cleared the bowl of meat before he even glanced at the grain. "And let me tell you that this certainly does *not* taste like chicken."

A good meal—a good portion of protein—always boosted his mental processes as well as his morale, and Jul found himself working out how to turn the metal tray into an implement or a weapon. Perhaps that was too obvious. They would know it was missing. What he had to do was escape from his cell, destroy the Huragok before they gave the humans too great a technical advantage, and then escape from this world. The last was least important even if it was what he wanted most.

He picked up the bowl of *irukan* and wandered around the cell while he ate it, looking over every panel, every conduit, and every seal. They would be expecting him to try to batter his way out. Osman would have told them how he raged and punched the bulkheads in her ship, and how it took two of their troops and a Spartan to subdue him. Perhaps the best strategy was to gradually give in and find a subtler way to get at the Huragok.

Where would they be, anyway? How many of them were

there? He needed to know these things. He had to destroy all of them, because the creatures were artificial, just like this world, and they could build more of their own kind. But he didn't know how much time he had. For all he knew it could already be too late.

How can I ask about the Huragok without arousing Magnusson's suspicion?

The *irukan* was really very good. The humans had actually managed to cook it correctly without turning it into gruel. Each grain burst on his tongue just the way it was supposed to.

They know they can't beat me into submission. They're trying to play on my isolation and convince me they mean me no harm. Why? What could I possibly give them?

He stood at the window watching the activity outside. More prefabricated buildings had sprung up in the last day. This was humanity's enduring pattern of behavior, to move into new territory that wasn't theirs, to fill it to overflowing with their buildings, and to strip whatever they could from it.

What would make them give him access to a Huragok?

We used to have teams of them. We never took much notice of them. They simply worked, and so did everything they touched.

Eventually there was a knock at the door. The daily ritual had begun.

"May I come in, Jul?"

"Please do, Dr. Magnusson."

She entered with her guard and took a few cautious steps inside, clutching her cattle prod, clearly still not convinced that he wouldn't lash out at her. He stayed at the window, adopting the same casual stance that humans seemed to when they were relaxed. It seemed to work. She glanced at the empty bowls on the table as she passed.

"And how was the meal?"

"Excellent. I see you managed to acquire everything."

Magnusson smiled without baring her teeth. "Yes, the Kig-Yar can be obliging for the right price. Let me know if the grain upsets your stomach."

"I've never had ill effects from *irukan*." Jul carried on with the polite, less confrontational approach. This ONI group believed they could break anyone and probably thought he was equally susceptible. So he would use that human arrogance against them. "What's happening on Sanghelios?"

"More fighting. The revolution has begun. Again."

"That's what you wanted. You wanted the Arbiter overthrown."

Magnusson raised her shoulders and dropped them. Jul found that shrugging gesture confusing, because it could mean too many things. "We thought 'Telcam was more likely to stay away from humanity. But now that's irrelevant. Capability matters more than intent. I think I might have said that before."

"Is there word from my wife?"

"No. Or at least not that I'm aware of. I can inquire, but we have very limited information from Sanghelios." She stood beside him and gazed out of the window as if she were searching for the same thing that he was. "We've just landed a special forces squad on Sanghelios so perhaps we'll be getting better intelligence from now on."

"That's impossible." She had to be lying. This was very crude, amateurish maneuvering. "You could never breach our defenses."

"I didn't say we did. The Arbiter gave permission, just as he did for Professor Phillips."

Jul's heart sank. The Arbiter was even more of a threat to his own kind than he'd imagined. Why did he have this foolish tolerance for these creatures? "Why?"

"Because we asked nicely. Imagine, a Spartan and some ODSTs wandering around your world."

"*Spartan.*"

"Naomi. You've met. I hear she knocked you down and throttled you."

Jul resisted the taunt. Yes, the Spartan had captured him, single-handed and unarmed. The shame was painful. "The Spartans are artificial. Like the Huragok."

"You're a sore loser, Jul. Yes, we enhanced humans to make Spartans. But they're still human."

"Even a squad of them can't achieve much on Sanghelios."

"Ah, that's your problem. You see us as maggots. You do, don't you? You used the word *nishum* a lot when you were cussing, according to the AI. Well, maggots might be small and soft, but they can strip flesh from bone eventually, given time." Magnusson's tone was almost friendly, simply telling him the way things were. "Look, I'll ask the squad to see what they can find out about your wife. Maybe the fighting hasn't reached your home yet. What's her name?"

"Raia," Jul said, without even thinking. Somehow he felt he had handed Magnusson a great deal of power that he now regretted.

"We're in touch with 'Telcam, so perhaps he knows."

That scared Jul even more. "'Telcam is a naive fool."

"Because he believes in the gods?"

"Because he believes in you."

"We'll see." She looked him up and down. The guard was still in Jul's peripheral vision. "We're generating our own crop of *irukan,* so that we don't have to keep running to the Kig-Yar every time we need groceries for you."

"That will take a season."

"No, not at all. We clone plants and accelerate their growth to *days*. We can engineer them to survive in any condition, to suppress weeds and pests, to produce specific compounds, to be any color. So we can easily grow some dinner for you. Who knows? We might make it suitable for humans, and then ONI can patent it and generate some revenue from it." She closed one eye in a quick, strange gesture. "We even imported some *colos* to breed. They're not exactly appealing, but at least you get fresh meat now."

Jul struggled with the idea of this generosity. "Why go to all this trouble?"

"I'm operating in a rapidly changing environment, Jul. You saw too much, so we had to stop you from warning the Arbiter, but then we weren't sure what to do with you. First you're a potential source of intelligence—but then we find the Huragok more than answered all our questions. Now you're a potential prisoner exchange. One day, we might need to swap you for one of our people. Or maybe the Arbiter will fall sooner than we think, and 'Telcam will take over, and you can go home. So why would we kill you until we know for certain that you're no use to us?"

"I could become a very embittered enemy."

"True, but if we shoot you now, I might regret it later. And I really don't get any thrills from mistreating prisoners. I'm not a sadist. I'm objective-driven. I do things solely to get results. Right now, understanding the Sangheili better is enough of a goal for me."

It might have been an elegant and oblique threat, but Jul didn't respect those. Even in translation, he felt he was shuffling through a minefield of unknown elements and misunderstandings.

"You fear you can't destroy us. Why else would you need to study us?"

"Jul, we know all there is to know about a bird called a dodo. We sequenced its genome from bones. But it's still been extinct for nearly a thousand years, and it's not coming back. We wiped it out."

Jul was lost now. He couldn't tell threat from comment from reassurance. He knew he had to stop worrying about Raia, because that would become a sore and then a vulnerability that ONI would exploit, but it was impossible to forget. He felt suddenly small and pathetic. It was even making his stomach feel heavy. This was how children reacted.

Isolation. This is how humans break down prisoners. They leave them to fret and imagine the worst, with nobody to comfort them or tell them the truth. I must resist this.

"I'll call someone about Raia," Magnusson said. "Is there anything else you need?"

Jul felt himself sliding. He'd been certain he would withstand years of this if he had to. It was more like days. He was weakening.

"I would like to walk in the sunlight," he said. "This room is too small for me to take proper exercise. But that's too big a request, isn't it? You must confine me."

Magnusson stared right into his face, into his eyes. He always found human eyes unsettlingly pale and watery even if the irises were dark. There was so much whiteness, like a terrified animal. It made humans look constantly hostile and agitated.

"There's no way off Trevelyan," she said. "But I don't trust you not to do a great deal of damage. If you're prepared to accept some restrictions, though, I might be able to give you outside access."

This was his only chance. Part of him really did want to breathe fresh air, though, even if it was as wholly artificial and managed as the rest of the planet.

"Very well," he said.

"I'll come up with something. Give me a day."

"One question. Why do you call this place Trevelyan *and* Onyx?"

Magnusson broke that intense and personal gaze, looking as

if she was weighing up what he might be seeking in the answer. "Onyx was the original name it was given when it was surveyed," she said. "We renamed it Trevelyan in memory of the Spartan who gave his life for it. That was his family name. I don't suppose you understand why that's so unusual."

"No, I don't. Many a Sangheili has given his life to defend his keep. Don't humans do that?"

"I meant the family name. Never mind. There's no reason why you should know."

"Were you just testing me?"

"Perhaps."

She nodded to the guard and he opened the door to see her out. Jul was left standing at the window, mulling over the temptation of a sunny day and open spaces. His heart really did feel heavy—*literally* heavy. He was made of stronger stuff than this, surely.

But I've never been alone behind enemy lines before. I've never been a hostage.

And that's not a sky. It's a roof.

The feeling was like a weight in his chest, pressing ever more heavily. The longer he stood there, the more urgent the pressure became. He dragged himself away from the temptation of illusory freedom and paced around the edge of the room to get some exercise, twenty-five paces along one wall, then twenty along the next, then twenty-five again, then twenty. He'd have to do this a hundred times a day to keep his circulation healthy.

Very well. I shall play this game.

He shut his eyes and visualized home as intently as he could. As he felt his way along the wall, he could see every pace as the path from the keep to the quarry, and then to the fields. If he concentrated, if he focused and made this real in his mind, the locked door didn't matter.

But he really did feel . . . strange.

It grew harder to concentrate. Now he was starting to feel too hot, prickly, disoriented. How many times had he walked this unreal path? How long had he been doing this?

He opened his eyes and suddenly found himself panting. Saliva flooded his mouth. His stomach cramped like a punch just as he swung around and tried to reach the basin in the corner of the room. It was too late: he vomited where he stood, knees buckling, and slumped to all fours.

It hurt more than he expected. He retched and coughed for several minutes until his jaws ached and he was just bringing up air and spittle. Before he could manage to stand up, the door crashed open and Magnusson was standing over him. He recognized the boots. She edged around the pool of vomit.

"Something must have disagreed with you," she said calmly. "Come on. Let's get this cleaned up."

CHAPTER
SIX

THE GODS ARE STILL WATCHING US, EVEN IF SANGHELIOS HAS TURNED ITS BACK ON THEM.

(THE SERVANTS OF THE ABIDING TRUTH, BDAORO CITY, IN DISCUSSION WITH BROTHER MONKS)

ONTOM, SANGHELIOS

"Osman says Phillips is in the temple and 'Telcam's told his minions to hand him over," BB said. "You can walk straight in."

"Not a wasted journey, then." Mal took a look around to check who was where. Sporadic shots led his eye to a low retaining wall on his left as one hinge-head popped up for a moment and bobbed back down again, then another. *Got to be a sniper somewhere. Why don't they just fry the whole area? This isn't like them.* When a chunk of brick just a whisper away from one of the Sangheili's heads exploded in a ball of dust and white light, Mal's guess was confirmed. "If they're going to keep this up, I'll get Dev to land the dropship in the temple compound."

"Is that all that's holding them up?" Vaz asked. "Why don't they put a few grenades up there?"

"Then they'll open fire on *us*." Normally, that wouldn't have been a problem. It would have been routine, even satisfying. But Mal was wrestling with a new political reality in which some Sangheili were fair game and some weren't. It was quicker to follow the rules for once. "Find a way around it. We're only here for Phillips."

"I still don't understand why they're not pulverizing the place." Vaz was persistent. "They've glassed each other's cities before now."

"If you had gunmen holed up in Canterbury Cathedral or Mecca," BB asked, "would you call up artillery to demolish it?"

"I thought hinge-heads were more pragmatic."

"Belief in the Forerunners isn't going to stop instantly just because the San'Shyuum were disgraced. Lots of them are still pretty touchy about Forerunner sites."

Mal eased himself up a little to take a longer look across the square. "Okay, so every stone is sacred. How do we exploit that?" The walls on both sides merged into the temple complex. He could see from the shape and precision of the blocks that at least a third of the wall was original Forerunner handiwork. "Grab a chunk of masonry and tell them to let us through or the brick gets it?"

Naomi squatted with her back against the wall, helmet tilted up as if she was sunning herself. "I've got a more diplomatic solution."

"Does it involve a cattle prod?"

"No. But I can take the Brutes."

Mal knew that when a Spartan said that, it had already been assessed and calculated. She'd taken on two Brutes single-handed before. She was also *fast*. The Mjolnir was more vehicle than body armor.

"Plan?"

"Get up to the top of the wall and hit them from above." It was a bloody big wall and there was a lot of open ground to cross to get to it, but not enough to make a Spartan think twice. "I can drop straight into the temple grounds from there, too. Give you cover if the Sangheili get overexcited and open fire."

Technically, they were here with permission from *both* sides—the Arbiter and the rebels. It should have meant a few tactful conversations and being allowed to pass, but life was never like that. Mal suspected the niceties of it would be overlooked in a stew of adrenaline and religious fervor, and whatever the squad did would now be taken as storming a holy site. But he couldn't abort the mission.

"Okay, do it," he said. "BB, you make sure you transmit Naomi's helmet view to us, because that's going to give us a lot of help."

"I'll tell you when to run." Naomi balanced on the balls of her feet, still squatting. "BB—no enhancing unless I ask for it. Got it?"

"I won't lay a finger on you, dear. Promise."

Naomi sprang up from the squat and burst from cover, kicking gravel against Mal's armor. No normal human could run like that. *Sixty kph. Holy shit.* She reached racehorse speed in seconds and made the far wall before he'd even had a chance to take it all in. Then she jumped, not even breaking her stride. She just launched herself in an arc with the armor's built-in propulsion and landed hard on the stone parapet.

Mal had never seen a Spartan actually fly before. The Brutes either didn't see her coming or didn't react fast enough, because she loped along the top of the wall and fired down—still running—onto the sniper position below her. Mal tried to keep one eye on her point-of-view feed in his HUD but she was moving too fast. He caught a blur of rubble and bodies before the output tilted into a stomach-churning view from a narrow, uneven path with a sheer drop on either side. Now he had an aerial view of the temple. It was a lot smaller than he expected and ringed by grounds that were a mix of paving and short turf.

Naomi kept running. Four hinge-heads stood up to watch and didn't even raise their pistols until she leapt off the end of the stonework and thudded down behind the temple walls. Something went *crack,* loud enough to echo across the plaza. The rocky cam feed steadied into a shot of stone slabs, a couple of them cracked from edge to edge, and then swung up to frame the heavy four-meter-high gates.

"*Wheeee!*" BB said. "Can we do that again?"

Naomi ignored him. "When you're ready, Staff." Mal saw her appear in the gateway just as her helmet feed picked him up in the distance. "Move it. I don't know what's behind me yet."

Mal and Vaz took a couple of careful steps into the open, just in case any quick movement made the hinge-heads open fire on a reflex. For a moment he thought the Elites were okay and just surprised to see a couple of ODSTs ambling around, but then they went into overdrive and started firing.

There was no more cover, nothing to do but run and hope that Naomi could keep the hinge-heads busy. Blind instinct was a great thing. Mal realized Naomi's shots were shaving past him and one quick but wrong move would kill him. Vaz overtook him just as he felt something hit his back-plate—one, two, three hammer blows—a second before he stumbled the last few meters through the temple gates.

The noise levels dropped instantly. For a moment he thought he was dead. Vaz turned him around by his shoulder.

"You've got some serious scorch marks," Vaz said. "Are you okay?"

"Fine." Mal tried to peer over his own shoulder to check. "Is there anybody home?"

He'd expected to be confronted by some of 'Telcam's gang but it was all remarkably peaceful, quiet as a churchyard, and all the more creepy for it. So Elites wouldn't trash a holy site like this, then. That was going to come in useful. Naomi and Vaz walked up to the temple with weapons raised and stacked either side of the door.

"Let them know we're here, BB," Naomi said.

"Can I use your helmet audio? I'll even do your voice so that it doesn't get too surreal for them. I mean, my manly voice, your body, very odd . . ."

"They can't see that I'm female in this armor. Just make sure they know who we are and that we just want Phillips."

"And *me*."

Mal was still keeping an eye on the open gates, just in case. Now that things had slowed down a little, he was starting to notice the bigger picture. He couldn't hear much because the walls seemed to soundproof the place, but he could see two columns of smoke rising about five klicks to the north, and half a dozen small vessels were tracking back and forth above the city.

"Here he comes," Naomi said.

Mal swung around. An Elite emerged from the doorway and stood staring, first at their weapons and then at their visors. Then Naomi spoke, or at least BB did, and Mal didn't understand a word of it. The Sangheili responded. They had quite a long chat.

"What did he say?" Mal asked, one eye still on the gates.

BB's voice was his own again, transmitted through the helmet comms. "His name is Olar and he says Phillips has gone exploring in the tunnels."

"Tunnels?"

"The temple's full of passages."

"It's not that big."

"That's what I said, but he says there's a complete warren underground that runs for kilometers."

Phillips must have been fine if he had the time and inclination to do a spot of tourism. "Okay, so ask him to bring him out."

BB switched back to his Naomi-speaking-Sangheili voice, but the tone didn't match Naomi's impatient body language. That must have confused the hell out of the hinge-head. "He says he's been gone for hours and he can't leave his post to go and retrieve him."

"Lazy sod. Okay, so we go in and get Phillips. He's going to let us in, isn't he?"

Mal could pick out two words of Sangheili on a good day but he knew hinge-heads well enough to work out when they were getting upset. Olar was. He gestured, slapping his arms down at his sides. BB sounded as if he was reasoning with him. Mal decided to call Osman with a sitrep while BB ironed things out.

"Kilo-Five to *Stanley*."

Osman must have been sitting on the comms. She responded instantly. "Receiving, Staff."

"Phillips is okay, ma'am. We're just negotiating access to the temple to get him out."

"Do you need me to talk to 'Telcam again?"

"Doesn't look like it. I'll report in when we've actually got him."

"Watch your backs when you exfil. We're only monitoring the northern hemisphere, but there's a fair bit of fighting going on."

"We'll be out of here in an hour or two. Kilo-Five out."

BB was still negotiating. Mal was getting fed up with the delay. He took another look through the gates and counted about thirty hinge-heads gathering fifty meters outside, so they'd obviously decided it was safe to come out and start the clear-up. Vaz stood back from the door and scanned the roofline.

"Come on, BB, what's his problem?" Mal asked. "Is this a setup or something?"

"He says we're not supposed to enter the temple, being unbelieving scum and all that. I'm trying to convince him that we won't touch anything and we'll be gone before he knows it."

"Tell him I'll make sure 'Telcam knows how uncooperative he's being." Mal took a couple of slow steps forward to make it clear that they weren't going away anytime soon. "Tell him I'll get Osman to call his boss right now."

Vaz shifted his attention to the gate and wandered away from the door. Mal was about to push his luck and just step past Olar when Vaz called out to him.

"Mal, you need to take a look at this."

"What?"

"Hinge-heads," Vaz said. "They're gathering outside the gate and they don't look very happy."

Naomi looked over her shoulder and BB carried on talking to Olar. She gestured at Mal, tapping her visor and pointing. *Look at that.* So Mal looked.

"Oh shit," he said. Vaz was right. There were a lot more Sangheili outside now, *right outside,* and they were snarling and gesturing toward the temple. The gates were three-quarters open. Mal didn't have to be a linguist to pick up the mood. "Is it us? BB, can you listen to this as well? What's pissing them off? Is it because we didn't wipe our boots or something?"

BB didn't miss a beat. Mal could hear him still arguing with Olar, but he managed to carry on a simultaneous conversation with the squad.

"They're arguing whether to come in and drag us out," BB said. "It's some theological debate about whether it's permitted to kill an unbeliever on holy ground, or whether they have to haul us outside to do it. You get a more intellectually rigorous class of violence here."

"Great. So we're pinned down."

"I think we should bar the gates, just to be on the safe side."

"There'd better be a back door out of this place."

Naomi broke off and ran for the gates, ramming one with her shoulder to slam it shut just as the grumbling outside turned into shouting and the Elites surged forward. They didn't open fire. That was all that saved Mal and Vaz as they struggled to slam the other door shut. Naomi slid the security bars into place and Mal held his breath for a few moments.

"Are they going to kick those doors down?" Vaz asked.

"They're still dithering about whether they'll be violating a Forerunner site," BB said. He shot out a stream of Sangheili at Olar and got an arms-spread gesture back. "Come on, get inside. I've told him to let us in and lock the door in case the faithful out there turn ugly. Okay, even uglier."

Mal brushed past Olar. The hinge-head was a head taller and he could have snapped Mal's neck in a heartbeat, but he seemed too overwhelmed by events to bar the way. He'd been left to mind the store and was probably now wondering how he was going to explain all this to his boss. They clattered down the passage into a vaulted chamber full of crates, tables, and equipment.

"Where are the rest of them?" Vaz asked. "Is this it?"

There was only one other Sangheili in there, a smaller male sitting at a communications desk. He looked up at Mal and didn't seem surprised. Whatever he was listening to had a firmer grip on his attention. BB, still using Naomi's helmet speaker, started talking to Olar again. Olar gestured to a doorway and threw up his hands.

"He says Phillips went that way," BB said. "And that we mustn't touch anything."

"Okay, first things first." Mal went ahead, following a line of overhead lights, and called Devereaux while he still had a signal. This was Forerunner territory and he couldn't take anything for granted. "Dev, we're inside the temple. He's in here somewhere."

"Is everything okay?"

"Yeah," Mal said. "We've got a tough crowd tonight. Take a

look at BB's plot of the area and check if you can land *inside* the compound."

UNSC *PORT STANLEY*, SANGHEILI SPACE

Osman had never been a people person, but today she felt the need for company.

Stanley was a very empty ship now and she'd grown used to having Kilo-Five around in all too short a time. She sat in front of the viewscreen to try to feel some connection with her team down there on that rust-red planet, a world that she could see but that couldn't even detect her vessel. That feeling kept creeping back. If she looked away, if she didn't keep an eye on that planet, then she was abandoning her crew. It was illogical but none the less insistent for that.

"Well, at least Phillips is okay, BB," she said. "Are you there? Oh, what am I saying . . . of course you are."

She looked around for the AI's avatar. Maybe if he'd remained a disembodied voice then she would have started to think of him as he truly was, as a distributed entity inhabiting not only every part of the ship but capable of extending himself across light-years on a carrier wave. Now he was pulling off that brilliant trick of being in several places at once in multiple forms but still functioning as a single mind.

The cube of blue light popped up from the console. "You don't enjoy sitting and waiting, do you, Captain?"

"That obvious, is it?"

"You'll be doing this a lot as CINCONI. You'll deploy your people and then all you can do is let them get on with it."

It was a sobering thought. Osman was forty-one, and she already knew that she'd be promoted to rear admiral in a few weeks. She wouldn't have to wait for the list to be announced like all the other hopefuls. Parangosky had told her what was to come, and what was not, and the only thing she didn't know yet was the date on which she'd succeed the admiral as head of ONI.

She preferred not to know. She wanted to think that it was still years away, and not just because she wasn't sure if she was ready for the top job, or because she didn't want to see Parangosky leave. Now that she'd had a taste of being in the field with a team, she found that she liked it, and she wanted a little more of it before she retreated to Bravo-6 and that big, big office to see out her career.

See out? I could be looking at fifty years in that post. God, fifty years. That's terrifying.

And that'll mean at least six more AIs after BB goes rampant. I don't think I'm ready for that, either. I don't even want to think about it.

"I should have gone down there with them," she said.

"And that would have been for your benefit, not theirs," BB said. "Which is why you didn't do it. You might not be an operational Spartan, but the characteristics that got you selected are still there. You're a doer. A scrapper."

"*Selected.* Love that word."

"Have you decided how you're going to handle Naomi's situation?"

"Awkwardly, BB."

"She took a massive risk by deciding to open her file."

"And I haven't. Is that the point? That you still think I should man up and take a look at mine?"

"As if I'd be so judgmental."

BB wasn't actually nagging her to relent and find out who she really was, but he'd raised it more than once. Sometimes she wondered if he was nudging her because he knew the contents would soothe her or make her happy, take away the guilt she felt at not trying harder to escape from Halsey and get back to her parents. But she was too afraid to open that file and find that she was wrong. The Pandora's box that Naomi had opened had made her even more reluctant to take the plunge.

"I'm wallowing now, BB," she said. "Make me do some work. I can't keep pestering Mal."

"Don't worry, I'm tracking them. I've still got a signal from me. I mean the Kilo-Five fragment. Not the Phillips one, of course." BB projected a hologram of the temple's interior, an incomplete mesh of multicolored lines that was growing steadily as Vaz, Mal, and Naomi progressed deeper into the maze and their telemetry was sent back to the ship. "Gosh, it's always fun deploying in Naomi's implant. It's so *physical*."

"Are you mooching around *Infinity* at the moment as well?"

"Indeed I am. You're going to love it. The Huragok are doing some extraordinary things."

"Where else are you?"

"Bravo-Six, naturally, and I'm eavesdropping on low-orbit transmissions to see what 'Telcam's fleet's achieving. Are we making conversation, or are you concerned about something?"

BB's matrix was based on a donated human brain. Osman sometimes found herself wondering how much if anything he had in common with the anonymous donor. She was sure she would have liked him—or her.

"How do you incorporate your past into your life, BB?" She did what she thought of as looking him in the eye, focusing on the front panel of his box. "When you're separated from a fragment and you catch up with it when you drop out of slipspace, it tells you what it's been doing, doesn't it? All the things you've missed. But it's still you. Just your past, even if it's microseconds."

"That's a good summary." The blue box didn't move. "Is this about *your* past?"

"Partly. But also about your fragment with Phillips. You're afraid it's been damaged."

"Yes, of course I am. I felt something go wrong."

"What if it's *really* damaged? Do you reintegrate it? Erase it? Select the best bits and delete the rest?"

"Depends. If it's so damaged that it compromises my function, I'd have to erase it, but I'd lose data, and that's a kind of scar. There's no avoiding it. One way or another, I can't ignore it and pretend it never happened." BB drifted slightly, so close that she thought he was going to settle in her lap like a cat. "But I do love a good analogy, and that was a very elegant one. I can't avoid my past. And neither can you."

"I was being literal." *Ouch. He's right.* "I know you're worried about what you're going to find."

"Aren't we all."

He lifted and spun away. Osman leaned back in her seat and popped her earpiece into place to listen to the translated voice traffic, although BB was monitoring it all in real time anyway. It was patchy and chaotic: the comms drones that *Tart-Cart* had launched into low orbit around Sanghelios were picking up everything from routine intercontinental calls to ship-to-ship messages. If this was a representative sample, then half the planet didn't even know there was an uprising going on yet. Vadam was busy, though. Sangheili were calling each other. There were a lot of messages going from Vadam to other keeps.

"What's going on between Chaura and Hilot?" she asked.

"The Vadam keeps are warning other cities," BB said. He processed information at such speed that he was now way ahead of her. "They're probably the ones that the Arbiter thinks are most loyal to him. There you go, Captain, instant intel. I'll map it. There's a cascade of calls now, city to city."

"Can you grab any visuals? We should be able to get imaging down to five meters without being detected."

"I'll divert some drones to Vadam now."

"Put one over Ontom, too, and patch it through to Devereaux. I don't want Mal walking straight into another firefight." She leaned over the console and opened the channel to Mal, even though she knew BB was synced up with the squad. She needed to stay in voice contact to feel she was doing her job. "*Stanley* to Kilo-Five. How's it going, Staff?"

Mal didn't sound as if he was in a stone tunnel at all. "Still no sign of him, ma'am. It's a case of trying every passage."

"Dumb question. Are you calling out?"

"We are. No response. Maybe it's the weird acoustics in this place."

"Okay. Be aware that the fighting's spreading. I won't overload you with data, but I'll keep Devereaux up to speed."

"I'm more worried about the mob we left outside, ma'am."

Osman checked her watch. They'd gone into the temple forty-five minutes ago. There was plenty of time. It was just idleness feeding her anxiety, the helplessness of being able to do nothing but watch while every minute dragged by.

"Here you go," BB said. "Here's a satellite-level view of Vadam. Can you see the smoke?"

"I'll take it on my datapad."

He punched up a two-dimensional image. Osman struggled to pick out the detail until he helped her out by enhancing the smoke plume and other features.

"I've put a thermal overlay on that," he said. "You can see the areas where there are fires, and those blobs on the top margin are the anti-air batteries. I'm picking up warships, too. See that red mark here?" He made the icon flash on her screen. "That's a ship that's been shot down."

"Abiding Truth didn't have much of a fleet to start with."

"Let me magnify this for you. Would you like it on the head-up display?"

Osman nodded. "We could intervene, but how much could we do?"

"Not much in a ground assault," BB said. The aerial view of Vadam now filled much of the viewscreen, diverting her attention from the red disc of the planet. "We'd need direct contact with 'Telcam's fleet to coordinate it, and it would be awfully hard to keep ONI's name out of that."

The image was now so magnified that she could see actual units on the ground in Vadam. Small vessels moved like dots along the roads and canals. A series of explosions suddenly flared in one area, rippling the ground with shock waves, and then a huge flash of white light wiped out half the screen for a few seconds before it died away to leave something belching smoke and flame.

"What was that?" she asked.

"Going by the thermal and blast patterns, someone's hit another ship and brought it down. I think we can assume it's a rebel vessel."

"Okay. Stand by to put a call in to Parangosky."

"Big upsurge in voice traffic, by the way. The Arbiter's allies are really getting those warnings out. I fear that our monk has lost the advantage of surprise."

'Telcam just hadn't gone in hard enough and fast enough.

But if he had, and he'd completely annihilated the Arbiter's allies, that wouldn't have suited ONI's purposes either. Now every city was on the alert, waiting for its own uprising to start. ONI had wanted a civil war but the last thing it wanted was for the Arbiter to crush it in days. Osman sat back and watched more firecracker flashing of artillery fire on the image.

"I think this is going to be over far too soon, BB," Osman

said. "And if 'Telcam's wiped out, it's going to be hard to start over on this."

Hard? It'd mean a completely new approach. Perhaps *Infinity* would change things entirely. What Osman needed right now was a stroke of luck.

TEMPLE OF THE ABIDING TRUTH, ONTOM

Phillips stood staring at the cartouche with his hand held just above the surface as if he was testing a hotplate to see if it would burn him.

"No, really, BB. I think I've done something stupid. Any ideas for rolling this back?"

BB considered the idea of a space-faring race so advanced that they could wipe out entire galaxies, and the possibility that one of those massively destructive Halos could be triggered by an illiterate alien casually fiddling with a panel. No, they would have built in more fail-safes than that.

Surely.

"Not yet," BB said. "But if this really does unleash destruction, it won't affect this location. If the Halos are spread over huge distances, then this has to be a remote control. Nobody would destroy their own galaxy while they were actually *in* it."

Surely . . .

Phillips kept running his hand over his beard, clearly agitated. BB's view of him was from chest height, looking up under his chin. "Really? How about kamikaze? Suicide bombers? Self-destruct mechanisms?"

"I really don't think this is one of those."

"Great. So I incinerate *another* galaxy. Fine. At least there'll be nobody left to come after us bent on vengeance."

And this man . . . he's my friend. He told me so. In another life, I know him, I can do all kinds of things I can't do now, and I know a lot more. But I can't recall most of it.

This is horrible. Am I going mad? And why am I thinking in terms of madness, not malfunction?

"I think we've translated it correctly, Professor. I'd leave it alone if I were you."

Phillips licked his lips nervously, unable to drag himself away from the panel. He recorded more images of the surface with his datapad, then ran his fingertips carefully over the plain sections of the cartouche. BB saw the status icon shift again. It had returned to its original form.

"There, it's reverted," BB said. "Panic over."

Phillips's gaze darted back and forth between the image on his datapad and the cartouche. Eventually he seemed satisfied that the symbols at the top had changed back to the way they'd been before.

"Okay, that's a few billion beings out there somewhere who owe me one," he said. "What I really need now is a team of ONI techies to examine this with a Huragok. In the absence of that, better hope I've recorded enough data for someone to make sense of this." He looked at his watch. "I'm just going to pop back along the passage and relieve myself, and then we'll press on. Would you mind sort of looking the other way? Oh, never mind. You're omnipresent in the ship, and I managed to get used to *that,* so . . ."

Phillips disappeared back the way they'd come, singing under his breath. BB wasn't sure why he picked one section of wall and not another. He looked around as if he was lost, then shrugged and got on with it.

"This is probably sacrilege to them, isn't it?" he said, zipping up. "Having a wee-wee in a temple, I mean. You know, I was

certain there was a corner up there. I hope I'm not getting disoriented."

He strode back to a curve in the wall and stood almost
touching it, then stepped back again, frowning.

"There *was* a corner there," BB said. "Perhaps the stone re-
configured itself, like the cartouche symbols. Perhaps it's a security door."

Phillips reached out and put his hand on the wall. "That's
very weird. It *feels* soft, but it isn't. I thought my hand was going to go right through it."

"You should check your blood sugar."

"You always say that."

"Do I?"

"Look, are you telling me that these passages are changing
while I'm walking through them?"

"It's entirely possible."

"Oh, shit. How do we get out again, then?"

"You won't know until you try."

Phillips looked at his watch yet again. He could have checked
the time on his datapad or asked BB, but he seemed to take great
comfort from that obsolete piece of jewelry. BB wondered why
the time mattered so much to him when he had no schedule.

"I'm going to keep going while I can," Phillips said.

He went on walking, one hand skimming the right-hand wall
while he looked at the left-hand one. "In case the Sangheili come
after me and drag me out before I'm done. Come on, BB. We're
looking for anything with those Halo symbols now."

*He could just ask. The lens on this camera gives me a
240-degree arc, so I'll see panels before he does anyway.*

After a few minutes, Phillips slowed down and stopped to
look up at the ceiling. Then he retraced his steps a little way.

"BB," he said. "There aren't any lights. I can still see just fine, but there aren't any lightbulbs." He pointed upward as if BB didn't get it. "Where's the light coming from?"

BB felt an urge to do something specific but wasn't sure what. The impulse tormented him, the pain of knowledge that he knew he had but that remained beyond retrieval. How could he possibly *forget* anything? He knew that he had to respond to that question by analyzing the environment in a certain way, but that was as far as he could get. It was both terrifying and uncomfortable.

"I don't know," he said. "But I know that I ought to be able to tell you."

"You haven't got any special sensors, have you? Never mind. Not much you can do when you're stuck in a radio."

Stuck in a radio. "I'll feel better when I'm back in . . . a vessel, then."

"Well, yes, because you'll be able to move at a zillion klicks a second and zap enemy ships. And stick your nose in anywhere you like." Phillips started walking faster. "Can you feel that buzzing sensation?"

"No, but I can see more panels about twenty meters ahead of you."

Phillips scratched the back of his hand. "It's making my hair stand on end."

BB found himself so disturbed by the gaps that he kept detecting in his knowledge that it began to distract him. *But if I can process information the way Phillips says I can, why can't I keep my mind on several things at once?* There was something very wrong with him. He wasn't sure whether it was getting worse or if he was just becoming more aware of it. He was thinking too much without acquiring new data to improve his decision making. He had to stop that right now and concentrate on the task at hand.

"Good grief," Phillips said. The passage opened out into a

large, rectangular chamber completely lined with carved panels. "I think this is going to take us some time. Come on, BB. Lots to process. Starting here . . . y'know, this is like a decorated burial chamber in a pyramid. Maybe it's just someone's life story. Or a control room. Or both."

BB had no opinion yet. He started recording and interpreting the symbols, hoping for clarity. Phillips moved along the four walls, facing them and taking slow sideways steps with his datapad held in the capture position. He didn't need to. Suddenly BB felt anxious. He couldn't define it, but this was troubling him.

"You don't trust me, do you?" BB said. *That's it. He's keeping it from me. He's humoring me.* "I'm recording all this."

"Oh, I trust *you*, chum. It's the hardware I don't trust. It's let us down once, and if it lets us down again, we'll lose all this." His heart rate was up and he was breathing faster. This seemed to be genuinely exciting for him. "I think this is a hundred thousand years old, like Onyx. Malleable stone. *Real* solid state engineering. What kind of technology does it take to create that? Could they manipulate stuff at a subatomic level?"

"What happened to them?" BB asked. "Perhaps someone pressed a Halo button and they wiped themselves out."

Phillips did an odd thing. He lifted the camera without unclipping it and stared into the tiny lens, as if he was looking BB right in the eye. His face was upside down until BB inverted it. It was a thoughtful gesture in its way: Phillips had obviously remembered that BB's view of the world was limited, and was trying to imagine what he could and couldn't see.

"You can be a very depressing little bastard, you know that?" Phillips said.

"Sorry."

"Ah, no worries. Look, start translating this for me. What is it? What does it say?"

BB wondered why any gloriously intelligent species—any

being—would destroy itself. Accidents, perhaps: carelessness. But deliberate destruction . . . that spoke of terrifying desperation. He wondered what that felt like to suddenly want to cease exploring, thinking, finding out, when all your existence before that point had been about the pursuit of it.

He matched and juggled symbols, trying out meanings and looking for patterns. The Halo symbols were repeated in here with the same status icons as the panel in the passage. There were other symbols, too, some identical to the ones in Halsey's lexicon, and some—*ouch*. BB tried again. He felt as if something within him had reached out and slapped him hard. He was following a pathway, certain that it led to something he already knew, but a barrier kept blocking him. It hurt. He received a dozen more smacks even when he tried to reroute.

"I know more than I can retrieve," he said. "I ought to be able to translate much of this, because I recognize it, but something won't let me access the meaning."

Phillips sighed. "That's probably because half of what Halsey found on Onyx ended up being classified. Don't worry. You'll sort it when you reintegrate with yourself. Do what you can for the time being."

"I've failed you."

"BB, humans are used to this. You go out drinking with friends. One of them gets completely hammered, does a few daft things, and next day he can't remember what he said. But he sobers up, everyone reminds him what a dick he made of himself, and everything's okay. It's just a temporary embarrassment."

That level of detail sounded almost autobiographical, but BB decided not to ask. "Very well." Phillips had complete confidence in him. BB hoped he had grounds for that. "We have what seems to be a repeater panel of the Halo status. And there's also another panel with a reference to the *regulator* or *regulations,* the one with the negative phoneme, except there's additional material."

BB re-ran every symbol in the room, every phoneme, every pictograph, every vowel point. So . . . *that* implied an agent, so *this* one didn't mean regulations. It meant someone who *imparted* them, taught them, instructed, and the negative phoneme . . . ah, there were *two* versions of it, one with the sense of not to be changed, not to be questioned, immutable, didactic—which seemed to be a noun—and one that was a command, an exhortation not to do something.

"Just tell me. Think aloud." Phillips was starting to sound impatient. BB felt he was the drunken friend being given leeway in the belief that he'd be sober in the morning. "I'm a linguist too, remember."

"There's a reference to an inflexible teacher, I believe. A dictator, in the literal sense. A didact. There's also a warning not to do something regarding that person—or rank of persons. It could mean anything, but it's repeated several times, and—oh, that's interesting. There's another occurrence of that *superior* idea."

Phillips had both hands flat on the wall now, but placed carefully in blank areas. "So, it's something like don't do X or Y regarding this rank or person . . . without the approval of a superior."

"That's a big leap, but why not?"

"It's a control room. Or a guard house. It's either the rules and regs written on the walls, or it's an alarm center. Okay, perhaps I'm thinking too human. But everything we've seen says they had a lot in common with us. They weren't methane-breathing globs of gel. Not that I'm being methanist."

"I believe some of the symbols are coordinates."

"Just grab everything you can. Once I'm out of here, I doubt they'll let me back in." Phillips pushed back from the wall and started pacing sideways around the edge of the room again. He recorded it all from a different angle. "For all we know, the Arbiter might blow this place up if 'Telcam doesn't win."

"Do you want 'Telcam to win?"

"Apparently, we want them *both* to win. And lose. A stalemate. A never-ending nil-nil draw that's gone into injury time and has an endless penalty shoot-out."

"Should I understand soccer, Professor?"

"You get the idea. We want to keep them busy."

Phillips stood staring at the wall for a long time without saying a word. Then he reached into his bag and took out something. It was food. BB could hear his jaws chomping and see the movement of his throat. Eventually he swallowed for the last time and went back to the wall, running his hand along it.

"Furry barrier . . . another furry barrier . . . and now the dictatorish didactic bit . . . whoa." As his hand passed over the panel that warned not to do something, whatever it was, the symbols changed conspicuously. One of them lit up, red and blue. "Christ, is that light right in the stone? That's some trick."

"I really think you should leave it alone."

"I hear you." Phillips took a lot more images of the panel, then touched the plain section next to it and the lights went out. "I hope it's not a burglar alarm. If we get a bunch of Forerunner cops kicking the doors down, you'll know what it was."

"There are no more Forerunners."

"You're never normally this literal. I could get pissed off with this if I didn't know you'd be back to normal soon." Phillips went on, touching every part of the walls that he could reach. He didn't seem deterred by the risk. Then, without warning, a piece of stone extruded from the wall as his fingers passed over it. For a second it looked like a plain brick, but then it took shape, developing intricate perforations and turning into a sphere.

"Doorknob?" BB suggested.

Phillips pressed his face close to it as if he was trying to peer inside. BB couldn't see his expression, but he heard the wet click as his jaws moved and the muscles under his chin tightened. He was smiling.

"No," he said. His fingers spun the sphere and BB could see that the doorknob was in fact interconnecting, nested layers. *"Arum.* Do you remember any of that? The Sangheili puzzle ball that's supposed to teach their kids persistence and that everyone has their allotted station in society. Except *arums* are completely smooth, and this has holes carved in it."

"And you're going to open it."

"Might as well try."

"Is that wise?"

"We'll see."

BB had to admit it was an impressive skill. It took Phillips under a minute to turn the spheres in such a way that something went *click* deep inside. That was very fast indeed for a slow-thinking entity like a human.

"Now what?" Phillips stepped back. "Don't I get a cuddly toy or a coconut or something? Ah . . . *look.*"

The panel in front of him was changing completely. BB watched the stone rearranging itself like coalescing mercury. Now the symbols offered a long list of options, locations judging by the string of numbers after each, and the engraving right at the top read . . .

"Doors." BB was pretty sure now. "Portals. Entrances. *Powered* in some way. Expressway? Elevators? No, Professor, *don't touch them.*"

Phillips took a deep breath and held it. "Let's give it a go," he said. "This might be the only chance I ever get."

"Don't you think that we should wait and—"

"Can't," Phillips said, and touched the first symbol on the list.

CHAPTER
SEVEN

THE MOST INTERESTING THING ABOUT THE FORERUNNERS AS FAR AS I'M CONCERNED IS WHY THEY'RE NOT AROUND ANY LONGER. SPECIES GO EXTINCT ALL THE TIME, BUT SOME OF THEIR RELATIVES USUALLY SURVIVE. A TECHNOLOGICALLY SOPHISTICATED, GALACTICALLY DISTRIBUTED RACE GETTING WIPED OUT TO THE LAST INDIVIDUAL, THOUGH—THAT RE-QUIRES INTERVENTION.

(ADMIRAL MARGARET PARANGOSKY, CINCONI)

VADAM, SANGHELIOS

So this was Jul's world; this was what he did, what he'd done almost every day since Raia had first met him, and it was nothing like she'd imagined. It was noise and shock and blinding light, and now it stank of blood, too.

She ducked as the bolt of white fire came right at her. It was pure instinct, absolute animal terror, but the missile detonated some way off *Unflinching Resolve*'s bow and never made contact at all. The shock wave did, though. The ship shuddered and bucked. Two strips of metal broke free from the bulkhead and shot across the deck, one bouncing down the polished metal, the other embedding itself like a blade in one of the warriors at the helm controls. He went down like a felled tree. The metal fragment vibrated for a few seconds, standing upright in his back. Two of his brothers rushed forward to drag him clear but Raia didn't see where they took him or even if he was still alive.

She cowered. Nobody on the bridge took any notice of her. She couldn't see what was happening outside, and the glimpses she snatched of monitors and sensors meant nothing to her.

Buran roared, exasperated, grabbing the helm. "We must withdraw, Field Master. Do you hear me? *We need to withdraw,* or move into orbit."

'Telcam stood at the console as if he hadn't even noticed the ground fire coming up at the ship. The deck shook again.

"And the Arbiter will pursue us into space, Buran, and where will we go from there?" he asked. "We have nowhere to retreat."

"We weren't ready to move."

"But we moved nonetheless, and the battle isn't lost yet. Come about. Bring the ship around."

Raia looked to her side. A young male was trying to repair a control panel that smoked and sparked every time he touched it.

"We've lost navigation, my lord," he said. "I can't repair it."

"Then we fly by sight, Dunil." 'Telcam stalked across the deck and went to the other viewscreen. "I need cannon. *Now.*"

Raia caught Dunil's eye. "Are we going to crash?" she asked.

"Possibly, my lady." He lowered his voice. "Bend your limbs and protect your head if we start to lose height. That might save you from breaking bones."

The booming sound was louder and the white-hot flashes were much closer together now. Then the whole ship lurched as if it had crashed into something. Raia felt the shock ripple back through the deck. Jets of white vapor began punching out of conduits that then burst and sent fluid gushing like a ruptured artery.

"Direct hit!" someone roared. *"Direct hit!* The hull is breached, we're losing height, we have no propulsion—"

The ship peeled off in a totally different direction, suddenly much quieter, and for a moment there was an illusion of things returning to normal, but everyone was rushing to console positions and Raia knew it was anything but.

"Crash landing," Buran yelled. "Brace for crash landing. Steer to the shore."

"Shipmaster, we can't—"

"I said steer for the shoreline!"

I won't survive this.

I'm going to die, and I'll never find Jul.

Raia braced as she was told, waiting second after second for an impact that would throw her into dark oblivion. *I'm sorry, Jul. I had to try.* Then there was a huge jolt, then another, and another, and the deck was bouncing her like a pebble on the skin of a drum. Metal screamed. Fittings tore from the bulkheads. The lights went out. Then everything stopped dead and she was flung into a row of bench seats.

Now I'm dead. Now I'll see for myself if the gods exist or not, and if they do I shall spit on them for abandoning us when we most needed them.

But she wasn't dead, or else she wouldn't have been able to feel the rip in her shoulder muscles as someone grabbed her and tried to pull her with them.

"Get out, my lady." It was Dunil. "We'll be burned alive if we don't run."

Instinct made her scramble upright and run with him, stumbling over bodies and not looking down to see who they were. She was swept up in the tide as everyone abandoned ship. Cool, fresh air hit her face and she was suddenly skidding down a torn sheet of metal the size of a raft, hot under her hands, then falling a short distance onto grass and pebbles. She had already run some way from the wreckage before she looked back to see what was cracking and groaning behind her.

Flames licked what was left of the hull for a few moments, then engulfed it. The last thing she saw before she fled for her life was jets of leaking coolant ignite and send columns of flame into the air like blowtorches. When had she last run like this, throw-

ing every muscle fiber into it? She'd been a child. She'd been playing chase with her brothers and sisters. As she grew up, she
learned that females didn't run. They had no need to.

But she needed to run now. Her legs pumped but she felt as if
she were struggling through mud. Her lungs screamed for breath.
Then a blast—silent, oddly silent—caught her full in the back and
lifted her off the ground. She landed hard and the last gulps of
air were knocked out of her. Noise and blisteringly hot air swept
over her moments later. All she could do was lie there, unable to
move, noticing just how many small black clouds of smoke were
hanging in the sky above her, and wait to die.

Someone grabbed her arm again and pulled her to her feet.
"Run, my lady." It was Dunil, the young male who'd been so
patient with her on the bridge. "We have to get out."

"Where's Forze?" She couldn't get her breath. "Where is he?"

"I can't see him. Everyone's scattered. Quick, find cover.
They're coming for us."

"Who is?"

"The Arbiter's troops."

All Thel 'Vadam's forces had to do was head for the crashed
ship, now a burning beacon on the edge of the city. There was
no hiding from them: if she tried to pass as a local in Vadam,
her accent and light skin would mark her out as coming from a
foreign keep. The entire crew was in the same position. They
would have to fight their way home. She found herself stumbling
through thorn bushes and then into trees, and only when she
ran out of breath and her legs wouldn't carry her any farther did
she stop, dropping to the ground. Dunil stopped with her.

"You have to keep going."

"Go. Leave me here."

"I can't."

Raia could think of nothing now but survival. Just when she
thought her lungs would burst and she could never stand up

again, a cold and intense clarity swept over her and stripped away every thought that wasn't devoted to the immediate moment. She reached into her holster and took the plasma pistol, checking the charge.

"I have several hundred shots in this, don't I?" She held it so that Dunil could see it. "Tell me. How many?"

"That model? Four hundred."

"More than enough."

"For what?"

"To kill any fool who tries to kill *me*." Finding Jul was a secondary issue now and she was shocked to find she felt no guilt for thinking that way. She was no use to Jul dead. "I have nothing to lose. What do we do now, regroup or press on?"

Dunil looked down at her as if she was mad. "Do you want the command view, or the real one? I could tell you that we press on and die gloriously, or I could tell you that the intelligent thing to do is to escape and come back another day with greater forces."

"Then we will do the *intelligent* thing," Raia said. She looked around, buoyed up on new clarity, and spotted some of *Unflinching Resolve*'s crew moving through the trees at a crouch, pistols in hands. "I have never traveled far from my keep. How do we get home now?"

"Ah, that's the question," Dunil said.

Forze came crashing through the undergrowth, smoke-smeared and angry. "Raia, come with me. We must get down the shore. Naxan's going to send Gusay to collect you."

"Is that it? What about everyone else?"

"Let *us* worry about that. You shouldn't be here. This is no place for an elder's wife."

"Don't start that argument again."

She could still hear the sporadic crack and hiss of cannon

somewhere in the distance. Then another sound began to drown it out, a ship's drives, and she assumed it was Gusay showing up to take her home. It was only when the sound multiplied that she realized there was a squadron of vessels somewhere overhead, and her assumption changed: this was the Arbiter's fleet, coming to hunt them down and finish them off. She wasn't the only one. She saw all the males look up and aim their weapons, pointless though it was to try to take on warships with pistols.

But she raised hers, too.

Then 'Telcam came stalking into the clearing just ahead of her. He held out his arms as if he was summoning his crew for an address.

"Do you hear that?" he called. "Do you hear it? Do you know what that is?"

He was taking a huge risk. Whoever was flying overhead would be able to see him. But he looked more than unconcerned. He looked *triumphant*.

"What is it, brother?" one of the monks asked.

"Listen to your communications," 'Telcam said. "Open the channel. The gods have come to our aid."

Raia's heart sank. The monk had lost his mind. She waited for a searing energy bolt to vaporize him where he stood, but she turned and caught the expression on Dunil's face and Forze's. All the troops were listening to something.

She had no communications equipment. She wouldn't even have known which channel to switch to.

"I'd call that a timely miracle," Forze said. His jaws parted and snapped together again with satisfaction. "And an apt one."

"What?" Raia stood in his way, demanding an answer. "What is it?"

Forze removed his communicator and held it out to her. "Listen to the sound of salvation," he said.

The mood had changed in seconds. The surviving crew were all standing in the open now, either listening to their communicators or roaring in approval as they looked up into the sky. She put Forze's device to her ear. Someone was talking to 'Telcam.

"We're not alone," the voice said. "Word is spreading, from city to city. The keeps are rallying. We might not be the most pious warriors, but 'Vadam has gone too far this time. Allowing *human troops* to land on Sanghelios, allowing them to defile a temple—that's more than enough to unite the keeps against him."

'Telcam had his miracle, then. Raia hoped it would last long enough to bring Jul home, wherever he was. She gazed at her pistol, now feeling more comforting in her hand than unfamiliar, and decided she wasn't going home to Mdama just yet.

Gusay would have a wasted journey. Forze could call him now and tell him to stay at home.

TEMPLE OF ABIDING TRUTH, ONTOM

Fifty meters into the tunnel, comms with *Port Stanley* began to break up. By one hundred meters, Vaz had lost the link completely.

"Can you still hear us, Dev?" Sooner or later, they'd lose *Tart-Cart,* too. BB hadn't been able to scan inside the temple from orbit, so there was a fair chance that something about the Forerunner structure was interfering with signals. "Everything okay out there?"

"No," Devereaux said. "Do you want to see? I've moved so I can monitor the lynch mob outside."

Tart-Cart's forward exterior cam fed Vaz a view of the plaza from ground level, just a few hundred Elites gathering and making angry gestures, but even in that big open space it still looked like a lot of hinge-heads. They hadn't plucked up the courage to storm the temple and piss off the gods yet. Judging by the body language of the ones closest to the cam, though, they were giving it some serious consideration.

The image relayed to everyone's HUD. Mal whistled to himself.

"Hinge-heads to the southwest," he said, putting on an exaggerated accent that Vaz didn't recognize. "*Thousands* of 'em, sir."

Devereaux huffed. She seemed to get the joke. "Yeah, funny, Staff, but I've got to move the ship. I'll take a big loop around and avoid going over their heads, because that really won't help matters. I'm going to set down at the back of the temple."

"Is there enough space?"

"I'll *make* space."

"Try not to damage anything, Dev."

"You just make sure you exit via the back door, okay?"

"Got it. You're breaking up now, so we're going to lose comms."

"*Tart-Cart* out."

Vaz replayed the footage as he walked. He wondered how long piety would stop the Elites storming the place. If they were anything like humans in crowds, the whole thing would boil over in a second and they'd be in here, bent on revenge. Narrow passages, nowhere to run—would they open fire, or would they be too worried about damaging sacred structures? Did it matter? They could rip Vaz apart with their bare hands and just mop up the mess later.

And Phillips might not have been the only person down here. Maybe they were all walking straight into an ambush.

"Phillips?" Vaz yelled at the top of his voice but there wasn't even the hint of an echo. "Come on, Phillips, where the hell are you?"

"He's come this way, because I can smell him," BB said. "And his fingerprints are on some of the surfaces."

"What do you mean, *smell* him?"

"Human sebum. Very persistent, full of heavy alcohols and hydrocarbons. No witty rejoinders, please, Mal."

Mal had his finger inside the trigger guard, so he was as worried as Vaz about what might be around the next corner—or behind them. "Is Phillips *all* you can smell? No Elites?"

"Just Phillips. At least in recent weeks."

"Are you using my nose?" Naomi asked. She sounded absolutely serious to Vaz. "How did you pick that up?"

"Your NBCD filters."

"Oh. Okay."

Mal stopped a few meters ahead of them. "So you're sure we haven't been down this one before, BB?"

"Positive. But Phillips has. Keep going."

"How far have we come?"

"Over three kilometers."

"Well, it's got to end somewhere."

"No," Vaz said. "This place could be in some part of slipspace for all we know."

He looked back to check on Naomi. He didn't trust Forerunner technology after what had happened on Onyx, so he walked back around the curve of the tunnel to look for her. He found her standing in front of a carved panel, tilting her head one way then the other as if she was trying out different filters. There was no telling what went on with her armor these days. It had some nanite system that upgraded it when it was idling, so her hardware was as much a voyage of discovery as the Forerunner ruins. It still looked like Mark V Mjolnir from the outside, but it definitely wasn't. Maybe she liked the retro style and wanted to keep it, like a shabby but much-loved pair of jeans. He wasn't going to ask right now.

"No wonder Phillips has gone on safari," BB said. He still

sounded as if he was doing a ventriloquist's act with Naomi as the dummy. Vaz wondered how long she'd put up with that. "Have you *seen* these engravings? I'm recording them, just in case."

"I hate it when you say that."

"These are control panels, like the ones Halsey found in the Dyson sphere, except this isn't an emergency shelter. It's more like a command center. A garrison building."

Naomi stepped back from the panel and walked away. "Hey, I haven't finished," BB said. "I need to use your visual feed."

"You can process information in a split second, and you can monitor through *anyone's* helmet."

"Oh, sorry I spoke—"

Vaz interrupted in to break it up. "So why aren't you fluent in Forerunner by now, BB? Halsey can't be smarter than you are."

"If you think that cereal-packet psychology is going to distract me from the inevitably unpleasant discovery that my fragment is utterly buggered, Vaz, it *won't.*"

Yes, BB was definitely strung out. "Okay, so tell me what it says."

"What does the word *link* mean in English? Anything from a comms channel to a shuttle service. Be a dear, Naomi, and touch the surface, will you? I need to analyze that shield that's covering it."

Naomi put her gloved palm cautiously on the surface. "What is it?"

"A job for a Huragok," BB admitted.

Nothing blew up, lit up, or made a noise. After a couple of seconds, Naomi turned, pointed forward in the direction that Mal had gone, and walked off. Vaz prodded the surface of the panel to check and decided it felt more like the bristles of an invisible silicone brush.

Mal was opening up a gap ahead of them, calling out like he was looking for a wayward cat. "Phillips . . . *Phil*-lips . . . come on, time to go home. Lots of angry hinge-heads outside."

"Left," BB said. "He went left. Right's a dead end, anyway. Look, Mal, let Naomi take point, will you? I need her sensors out front."

Mal stopped and turned slowly around, cradling his rifle. "Right away, sir. Any other orders?"

"You know I mean well."

"Yeah."

Naomi strode past Mal, leaving Vaz on tail. Vaz was now starting to worry whether he'd actually hear anyone coming up behind him. The passages swallowed sound. He was waiting for the outraged faithful to jump him from behind: it was beginning to feel like a jungle patrol minus the trees. He turned around every few meters and walked backward for a few paces.

"Ick," BB said. "You don't need sensors to detect *that*."

Vaz faced forward and inhaled. He couldn't pick up anything through his filters, so he lifted his helmet and sniffed again. It was a very familiar odor. "Smells like the heads."

"Oh dear, the Prof's let the side down," Mal said. "Peeing in a temple. I'll be writing to *The Times* about this. You still on the trail, BB?"

"Yes. He went down there—ahhhh. Look at that." It was another panel of carvings. "That's like the one in the Dyson sphere. The storehouse-garage-sarcophagus symbol. And lots of negative symbols. I might have to send this back to the Admiral and ask for a Huragok to take a look at it."

"What makes you think they'd know?"

"Why leave a janitor with instructions he can't read?"

"But why wouldn't they volunteer that information?" Naomi asked. "Were they ordered *not* to, or is it a case of just having to ask them for every damn thing?"

Vaz caught a quick burst of static on his radio, as if someone was trying to contact them but unable to get a stable signal. It had to be Devereaux. Mal turned around. He'd heard it, too.

"I'm going to assume that was Dev," he said. "And that something's wrong. Because it usually is."

"Skip the survey, BB." Naomi started jogging. "Just follow Phillips." She speeded up, sounding like a trip-hammer even with the sound-deadening acoustics of the passages. *"Phillips!* Come on, Phillips, answer me."

All Vaz could do was run after her. Mal broke into a sprint. Vaz found himself trying to calculate how long it would take a hinge-head to cover three klicks, based on the length of stride, and the worrying answer was that it would be a lot sooner than he thought. He was pretty certain now that at the end of the trail of Phillips's unique cocktail of odors, he'd trip over a body.

"You realize that wherever we are, we're going to come up a bloody long way from the dropship even if we find a way out," Mal panted.

"So we retrace our steps."

"Hey, what happened to the lighting?"

"It's still—oh. Yeah." Vaz noticed there were no more visible light fittings hanging from the ceiling, but somehow there was still light. "How do they do that?"

"I think we're entering Weirdville now."

Vaz couldn't see Naomi. The passage curved around to the left and then there was a sharp corner, but BB's voice came over the radio before Mal got there.

"I've lost the trail," BB said. "It's just stopped dead."

Mal let out a long breath and kept going. Vaz was right on his heels, still checking over his shoulder for enraged hinge-heads. When they caught up with Naomi, she was standing at a T-junction in the passage. Vaz felt that buzz in his earpiece again, like radio interference or a failing loop-suppressor, and stopped to look in both directions.

"No scent?" Vaz asked. "It doesn't necessarily mean he hasn't been here, does it? Where else could he go?"

Naomi prodded the stonework. "This isn't like Onyx. This is solid. He's gone one way or the other."

"Okay." Mal pointed left. "Naomi, you take that passage and we'll take this one. Keep broadcasting and turn back if you lose the signal. I don't want to misplace anyone else."

Vaz was now starting to imagine cuffing Phillips around the ear when he found him rather than slapping him on the back with relief. Once they found him, they still had to exfil. Vaz hoped that whatever Phillips had found was worth all this crap.

"*Door,*" Naomi said. "I've found a door. I'm waiting here until you come to me."

"You heard the lady." Mal did a U-turn and gestured at Vaz to go back. "I'm going to kick his arse into the middle of next week."

"I hope you realize how many panels I've *not* been able to find and record," BB said irritably.

"That's all right. Adj can fill in the gaps."

It was a door all right, like a smaller version of the one at the front of the temple, with an actual locking mechanism rather than a button. Naomi stood beside it, running her finger around the frame while she checked the TACPAD on her wrist.

"It's just a door," she said. "Better open it."

"Live dangerously." Mal raised his rifle and aimed into the doorway. Vaz stood to the other side. "One, two . . ."

Naomi turned the circular handle and it swung outward. For a second, all Vaz could see was a patch of light and absolute black shadow until his visor adjusted. He could hear crowd noises but they sounded distant, and—more important—there was the familiar and comforting whine of a dropship's idling drive. But there was no sign of Phillips.

"Now I'm getting really pissed off with him," Vaz said. "Didn't he realize we were coming?"

"Evidently not." Naomi went ahead and stalked up the short passage. "Permission to grab him and cart him off, Staff?"

"By the nuts if you want to," Mal said. "Dev, can you hear me?"

"Got you, Staff. Meter's running. Where are you?"

"Where are *you*?"

"Right behind the temple. I've got two meters' clearance on both wings."

BB was still griping. "I can't pick up any odor. Opening the door might have diffused it, but I doubt it."

Naomi reached the end of the passage and stepped outside. Then she held her hand up to stop. "I think we've come in a circle," she said. "I can see the wall in the plaza. And no Phillips."

"Oh, for Chrissakes—Dev, has he come out near you?"

"No Phillips here, Staff."

"We're going to have to search the grounds." Vaz didn't feel very comradely right then. "Quietly. Are those hinge-heads inside the walls yet?"

They stood outside for a few moments, looking and listening, just in case Phillips decided to pop up from a hiding place and they could run for it. But it was a few seconds too long. Vaz edged beyond the building and held his breath. He was looking at maybe a hundred Elites as they clustered around the front door, right inside the compound. Someone was arguing with them. It wasn't Phillips. It looked like Olar, the hinge-head they'd met going in.

And then one of the Sangheili turned to face Vaz.

"*Nishum!*" he roared.

Vaz didn't need a translation. The hinge-heads surged forward and he ducked back. Mal and Naomi got the idea instantly. They started running down the side of the temple building toward the rear, followed by a roaring that sounded like the surge of a tidal wave.

"Dev, here we come," Mal said. "Plan B. Up and out, fast as you can."

The noise of the drives suddenly rose into a high-pitched whine. It was going to be a rough takeoff. Vaz skidded around the end of the wall just behind Naomi, who reached into her belt and flung something back over her head without even looking. Vaz caught a glimpse as it arced over him.

"Just smoke," she said. "Every second counts."

The smoke grenade went off behind them with a loud bang and Vaz spotted *Tart-Cart*'s velvet gray nose up ahead. The next thing he saw was half a dozen Elites between him and the ship. The dropship's side hatch was open. If this wasn't 'Telcam's guys coming to help them out, it was going to turn ugly pretty fast. Then one of the hinge-heads answered the question by aiming his plasma pistol, and a green bolt of energy sizzled off Vaz's shoulder plate, almost bowling him over. Something caught him and shoved him upright in a second—maybe Naomi, maybe Mal—and his body did what it had learned to do without thinking: he returned fire, and kept firing as he ran, crashing into one Sangheili so hard that the impact hurt deep in his sinuses. He didn't realize how high he could jump until he landed in the open hatch and smashed onto the coaming. He rolled clear and grabbed the first arm he could see. Mal hauled him through the hatch and Naomi jumped onto the step, holding on to the hull.

"Go, Dev," Mal yelled. *"Lift*. Go go *go."*

The dropship shot up vertically like a mortar. Vaz found himself on his back, looking through the open hatch at a fireworks show of green and white streaks zipping past Naomi, framed in silhouette for a second. The hatch shut and sealed with a *fwoomp* of air.

"So," Devereaux said. "No Phillips. If he'd been outside, I'd have found him."

"If he'd been inside, *we'd* have found him." Mal leaned over Vaz and checked him out. "So, apart from explaining to Osman how we managed to start a riot and kill a few hinge-heads on holy ground, I think we ought to start an aerial search."

Vaz's ribs were starting to throb where he'd fallen against the hatch. "He can't have gone that far. No more than thirty klicks, even if he was running."

Naomi looked down at him and BB's voice emerged from her helmet. It didn't look as funny as it had an hour ago.

"That," BB said, "depends on how he left the temple."

SANGHELIOS: EXACT LOCATION UNKNOWN

"That didn't happen," Phillips said. "Did it?"

For a moment he thought he'd stepped into the temple grounds, but his stomach was still cartwheeling as if he'd done a somersault. A breeze played on his face.

Ontom was gone. He had no idea where he was.

He stood in a ruined building—no roof, no windows, just three crumbling stone-block walls—in the middle of nowhere. Hip-high, dark green grass rolled and swayed like an ocean for a couple of kilometers ahead of him. He turned around slowly, taking in a small town in the distance, and decided that his only chance of getting out was to walk to the nearest keep and beg for help. Maybe a little sleight of hand with an *arum* would be his passport.

If only BB would suddenly snap back to normal.

"That was a portal," BB said.

"I sort of worked that out." Portals were routed all over the place, usually not on the same planet. The sky looked the same; the air smelled familiar. "But we're still on Sanghelios, aren't we?"

"I believe so. I still have my positioning system."

"How far from Ontom?"

"I estimate eighty kilometers."

It seemed a pointlessly short journey for a portal given the energy needed to power it. But perhaps it made sense when the Forerunners were last here, and at least the thing still worked even though the exit end was in ruins. Phillips took a look around the structure and wondered whether it was worth risking an unencrypted broadcast. He didn't have any protection from the rebels now, no top cover as Mal called it, and announcing that he was a good pal of the Arbiter might get him killed with equal speed.

The ODSTs would definitely come looking for him sooner or later. He had to make it easier for them to find him.

"I can't hide, BB." There was a panel of carved symbols on a slab of masonry but half of it had crumbled away. Phillips recorded a few images anyway. "So I might as well make myself conspicuous. Nice brisk walk into town."

"I think that's a collective of keeps called Acroli. But I can't tell what its loyalties are."

"I have a feeling it's not going to make much difference. I'm a worm. An *arum*-solving worm."

"Professor, I find I'm having to revise my translation."

Phillips was sure he could see smoke in the far distance. He checked his datapad map, which wasn't exactly reliable. He should have asked the Arbiter for an accurate chart. "Is that a problem, BB? Because I think you got the word for portal right."

"Coordinates," BB said. "I must have interpreted the numbers wrongly. Or Halsey did. This location doesn't correspond to the position I would have expected."

"Back to the drawing board."

"It's important. I need to work out how the Forerunners navigated, or else you won't know the locations of the Halos."

"How come your security thingie hasn't wiped your awareness of Halos?"

"I don't know. It's very distressing."

Phillips didn't know what to say to comfort him. He wasn't even sure if changing the subject worked. "We'll sort it out later," he said. "Let's get home first."

Somehow he'd always expected the Sangheili to have sophisticated security that could pick up an alien incursion anywhere on the planet, but here he was, ambling through a meadow within sight of a town, and nothing had swooped on him, shot at him, or detected him yet. He was used to a world where security cameras picked him up two hundred times a day just wandering around Sydney and where his bank and comms provider knew his every desire, habit, and movement, let alone all the government snoopers who'd probably been keeping tabs on him without his knowledge. *Yes, but* I'm *a snooper now.* ONI was right about the technological infrastructure going down the pan with the San'Shyuum. They'd only been gone a few months but they'd left a massive hole.

The town was getting closer. So were the palls of smoke behind it. Phillips started to rethink his perspective, wondering if the smoke was actually closer than he'd first thought and that he was walking into trouble. But there was no other place to head to. He felt in his bag to see if he had anything sharp that he could use to defend himself. *Okay. Two-fifty centimeters of Sangheili, one-meter-seventy me, and the winner would be . . . not me.* Then his fingers touched cool, polished wood, and he took out the *arum* that he'd been clutching before the explosion, the one that had contained the message from 'Telcam. That would get him out of more tight spots than any knife. He spun the nested spheres, got it open, and bent down to pick up a small stone to place in its heart. All he had to do when confronted was rattle it and dazzle his enemy with his dexterity.

"What's that?" BB asked.

"You know what this is, BB." *Oh God, is the rest of his memory failing, too*? "It's an *arum*."

"I mean *that* up ahead."

Phillips had been too wrapped up in the *arum* to notice. He scanned along the radio cam's line of sight, looking for whatever had grabbed BB's attention. The grass was moving about fifty meters ahead of him, and it wasn't the wind. Something was wading through it. There must have been wildlife on Sanghelios, even livestock, but he knew nothing about it. He decided to assume it would sink its teeth in him.

"What do you think it is, BB?"

"Something short."

"Or something with its head down, stalking us."

"I'm just the radio cam, Professor. It's stalking *you*."

Phillips started thinking what he'd do if the thing — whatever it was —came at him. Okay, he had a bag, and he had a lump of wood, and he could swing that like a sock full of coins. Yet again he thought how helpless he was compared to Mal or Vaz. Vaz would probably have head-butted the thing and then eaten it raw. Nothing scared him. Christ, even Devereaux wouldn't have broken a sweat: pilot or not, she'd been through exactly the same training as the two guys. Phillips envied their absolute physical confidence.

He noted that he didn't compare his lack of survival skills to Naomi's, though. Naomi was beyond human. Nobody expected him to shape up to a Spartan, not even his ego.

"Professor, I think there's more than one," BB said helpfully. "The grass is moving in several places."

"Pray for sheep." Phillips put the *arum* back in the bag, transferred everything breakable to his pockets, and began twisting the fabric to make a long handle. His heart started pounding. *Swing it nice and hard. Whack.* Really *hard. Job done.* "Or whatever Sangheili rear for dinner."

He was ready. He really was going to take a swing and brain whatever came at him. He was in full primal mode, about twenty meters away from the target, and pumping up a good head of adrenaline to carry him through. Then something bobbed above the top of the grass. It stood up. It was deformed and comically ugly, or at least he thought it was until he realized it was wearing a breathing mask and the hump on its spine was a backpack.

"Unggoy," BB said. "Grunts. They breathe methane."

Two more masked heads popped up. Phillips had never seen a Grunt in the flesh before. It was nice to be taller than an alien for a change.

"Yeah, and methane's flammable." The Grunts just stared at him. "Do they fight?"

"Some do. Most are just manual labor."

"Okay, silent routine, BB."

This was no time to make new enemies. Phillips lowered his bag slowly and tried to look nonthreatening. They'd speak Sangheili. He could dazzle them.

"Hi," he said. "My name's Evan. I'm lost and I need help. I was invited here by Thel 'Vadam and I need to contact his office."

The Grunt looked up at him through slit-like eye-pieces. "You talk funny. Fancy, but *funny.*"

"Do you work here?"

"Yeah."

"Is this a farm?"

"Yeah."

Okay. This is going to take some time. "If I knock on the door, will the farmer help me?"

"Nah," said the Grunt. His two buddies padded a little closer. "He's a bastard. They all are. Elites. Hate 'em."

"I just want to make a call to the Arbiter."

"You want to go to the keep?"

"Yes. Please."

One of the other Grunts shuffled through the grass and stood in front of Phillips. He pointed into the distance with an oversized hand. Whatever they looked like without the masks, they probably weren't much prettier.

"Wassat smoke?" he asked. "Humans invading? You're a human, yeah?"

So they didn't even know there was a coup going on. Why should they? They seemed to be just farmhands. "Yes, I'm human, but no, we're not invading."

"Oh. Pity. Our ancestors tried fighting the Elites. But the bastards glassed them."

"And gave us all the shitty jobs," his buddy added. "We hate 'em."

"So you said." The smoke was looking way too close for Phillips's comfort now. He could hear drives whining in the distance, but the vessels could have been anything from civilian transports to crop sprayers. For a Sangheili expert, he still had a lot of gaps to fill. "Look, I'm going to walk down to the keep. What's the elder's name?"

"Jicam," said the main Grunt. "You ought to shoot him."

"Don't take any notice of Dengo," his buddy said. "He's sucking too much infusion. Passes the time in this job, you know? Just approach nice and slow. You want us to walk with you?"

"Okay." Phillips thought that would make getting shot on sight less likely. "What's infusion?"

"It smoothes the day out. You want some?"

Oh. Dope. Alcohol. Whatever. "No thanks, I don't think I've got the right body chemistry."

Phillips started walking and the Grunts trotted along with him, two at his side and one some way behind. When he pushed through the grass, he walked straight into a mown area and realized they'd been cutting whatever the crop was and decided to take a very long break. They grabbed any excuse to stop working for a while.

So I'm making friends with Unggoy. Wow. That's got to be worth another paper. Professor Evan Phillips, alien pundit, part-time spook. Oh, the lecture tours . . . the TV gigs.

And the obituary, if I'm not careful.

He could hear a vessel approaching from behind and looked over his shoulder to see a purple streak that could have been a Banshee zip overhead at high speed in the direction of the smoke. Now it was starting to worry him.

I really should have thought a bit harder about that smoke.

"They got trouble," Dengo said. "Hah."

Another Banshee shot overhead, then another, and another. Five seconds later, instant bolts of green light punched down from the sky and sent balls of flame and black smoke roiling into the air. It wasn't the town. They definitely hadn't hit the keep. They *couldn't* bomb the keep, he needed it in one piece, he *had* to make that call to the Arbiter's office, or else—

"*Get down*, Professor," BB said. "I know you told me to be silent, but *take cover.*"

The Grunts swung around to see where that foreign voice was coming from. Phillips watched four small specks in the sky getting bigger by the second, probably the Banshees on the way back from their sortie. But there was one too many, and then one of the roofs on the keep exploded, sending masonry and glass high in the air. This time he ducked. He hit the ground facedown in the grass. There was a deafening *zzipppp* that sounded as if someone had ripped a giant piece of fabric right next to him, the smell of burned air, and an explosion like a grenade. Dirt and water rained on him.

The Grunts went crazy, or at least two of them did. It wasn't water. It was blood. Phillips lifted his head a fraction and he could see it. He couldn't work out what was going on now because the Grunts were screaming, but he knew they'd lost one of their buddies. Curled and misshapen pieces of metal lay in the grass a few meters from him, still hissing. So that was what happened when you hit a methane tank.

Phillips waited, still clinging to the ground, but he couldn't hear the Banshees now. He risked pushing himself up on his hands and looked around again. The Grunts were hunkered down, now chattering furiously.

"Hey," Phillips barked. "Hey—guys, get a grip. We can't just sit here all day. Come on. Let's get to the keep."

"They killed Sensen," Dengo said. "Bastards killed him."

"You don't know *which* bastards." Phillips knelt up. *What would Mal do? What would Osman do?* "They're fighting each other. But you work for the keep, yes? Then we go there. Even if it's just to arm ourselves. Okay, you're Dengo—what's your name?"

"Gikak."

"Move it, Gikak."

Phillips got to his feet and started walking. If he was honest with himself, he was close to loss of bowel control again, but he'd lived through this once and that meant he could live through it again. Even 'Telcam thought the gods were looking out for him. Sometimes telling yourself a really big lie was as good as the real thing. When he looked behind him, Dengo and Gikak were following obediently.

"You better knock on the door," Phillips said. "I might be too much of a surprise."

He could see what the smoke was now. It was a downed vessel, something small, fighter-size; he could pick out the shape of the hull between the trees. With any luck, whoever had done the strafing run wouldn't be back. He couldn't see anyone as he approached the keep—small, tatty, nothing like the Arbiter's imposing headquarters—and the Grunts did as they were told and went ahead.

"Just observe, BB," Phillips whispered. "Let me do the talking."

The huge double door didn't open for a few moments and the Grunts just stood there looking lost and confused. Then one side eased half-open, followed by the muzzle of plasma pistol.

"My lady Elar," Gikak said. "Sensen's been killed. We found this human. He's lost."

The door opened fully. Phillips had never been up close to a Sangheili female before. They were almost as big as the males and this one seemed to know how to handle a weapon.

This was hands-on anthropology, live and raw.

Charm. Courtesy. Oh God. Do it.

"Hello, my lady," Phillips said, terrified. "May I come in?"

CHAPTER
EIGHT

YOU NEED TO DO MORE THAN OVERTHROW THE ARBITER.
YOU NEED TO WIPE BOTH HIM AND VADAM FROM THE FACE
OF SANGHELIOS, BECAUSE AS LONG AS THAT STATE EXISTS,
IT WILL REMAIN LOYAL TO HIM, AND IT WILL EXERT ITS POWER
AND INFLUENCE.

(SHIPMASTER BURAN 'UTARAL TO AVU MED 'TELCAM)

UNSC *PORT STANLEY*, IN SANGHELIOS ORBIT

"I'm sorry, ma'am," Mal said. "It was a bit of a balls-up. But we had to open fire."

Osman hoped that her dismay didn't show on her face. She steeled herself to sit well back in her seat and not lean forward toward the cam mounted on the console. They'd done all they could, and she certainly couldn't have done any better. She needed to project her confidence in them.

"You're entitled to defend yourselves," she said. "We can only take diplomacy so far. Is Vaz okay?"

She could see movement behind Mal in the crew bay. Vaz was sitting up against one of the bulkheads in his tank top with one arm folded across his chest, fending off Naomi's first aid. The Spartan ran out of patience, grabbed him by one shoulder, and pinned him while she sprayed salve on his burns.

Mal glanced around as if he was checking she hadn't handcuffed him. "He took a couple of bolts at close range and got burned, but he smacked himself up when we banged out."

"Ma'am, it's just bruises," Vaz called, indignant. "I landed hard and it rammed my chest plate into my ribs. I'll live."

"So anyway, I think we dropped four of them," Mal went on. "We didn't stop to count."

Osman shrugged. "Probably didn't make things any worse."

"No, they went mental when they realized we'd entered the temple. Maybe I should have made the hinge-head go and get Phillips."

"And if he'd told you he couldn't find him, you couldn't have taken his word for it. Besides, you've inadvertently helped boost support for 'Telcam."

Mal rubbed his nose thoughtfully. He seemed to be looking for a tactful response. "Well, I think that's what used to be known in the Corps as a self-adjusting cock-up."

"Okay, stay airborne and keep looking. How far could Phillips get?"

BB interrupted. Osman could see him out of the corner of her eye, hanging motionless above the helm controls. "You're not going to like the answer," he said.

"Try me."

"I believe I've cracked some of the inscriptions, which I'd prefer to call *signage,* seeing as that's what most of it is."

"And?"

"Portals. Lists of portals. Chances are he's activated one, seeing as he can't leave things alone. Which means he could be anywhere in the galaxy."

Osman's scalp tightened. *Poor Evan. Poor bastard.* At the same time, the pragmatic ONI part of her patted her on the back and said it didn't matter where Phillips was, as long as he wasn't in enemy hands on Sanghelios having the truth beaten out of him. She didn't know which was the real Serin Osman and wasn't sure that she wanted to find out.

"If you know they're portals," she said carefully, "then can you work out where they go? We could at least narrow down the locations."

"Well, you can forget names, because they won't correspond at all, so I'm relying on coordinates. But I can't work those out until I compare a portal with an actual exit location. Because, rather inconveniently, they didn't use UNSC chart conventions."

"Yes, okay, BB, point taken. Now tell me something useful."

"I vote we keep looking, ma'am," Mal said. "Rule out Sanghelios, if nothing else."

"It's a damn big planet."

"We'll keep going until you call us off."

Any deadline she set now would be an artificial one of her own making, but doing nothing and hoping for the best wasn't an option. There was always the possibility that Phillips had escaped under his own steam and made a run for it, and he was no fool. Even with his BB fragment dead, he'd find another way to send a signal. Osman couldn't just shrug and head back to Venezia even if she wanted to. It was lethal for morale, if nothing else.

No man left behind. That's what the ODSTs expect. Naomi, too.

She checked the real-time chart. *Tart-Cart* showed as a small blue icon even in stealth mode, for *Stanley*'s electronic eyes only. "So you're twenty klicks outside Ontom."

"It'll be dark soon. We can use thermal imaging and not invite pot-shots. Shame he hasn't got a neural implant, though."

"I'll shove one in him personally for the next time he goes missing. The hard way."

"Just a thought," BB said. "If portals go anywhere at all on Sanghelios, they'll probably route to other Forerunner sites. Can Admiral Hood sweet-talk a chart of relics out of the Arbiter? It would save me a lot of survey time."

"I'll ask. How are you doing for rations, Staff?"

"A week's worth if we're careful," Mal said. "No problem with water, because there's any number of rivers down here."

"Okay. Next sitrep on the hour."

The video link closed and Osman was left staring at the ONI ident screen. BB drifted closer and sat on the console as if he was going to have a heart-to-heart with her.

"You prefer to hear it direct from them, don't you?" he said.

She nodded. "No offense. Instant data is wonderful, but I need to look my people in the eye." She clapped her hands on the armrests of her chair. "Okay, let's crack on with this. Tell me what's happening with the Arbiter."

"He's struggling to hold Vadam. Want to listen?"

BB switched the bridge audio to the output from the orbital surveillance drones. Osman could only guess what the actual transmissions sounded like—a dozen different channels eavesdropping simultaneously—but BB's breathtaking speed meant that all she heard was one voice at a time, already translated into English. It was still hard to follow. She listened for names. One in particular leapt out at her.

"The ship isn't responding. . . . Is *Unflinching Resolve* down? . . . No matter, we can do this with or without 'Telcam, if we have the will . . . locate *Pious Inquisitor* . . . we have fifteen more vessels joining us . . . then move the artillery, you fool, move them up to the keep. . . ."

Whatever happened to that well-oiled war machine? *No San'Shyuum. Still finding their feet again.* She glanced at BB. "So *Pious Inquisitor*'s back. I wondered what had happened to her. I keep forgetting how willing they are to glass one another."

"They're running low on big ships. It looks like they're losing the few they've got, but they don't need much to take out the Arbiter, because he's as short of resources as they are."

"Is he losing?"

"Yes. He didn't see this coming. Lack of organization has its advantages."

"So other than monitoring, what else can we usefully do at the moment?"

"I've brought the Admiral up to speed."

"And?"

"She's still leaning on Hood to give *Infinity* a run, for reasons so Byzantine that I fell to my virtual knees in worship. She's asking Hood if it isn't time to go and help his Sangheili chum. We could well have a flagship plus both commanders out here soon."

"What, she's planning to come out here with *Infinity*? Hood as well? Good God."

"ONI does house calls."

"Are they even allowed to deploy together? Sounds like a recipe for a power vacuum at the top if anything goes wrong with all the untested technology."

"I doubt either would let the other have the keys and take the ship for a spin alone. Anyway, ONI would be fine. You're the heir apparent. Fleet would be rather inconvenienced, though."

They didn't need a warship like *Infinity* to back up an extraction like this, not when Sanghelios was still groping for a new direction and mired in problems of its own. Osman realized that she would have done the same thing in Parangosky's position, though: an early test of what the ship could now do, a timely warning to the Sangheili that they were no longer top dogs, a more serious shake-down of the crew to find any weak links, and a perfect excuse to take out a few more Sangheili ships that might one day trouble Earth.

Do it, ma'am. Take the risk. But just remember you're not a kid anymore.

"It's amazing how tolerant families are of these long mystery deployments," Osman said.

"Lots of young, single officers."

"I did wonder. UNSC *Lonely Loser*."

"Oh, there'll be seventeen thousand shipmates before too long, and nothing much else to do . . ."

Two-edged sword, families. Something to fight for, or something to lose and grieve over. But I'll never know.

Osman watched the displays, keen to forget the family complications that might end up plaguing Kilo-Five. She switched to the drone view of Vadam, trying to work out which pall of smoke was *Unflinching Resolve*. That probably explained why she couldn't raise 'Telcam. Was he dead? She'd have to find another way to keep the plates spinning. He couldn't be the only religious Sangheili ripe for exploiting.

"It must be very hard to have normal relationships in this job," BB said suddenly, obviously still pondering on *Lonely Loser*. "And not just because the clear azure pool of eligible men contains so many rotting leaves of the Captain Hogarth variety."

Osman almost shot back a heartfelt response but found herself frozen. The most unsettling thing about a conversation with BB was that he almost never had to ask her a question, because he knew her past: he had every conceivable piece of information ever recorded about her, including the stuff she didn't even know and wasn't willing to look at for herself. He remembered it flawlessly, too, all the dates and names that she forgot, even though she prided herself on a pretty sharp memory by human standards. But so much conversation was about the past, the wealth of detail and incidents unknown to the other person that could be dredged up and discussed, or asked about politely, and BB was incapable of being surprised by any of it. BB's past hardly existed. And the things that fascinated her most about him as an entity, as a *person*, were whatever linked him to his donor and how he handled knowing that he'd cease to exist in an unfairly short time.

He rarely knew how she'd *felt* about things, though. The records didn't cover that, which was why many of his little chats were eye-wateringly intrusive. It was all that was left to really talk about.

"You're right," she said. "There's only one bigger blight on a girl's social life than being ONI brass, and that's being a Spartan. Have you had this conversation with Naomi?"

"Not while my data chip is still lodged in her head. . . ."

"Very wise."

Osman almost asked if he knew anything about his donor, but lost her nerve. BB was now her closest confidant. She wasn't sure if that was sad or miraculous. "I'm going to grab a coffee while I can," she said. "I'll take root in that damn chair if I don't walk a few more decks during the day."

Port Stanley felt bigger and emptier than ever. In the wardroom, one of the few communal spaces that was small enough to feel comforting for a crew of six, she poured herself a cup of the best Jamaica that Parangosky had laid on for the squad and smiled at the memory of Adj endlessly tinkering with the coffee machine until he'd perfected it. But the next thought leapt back to Phillips, and that was nothing to smile about.

It's just a few days. The rebellion isn't affecting every city. He'll come through it.

She shut her eyes and sipped. For a few moments she was so far away that BB's voice almost made her choke.

"I thought you'd like to know that I've located 'Telcam," he said, "or at least some of his crew."

Osman slammed the cup down on the counter and set off back to the bridge at a jog. "Can you get a call in to them?"

"I'm trying right now. His ship's burning, but he seems to have set up an operating base outside the keep."

By the time she got to the bridge, BB was talking to someone

in Sangheili. She could also hear the simultaneous English translation.

"Shipmaster, I insist," BB was saying. "We must speak to 'Telcam. Get him." He dropped one voice to a whisper. It was impressive to hear him speaking with three voices simultaneously.
"I've fed them bogus data to make us look like a Kig-Yar ship.
I'm clever like that. And you'll sound convincingly authentic to
them."

Osman sat down and tried to think like a mercenary heron.
There was no point banging the table and telling them that
their ONI quartermaster had arrived. "Shipmaster," she said,
trying to project Kig-Yar disdain. "I demand to speak to Avu
Med 'Telcam."

BB formed a small yellow note and positioned it in her eye
line. IT'S FORZE, it read. REMEMBER FORZE? JUL'S FRIEND.

"And who are *you*?" Forze snarled.

"All you need to know is that I've kept him *supplied*."

"Unless you have a spare *warship* at this very moment, then I
suspect he's too busy to talk."

"Tell him," Osman said quietly, "that he'll need me very soon
when 'Vadam's allies show up." It was worth a gamble. It was
only words. "Get him. Or is he dead already?"

The channel went silent. Osman waited: BB rotated slowly,
his equivalent of finger-drumming. Then a familiar voice came
over the audio. It was 'Telcam, and he wasn't amused.

"Where is *Pious Inquisitor*?" he demanded. "We've been
signaling you for an entire *day*."

The question was both unexpected and utterly fascinating.
BB had played the Kig-Yar card very well indeed. In one sentence, 'Telcam had revealed a world of information, the most
significant of which was that the Kig-Yar had control of a battle-
cruiser. Damn it, they had *Inquisitor*.

"This is Osman," she said. "Where's Phillips? He's missing. My people went in and he was *gone*."

'Telcam took a couple of breaths. He couldn't admit he had human allies, not with the company he was keeping now. He'd keep his mouth shut.

"We don't have him."

"Then damn well find him, or you're on your own."

"We are *winning*."

"For the moment."

"What are you telling me?"

I'm bluffing. Almost. But you're in chaos, lucky or not, and you can't afford to ignore me. "I want Phillips back. Put the word out. Do whatever you have to do to find him, and I'll do what I can if the battle turns against you."

"You know something."

"Find him. And tell your people not to fire on my team, understood? Osman out."

BB cut the comms. Osman expected her pulse to be racing, but it wasn't. She was in control again. It felt good.

"Remind me never to play poker with you, Captain," BB said. "And not just because I haven't any hands."

"Well, *that* flushed out some surprises. Good spoof, BB."

"And he's misplaced a battlecruiser. Oops. Don't you just hate it when that happens?"

Osman had backed herself into a corner over Phillips, but it was a position she realized she would have found herself in sooner or later. Kilo-Five was there for one purpose: to keep Sanghelios divided, and that meant there could be no outright winner.

So . . . Pious Inquisitor. *Now, what do the Kig-Yar want with her?*

"I have a feeling that we ought to keep an eye out for her," Osman said. "Just in case."

ONIRF TREVELYAN

Dr. Magnusson held out her hand. "I think we should do a blood test," she said. "You're not improving."

Jul sat on his bunk and struggled to hold his head up. It was a disgrace to show weakness in front of a human, but he hadn't been able to keep down food for two days and he was finding it harder to stay alert.

"You don't know what you're looking for," he said. "What do you know of Sangheili biology?"

She folded her arms. It took her a few moments to speak. "Quite a lot now, actually. You can learn a lot from dissection."

"So you found a use for our fallen."

"Wouldn't you?" She held out her hand again, palm up. "Come on. It won't hurt."

She held a small stylus in her right hand. He thrust out his palm, not sure what to expect, and she simply touched the stylus against one of his fingers. There was a brief feeling of suction, nothing more.

"There," she said. "All done. We'll take a look at that and see if we can find out exactly why you're so sick. In the meantime, I'm going to put you back on your old diet. Gas has to be preferable to diarrhea and vomiting."

"I'm not hungry."

"You will be, sooner or later." Magnusson leaned over him. He wasn't sure that he still had the strength to throttle her even if he decided to. "Now, you said something about going outside."

She'd made a half-hearted promise, but he never expected her to try to keep it. Humans lied so easily that they didn't even seem to realize they were doing it.

"Are you going to tell me it isn't possible?"

"I did promise," she said. "But I have to take security precautions."

"I can't escape from this world." Right then, he'd have had trouble trying to escape from a warm bath. "You said so yourself."

"You could still cause a lot of damage, and you could certainly meet with an accident on Trevelyan. And I do mean an accident—we don't know most of what's out there yet. Think of it as a compromise."

She stood back and went to open the door. A Huragok drifted into the room carrying something all too familiar. It was an explosive harness of the kind that the Brutes had sometimes fitted to Huragok to stop them from falling into enemy hands.

Jul doubted that the creature enjoyed the irony or even understood it. It approached him with the harness and stopped just in front of him with it draped over its tentacles, like a servant waiting for him to try on a new tunic.

"The device will only be detonated if we can't find you for an extended period," Magnusson said. "And we now have complete satellite coverage, so there's no escaping it." She went to the window and looked out, one hand flat on the toughened pane. "What a gorgeous day. It always is, though. It's a very impressive climate management system."

Jul was repelled by the idea of the harness but the more he looked at it, the more an idea began to form, a new possibility— not the one he wanted, but a fallback position that might achieve his aim if all else failed. How many Huragok were there? Could he contrive a way of getting them in one place and somehow triggering the device?

But I don't want to die. I want to go home. I want to see Raia again, and my keep, and my kin.

"I refuse to wear this," he said. "I'm not an animal."

"It's the only way you're going outside. Would you do any differently if I were your prisoner?"

Getting out of this cell was his priority. The rest was detail that he'd have to work out as he went. The opportunity was too important to let pass, and he knew his resolve was being eroded hour after hour by this painful, debilitating illness. He debated whether to submit quietly. That would either placate her or make her more wary, but in the end, he wasn't sure that it mattered.

"Very well." He held his arms out from his sides. "I can't stand these four walls any longer."

The Huragok hesitated for a moment, then rose to place the collar section over Jul's head. He could see its tentacles working frantically and feel the slight movement of air that they generated. The creature was remaking the harness as it went. The collar was heavier than Jul expected.

"Can this thing understand me?" he asked.

"He has a translation device, yes. Whether you want to understand *him* is another matter." Magnusson glanced at her datapad, smiling. The Huragok was obviously communicating with her. "He says he's heard that Huragok have worn them with no ill effects. Until they go off, of course."

Jul was still coming to terms with human humor. He understood sarcasm a great deal better. Perhaps that observation had come from her, and maybe it really had come from the Huragok, but either way they were mocking him. The idea of a Huragok with a sarcastic side was more than he could accept. They were *machines*.

The creature finished securing the harness. Jul could see no clips or closures, no obvious point at which to unfasten the straps, and he was sure that trying to cut or tear them would trigger the explosive.

"Ask it a question for me," he said.

"Ask him yourself. His name's Prone. Short for Prone to Drift."

"If you insist." Jul found it impossible to make eye contact with it. It had too many eyes. "If you can put these devices on, why couldn't you remove them from yourselves?"

Prone floated over to the window and peeled Magnusson's datapad from her hand. She seemed amused by it—*him*—and perhaps even a little fond. Huragok dismantled and rebuilt equipment so fast that it was hard to see exactly what they were doing. Prone's cilia were a translucent blur for just a few seconds before he appeared to extract something the size of a claw from the screen of the datapad itself and returned the device to Magnusson. He drifted back toward Jul, holding the tiny fragment in one tentacle.

"What's that?" Jul demanded.

Prone placed the object on Jul's harness, where it merged instantly with the fabric and sat there like a decorative silver thread.

<A modification so that you can listen to me.>

Jul didn't so much hear the words as feel them. It was like having a communicator buried in his skull. "I understand you."

<They tell me that my brothers were assured it was for their own good. They were told that the humans would force them to destroy Forerunner creations if they captured them alive.> Prone paused. *<They now know that was untrue.>*

Jul wondered if he detected a little vengeance in there somewhere. No, Huragok cared only about repairing and building. If they had any emotion, it was a response designed into them by the Forerunners to ensure that they were moved to compassion by the plight of faulty machinery. Had they been human . . . he knew humans well enough by now to realize they would exact revenge whenever servants became masters.

Magnusson checked something on her datapad. "Got you. I can track you anywhere."

"May I go outside now?" Jul asked.

"Yes, but be careful of the traffic." It seemed like foolish advice, but she started laughing. "Prone was one of the custodians of this place, so I'm sure he'll be your *tour guide.*"

The words didn't translate into Sangheili, but their meaning seemed clear in context and Jul made a note of them. He was picking up English a word at a time. *Hinge-head.* He'd finally worked that out.

The armored guard stood back to let him pass with a completely blank expression, but his chin was drawn back a little as if he found Jul repellent and was trying to hold his breath. The man would probably have killed him if he hadn't had orders not to. Suddenly Jul was in a narrow, featureless corridor with a door at one end and a rectangle of bright, beckoning sunlight set in it. His stomach was cramping and sore and his legs felt unsteady, but he drew himself up to his full height and strode toward the door with as much dignity as he could muster after vomiting and soiling himself for two days. The door opened as he approached it.

The air was so sweet and fresh that it tasted like perfume. Jul sucked it in gratefully. Now he was standing in a quadrangle of prefabricated buildings around a central area of grass dotted with wild flowers. Through the gaps between them, he could see open downs dotted with more gray and steel blue buildings, and, in the far distance, elegant towers that could never have been made by humans.

Magnusson shoved him gently in the small of his back.

"Go on," she said. "Go for a walk."

"Where?"

"Go look at the Forerunner ruins. Be inspired. And Prone can show you where we're growing the *irukan.*"

Why was she doing this? Jul had asked himself that question a hundred times a day and none of the answers convinced him. She was far too compliant, far too soon. *And that's the same*

*face that I present to her. But what if that's what she wants?
What if she's observing me for some reason; what if this is exactly what she wants me to do?* But that didn't matter. He'd
taken a vital step toward getting out of Trevelyan.

He could waste the rest of his life asking himself endless questions and taking no action. It was time to act. He set off across
the grass, unsteady and uncomfortably aware of the Huragok
trailing a few paces behind him, but he kept going through the
gap between the buildings and out into open land. He passed
humans in pairs and groups, some of them wearing baggy single-
piece garments in various drab colors with rank markings he
didn't understand, others in uniforms with gold trim that were
more familiar. They looked at him with expressions that he'd
learned to recognize—loathing, suspicion, dread—and some
that he hadn't. But none of them seemed startled or afraid. He
wasn't the victor here, the conqueror, the invader: he was their
prisoner, a curiosity at best and an object of contempt at worst.

When he finally stopped, his legs were shaking. He turned to
look back on the human settlement and noted again how rapidly it had spread.

<You do not know where you are going,> Prone said. *<Do
you want to see the Forerunner buildings? The nearest is a kilometer from here. The* irukan *crop is much closer.>*

"Show me that first, then."

Prone did no more than lead him in the right direction.
Huragok generally spoke when spoken to and volunteered nothing. But why would they? They were just machines. Jul could see
the *irukan* now, a long, broad strip of yellow-green leaf topped
with white spikes of seed heads that stretched over the brow of a
small hill. That in itself was incredible. The crop took two sea-
sons to mature, but here it was, growing and ripening in what
could only have been days. It took longer than that to germinate.
He remembered playing in the fields around Bekan as a child,

digging up the seeds from the furrows while the Grunts who were still busy sowing it made angry gestures at him.

"How did they achieve that?" he asked. "How did they make it grow this fast?"

<Many techniques,> Prone said. <And we created a bubble for them.>

Jul struggled with the word bubble. "A glass house? A plant shelter?"

<Slipspace. A time out of this time. Sometimes slower, sometimes faster.>

No Huragok he'd ever come across could manipulate time. That made these creatures even more dangerous as a weapon for the humans to use. Jul couldn't yet imagine all the ways that could be misused, but he was certain that it would be. He walked through the crop, half expecting to find that it was somehow artificial, but the leaves smelled strongly when he accidentally trod on them. When he reached the top of the hill he looked down on another familiar sight that shouldn't have been here in this outrageous lie of a world: colos, wandering around in pens with high fences that seemed to be woven loosely from strands of metal. The pens had concrete floors, and the animals nibbled at irukan plants piled in a mesh trough.

It took him a few moments to work out what he was actually looking at. In one pen, the colos appeared strong and healthy, with thick, glossy coats. In the other, they looked thin and listless. Some of them were stretched out on the floor, flanks heaving. He wasn't sure why the humans had separated the flocks.

"Do the humans know how to take care of these animals?" Jul asked. He didn't, but any fool could tell what a sick colo looked like. "What's wrong with the ones in that pen?"

<They are unwell,> Prone said. <The others are not.>

Prone clearly had a talent for being annoyingly enigmatic. Jul would have to get more answers from Magnusson the next time she visited. He wondered if the colos were infected, and whether the same sickness was causing his symptoms. He carried on past the pens and Prone speeded up to head him off.

<Wrong direction.> The Huragok was remarkably insistent. *<The nearest Forerunner buildings are in the other direction. You are too weak to walk to the others.>*

Jul wanted nothing more than to curl up in a dark corner and sleep, but he was relatively free now and he was determined to make the most of it.

"Take me to the nearest ruins, then."

<They are not ruins.>

Perhaps it was reverence. The word might have sounded disrespectful to the Huragok, and Jul knew just how sacred even the most derelict heap of crumbling stone was to the monks back home. Interfering with those relics could still mean death. He followed Prone in silence, getting closer to the elegant towers that he'd seen from a distance, until he could pick out the shapes of the gold stone blocks and the smooth curves. The buildings looked as if they'd been constructed yesterday. They were perfect.

"So they're not ruins," he said. There were many remains of the Forerunners that were in excellent condition, but none like this. "What are they? What did they do?"

<They still function,> Prone said.

"Function?"

<Function,> Prone said, and didn't elaborate.

NES'ALUN KEEP, ACROLI, EIGHTY KILOMETERS FROM ONTOM

"What are you?" Elar demanded. More females clustered around her, all armed and all staring at Phillips as if they were sizing him up for cuts of meat. "And how can you speak our language?"

Phillips had no strategy to fall back on except harmlessness. He could see youngsters creeping into the hall to check what their mothers were doing. With any luck, the females wouldn't open fire with kids around.

"My name's Evan Phillips," he said. Now came the big gamble. Whose side was this keep on, if any? He prepped for some creative embroidery. "I'm . . . a language scholar. The Arbiter gave me permission to visit sacred sites to study the inscriptions. But I got lost."

The females loomed over him. Some of the kids were as tall as he was. But it was the plasma pistols that worried him most.

"How, *Efanphilliss*?" Elar said.

Phillips waited for a chance to play the *arum* card. Maybe one of the kids would have one. "How did I get lost?"

"Yes. Nobody strays here by accident."

"I did. I stepped through a Forerunner portal in the temple at Ontom."

It had far more effect than he bargained for. Elar leaned over to stare into his eyes. It was that awful moment when you felt an animal's breath and didn't know if it was going to lick you or sink its teeth into your face. "Not possible. No monk does this. No *human* ever could."

Dengo butted in. "He did, my lady. I saw him. He just popped up in the holy ruins. Out of nowhere."

Everyone took a step back from Phillips. It was like the sun coming out. He would have preferred them to hail him as a miracle worker, but instead they just seemed more hesitant about ripping him limb from limb. He decided to quit while he was ahead.

"It had a lock like an *arum*," he said. "I opened it. Do you want me to show you?"

They looked blank. He'd been sure that the *arum* was universally understood, but maybe not. Then one of the bigger kids stepped forward and thrust a polished ebony ball into his hands. Phillips smiled, utterly confident, and began to rotate and click the parts. The stone at its heart rattled invitingly.

Click . . . click . . . click.

This was taking longer than he expected. He could feel the parts moving and hear the whisper of wood on wood as the sections rotated and moved apart deep inside.

Damn.

He looked up for a moment into disbelieving eyes. This was a really bad time to find he'd lost his magic touch. Even the Grunts were watching, transfixed, as he gave it one more quarter-turn in its vertical axis. Then a sudden, reassuring *chonk* indicated that the core had opened. He shook the stone out into his sweating palm. It was scarlet shot with black veins, the size of a marble.

"I think the *arum* was based on those locks somehow," he said. "It's a little link with the Forerunners."

Elar looked him up and down again. "Clever, but I hope you can make yourself more useful than that. You don't look like a warrior. And that's what we have most need of."

She caught him by the shoulder and steered him up the hall toward a window. The keep was all rough stone blocks, uneven flagstones, and heavyweight rustic wooden furniture, nothing like the polished minimalism of the places he'd visited in Vadam. When he looked through the long slit of rippled glass, he was staring down a shallow valley at a thick layer of smoke. Now he could see more buildings in the distance. That had to be the town itself.

Elar leaned over Phillips as if she was checking what he was looking at. He'd never been stuck in a room with a group of Sangheili females before, and they smelled of clean feathers, distinctively different from the leather upholstery scent of the males.

The youngsters were watching him intently with unnerving little head movements that reminded him way too much of baby mongooses being taught to hunt snakes. He felt like prey.

"Our husbands have gone to fight the Arbiter," Elar said. "And in their absence, the elder of Lacalu keep has come to seize our land because he's a coward who can only fight females and infants."

Oh dear. I should have kept walking and found the Arbiter's guy. "He's loyal to the Arbiter, is he?"

"He's loyal to whoever enables him to claim our territory." She let out a long hiss. "They'll be back soon."

"Back?"

"I thought you could speak Sangheili."

"I understood you. I'm just worried."

"Then this will comfort you. Shobar, give me that." Elar held her hand out to one of the other females and took a pistol from her. She slapped it in Phillips's palm. "Can you handle this?"

It was far too big for him. He had to grip it in both hands like a submachine gun, which made him feel pretty warry until he saw how easily a bunch of housewives hefted the weapon in one hand.

"You'll need to show me how it works," he said. *Like I know the first thing about firearms. You promised to teach me, Vaz.* "Is this the trigger?"

"Yes. At least a hundred rounds. If you hold it down, though, it overcharges and you can destroy larger targets—provided someone doesn't kill you while you're waiting."

"I'll stick to single shots, then."

"Most sensible."

Phillips thought of those screaming fighter craft zipping overhead. "Is this going to be any use against Banshees?"

"They won't use aircraft now they've cut us off from the town.

They want this farm in one piece. This will be a siege. Especially as we shot down one of their smaller vessels."

Siege. No. Not again. This is not happening. Now I'm holed up with Ma Baker and her sisters.

How the hell did he end up walking into another crisis after walking out of the first? He couldn't take his eyes off the pistol. It was probably more of a danger to him than to the enemy. How fast would he burn through a hundred rounds?

"I need to tell my ship where I am," he said. "Will you let me contact the Arbiter?"

"He won't be able to save you." Elar held up her free hand for silence, head cocked as if she'd heard something. "Shobar, go to the rear doors and take the Unggoy with you. *Efanphilliss,* your call will have to wait."

Bang. Something crashed against the heavy doors behind him, shaking off particles of varnish. Smoke curled in around the cracks. Most of the children fled up the stairs but the bigger ones stayed, some armed with wooden staves, others with small pistols. *Why not give me one of those?* Maybe they weren't real. If a battalion of crazed Sangheili commandos stormed the keep right then, though, Phillips didn't know if he had what it took to pull the trigger. He wasn't even going to get a chance to practice. One thing was certain. Whoever was outside wasn't going to care if he was a human or a Sangheili in the heat of the moment, and most of the planet would still see him as the enemy.

Bang. The door shook again. It sounded like lightning cracking overhead, not a battering ram. He guessed someone was using a plasma weapon on the doors. *Bang.* Elar and a couple of the other females just stood there calmly and slowly raised their pistols. *Bang.* And then one half of the door burst off its hinges.

Phillips saw an arm poke through, but that was as far as it got. From that moment on he couldn't take his eyes off the door or look to either side. Bolts of brilliant light poured in. He squeezed the trigger instinctively instead of ducking, and then his entire field of vision was a wall of what looked like continuous tracer fire. If there were any people—bodies—on the receiving end, he only saw them as vague dark shapes. The noise, the smell, and the smoke made him reel. He was holding the pistol so tightly that his right hand was starting to go numb. He only stopped when a big Sangheili hand slapped down on him and he realized the noise and plasma bolts were now coming from him and nobody else. There were a couple of bodies in the door frame, smoke curling off their backs, and the door was mostly charcoal splinters.

"Stop," Elar barked. "The door is *dead* now."

Phillips still couldn't see a thing. His vision was dappled with bright red spots wherever he looked, the aftermath of staring into those points of light, but he felt charged up and hyper-alert again, almost shaky. God, he loved that feeling. He was scared shitless, but he could feel every nerve and muscle fiber in his body. He could almost *see* them. Elar stalked over the debris of the firefight and turned one of the bodies over with her boot.

"So, you attack women and make a mess of my clean floor, you *filth*," she snarled at the corpse. "Come on. We must barricade this doorway while we still can."

Phillips tried to take a look outside, but Elar batted him back with one hand. Youngsters and adult females swarmed back into the chamber dragging furniture, planks of wood, and sheets of composite that made odd wobbling noises, then began frantically boarding up the doorway. They clearly had a defensive drill and everyone seemed to know their part in it. Phillips wished he'd counted how many rounds he'd squeezed off. He stared at the pistol, lost.

Oh God. Do I recharge this thing, or does it have power packs? How long does that take?

He didn't have a clue. For all he knew, he could have killed a dozen Sangheili and not even seen them fall. The red splotches still danced in front of him. He hoped it wasn't permanent retina damage.

"Professor," BB said quietly. "Your heart rate is worrying me."

"Sssh. I'm fine."

"Professor—"

"Do some translation. Record some stuff."

Phillips moved at a crouch to the back window and rested the pistol on the sill as best he could. It was more like a horseshoe in shape, no muzzle as such to poke through small holes. He squinted with one eye to try to see past the red lights. Someone walked up behind him.

"Head down, *Efanphilliss,*" Elar whispered. "And *wait.* We will now contact someone to tell them you're here."

"The Arbiter?" He was going to get out. Shame, really: he was starting to feel invincible. He wanted to get *good* at this. "Oh, thank you. Thank you."

"No." She put a huge hand on his head and shoved him down below the line of the windowsill. "The Servants of the Abiding Truth. If the Arbiter values you enough to let you come here, then you may well be a valuable hostage for them."

His stomach lurched and fell. *So . . . right back where I started. Terrific.* But there was an equal chance that he'd end up with his head incinerated by a plasma round from a Sangheili who didn't know him and just wanted a few hundred more hectares of prime arable.

"Okay," Phillips said. "I better not get killed, then."

CHAPTER

NINE

PEOPLE MAKE STUPID DECISIONS IN WARS. WRONG KIT, WRONG ASSETS, WRONG PLACES, EGOS TAKING PRECEDENCE OVER COMMON SENSE, POLITICS—THE MEN AND WOMEN AT THE SHARP END UP DYING WHEN THEY DON'T HAVE TO BECAUSE SOMEONE FARTHER AWAY FROM DANGER IS MORE CONCERNED ABOUT BUDGETS OR VOTES OR AMBITIONS. WELL, WE'VE CUT THE POLITICIANS OUT OF IT. WE'VE ONLY GOT OURSELVES TO BLAME NOW.

(COMMANDER THOMAS LASKY, XO, UNSC *INFINITY*)

VADAM, SANGHELIOS

Vadam keep had stood for a thousand years, they said, but Raia wasn't sure that it would survive much longer.

She did as Forze told her and kept her head down behind the barricade of Ghosts, Revenants, and Spectres that marked the forward rebel position six kilometers from the keep walls. The keep itself was more rock than masonry, one wing set into the lower slopes of Mount Kolaar itself. A huge hole in the east wall now gaped like a mouth open in outrage that anyone would dare to attack it. The Arbiter was being brought down a stone, a brick, a branch at a time, not by overwhelming technology or the firepower of capital ships, but by the sheer number of small groups with a single bitter grudge. Raia wondered if any of them would have anything in common once the task was accomplished, but for the time being, they were united.

For them it was bad enough that Thel 'Vadam had turned his back on the gods, but he compounded the betrayal by appeasing the humans. He'd fought alongside them, defended them, shaken hands with them, and now he'd allowed them to trample on the spiritual heart of the world. He had to pay for that sacrilege.

Raia no longer believed that ritual could please or offend real gods, or make any difference to imagined ones. She wanted her husband back, and then she wanted her nation restored, able to shape its own destiny for the first time in millennia. But it was hard to think beyond her family when she was cold, hungry, and in the middle of a battlefield.

Forze leaned over her. "You should go home now and wait for Jul. Wherever he is, when the Arbiter falls, he'll be found or freed. I can find someone else to take you back to Mdama."

"I have to stay," she said. "I have to see this through."

She raised her head over the barricade and looked around. She'd expected a violent uprising to be continuous shooting and shelling, but it was confusingly disjointed. There were long, quiet lulls: warriors, veteran and young alike, stood in discussion, watching and waiting, some taking the opportunity to eat hurried snacks. From time to time, the hiss and crack of plasma fire would send everyone running for cover or returning fire, or a Banshee—sometimes one from the keep, sometimes one attacking it—would zip overhead and explosions would shake the soil beneath her feet. This was one of those moments. A purple metallic streak caught her eye and the sound hit her a heartbeat later. A pulsed stream of fire went up from a Revenant and caught its tail section. The Banshee belched flame and smoke before skimming the walls of the keep and disappearing behind the mountain. Then an explosion she couldn't see sent smoke high into the air. Firing started up on both sides again.

Forze pointed away from the front line. "As I said—go home."

Raia ignored him. Sooner or later the rebels would storm the keep, and she'd go with them. She'd kill anyone who got in her way, and she'd find the cells and locked rooms that such a keep would certainly have, and then she'd search for Jul in every one. If he wasn't there and he still didn't come home once the Arbiter was gone, she'd know he was dead.

But she knew nothing of the kind, not yet.

'Telcam walked along the barricade with the air of a kaidon surveying his territory. He stopped when he got to Forze and Raia.

"I have a task for you, Forze," he said. "I need a guest collected."

Forze thrust his head forward. "What kind of guest?"

"Someone whose safety I need to ensure—a human who's on Sanghelios with the Arbiter's permission. He's at Acroli with a loyal keep that's been attacked. Go and get him. Bring him to me."

"Why would you need to keep any human safe?" Raia asked.

"Because I have a promise that I need to honor to continue doing the will of the gods. He has considerable value."

Forze didn't question the situation. Raia wanted to but thought better of it.

"Very well, I'll collect your hostage, but what about Raia?" Forze asked. "I can't leave her here without protection."

"She can go with you."

Raia objected. "But I've come to find my husband."

"He could be anywhere, and there's little you can do here." 'Telcam looked around impatiently. "It's your choice. How long will it take you, Forze?"

Forze spread his arms. "It's a short flight—we can be back here before the next meal."

"There, my lady, you can go with your protector and still be back in time to watch the fall of the blasphemer," 'Telcam said. "And my conscience will be temporarily soothed. I would prefer not to have the shame of a female dying on my battlefield."

Raia realized she no longer had any leverage. She'd lost it the moment that 'Telcam had taken his ship from her quarry, and now even the ship was gone. If she wanted to carry on her hunt for Jul, then it would require 'Telcam's blessing. Forze would bring her back. She could rely on him. So she would concede, a tactical withdrawal.

"Come on, Raia," Forze said, beckoning to her. "Field Master, where is this keep?"

"Dunil will program the coordinates for you." 'Telcam walked away. "Take one of the Phantoms—the least equipped one, mind you, but I want the human alive and well. No foolish mistakes with the locals. His name is *Philliss*."

Raia followed Forze through the ranks of rebels and vessels that were assembling in ever greater numbers on the lowland facing Vadam keep.

"Look at that," he said. "It still worries me when we assemble too many assets in one place. But who's left to take advantage of our vulnerability? Nobody."

It looked as if half the keeps in the northern hemisphere had sent a few warriors and a vessel of some kind. There were now so many packed in the coastal strip between the keep and the sea that Raia felt she'd walked several kilometers simply to pass through them and reach the Phantoms. Jul had said that keeps had commandeered ships and hardware when the Covenant collapsed, but this was the first time that she had fully understood how much had been spirited away. Much of it was battered and looked poorly maintained without the Huragok to take care of it, but it was almost as if the great righteous army had come together again.

We can do this. We have far to go, but we can become a powerful nation again. We can relearn what it means to be great.

For a moment, she wished she had brought her young sons to see this. The sight of all those vessels and warriors, however down-at-heel, however divided they were by petty domestic feuds, was as eloquent a lesson in nationhood as any long speech that Uncle Naxan could have given them.

"This human must be very important," she said.

"Ah, politics." Forze shook his head. "Just another worm. This must be the one Buran said they had taken to the temple. There must be a very special ransom for him."

The human didn't matter at all. "Can you fly a Phantom?"

"Of course I can. It's only a dropship."

"But I can't operate its weapons." Raia could see it clearly now, a curved and polished blue hull like a squat insect. "Will we need them?"

"It's simply a plasma cannon," Forze said. "Leave all that to me. As if we'll need it against farmers."

He sounded very casual, but then he was used to cruisers and battles involving entire fleets. This was a minor diversion for him. Dunil met him at the ramp. The Phantom assigned to them wasn't the one she'd been looking at, but its less glamorous twin—short on polish and the worse for wear.

"Only the fore cannon works," Dunil said. "The other two are awaiting repairs."

"Let's hope the farmers have no large rocks, then," Forze said. He ushered Raia to the cockpit. "Touch nothing. Even if it doesn't work."

In the last day she had forced her way onto a warship, survived a crash landing under fire, and watched the beginning of the end for Thel 'Vadam. Now she was sitting in the cockpit of a Phantom, preparing to collect an alien, an enemy that had fought the Covenant for an entire generation. It would be hard to look the creature in the eye and not want to kill it.

"Have you ever met a human, Forze?" she asked as the dropship lifted off. The drives sounded *irregular.* She could describe it no other way. "Have you touched one? A live one, that is."

Forze rocked his head from side to side in a shrug. "Only from a great distance. They're very small. When they take their helmets off, they have these strange, flat faces that look as if something has been cut off them."

"Horrible," Raia said. "And this one speaks Sangheili. Do they all?"

"No. It's too difficult for their little animal brains. Some warriors had to learn their language simply to insult them properly."

So this *Philliss* creature was unusual. Raia was curious. It would be something to tell Jul about when she'd found him and brought him home, another way of showing him that she finally understood his world and would be more understanding in the future of what drove him.

"Don't get too comfortable," Forze said. The sea churned beneath them as they crossed the coast at Vadam Harbor, completely deserted today. "We'll be over Acroli before you know it."

UNSC *TART-CART*, SEARCHING THE ONTOM COAST, SANGHELIOS

"Got him," BB said. "Got him, got him, *got him.*"

His blue box did a flip and a twirl in the middle of the cramped crew bay, catching Mal's shoulder. It was weird, not only because it didn't *feel* of anything, but because BB was too precisely controlled to misjudge a movement even with his hologram. All heads turned. Devereaux made a *yeee-hah* noise.

"Where?" Mal couldn't see anything on the recon display. The dropship was skimming low over the deserted shoreline, just in case Phillips had decided to wait it out in the least populated open ground. But even on the thermal screen, nothing showed up except some kind of four-legged eels basking at the water's edge and slapping their tails. "Alive, yeah?"

"He's just shown up at a keep in Acroli and they've called 'Telcam to pick him up."

"Better get there before the mad monk does, then." Mal slapped the bulkhead. "Acroli, Dev, and don't spare the horses. Where is it?"

"Here's the coordinates," BB said. The dropship banked and swung out to sea. "Lian, you'll probably want to fix your hair before we pick him up."

"What's he doing in Acroli?" Devereaux asked, ignoring the jibe. "That's eighty klicks away."

"*Por*-tal," BB trilled. "Lucky that I'm phenomenal, or else we'd still be twiddling our thumbs waiting for Hood to send that list of sites. You just can't get the staff these days."

"I don't think the Arbiter's taking calls at the moment."

Mal batted at BB's hologram to get his attention. "Are you going to tell us what went on?"

"Phyllis popped up in the middle of a field and some Grunts took him to a farmer's keep. Hah. They really can't say his name."

"And?"

"The keep's been under attack. But everything's fine, because the ladies of the house have beaten them off."

"Oh, *now* we get the detail." Mal trusted BB to give them the intel they needed when they needed it, but sometimes the AI liked to indulge in a bit of theater. At the moment, though, it was hard to tell if he was amusing himself or just trying not to worry about what he'd find when they hooked up with Phillips again. "So this is an opposed extraction, is it?"

"Probably not. Depends what's happening when we get there."

"We'll be there in *minutes*, BB," Devereaux said. "Is there a fight or not?"

"At the moment, it sounds like not. Look, I'm just listening in on a very unreliable comms link. I'll have to move a surveillance drone to actually see anything, and we'll be in Acroli long before it's in position."

"I hope you've got an exact location."

"Nes'alun keep. It's not marked on charts."

"But it's a small town."

"Yes."

"Okay, we'll worry about how we knock on doors when we get there. A keep's got to be obvious, right?"

Vaz made a noisy show of clipping down his armor plates and reloading his rifle. "Females." He checked the optics. "Remind me, have I ever seen a female hinge-head? Do they look any different?"

"Not a lot," BB said. "You won't want a date. It's the jaws. Ghastly kissers."

"Then they'd better hand *Phyllis* over." Vaz was immune to being cheered up. "I believe in equality. I'll shoot anyone."

He got up and walked to the front of the compartment, grabbing the safety rails as he went. Naomi still had the shutters up. She hadn't taken off her helmet and sat staring at the bulkhead, arms folded, which probably meant she was watching something on her HUD. Mal placed a mental bet that it was the latest ONI reports on Venezia. It was too easy to forget that once they'd retrieved Phillips, a queue of other messy problems was still waiting patiently for them.

"So remind me what the strategy is," Vaz said. "Are we playing nice with 'Telcam or not? How do you think he's going to react when we grab Phillips?"

"Well, there's the interesting thing," BB said. "Osman told him to find Phillips or else no more arms, but they're using words like *hostage* on the comms channels."

Naomi lifted off her helmet and tidied her hair with one

hand. If Mal hadn't known better, he'd have thought she'd just woken up. "Even if he doesn't think Phillips is a hostage, the others might. We're not dealing with one tidy group here."

"I always assume the worst," Mal said.

"So do I." Devereaux sounded as if she'd leaned out of her seat. "It's you-can't-see-me time."

A row of unfamiliar status lights flashed up on the bulkhead repeater. "Deflective camo, Dev? That's nostalgic. I didn't think we still had it."

"Just because it didn't fool Covenant sensors doesn't mean that Farmer Giles can spot us," she said. "There's still value in hiding behind a tree, you know."

Mal caught himself teetering on the edge of praying that nobody would wonder what that funny whining noise was overhead, as if any god would care about what happened to one ODST. Carbon nanotube cloaking was very old and largely useless now, but Kilo-Five wasn't going up against a high-tech enemy. This was pitchfork country. It would do.

"It doesn't make us *completely* invisible," he said. "Or silent."

"No, but it makes us pretty damn hard to spot at two hundred meters." Devereaux made a few grunting sounds, as if she really was combing out tangled hair. BB didn't comment. "Did you think he was dead?"

"Phillips? No. I never gave him permission to die."

Naomi flipped her helmet over between her hands like a basketball. "I don't believe anyone's dead until I see a body."

It wasn't like her to join in unless she was asked a specific question. Mal's first thought was that she meant her father, but then he remembered that she'd been really cut up to hear that the Master Chief was officially MIA with a strong unofficial dash of KIA. Maybe she meant him. It was hard to tell with so many dead and so few bodies brought home.

"We'll be over Acroli in six minutes." Devereaux still seemed more worried about Phillips than she'd admit. "Ideas on how to identify Nes'alun, BB?"

"Well, a farmhouse with a lot of damage, probably."

"You're a natural-born navigator."

Six minutes was a lot longer than it sounded. Mal sealed his helmet and checked the video feeds. One was the exterior cam mounted under *Tart-Cart*'s nose, showing a lot of greenery that threw long shadows in the late afternoon and a little stone-built town beyond. It looked like half a dozen small, walled keeps and a few big barns. But as the town rushed up on them, Mal saw some serious damage—big holes in some of the walls, missing sections of roof, and the charred remains of a fighter or something gouged into the ground. It wasn't exactly pitchfork fighting, then.

"Well, it's *all* damage, BB," Mal said. "Next idea?"

Tart-Cart slowed and looped around the settlement at three hundred meters. There were some Sangheili trying to salvage their property, and a couple of them looked up as the dropship passed overhead, but they went back to clearing the rubble. They'd heard it but they couldn't quite see it. They probably thought the noise was coming from another direction.

"'Telcam's got to have coordinates to find the place," BB said. "If I could get hold of him. Acroli is largely Arbiter supporters."

"*Location.* Any clue at all would do."

"Wait one."

"See, BB, when we were baby ODSTs in training, the sarge impressed on us the importance of observation and planning when retrieving hostages."

BB went a little acid. "You can go back and ask *Sarge,* then, Staff."

A rough stone building that looked like a kid's idea of a fort stood a couple of klicks away from the settlement.

"Okay, what's that over there?"

"Another keep."

"And what's that muzzle flash?" Mal knew perfectly well what it was. He'd seen enough plasma fire to last him a lifetime. "I bet that's Nes'alun."

As *Tart-Cart* slowed to sweep wide around the fields, Mal could see that it wasn't so much a firefight as a sporadic exchange of shots. About twenty hinge-heads crouched in the cover of low walls and shabby outbuildings, focused on the main structure, but they seemed to be playing a waiting game rather than launching an assault. A couple of shots spat out from a narrow window. The hinge-heads laying siege ducked, then fired back. Then it went quiet again.

This had to be the farmhouse. The dropship changed course again and now Mal could see the state of the main doors. The opening was blocked with all kinds of wood, and black smoke streaks radiated from the stone door frame like sooty petals. It looked like they'd tried to storm the place and failed.

"So the women are defending the keep because the blokes are away fighting, I suppose," Mal said. "Which means they could be back anytime, so the ones down there can't wait forever."

"What do you want to do?" Devereaux asked. "Set down and observe for a while?"

"No, let's clear the area. Come around and approach from the east. Lay down a bit of fire and push them back."

Whoever the Elites outside were, they'd almost certainly open fire on any humans they weren't expecting. The Arbiter hadn't exactly broadcast a plea to treat all human tourists as welcome guests. Sanghelios didn't even seem to have a public network, so how they circulated general information these days was anyone's guess. For all Mal knew, most hinge-heads would still see humans as the vanguard of an invasion.

Come to that, whoever was inside the keep would probably see things that way, too.

"Okay, do it," Mal said. "Buckets on. Get ready to drop."

Devereaux banked the ship. "I haven't actually done this before, but I'm told it's the most fun you can have without getting arrested."

Mal scanned the nose cam view. The hinge-heads were still facing the keep. *Tart-Cart* was coming up to the rear and flank, unseen, dropping to seventy meters. "What d'you mean?"

"Like this . . . *surprise!*"

The deflective camo warning light went off. Twenty hinge-heads looked up at once. Devereaux hit the chin gun and Mal's view of the ground was lost in cannon flash, flying debris, and smoke. One second the Elites had been scratching their backsides and waiting for hinge-head Christmas, and the next the sky was full of angry dropship. Devereaux kept up the fire while she dropped low enough for Mal, Vaz, and Naomi to jump out of the side hatch and run for the keep. Mal found himself up to his ankles in churned mud. A couple of plasma bolts shot past him, too wide to worry about.

"We're in position, Dev," Vaz said. "You can pull back now."

Tart-Cart rose to a hover above the keep and broke up like a mirage into a shimmering patch of nothing. Now they had to check that they had the right keep. Mal wasn't counting on any gratitude from whoever was inside.

"Here's the fun bit," he said. "No door to knock. BB, can you do some shouting?" He edged around to the side of the building. "Ask them if they've got Phyllis in there—very loudly."

"I can pick off the Elites, Staff," Devereaux said over the radio. "I don't think I actually killed any, but I can remedy that."

Bloody diplomacy. Mal could imagine the grief he'd get if he ended up killing a bunch of the Arbiter's allies and they'd hit the wrong keep anyway. "Wait for me to call for support. I'd hate to get a stiff memo from CINCFLEET." He reached behind him and tapped Naomi's arm. "Window. Slap a cam on that. See what we've got inside."

Naomi shot off, drawing a hail of plasma that didn't seem to slow her down. A few moments later, an icon activated in Mal's HUD and he was looking at a color-enhanced view of a hall full of moving shapes, some big, some small. Hinge-heads: hinge-head kids, too. He'd never really thought of them as having families. When he refocused, Naomi was squatting next to him again.

"That was quick," he said. The adults all had plasma pistols and a couple had storm rifles, too. "Well, I'd say that's the girls. Ten, maybe. Six kids." He listened. The cam also picked up sound waves flexing the windowpane from inside. "Got that, BB?"

"They're very quiet."

Vaz checked the feed too. "Can't see Phillips."

"What about the kids?"

"They're armed," Naomi said. "Legitimate targets."

What else did Mal expect her to say? She'd been handed a weapon and trained to kill at six years old. She didn't have that taboo ingrained in her.

"Who'd like to be my mouthpiece?" BB asked. "Your turn, Mal. Shall I do the talking, or just render you comprehensible?"

"Just translate." This was the weird bit. Mal wasn't sure that his brain could handle saying one thing and hearing another. *Ah well.* He gave it his best shot. "This is UNSC forces—we've come for Professor Phillips. Have you got him in there?" No, he couldn't do it. He struggled to find the next word. "BB, kill the external audio. It's confusing me."

"Of course it is. Try again."

"*Ladies!* We've come for Phillips. Have you got him?"

That was better. As far as Mal was concerned, he was outside the door, yelling in English. To the Elites, he was shouting in fluent Sangheili.

"We have," a female voice shouted back. "We're handing him over to the holy monks."

"And the monks are going to hand him to us. So let's save ourselves some time."

"Get away from the door or we'll open fire."

"We just drove off the Arbiter's allies. The ones attacking you, remember?"

"They're still out there. And so are you."

There was a line of small arrow-slit windows on the upper floors above him. Plasma fire spat out of one, frying the ground a little way from him. Whoever was firing couldn't lower the angle far enough because Mal was too close to the wall.

"Bring him out," Mal yelled. "Don't make us come in."

"Fool."

"Would you like to meet a Spartan? A demon?"

Naomi moved around to the doorway and gave him a thumbs-up. She was gagging for a fight. Vaz edged over to the other side of the door, ready to storm it.

"We have children here. You *bluff*."

"Bring Phillips out and we can all go home."

Naomi stood up slowly and pressed against the barricaded door with one hand flat on it as if she was testing it. Her other hand gripped her pistol. Mal wasn't going to lecture her on rules of engagement.

She nodded. "Ready when you are, Staff."

"Last chance," Mal called. "We don't want to hurt anybody."

He didn't have to raise his voice, but it always psyched him up. This wasn't how it was supposed to be done. You hit a building hard and without warning, shot anything that didn't obey the warning to get down and stay down when you burst into the room, and then you grabbed your hostage and got out. But that couldn't happen now. There was no element of surprise, and there were kids. It shouldn't have mattered, but Mal had to think of the consequences if he killed any. Just walking into a bloody temple had sent hinge-heads rushing to fight the Arbiter.

"Mal? Mal, don't crash in here. Please."

That was Phillips, all right. Mal now couldn't tell if he was speaking Sangheili or not. "Phillips, are you okay?"

"Fine."

"We're coming in."

"No, don't. Nobody shoot, do you hear? Just don't. None of you."

"It's not your call, mate." Mal nodded back to Naomi. "You're coming out, one way or another. Stand back from the door."

"No, hold your fire. All of you." Phillips was still talking. "You too, Elar. Everybody *relax*. Everybody calm down—"

Naomi drew back her arm and simply punched her fist into the barricade like a power-hammer. Mal jumped up behind her, almost crashing into Vaz as the Spartan drove a huge hole in the wood and metal and sent the debris clattering into the hall. Mal braced for a blinding hail of plasma, but the first thing he saw wasn't the hinge-heads but Phillips, standing in front of them with a plasma pistol raised two-handed, right in the cross-fire zone. Everyone froze.

"Don't you bloody *dare*," Mal said.

"I'm stopping them from shooting you."

"Great. Thanks. Now get out of the way."

The Elites had formed a barrier in front of their kids, with one big female slightly out in front with her pistol aimed squarely at Mal. He looked into her face for a moment and saw small, angry, animal eyes and flaring nostrils. They must have thought Phillips was worth a lot if he was all that was stopping them. Naomi didn't seem to give a damn and held her pistol on the Elites as she stalked along the line. Some of them stared at her as if they didn't believe humans came in that size and shape.

"Ladies, we've got a warship right overhead," Mal said. "If we'd wanted to kill you, we could have reduced this keep to rubble from a safe distance. Now we're taking our man and going. Okay?"

"They're under attack," Phillips said. "You've seen what's outside."

Vaz jerked his head toward the door. "That's not our problem. You ready, Dev?"

"Standing by."

"We can't abandon them," Phillips said.

Mal was running out of patience. At any second, a hinge-head kid could start firing, or one of the jumpier females, and then it would be a bloodbath. "We can, Prof, and they're big enough to take care of themselves. Move."

This was the tricky moment. They'd have to turn around. Naomi started backing out. They were seconds away from getting out of this shit hole. Mal grabbed Phillips and pulled him toward the door, keeping his eyes on the big female at the front. They were picking their way over the debris from the barricade when two voices filled Mal's helmet—Devereaux's and BB's.

"Enemy vessel approaching."

"Abort that, Mal. Take cover."

"*Two* enemy vessels approaching."

"We've got 'Telcam's team and some other joker."

Mal stuck his head out of the door just as a volley of bolts skimmed past. "Shit, why isn't anything simple these days? Everybody *down*."

Phillips dropped prone as if he'd been shown how to do it.

He aimed out the door. "Told you so," he said. "The other keep wants their land and buildings. It's nothing to do with the war."

Mal stopped short of smacking him around the head. It was a technicality. Wars were always great excuses to settle all kinds of personal scores.

"Well, you tell that to the plasma round that cooks your frigging head." He signaled to Vaz and Naomi. The hinge-heads were already in position at the windows. "You've got to work out which side you're on, Phillips, and here's a clue—it's *ours*."

UNSC *INFINITY*, OORT CLOUD

Parangosky watched the discreet icon on her datapad switch from green to blue. It was a shame to stop young Lieutenant Priselkov when she was in full flood about the slipspace comms tests, but Parangosky trusted BB to know better than any human what was truly urgent and what could wait for a presentation to end.

"My apologies, Lieutenant," she said, getting to her feet and sliding the pad off the table. "May we resume this a little later? Something's come up. I'll be back as soon as I get this resolved."

It was always educational to watch their faces. She cast a benign glance around the table and noted who looked worried, who looked intrigued, who looked irritated, and who was doing their best not to betray any reaction at all. This project had consumed their lives for the last year or two, cut them off from everything they held dear on Earth, and—since the Huragok had arrived and changed everything in a frantic whirlwind of modification—most of them hadn't been able to grab more than three hours' sleep a day. She watched them wondering whether she understood all that.

"This is quite a serious situation," she said quietly. "I wouldn't interrupt this meeting for anything less." It did them no harm to think she was a mind-reader as well as omniscient. She nodded at Hood. "Excuse me."

Hood had a way of watching her without actually moving a muscle, not even his eyes. The doors closed behind her and she slid onto the buggy's seat to ride to the closest secure space on this deck.

"She's too big, BB." Parangosky propped the datapad on the dashboard and whirred down the passage. "Just my personal taste. She's a flying city, not a ship. I'll always be a frigate scale of sailor."

"I didn't want to upset Aine again by asking her how things were going."

"She's rather unsettled by the Huragok, I'm afraid. They don't document their modifications. She has no idea what they're doing sometimes."

"That sounds astutely unionized of them."

"Yes, let's not fall into the same seductive trap that the Sangheili did, because once you lose the services of the little darlings, you're scuppered."

She could see the compartment door up ahead, marked SECURITY TESTED. She'd take BB's word for that. The seal sighed as she closed the door behind her, leaving her leaning on her cane in a conspicuously quiet compartment with generic power outlets and data feed sockets on the bulkheads. It didn't even have any floor covering, just the bare gray composite of deck sections.

"Okay, Admiral, we have a mixed bag of news for you, and I'll be patching you through to Captain Osman in a moment," BB said. Parangosky's datapad flashed up an ONI holding portal. "We've found Phillips, but Kilo-Five is still trying to extract him. The fascinating news is that it might be a perfect time to offer the Arbiter some help with his little local difficulty."

Parangosky didn't rely on God or luck, but she was prepared to accept that the reward for being permanently on the lookout for opportunity sometimes resembled an answered prayer.

"We're half-finished," she said. "But that also means we're half-ready. The important thing is that all the combat systems are operational, so we can manage without a sauna or two." She watched the portal screen change to *Stanley*'s bridge. "How's it going, Captain? Is Kilo-Five all right?"

"They're with Phillips now, ma'am." Osman kept looking up past the console camera. Parangosky guessed she'd projected charts onto the viewscreen like a HUD. "Just small-scale resistance. I think it's a case of wrong time and place. You really need to see the latest from the drone cams, though—things don't look encouraging for the Arbiter. You might want to show this to Hood. Do the honors, BB."

It was an aerial view of Vadam, something that Parangosky still regarded as a watershed in her life. Sanghelios had been a closed world until the last couple of months. The first limited scans gleaned from Hood's diplomatic mission were keeping ONI analysts busy, and now the information was rolling in via *Port Stanley* and BB. The view of Vadam looked almost mundane. There was Mount Kolaar to the right of the image, with the wartlike gray keep on its lower slopes. To the right of frame, the land merged into grass and woods. The detail was partially obscured by white smears.

"Cloud or smoke?" she asked.

"Smoke. Zoom in. This is only drone imaging, so it's not perfect, but you can see that Vadam keep is surrounded on three sides."

Parangosky took her weight off her cane for a moment and tapped the image a couple of times with her right hand. It was hazier now, but the first thought that struck her was *cars*. It was an instant and unedited reaction: cars parked at a grassy picnic site. The area facing the keep was dotted with blurred patches of color—red, blue, purple, black—but then she adjusted her mind to the actual scale and realized the patches were Covenant military vehicles and other craft. Some were substantial, dropships and larger vessels as well as mobile artillery pieces.

"BB's streaming the comms chatter back to Bravo-Six for analysis," Osman said. "But to cut to the chase, the Arbiter's been caught out by the numbers that have turned on him. A lot of that was outrage at him allowing Phillips and Kilo-Five to enter the temple at Ontom. So . . . he needs a friend."

ONI was spinning an increasing number of plates. Parangosky fully expected 'Telcam to launch a holy war on Earth after he'd dumped the Arbiter. "What's the situation like off-planet? We're not picking up any intel on actual warships."

"The Arbiter's forces shot down *Unflinching Resolve,* but she was a minnow compared to what else must still be out there. And *Pious Inquisitor*'s still missing, possibly seized by Kig-Yar. I doubt they'll be joining this uprising, but they might sell her to the Arbiter."

Pious Inquisitor had too much history for Parangosky's taste, both as enemy and ally. The ship had glassed colonies; she'd also destroyed a Flood infestation in Africa. Capability was always what mattered, though, not intent. Parangosky had to plan on the basis that *Inquisitor* could be turned on Earth again if she fell into the wrong hands.

And the Sangheili will always be the wrong hands.

"Anything else?" she asked. "I think now would be a good time for Terrence to call the Arbiter and offer *Infinity*'s immediate support."

"Superb timing, ma'am," Osman said.

"It is, isn't it?"

"But will she get here in time to make a difference?"

"Serin," Parangosky said, "I think your charming staff sergeant has a phrase for it. She's faster than a greased weasel. Much as it sticks in my throat to thank Halsey, I may have to." She glanced at the time on the pad. "Give me two hours, and keep me updated on Kilo-Five."

"May I ask you something, ma'am?"

"Certainly."

"Do you think it's a good idea for both you and Admiral Hood to be embarked if *Infinity*'s flying into a civil war?"

"I think it's a case of both of us or neither," Parangosky said. "And I've been far too out of touch with the front line for too long, my dear."

"Understood."

So it was an eccentric choice. So was sending a ship in refit to do a little gunboat diplomacy that might actually have to be backed up with action. But this was the best excuse they might have for years—and at the best time.

Parangosky climbed onto the buggy and headed back to the meeting room. Hood gave her a slyly meaningful look as she made her way back to her seat, commanding instant and reverent silence from the table.

"Don't let me interrupt," she said, knowing damn well that things tended to revolve around her whether she wanted them to or not. "I have plenty of questions, though."

Glassman tapped his datapad and the display on the bulkhead rolled backward. "Ma'am, I was just bringing everyone up to speed with the drives. I apologize for the lack of technical rigor, but interfacing with the Huragok is an act of faith. I'm not sure if they're just not used to being asked to show their workings, or if they're too . . . *enigmatic* to explain things. Sometimes they look at me as if I'm asking them to explain what blue looks like."

"I admit they're a mixed blessing," Hood said. "Midas springs to mind. Being able to turn everything you touch to gold sounds wonderful until you need to visit the bathroom."

Aine spoke up for the first time. "I realize security isn't my department," she said, "but they absorb and share all the data they find. We could end up like the Covenant. How can we let them work on other UNSC ships when they have so much classified data on *Infinity*? We need to start controlling their associations."

"Excellent point, Aine," Parangosky said. She knew she hadn't worried about it enough, not yet, but the immediate benefits were too great to put everything on hold. "Which is why Admiral Shafiq might have to wait longer for his dream of a Huragok in every ship. We'll need to find another separate population for that. For the time being, Huragok are confined to a handful of classified projects."

"As long as we're aware, ma'am," Aine said.

Aine always did what was asked of her in such a put-upon and resigned tone that Parangosky almost felt sorry for her. She didn't politic or scheme like an ONI AI. All she did was prepare ships for deployment, the Queen of the Thursday War. She manifested herself at the side of the meeting table as a small figure of a thirty-something woman wearing baggy white overalls, safety goggles parked on the top of her head, and a resigned expression.

"So when can we put *Infinity* through her paces?" Parangosky looked straight at Glassman, not Hood, and prodded his ego. "Are we ready to see if this gamble is worth it?"

Glassman had a lot in common with Halsey, which probably played a part in the friction between them. He was professionally vain, massively ambitious, and in constant competition with life. Any suggestion from Parangosky that she wasn't dazzled by the speed and brilliance of the modifications was guaranteed to scrape the right raw nerves.

"We've changed the entire technology of slipspace propulsion and associated systems in a matter of days, ma'am," Glassman said stiffly. "And I'm happy to put her through her paces right away."

Gotcha. Who says humans aren't ninety percent programming?

Hood let out a breath. "I'm still anxious to draw the line between exploring the cutting edge and belief in magic."

"Ah, but I have a reason for asking," Parangosky said. "May I brief you privately, Admiral?"

"Certainly, *Admiral*." Hood did one of his tight, polite smiles at the assembled staff. "Let's break for an hour. Caffeine levels are critical. You too, Aine. Go and check that BB isn't rifling through your tool locker."

Aine just winked out of existence, leaving a brief darkness behind her, and everyone filed out in tactful silence to leave the admirals to their discussion. Hood didn't say a word for at least thirty seconds after the doors closed. Then he ran his hand over his face, brow to chin, weary.

"You're railroading me, Margaret. Why?"

"I want you to take a look at some recon data from Sanghelios." She pushed her datapad across the table to him. "Thel 'Vadam could be deposed in days, and where's your peace treaty then?"

Hood spent a few minutes looking through the images. His dismay showed on his face. "Not good. I never did back winners, did I? Found Phillips yet?"

"Yes, but the spec ops team still hasn't managed to extract him. Don't you think it's time you offered the Arbiter some help? He won't ask for it."

"What's in it for you?"

"We could destroy a few ships." She didn't specify whose. "How else are we going to remove potential enemy assets now without starting another war of our own?"

"True. And?"

"You really don't want to see a Sanghelios run by the rebels. This is an antihuman movement, Terrence. Put them down, and put them down firmly on their own turf, with a piece of technology that will—if you'll excuse my vernacular—make them shit their pants and resolve never to trouble us again."

"I don't think their bowels are that easily moved. But you're set on this, aren't you?"

"We could be there tomorrow, and also give *Port Stanley* some backup. I want my people out of there in one piece." Parangosky lowered her voice. "Phillips has earned his keep. There's no telling what else he's going to bring back for us, either."

Hood leaned back in his seat and looked up at the deckhead.

"So we've got every reason to give it a run and very few not to," he said at last. "But remember we have joint control—she's *our* ship, not yours. Without alienating Del Rio, of course."

"It's a Thursday War. He'll understand. Nothing odd about having admirals along for historic trials. Let alone mercy missions."

"You know, I've never had a working-up exercise that involved actual warfare."

"Times change, Terrence."

Hood just gave her a look and eased himself out of his seat. "I'll patch you in when I make contact with the Arbiter," he said. "It's going to be delicate."

Sangheili had their buttons and raw nerves, just like humans, and they could all be pressed. Parangosky went back to the bridge to make her presence felt and soak up the informal briefings that the more junior crew members would volunteer, and waited. She was back in her cabin sipping her fourth coffee when Hood rapped on the door and walked in.

"Want to listen in?" he said.

Parangosky nodded at the screen and slid out of its range.

The Arbiter didn't need to see her there, even if he wouldn't recognize her. "Go ahead."

It took a few moments for the Sanghelios end of the link to appear. Parangosky almost expected to see the Arbiter sitting in ruins with shattered plaster and smoke everywhere, but the cam showed him in his tidy chamber much as before, apparently unmoved by events that she knew damned well were ripping up the city around him.

"Thank you for taking this call, Arbiter," Hood said. "I won't delay you. I'm very aware of the difficulties you find yourself in at the moment. I still have a team on Sanghelios."

"I regret I have no resources to devote to helping you find Professor *Philliss*, Admiral."

"I know, which is why I have an offer for you. You need support, and I can give it. Let me help put down your rebellion."

The Arbiter paused. He was hard to read, even for a Sangheili. "That's not possible. But I value the kindness."

"Oh, it's possible. I have new ships. You've kept your word. Now let me keep mine, and do what I can to preserve the peace."

"And retrieve your people, of course."

"That, too."

"And you're certain you can do this."

For a moment, Parangosky was surprised by the ease with which the Arbiter seemed to be agreeing to human assistance. It was a long shot at best, but she'd expected more wrangling and even a refusal, and she was prepared for plan B, which was showing up uninvited.

Ah. He doesn't think we can do it. He's humoring us. Like letting a child help you bake a cake by spilling flour everywhere.

"I'm certain," Hood said.

"And Earth would send its most senior officer into combat for me."

"Well, I haven't forgotten that you fought alongside the Master Chief. . . ."

"So I did." The Arbiter bowed his head. "Thank you, but please attend to your own safety. I might not be able to protect your ships."

Hood smiled. "I shall see you very soon, then. Hood out."

The comms link closed. Hood shoved his hands in his pockets and looked sideways at Parangosky.

"Still thinks he's master of the galaxy. He doesn't believe us, does he?"

She shook her head, stifling a grin. "That's even better. And your conscience is still spotless, Terrence. How *do* you do it?"

Hood ambled toward the cabin door, looking pleased with himself, but he was too much of a gentleman to smirk. "I'll let you incur all the stains, Margaret. That's why ONI uniforms are black, aren't they?"

She smiled at his retreating back. "I'm glad you're a little bit of a bastard at heart. I can't stand boy scouts."

Most senior commander. Parangosky chuckled to herself. Sanghelios still didn't seem to grasp the political reality of ONI. And that was fine by her.

THERE'S NO BETTER TEST THAN TRYING OUT A NEW ASSET ON REAL ENEMY TARGETS ON THEIR HOMEWORLD, AND ALL WITH THEIR PERMISSION.

(ADMIRAL MARGARET PARANGOSKY, CINCONI)

NES'ALUN KEEP, ACROLI

"Identify yourself," BB said. Vaz listened to the comms chatter feeding straight into his helmet, mouth instantly dry. "Phantom, *identify yourself.*"

For a moment, the shooting stopped. It was the eye of the storm, probably only seconds, but to Vaz it felt a lot longer as he waited for something to take the roof off the keep. He crouched next to a window, one of the larger ones that gave him a wider arc. At least he could spot something coming from this position.

It took him a moment to realize that a Sangheili kid was standing right next to him. He didn't know if it was male or female, and he didn't feel any instinct to take care of it or save it from harm. It wasn't a kitten: it was the enemy. It would grow up to hate humans and kill them. If he looked into an animal's eyes he could usually see some kind of *self* within, some living connection, but he couldn't see a damn thing in the Sangheili's. The eyes were empty and alien. He wondered if it was thinking the same about him.

"Phantom, identify yourself."

"BB, I've got to shoot or move," Devereaux said. "We've got Banshees inbound."

"Shoot what you have to," Mal said. "Who's who?"

"Stand down in the name of Field Master 'Telcam." It was a new voice on the radio, probably the Phantom pilot. "Stand down."

BB chipped in. "One Phantom from the mad monk, three Banshees from the local yokels."

"BB, tell him we're fine collecting Phillips but he can knock himself out on the Banshees if he wants."

"He heard that."

"Mal, check your ground feed. Elites on foot. About fifty."

"Can Osman hear this?"

"Only the essential bits," BB said cryptically.

Everything was being fed into Vaz's HUD, and it was disorienting him. There were too many extras to watch and listen to when all his brain wanted to do was focus everything on the firefight. He couldn't stop it. Even if he hadn't been drilled to do that until it became automatic, a million years of evolution refused to hand over the controls anyway. For a second he envied Naomi. Maybe all that messing with her brain was worth it for a clear view of the battlefield.

Boom. An explosion shook the ground and dust fell from the beams above his head, rattling on his helmet. The eye of the storm had moved on.

"Dev, are they bad shots or are they avoiding the building?" Mal asked.

The big female interrupted. "They want the keep and the land, you idiot. They won't destroy anything they don't need to. And you're outnumbered."

"Yeah, I can count, missus."

"My name is Elar 'Nas. You're in my keep now and you will show me respect. I could kill you where you stand."

Vaz turned around with his rifle aimed. *Why did I think I could turn my back on these things?* But Naomi was already on it. Elar was staring up the muzzle of Naomi's pistol.

"But you won't," Naomi said. "Because I'm a lot faster than you. Now let's all *cooperate.*"

Vaz looked up at the ceiling. His HUD chrono had moved on by a minute, one lousy *minute.* The hinge-head kid was still staring at him.

"Watch the damn window, not me," Vaz snapped. The kid was almost as big as he was. "Here they come."

'Telcam's pilot was on the radio again. *"Stand down, traitors. Shipmaster Forze 'Mdama demands it."*

Small world: Vaz remembered *that* name. "Is that a coincidence, Phillips, or does he know?"

Vaz could only see the professor's backside as he lay behind the frail cover of some beams the size of ancient railway sleepers. "We just plugged into the right network," Phillips said.

"Know what?" Elar demanded.

"Never you mind," Vaz said. "Just cover the windows. We'll take care of the door."

"He doesn't know," BB said in Vaz's earpiece. "Osman's already run into him on the comms net. No time to explain it all, but I'd have heard by now."

Vaz kept looking between Mal and Naomi. There'd come a point where the only option would be to call Devereaux to a low hover to lay down fire, grab Phillips, bundle him outside, and just bang out. The tricky bit was creating the space to do it without getting a chestful of plasma. *Crack.* Something zipped overhead like a thunderstorm right on the roof, shaking Vaz down to his teeth. The whole hall lit up with brilliant white light. A second later, a shock wave crashed over him followed by a curtain of black smoke. He scrambled for the door and dropped down beside Mal and Phillips.

"One Banshee down, Mal," Devereaux said. "The others have looped off with the Phantom up their asses."

"Can't see the ground troops."

"They're forming up into four groups." BB didn't usually interrupt with tactical input unless he was sure they hadn't reacted to what he could see. "One at each wall. They've left a dozen right in front of you. That's east. You know you're facing east, don't you?"

"Yeah, thanks BB." Mal tapped Vaz's arm. There was another big *whoomp* and a ball of white light flared beyond the trees in the distance. "Who's down, Dev?"

"Another Banshee. Here comes the Phantom again."

"Human vessel, get out of the area."

"Oh dear. And he was doing so well for us."

"Human vessel—get out."

Maybe he was being thoughtful and telling Devereaux that he'd got it covered, but maybe he didn't plan to let them take Phillips. It was impossible to tell. Vaz had room for only one worry at a time, and that had to be the hinge-heads who suddenly decided to rush the door. Everything in front of him was white light. He poured a full clip into the blur without stopping, but a loud crack of superheated air next to him made him swing around to fire before he realized it was Phillips squeezing off his hinge-head toy. Then something crashed in behind him. He rolled over just as one of the larger windows smashed and all hell broke loose. Naomi waded in, firing, and body-charged one Elite male so hard that he hit the wall. The females went crazy. Vaz tried to get a shot in but it was a chaotic rugby scrum in the hall, a tangle of Naomi, the females, the kids, and even a couple of Grunts. Jesus, he'd always thought hinge-heads were animals but now he *knew* they were. Three of the females got a male down, snatched his pistol, and pounced on him. They could have just shot him. Instead they tore into him like lionesses, roaring and hissing. It was two hideous seconds before Vaz's attention was slapped back to the door by more outgoing carbine rounds and he realized he'd spent those transfixed moments reloading his own rifle without noticing it.

"They're in, Dev, they're inside," Mal yelled. "Can you get in close?"

"Trying." The dropship's drive whined up the scale, so close now that it sounded like it was in the room. "If that bastard Phantom backs off."

"He *can* see you, right?"

"Er—you bet."

"Tell him to sod off."

"I'm repeating it with a warning shot. Can anyone call 'Tel-cam?"

"I'm trying to get him," BB said. "Sorry to take over . . . Shipmaster Forze, stand down. Talk to your commander. We have this covered."

"I hope that sounds more bloody urgent in Sangheili." Mal elbowed Vaz and looked back from the door. Elar and her kill-crazed sisters were at every available window slit, hosing whatever was out there while the unlucky Elites who'd managed to breach the building were a messy heap on the floor. Some of the smaller kids clustered around to look, as if there wasn't a pitched battle going on. "They've got to be running out of men soon."

Devereaux cut in on the circuit. "Mal, I'm going to push them back the hard way. They're right at the door, so watch for shrapnel."

Meters from the door, stone and soil fountained into the air in a stream of explosions like firecrackers detonating. Vaz saw the hinge-heads outside dive for cover. Some made it; some didn't. Behind him, the snarling and fighting continued but the firing had stopped dead. Naomi thudded down beside him.

"Now," she said. "Move *now*. There's about twenty left out-side. We can take them."

Boom. Something detonated above their heads. BB said some-thing, but Vaz didn't catch it. Then he saw a Banshee streak east again, skimming the tree line, and Dev started swearing blue murder.

"Bastard hit my tail," she said. "I'm losing coolant. Hey, ass-hole, you want to make yourself useful? Go get the goddamn Banshee."

Vaz heard a painfully high-pitched shriek of an engine as it pulled away. "Dev, can you drop an Anvil out front?"

"If you want to risk bringing down the keep."

"Just clear a space."

BB cut in. "Everybody *cover*," he said.

An Anvil missile was the last thing Vaz wanted to see deto-nate on his front doorstep. *Phillips. No armor.* The thought overrode everything else and he flung himself on the professor just as the blast hit his visor like a blizzard. The debris seemed to rain for ages. He tried to get up and found himself springing to his feet with easy, unexpected energy.

But it was Naomi. She held him up by his webbing. "Get go-ing," she said, and scooped Phillips up under one arm like a naughty toddler who was now in serious trouble. He wasn't dead or bleeding, anyway. He was still moving. "Dev, we're coming out."

Mal was up and running. Vaz stumbled after him. He couldn't see where the Banshee or the Phantom had gone, but he could see *Tart-Cart* waiting on the other side of a crater twice the size of a swimming pool, and Naomi sprinting toward it with Phillips. Then a huge hand clamped down on Vaz's shoulder and spun him around. Elar, the mouthiest of the hinge-head girls, loomed in his face.

"You destroy our land and then you run away." She pointed

behind her but he couldn't see anything. He could hear more Elites shouting as they ran, though, male. "My children and my sisters can't defend themselves against an entire keep."

It wasn't Vaz's problem. He shook her off. "Not my war," he said. "I've got one of my own. Sorry."

She could have ripped his head from his shoulders. He knew that for sure now. But she didn't, and he ran for the dropship. Mal pulled him into the crew bay and Devereaux took off so fast that he fell across the seats. The last thing he saw below was an all-too-familiar sea of armored heads thrust forward from massive shoulders as another wave of hinge-heads made their way to the keep.

"I've got to fix this leak," Devereaux said. "BB, let me know when you see a quiet spot where I can set down. Otherwise we're not going to make it out of orbit."

Phillips was almost forgotten for the moment. He sat on the bench seat, still clutching his plasma pistol and looking up at Naomi like he was expecting her to put him over her knee and slap his ass. She took the pistol off him.

"Thanks," he said sheepishly. "My radio went down and BB's fragment is totally screwed, but you should see some of the stuff I've found. *Halo* data." He looked past Naomi at the hatch, still open to the air. "They're going to be slaughtered down there. Can't we do anything?"

"We're not here to do peacekeeping. We came to save your arse." Mal lifted off his helmet and tried to peer out of the hatch. "Where's that bloody Phantom now?"

"Following us," said Devereaux.

UNSC *INFINITY*, SOMEWHERE IN SLIPSPACE

Andrew Del Rio sat at the comms console with an expression of confidence welded seamlessly to his face, but it didn't fool

Parangosky one bit. He clenched his jaw for a moment, then opened the ship's broadcast system.

"Safeguard in force," he said. It was the signal to all hands that the exercise was suspended and that they were deploying for real. This was no longer a drill. "Safeguard, safeguard, safeguard."

He *had* to be terrified. He had a temporary AI, a skeleton crew, two admirals breathing down his neck, and a new, largely untested ship running on alien technology that didn't have a manual.

And when *Infinity* dropped out of slip—if things went to plan—she'd be right in the middle of a civil war, tasked to defend a former enemy.

Now that's what I call the pucker factor.

"Bracing, isn't it?" Parangosky walked up behind his seat more slowly than she actually needed to and leaned close enough to his ear for him to feel her breath. "I haven't been on deck for a shooting war in *decades.*"

Del Rio was staring into the unbroken blackness ahead. She watched his Adam's apple slide just a fraction as he swallowed discreetly. When she was thirty and good-looking, it was a tactic that could be misunderstood, but now that she was beyond old and her glitteringly black history of vengeance was known throughout the fleet, it could only be interpreted as menace. Del Rio got the message loud and clear.

"I'm glad that you trust my abilities enough to take this risk," he said.

She inhaled silently: sandalwood soap, coffee, and mint. "I wouldn't miss this for the world, Andrew."

She straightened up and took a seat to his right just as Hood arrived on the bridge. Lasky was standing at the navigation console with Glassman and Nguyen as they watched the readouts, hands together and forefingers resting on his top lip. He looked like a small boy praying for a bike for Christmas. This was the test. This would prove whether the Forerunner drive enhancement and slipspace plotting would drop them exactly where and when they'd planned to be. Parangosky almost allowed herself a little shiver of excitement. One of the Huragok came onto the bridge and drifted along the rows of instruments like a highly decorative ghost.

"Fifty seconds, sir," Lasky said. "Engineering stand by . . . forty . . . thirty . . ."

Aine took over the count. Lasky didn't seem to be expecting that. She was probably making the point that she still had a job to do, civil war or not.

"Twenty-nine . . ."

"Sorry, Aine."

"Twenty . . . ten . . . five, four, three, two . . . and we're back."

Parangosky didn't feel the slightest hint of giddiness as the ship dropped back into realspace. One moment *Infinity* was in one dimension and the next she was in another, as smooth and instant as a blink. The black void filled up with stars and skeins of glowing gas.

But that was just the backdrop. Sanghelios hung in the foreground, a fox-red crescent curled around a handful of brightly lit cities, the first time that Parangosky—or any of the ship's company, come to that—had seen the enemy homeworld with the naked eye.

"Positional deviation—less than one kilometer, relative to target," Glassman said. Somebody out of Parangosky's eye line clapped a couple of times. "Time deviation—under one second. We're on the nail, sir. Absolutely *on* it." Glassman turned around and smiled at Parangosky, either being politic or acknowledging another member of the Halsey Haters Club, and then at Hood. She noted the order of precedence there. "How's that, ma'am, sir?"

"Worth the wait," Hood said. "Congratulations. Please pass a sincere Bravo Zulu to your team."

Del Rio stood up, looking ten years younger. "Well, god-damn, it *works*," he said. "That and the comms. Shame we can't roll back time and fight this war again."

"At least we won't have to fight another one at a disadvan-tage." Parangosky caught Lasky's eye and winked. "And I'm sure the Arbiter will gaze upon our capacity, and learn to wind his damned neck in lest we come back in a less friendly frame of mind."

The bridge was full of young lieutenants. They looked at her as if she'd revealed God's middle name. Hood gave her his don't-corrupt-the-children look.

"I need to talk to Captain Osman, so I'm going to scuttle off to my cabin," she said, easing herself up with the aid of her cane. Nobody expected ONI to discuss anything in front of Fleet, not even the sports results. "I'll be with you shortly. And I'll expect a fresh pot of coffee."

Even with a buggy, it took longer than she liked to reach the senior officers' cabins. When the door recognized her and let her in, BB was already in the system and waiting to patch her through to Osman.

"BB, I hope you haven't been irritating poor Aine again." She sat down on the sofa and beckoned the screen to move across to her position. "You know how uneasy she gets about things she can't catalog."

"I've been as good as gold, ma'am. She didn't even know I was there."

"Secure voice-coded link, please."

"Right . . . Captain Osman for you . . ."

Osman's seat was empty when the link activated. Parangosky heard the rustle of fabric and the captain slid into the seat, look-ing interrupted.

"Sorry, ma'am," Osman said. "I had to see it for myself. I was looking at *Infinity*. Six klicks long doesn't hit home until you see her at relatively close quarters."

"Impressive, isn't she?"

"I take it that wasn't meant to be a stealth approach. Because that was one hell of an entrance."

"Absolutely accurate reentry. I'll be cross-decking some goodies for you later."

"Kilo-Five's pulled Phillips out, by the way, but they've had to land to make repairs."

"No injuries, I hope."

"None that they're admitting to."

"We're standing by if they need help." Parangosky wondered if that might be a job for Adj, but it was a huge risk now to take him into Sangheili territory. "I haven't had time to look at the sitrep on 'Telcam, but I take it he's still making inroads. How many cities involved now?"

"From what we can see, it's certainly not global. But it's six major centers, still concentrated on the Vadam region. The Arbiter can't hold out much longer."

"Well, Hood's come to the rescue, but you're going to have to make sure that he's not *too* successful."

Parangosky had never been too squeamish to thwart other branches of UNSC to achieve ONI's aims, and she knew damned well that any of her opposite numbers would have done exactly the same to her given half a chance. But ONI had never pulled a trigger to counter them during the Covenant War, even via a third party. Now she'd be doing exactly that, even if she wasn't going to target *Infinity*.

"I know, ma'am," Osman said. "I've been wargaming the worst scenario."

"We can have the best of all worlds. We need to degrade what's left of Sangheili space capability, but we have to degrade it equally on both sides, which is generally harder in practice than it sounds."

"Understood. But concealing that from *Infinity* might be hard."

"I'll take care of that. I'm sure BB can muddy the waters somehow. Now, what about Kilo-Five?"

"I don't want them stranded down there after we're seen to take sides and kill Sangheili." Osman looked down at her hands for a moment. Maybe she was checking for that ONI stain. "They've gathered some useful data from the Forerunner structures that might be about the remaining Halos. BB's got the file. The Huragok might be able to unpick it further. We've not had a chance to extract Phillips's data yet because of the problem with BB's fragment."

"Are you all right, Captain?"

"About killing Sangheili allies? Yes. Absolutely. They were ready to wipe out every last human in the galaxy. Nothing's really changed. I know my duty. Humans first."

"I meant your people on the surface."

"I can handle that, ma'am." Osman forced a smile but it wasn't convincing. "By the way, still no word on *Pious Inquisitor.*"

"She's too big to sneak up on us," Parangosky said. "Now, we need to move fast. I've got two Huragok for you, and they're going to give *Stanley* a first-class makeover. Be ready to receive us in fifteen minutes."

"Understood, ma'am. Thank you. It'll be good to have Adj back."

"I'll bet. Parangosky out."

She leaned back against the upholstery and rehearsed what she'd say if *Stanley* was caught shooting down one of the Arbiter's vessels. The corvette could operate in stealth mode, but *Infinity* had new sensors, and it was hard to keep up with every change the Huragok made. That complicated matters. But once a ship was destroyed, it would never be used against Earth again, and the Sangheili wouldn't be able to replace ships for many years, if ever.

Asset denial, Terrence. It doesn't matter how betrayed the Arbiter feels if he doesn't have the capability to do anything about it. You'll thank me one day.

Parangosky didn't feel guilty about any of it. They were only Sangheili, and slaughtering humans for being humans meant that all morality and consideration of Sangheili as individuals were suspended. This was about the survival of her species. It wasn't a legal debate.

"BB," she said, "I need to ask a favor of you. A little extra assistance for Osman."

"Certainly, Admiral. I think I know what's coming."

"Could you leave a little of your inimitable self in this ship to counter Aine's sensors? You're awfully good at planting false information."

"I'm a *prince* amongst framers, ma'am. I could incriminate the Archangel Gabriel for armed robbery if you needed me to."

"I know. If *Stanley* shoots down anything, I'd like the sensors to record that the fire came from a Sangheili vessel. Perhaps even Kig-Yar. They're already in 'Telcam's bad books, aren't they?"

"Already taken care of, Admiral. Aine's a very good mechanic, but she lacks a certain imagination."

"Bless you, BB." Now it was time to be the matriarch, wise and comforting. "Look, you're going to be all right with this damaged fragment. Don't fret about it."

"I won't. I just feel a little too squeamish at the moment to take a look at it."

"I can understand that. But you'll cope with it. Parangosky out."

She checked her watch, then got up to get a bag of crystallized ginger from her grip. Osman wouldn't need it when every ship in the fleet had the new drives, but for the time being Parangosky would make sure that she knew somebody cared that slipspace jumps made her nauseous. Morale was built on those things. So was trust and friendship.

She tucked a bottle of cologne in the bag as well, then pressed the comms key.

"Engineering," she said. "This is Admiral Parangosky. Ask Adj and Leaks Repaired to report to the shuttle, please. And don't mention it to Dr. Halsey."

There was one more job to do before she could join them. She needed to talk to Mike Spenser, the man who would know only too well what the Kig-Yar might do with a former Covenant battlecruiser.

THIRTY KILOMETERS NORTH OF ACROLI, SANGHELIOS

"Right, BB," said Mal, stabbing a finger in the direction of the Phantom waiting on the other side of the field. "I want the chingun kept trained on that bloody thing, and I'm going to sit on the door gun until Dev's done her repairs. Got it?"

"Let me talk to them," Phillips said. "I can smooth this over."

He tried to stand up but Vaz pushed him back down in the seat as kindly as he could. The Elite dropship had landed about a hundred meters away but nobody had climbed out of it yet. Vaz watched it, waiting for the trouble to start.

"Evan, if you get taken again, they could sell you on to any bunch of thugs or nutters." Vaz didn't seem to be able to get it across to him that he'd been lucky to survive this far. "You've got a value now. You know things. Do I have to spell it out? ONI's gone in and *killed* agents to protect information before."

Phillips didn't bat an eyelid. "I know the Sangheili better than you do."

"No, you don't." Vaz pulled his helmet off and jutted out his jaw to remind Phillips of his scar. *"That's* who they are. You saw New Llanelli, all the glassing—*that's* who they are. You can play with that damn *arum* and quote their poetry all you like, but they exterminate humans. It's what they do."

Phillips went to get up again. This time it was Naomi who smacked him down in his seat.

"You need to concentrate on what you came here for," she said. "Get your data uploaded. What about BB's fragment?"

"Oh, better leave that," BB said, unconvincingly casual. "If there's a problem reintegrating it, I could end up compromised. I need to be back on board *Stanley* to run diagnostics."

"Is that my other persona?" a voice asked. "Am I going to be all right now?"

"Sorry. I'd told him to shut up." Phillips looked down at his jacket as if he'd spilled food on it. "The radio cam was damaged and I tried to fix it, but I think it triggered the security purge. This BB doesn't remember anything except the nonclassified stuff. I've tried to explain who he is so that he's not too traumatized when he . . . well, whatever you do when you reintegrate, BB."

Vaz squatted in the doorway, peering out under the port wing. It was weird to hear two different BBs talking. The one in Phillips's radio sounded like a stranger. Vaz almost didn't want to listen because it felt intrusive, like hearing his grandmother going senile. BB could delete it, though, couldn't he? He could just take out the data segments and ditch the rest. *If only organic brains could do that.* Mal shoved into the space next to him, switched the door gun to manual, and swung it into position.

"Okay, Dev, you're covered," he called. "Out you go."

Devereaux jumped down from the starboard door with a canister of metal foam and ducked under the wing. Naomi followed her. There was still no movement in the Phantom. Vaz wondered if the hinge-head was flying it on his own and didn't like the odds.

"How's it looking, Dev?" Mal asked.

Devereaux sounded as if she was scrambling up the hull. "I can fill in the skin, but it's going to take some time to repair the conduits. I might have to just seal off the lines and risk overheating. Anything beats letting the Sangheili get their hands on her."

"Or us." Mal switched over to *Stanley*'s channel, triggering the feed in Vaz's HUD. "Ma'am, are you getting this? Dev's trying to fix the coolant."

"I can see it, Staff," Osman said. "BB's monitoring the comms. Forze's trying to contact 'Telcam."

"What's he asking?"

"Whether he should let you go or stop you leaving."

"We could just fire an Anvil up his turbine now, ma'am. That might attract more of them, though, and we can't make a fast getaway."

"Just let me talk to them," Phillips murmured.

Osman carried on like she hadn't heard him. "We can probably give you some assistance if you need it. The cavalry's arrived, all six kilometers of it. Well, five and a bit. We've got some pruning to do to make sure the Arbiter–'Telcam game is a draw, so I'm anxious to get you off Sanghelios pronto."

"Oh. *That* cavalry. Is her paint dry yet?"

"Maybe not. No carpets, but she's fast and nasty."

"We'll let you know if we can't fix it. The fewer people we have to extract, the better. Keep it simple."

"Don't take any more risks. I've told BB to spy on you and alert me if you do."

"Understood, ma'am. Kilo-Five out."

Vaz watched Mal's expression brighten. He could put on a brave face at the end of the world, but there was resilient, and then there was pleased. He was verging on pleased.

"They haven't sent *Infinity* all this way for us," Vaz said. "Seriously?"

"Nah, they're rattling the galaxy's biggest saber."

"Saber wasn't the word I had in mind."

"Yes, it's all very Freudian. Ours is bigger than theirs." Mal leaned on the door gun again. "Let's just get this done and RTB. Oh . . . here we go. Look."

The ramp of the Phantom began to lower. Vaz sighted up. He had no idea how many Elites were in there, one or a whole platoon, but he'd make sure he got them before they got him. Mal's grip tightened on the trigger.

"It's not like them to hang around," he said.

Two hinge-heads came down the ramp, one in a shipmaster's armor and the other a smaller figure—possibly a female—in a fabric tunic. The female stopped at the foot of the ramp while the shipmaster carried on toward *Tart-Cart* with his pistol held at his side.

"They're heading this way, Dev," Vaz said. "You two want to get inside?"

The shipmaster suddenly looked toward the tail of the dropship. It must have been Naomi. A Spartan could always get a hinge-head's attention. He slowed down and finally stopped about thirty meters from *Tart-Cart*.

"Okay, BB, translate for me," Vaz said. He slid down from the door and took a couple of paces toward the shipmaster. "So you're Forze, are you?"

"I am," said the hinge-head. "'Telcam told me to find *Philliss* and bring him back, because he needs to honor a promise. Who are you?"

"We're UNSC marines," Vaz said. "Does ODST mean anything to you?"

"Ah, the fools who arrive conveniently packaged in their own coffins."

"Well, we've got Phillips, and we're heading home as soon as we're ready." Vaz thought he was doing really well. He was having a civilized conversation with a hinge-head when all he really wanted to do was open fire and make sure it never got the chance to kill another human. "What are you waiting for?"

"Because I don't know why 'Telcam would do a favor for humans, and that's a question that would have troubled a comrade of mine."

Mal said nothing. Naomi walked into Vaz's peripheral vision from the left, slow and deliberate. This was the awkward bit: 'Telcam couldn't tell his pals that he was getting arms from ONI. Vaz could see why all this looked dodgy to them. Forze meant Jul. Jul had followed 'Telcam to a handover and that was when Naomi had jumped him. The monk didn't seem to inspire trust in his sidekicks.

"Forze, it's okay." Phillips stuck his head out of the door. Forze stared at him. "These are my friends. Ask 'Telcam. He needs me to get home safely. Go on, ask him."

"Get back inside, Phillips," Mal whispered. *"Now."*

Vaz kept a wary eye on the female. This could have been a clever distraction, and he'd seen what hinge-head women could do in a fight. She was watching, head cocked, very intent. She had a plasma pistol in her belt, though. That was warning enough for Vaz.

"Is that your wife?" he asked. He couldn't judge the age of Elites and he wasn't worried about offending them. "Daughter?"

Forze didn't look around at her. Vaz didn't blame him for not turning his back on humans.

"My friend's wife," Forze said. "She came with me to search for him. Why?"

Phillips was still being a pain in the ass. He wouldn't get back inside and Vaz was on the verge of shoving him out of the way. The best he could do was to raise a discreet warning finger.

Keep it zipped, Prof.

"What was your friend's problem with 'Telcam?" Phillips asked, taking no damn notice.

"He wanted to know where he got his supplies. Jul always asks awkward questions."

He'd let the name slip. Well, that didn't take them any further. They knew all the connections.

Phillips still went on, though. "So this is Jul's wife."

"What does that matter to you?" Forze asked.

"I'm trying to work out what I need to tell you to convince you that these are the people 'Telcam was going to hand me over to."

Forze looked down his nose at Phillips. Vaz stood by to cut off any more conversation. Then Forze turned for a second and called out to the female. "Raia, try to contact 'Telcam again. Tell him there are coffin-worms here who say they have a right to take Phillips."

"Say the name Osman to him," Phillips called. Vaz decided enough was enough and got back into the crew bay to shove him out of sight. "Then he'll know it's okay."

"Phillips, shut up, will you?" Vaz bundled him inside and held him back. "What the hell are you doing?"

"Authenticating." He seemed upset, looking from side to side. "And realizing what I am."

"*Alive.* That's what you are, so let's keep it that way." So that was Jul's wife. It wasn't a happy thought and he could see that it upset Phillips, but that was just too bad. Nobody had asked the hinge-heads to start a war with humans so now they had to live with the consequences. "Stay inside and shut up."

Phillips looked a little hurt. Vaz went back to the door and squatted beside Mal. Forze was just standing there, arms at his sides. There was no sign of the female.

"Where did she go?" Vaz asked.

"Back in the ship," Mal muttered. "Christ, this is bloody weird. I'm not cut out for this secret squirrel stuff. What's Phillips up to? Trying to forge some bond with them so they don't blow the crap out of us?"

"He's feeling guilty and trying to fix things."

Mal got on the radio. "Talking of which, Dev, how are we doing?"

"I need something like a length of fuel line or polymer tubing," she said. "I can't tie off what's left. It's too short. I might be able to clamp a new section in, though."

"Are you telling me we're stuck here?"

"Maybe."

Mal didn't say anything but dropped his head for a second or two. Vaz patted his back. "Hey, remember when we hijacked that Spirit on Imber?"

"You're not suggesting we nick the Phantom, are you?"

"We could. We'd have to destroy *Tart-Cart,* though."

"I heard that," Devereaux said. "And the answer's *over my dead body.*"

"What about trashing the Phantom for parts? Hey, BB, you're not translating all this, are you?"

BB sighed. "Vaz, have you got enough fingers to calculate my IQ? No. Oh, look . . . here comes Mrs. 'Mdama. Is she smiling? It's so hard to tell."

Jul's wife strode across to Forze and said something to him. Forze held out his arms, whatever that meant, and took a few steps closer to *Tart-Cart.*

"'Telcam says he understands but he also expects agreements to be honored."

Mal nodded. "We'll pass that on."

"He's told me to offer you help with repairs."

"Pipe," Devereaux said instantly. "Ask him for a couple of meters of solvent-proof flexible tubing, about fifty-millimeter diameter, and any composite solder he can find."

"Forze, have you got any fuel line?" Mal asked. He held his fingers apart. "This wide. And composite solder."

Forze rolled his head and walked back to the Phantom in silence, Raia 'Mdama trailing behind him and occasionally looking back at the dropship. He came down the ramp again with a snake's wedding of pipes and wire coiled in his arms and walked right up to *Tart-Cart* to dump them in a heap on the ground.

"I know little of mechanics," Forze said. "We had *Engineers* for that. This is all I could find."

"Thanks." Mal gave him a thumbs-up and Forze walked off, apparently confident that Vaz wouldn't shoot him in the back. Devereaux appeared from under the wing and began sorting through the pile.

"Great," she said, whipping out a pocket gauge and measuring the diameters. "If I ever get back to the mess, I'll tell this story and I'll never have to buy another beer as long as I live."

"Does any of it fit?" Vaz asked.

"This bit might."

While they waited, the Phantom's drives started up and the ship lifted off. Naomi watched it out of sight and then climbed back into the crew bay. Vaz followed her inside and sat down between her and Phillips.

"She doesn't know where her husband is," Phillips said. "Doesn't know if he's alive or dead. That's my fault."

Naomi folded her arms. "I did it, actually. So you can stop beating yourself up about it."

"Yeah, they'd have glassed Sydney and everything else if they'd had a chance," Vaz said.

"And the females and children at Nes'alun. What the hell happened to them? I just abandoned them."

"Prof, it's hinge-head on hinge-head violence. None of your business." Vaz tried to bite down on his temper. Here they were, marooned in a damaged ship behind enemy lines, and Phillips was worrying about Elites who would have used him for target practice without a second thought. "We didn't start it and we won't finish it. *Usyok?*"

It was rude, and even if Phillips didn't speak Russian he could understand the tone. He shut up. Vaz suddenly felt guilty for snarling at him. The guy was just a civvie. He'd done pretty damn well for someone who didn't know how to use a weapon or carry out recons. Vaz reached over and slapped his back to make amends, embarrassed.

"Sorry, Prof," he said. "You must have been scared shitless. You did a great job. You even grabbed a souvenir. Not that we needed any more plasma pistols with a hold full of them, but they say provenance adds value."

"I didn't know you were coming for me," Phillips said meekly. "I thought I was supposed to try to escape."

"We never leave our people behind. Not even the annoying ones."

Vaz debated whether to lance a few more boils and raise the topic of BB's fragmentation issues, but it didn't feel like the right time. BB didn't seem to be joining in the conversation at all; he didn't even manifest himself. Vaz watched the time tick by in his HUD, then took off his helmet and went outside to pass the time, watching creatures that could have been birds or even disturbingly big insects wheeling around overhead on the thermals.

"Vultures," Vaz said.

Mal didn't blink. "Bluebirds of happiness."

Naomi squeezed past them and jumped out to stalk around

the edge of the wing. "Someone's got to secure the ship," she said. "Just in case."

"Okay," said Mal, "a paranoid, a depressive, and an incurable optimist walk into a bar, and—"

Devereaux cut in on the radio. "Someone get off their ass and give me a hand with this, please."

"Coming, dear." Mal pushed the door gun over to Vaz and trotted off. "You want a big strong man to do it for you?"

"Yeah. Find me one, will you?"

The hinge-heads could come back at any time so Vaz didn't plan to relax. He put his helmet back on to check the feed from the drone cams, most of which seemed to be focused on Vadam. It was hard to square the memory of Manny Barakat and all the other ODSTs who hadn't made it home from glassed, murdered colony worlds with a hinge-head like Forze helping out with spare parts, or the mother Elite defending her kids to the death. Gray areas were interesting, but Vaz couldn't live his life in them. There was one side, and there was the other, and he knew which one was his.

He still felt worse about not shooting Halsey than leaving a bunch of hinge-heads to fight for their lives.

CHAPTER
ELEVEN

THE PROBLEM FOR AN AI ISN'T DOING A THOUSAND THINGS
AT ONCE. IT'S SLOWING DOWN AND IMPARTING ALL THAT
INFORMATION TO HUMANS. I LOVE YOU ALL TO BITS, BUT
YOU'RE SOMETHING OF A BOTTLENECK IN MY PROCESSES.

(ONI SPECIAL OPERATIONS AI BLACK-BOX, EXPLAINING
IMPATIENCE TO HIS ORGANIC COLLEAGUES)

UNSC *PORT STANLEY*: HANGAR BAY

"The first thing I'm going to do is to put Adj and Leaks to work
on upgrading the comms," BB said. He realized he'd missed the
Huragok touch around the place. "Then the drives. Then they
can work on the drones."

Osman fastened the collar of her jacket as if Parangosky's
arrival was an admiralty inspection. The Pelican settled in
Stanley's hangar bay and the outer doors sealed, accompanied
by the hiss of repressurization and flashing vacuum hazard
lights.

"Aren't you even going to offer them a cup of nutrient sludge
first?" she asked. "They're ship's company now. Besides, we can't
afford the downtime at the moment."

"They'll take *minutes*. Okay, an hour, perhaps. We've got
plenty of material they can use."

"You're a slave driver." She snapped to attention. "Admiral
on deck. Look sharp."

The hazard lights stopped and the inner doors parted. BB

put all thoughts of his damaged fragment out of his mind and positioned his avatar to one side of the ramp, honor guard style, with his box edges extra-defined in lieu of standing to attention.

If the two Huragok were going to be a permanent addition to the crew, he'd have to find a way of firewalling his more sensitive sectors. The creatures were just too thorough for his liking. Adj had behaved himself on his last stay and heeded warnings to stay away from certain things, so perhaps BB could get around the problem by just giving both Huragok a stiff talking-to. If that didn't work, he'd have to add partitions to his matrix. The thought of them poking around in his code and knowing his most private processes was rather . . . creepy.

Hoist by my own petard. Now I know how the crew feels.

The ramp lowered and Parangosky stood at the top, clutching a small candy-striped bag. Somehow arriving with gifts did nothing to make her seem less fearsome. She made her way down the deck and placed the bag in Osman's hand. *Ginger.* It had to be crystallized ginger. There were things that even BB didn't know.

"Just a very quick visit, Serin." She used Osman's first name more often now, as if the captain was making the transition from protégé to peer. "Ginger. Let me know when you run out." Parangosky turned around and looked back at the open door. "Come on, don't be shy, Adj. You know Captain Osman."

Adj drifted out of the dropship, leading another Huragok by one of its tentacles. It was quite touching: they looked like refugees. They drifted to a halt in front of Osman and gazed around the hangar, probably working out what to completely rebuild first.

"The other one's called Leaks Repaired," Parangosky whispered, as if they wouldn't hear her. "They've both consolidated the Forerunner knowledge from Onyx, so you can safely let them loose on BB's translation project now."

"Welcome back, Adj," Osman said, holding out her hand.

Adj wrapped a tentacle around it but didn't quite manage to shake it. Still, it was the thought that counted. "Hello, Leaks. This is BB. He can do Huragok sign language."

BB extruded a set of holographic tentacles. <*Don't you dare touch anything until I brief you. If you think* Infinity's *classified, she's an open book compared to* Stanley.>

"There, everyone's made friends now." Osman seemed to think it was a greeting. "What's the plan?"

"Hood's making contact with the Arbiter about now," Parangosky said, checking her watch. "It's all going to be about timing. The more rebels who show up at Vadam, the easier it is to give them a MAC surprise, so we need to work out how and when to tip off 'Telcam. We'll be in BB's capable hands for comms monitoring."

"*Infinity* too?"

"Aine's not a combat AI, let alone spec ops or intel."

"But she's going to have to manage the firing solutions, surely."

"She has dumb AI capability for that. She won't mind BB carrying out the intelligence functions."

"Trust me, Captain." BB drifted off after the Huragok, who'd started exploring the hangar. "She won't even know I've been in her underwear drawer. Now come along, you two." He signed flamboyantly. <*Don't touch. Plenty to do later.*>

Parangosky took out her datapad and scribbled. "Handy."

"Believe it or not, Kilo-Five ran into Raia 'Mdama," Osman said. "She was with Forze, looking for Jul."

"My, my. Stand by your hinge-head. I'll pass that to Trevelyan."

"How's Magnusson doing with him?"

"She got the bioweapons team to modify the proteins and saccharides in some of their staple foods and tried them out on him. And on some Sangheili livestock."

"That was fast. What happened?"

"It made the grain indigestible. The livestock are dying, and he was as sick as the proverbial dog until she called a halt. She wants to introduce the modified seed to Sanghelios to starve them out. But I'm not too keen. I don't want to risk accidental contamination of similar crops when we recolonize."

Osman didn't even flinch. BB had to admire that detachment in the face of plans for global extinction. "Well, at least we have it in reserve if all else fails."

"Indeed. Look, I have to be getting back now, Serin, but when we've finished mopping up and things are less fraught, come over and take a look at *Infinity*."

"I will, ma'am. Good hunting."

BB tried to herd Adj and Leaks toward the compartment he'd set aside for them. There was no point locking them in, because they'd just rebuild the locks. He'd learned that as long as he explained everything to them and made his instructions explicit then they did as they were told. They didn't have time to defy him and they didn't get offended. Life for them was about fixing and building and improving anything from equipment to injured organic tissue. It was all they wanted to do.

He barred the Huragok's way and held up virtual tentacles. *<I want you to look around, but don't access any of my systems or modify anything yet.>*

Adj signed back. *<We'll wait. Where are the marines?>*

<They'll be here soon. Show Leaks the galley. Mal left a container of nutrient in the freezer.>

<Mal feeds us.> Adj seemed to be explaining that to Leaks. *<BB is impatient but clear-thinking. The Spartan does not allow access to her armor. Vaz is fast enough to catch you and trap you. Osman and Devereaux don't interfere with your work. Phillips will try to engage you in long conversations.>*

It was always sobering to see yourself through the eyes of

others. BB was about to explain how ultra-fast processing inevitably made an AI impatient, but Adj was simply stating facts to the new kid, not passing judgment. Osman overtook BB, chewing contentedly and trailing a haze of zingerone and a few other fascinating volatile oils. He could smell the ginger via the ship's chemhaz monitoring.

"You realize most officers would be too scared to eat anything Parangosky gave them," he said. "Like accepting mushrooms from Agrippina."

"The mushrooms are a *great* tip. Thanks." She settled into her seat and held her finger just above the comms link. "Okay, BB, we're fighting this ship alone. Ready?"

"Of course I am," he said. "I have full tactical capability in case the crew's incapacitated. But I know you like to feel useful."

"It's been a long time since I fired a shot in anger."

"Oh, it's like riding a bike. You never forget. And all you have to do is set objectives and I'll achieve them for you."

"Okay. See if you can get hold of 'Telcam."

BB could maintain monitoring on as many situations as he needed to, as long as he could establish a link with the relevant system. But as far as he was concerned he was actually present in all of them simultaneously. *Tart-Cart* was still grounded, and he was down there with Devereaux checking the diagnostic feedback; he was in *Infinity* scrutinizing targets around Vadam, using her imaging and dodging around Aine, just as he was wandering around Bravo-6 keeping an eye on Hogarth and Harriet, spying on Halsey out of sheer fascinated horror, and—intermittently—lurking in the makeshift rebel command center south of Vadam keep.

He could see all, be everywhere, and, if human beings acted as his hands, he could also do everything. But this was the humans' war: they had to be the ones to take action and give one another information, not him. It was more than courtesy that made him leave Osman to tell Parangosky about Raia. Once he started driving those decisions himself, it became *his* war, and if a war was left to AIs, then he suspected it would only last seconds before they all decided it wasn't worth the effort and went home to raid databases and play with fascinating theorems.

BB existed to protect Earth, and Osman in particular. Part of that protection was to accept that this was how they wished their world to be. Like a soldier, he was the instrument of the elected government, and he couldn't simply pick the parts he agreed with.

Their choices are what make them human—good or bad. If I take away their choices, I take away their humanity.

In the space of a second, he watched it all, spread across space. Devereaux dropped a connector and swore in Cantonese. Halsey put her head in her hands and cried quietly while she repeated the name *Miranda.* Phillips watched Mal loading his ammo pouches, trying to find the right moment to start a conversation. On the ground in Vadam, BB detected a radio signal that connected a ship called *Promised Revelation* with one of 'Telcam's lieutenants, Buran.

He resisted the urge to ride the carrier wave in case the signal was interrupted and he found part of himself stranded again.

"This is Avu Med 'Telcam," a voice said.

"Captain, I've got him." BB switched the channel through to Osman. "Go ahead."

If Osman had any doubts, they didn't show. She sat back in the seat, confident and in control. "Field Master, thank you for your assistance in recovering Professor Phillips. Now let me help you out in return."

BB projected *Infinity*'s aerial recon image of Vadam onto the viewscreen right in her eye line. The wooded area in front of the Arbiter's keep was now a solid mass of infantry behind a line of artillery pieces. Smoke blew back across them, kicking the image into thermal mode to maintain detail, and then one, two, three of them fired, dotting the image with flares of hot light. Explosions peppered the walls of the keep.

"You offered help before, but I think we're doing better than we expected . . . Shipmaster." Maybe 'Telcam had someone within earshot. "The Arbiter's sympathizers seem unwilling to join the fight."

"Let me tell you what I can. There's nothing I can do to prevent this, but your situation's going to change radically in the next few hours. What I *can* do is assist and try to save some of your assets. I don't know what form that'll take yet, but I've got enough firepower and intel to stop this turning into a rout."

'Telcam went quiet for a couple of seconds. "Any advice, Shipmaster?"

"How many warships do you have?" Osman didn't need to ask, because BB snatched the data from *Infinity* and overlaid it on the viewscreen. It was more a test of 'Telcam's honesty. "Not small vessels—proper warships. And where are they?"

"I have seven frigates and a cruiser. Four of the frigates are deployed to other states, and three are east of Vadam awaiting orders. The cruiser is still over Ontom. I want to avoid destroying Vadam itself, but if the Arbiter doesn't surrender, I'll use the ventral beam."

"You've lost one ship, so I'd take good care of the others if I were you."

"The Arbiter only has a call on five small cruisers."

"Just be ready to change your plan. Take a look at what's just shown up in high orbit, if your long-range sensors are still working. Trust me. Osman out."

BB shut the link. 'Telcam really had leveled with her.

"I don't believe I said that." Osman ran her hands over her face. "*Trust me.* Christ, BB, I wouldn't, not if I were him."

"You haven't actually stitched him up yet, Captain."

"So where's the rest of the fleet gone? I know they've lost plenty of hulls one way or another, but is that all they've got?"

"No, but it's all that the keeps are willing to commit. Like Earth's civil wars. In many of them, most people stayed out of it and let two factions slug it out. Most of Sanghelios is probably waiting to see who wins."

"The more I see, the more I think that Magnusson's crop killer project makes sense."

"Ah, but it's not the navy way, is it?" BB had a close eye on the decisions being taken on *Infinity*'s bridge, where Del Rio was waiting for the word to deploy the MAC against the rebels. "I'll update the Admiral."

"Hood does know we're here, doesn't he?"

"Of course, even if he can't see us."

"Remind them that we still have Kilo-Five stuck on the ground."

Parangosky already had. Del Rio was happy to wait, and the Arbiter hadn't responded to Hood's latest message yet. BB watched Devereaux from the aft section safety cam.

"I think they'll be able to move in a couple of hours," BB said. "But it might end up being a salvage operation once they take off. It's a good time to mention that to—oh, hang on." 'Telcam was trying to make contact. "It's 'Telcam again."

Osman nodded. "Go ahead, Field Master."

"Osman," he said. His voice sounded very distracted, very different. And he rarely used her name. "I took your advice. *Promised Revelation* has just sent me a sensor image, and . . . when did you acquire *that*?"

He'd spotted *Infinity*, then. It was very, very hard not to.

ONIRF TREVELYAN

The first lesson that Jul had learned from humans was deceit, and the second was sly patience. Every day, they would chip away at whatever frustrated them, sometimes boldly head on, mostly sneaking up behind it, until it crumbled and gave way.

Every day, then, he would do the same. He felt better this morning. The food was back to the bland menu he'd been given before Magnusson's inexplicable attempt to make him feel at home, with the exception of the *colo* meat. He stared at the bowl for a long time before scooping up half a mouthful of food and tasting it without swallowing, ready to spit it out if his instincts told him it was going to make him ill again.

It was the food. He *knew* it was the food. When he'd tried to eat yesterday, the very smell of it had made his stomach churn. But now . . . he felt fragile, but hungry. He cleared the bowl and waited for that awful cramping and nausea to start again. But after a couple of hours he still felt well.

Magnusson rapped at the door. She waited a few moments and then walked in without waiting for a response, accompanied by a guard and Prone to Drift. The Huragok carried the explosive harness.

"Hello, Jul," she said. "Do you want to go out for a walk today?"

Jul got the feeling that there was some humorous undercurrent to that at his expense, but it was irrelevant. His plan was crystallizing and he wasn't going to be distracted. He needed to spend time with the Huragok.

"I do," he said. "I want to see more Forerunner relics."

"Well, there's enough to keep you busy for years. We haven't even surveyed five percent of the surface yet." She gestured to Prone to attach the harness. "By the way, one of our colleagues saw Raia the other day. I hope I pronounced that right."

Just when Jul thought he finally had the measure of humans and how to deal with their games, one word could cut his legs from under him. He steeled himself not to react or start babbling questions. Magnusson appeared to notice that anyway, because she smiled.

"She was with your friend, Shipmaster Forze," she said. "I thought you'd like to know."

She didn't wait for his reaction. She walked out and the guard stood beside the door, his rifle held on its sling.

I must not be diverted.

She wouldn't have mentioned Raia unless she thought that her being with Forze would worry me.

And she wouldn't want to worry me unless she wanted something.

Jul followed the Huragok outside and accepted that he was very worried indeed, but that the way to deal with it was to let Magnusson make the next move. Perhaps they'd picked up the information by intercepting communications, nothing more. It didn't mean anything.

<Where do you want to go today?> Prone asked. *<There are entire towns here, empty, waiting for the Forerunners to return. I have been told that they never will.>*

Jul wondered what the Forerunners would have made of the humans if they had. "Why does it all look so new? Because of the way the sphere suspended time, or the perfection of the technology?"

<Both.>

Prone didn't elaborate. Huragok were devoted in every sense to Forerunner artifacts. They cared about their welfare like other creatures cared about their kin, so it was a strange brief answer to give about the entire focus of their life. Jul was willing to invest time in gaining the Huragok's trust, though, and there was a certain truth in what he'd said: he really did want to see more of the Forerunners' legacy. They might not have been gods—and he'd come to terms with the universe having no guiding direction—but they were still remarkable, and still able to change the fate of the galaxy even from the grave. Their machines and buildings had a kind of immortality. He would settle for that in lieu of a divine eternity.

Jul had little else to do but walk and explore, but it was an illusory freedom. His eye was caught by an object in the flawless turquoise sky. When he looked up, it wasn't a bird: it was a small device, flying under its own power. There seemed to be two kinds, one a gray, featureless cylinder, the other a more intricate metal egg that looked much more like human technology.

"What are those?" he asked.

<Monitoring devices,> Prone said. <They observe and measure. They look for Flood contagion. The ovoids are human surveillance machines.>

The more Jul checked the sky, the more he realized that there'd always be something watching him. Between the spy drones and the explosive harness, he was still in a cage. How many humans were working here? There seemed to be more every day, more uniforms, more instant boxlike buildings, more little vehicles pottering around or skimming the horizon. But Magnusson had said it herself—this was an entire planet, albeit an inverted one, and the humans had only just started exploring it.

If it was a sphere . . . Jul looked up and down, orienting himself. If it was a sphere with the sun at the center and he was inside it, then space was beneath his feet. He'd thought about this many times at night, unable to sleep, and he reached the same conclusion. The only way out was down.

He carried on walking along the same path he'd taken the day before, planning to walk for a few more hours beyond his previous limit. Why had the humans chosen to locate their camp here when they had a whole world to choose from? He made a mental note of two curved stone towers that dominated the landscape. Prone stayed at his side, silent unless Jul spoke to him.

"What are the towers?"

<*Environmental maintenance. The control of atmosphere. The well-being of life within. This is our task.*>

Jul found that interesting. Could it be sabotaged? That might destroy this whole facility. "Do the humans control it?"

<*It is our task. They let us continue our work there.*>

So sabotage would rely on manipulating Huragok. That was beyond him. The creatures wouldn't cooperate, and he didn't have any scientific knowledge to guide him anyway. He dismissed that idea and went back to the next thing available to him, the destruction of the Huragok themselves.

"I'm watched wherever I go," he said.

<*Everyone is. This is for safety.*>

"Can I be heard?"

<*Yes, via your translation receiver. In case you need to call for help.*>

Jul would have to be much more careful about his line of questioning. What would humans believe most easily about a Sangheili? A little religious fervor.

"I want to know about the Forerunners," he said. "I need to understand who and what they were. They were—are—our gods. Our lives were centered on them. But now we're told they were never gods, and everything we believed in and sacrificed was for nothing."

<*What do you want to know?*>

"Were they like us?"

<*Not like you, and not like us. More like humans.*>

That rankled. Humans always seemed convinced that they were unique and special, not simply one mediocre creature out of many species. "Do you remember them?"

<We remember, because we remember everything, but the memory is not direct. It has been shared many times over the years.>

"How many of you does it take to manage this world?"

<All of us.>

Jul would have to be more subtle. "I meant are there more towers in other parts of this world."

<That option exists.>

Prone might not have understood the question, or his answer might have contained more information than Jul could grasp. Or he might have simply given an evasive answer because Magnusson or even the Forerunners had told him to. If Jul questioned him more specifically, then whoever was monitoring him would guess his plans. It was time to change tack.

"What did the Forerunners want from us?"

<Nothing.>

The conversation had taken Jul to the bank of a river and much closer to the environmental control towers. The landscape was all gentle hills and orderly woodland, not rugged wilderness like Sanghelios, the kind of soft, tame terrain that humans liked. It would take him a brisk walk to reach the first tower. There were no guards in sight.

If he could get inside, that was where he'd probably find the other Huragok. If he still dared think in terms of detonating his harness, a confined space would mean maximum destruction.

But Raia's still out there. Death should be a last resort. We never admit this even to ourselves, but we're too afraid to say it aloud: we want to survive.

He could see a huge open doorway, temple-sized. Yes, this would have been called a temple on Sanghelios. How many of the sacred sites there were actually just warehouses, or barracks, or maintenance areas? This was the problem when trying to read the minds and intentions of gods. It wasn't possible. The Forerunners probably didn't even realize they would be distorted into divinity and used as motives for galactic war. They couldn't have known that their mundane buildings would be declared holy or that devices designed to protect them from a plague would become mystical gateways to eternity. It was all very disappointing. Jul had enjoyed the majesty of the unknown as a boy. The known always fell short.

He resisted breaking into a run. He was sure that would attract the attention of the surveillance drones. But he speeded up as much as he could and stood at the threshold of a hall whose ceiling was so high that it vanished into darkness. There was a wall to his right. When he took a step inside and his eyes adjusted to the light, he could see that the wall was covered with illuminated symbols, some stable and some constantly changing.

"Air conditioning," said a voice behind him. "Fancy, but it's still air conditioning."

He spun around to find himself looking down at one of the guards. He hadn't even heard the man approach. The guard held his rifle one-handed, not exactly aiming it, but he had a small device in one hand and tilted it so Jul could see it.

"If you ever see me back away fast," the guard said, "it probably means I'm going to press *this*. We've all got one. And then the jellyfish guys will have to repair everything."

So it was a remote detonator for his harness. It was another thing Jul might work on acquiring, but this wasn't the right time. Very well; he would play this game and live up to the human expectation of a Sangheili.

"This is the work of the gods," Jul said, playing his role with gusto. Blasphemy was an imaginary crime now. There was nobody up there to offend. "Show respect."

"Whatever you say." The guard stabbed a finger toward Prone.

"You're supposed to keep him out of operating areas. Do you understand?"

<He can do no harm here.>

Prone drifted away, looking back as if he expected Jul to follow him. There was no point pushing the issue with the guard, because that would almost certainly end in being confined to the cell again. Jul walked off.

It was a tactical withdrawal, nothing more.

"So I'm not allowed to go into *operating areas*," he said. "Where *can* I go?"

<Go where you wish. If it isn't permitted, you'll be made aware.>

"By being blown up."

<I don't know. But there is nothing you can damage here.>

Prone had said that a few times now. Jul decided that simply getting a better idea of the layout of the area would be time well spent. He moved off into open country and away from the towers, heading for the deserted town some distance away. As he reached the top of a ridge, he could see Warthog vehicles making their way slowly in the same direction, with a soldier on the back of one of them manning a gun. Two more Warthogs converged on a point and drew up side by side but facing opposite directions while their drivers talked. Perhaps the humans were drawing some conclusions by watching where he went and what he did.

<Nobody ever came back to live in the cities,> Prone said suddenly. It was the first time he'd opened a conversation. *<It was all made ready for them.>*

The closer Jul got, the more wonderful the buildings looked. The structures were silver-gray and smooth, all heights and shapes, almost inviting exploration. He could hear the Warthogs in the far distance. He expected one to come roaring down the road that led into the city to head him off and tell him he couldn't enter, but nobody intercepted him, so he carried on between the buildings and into a large square. The first thing that struck him were that the doors were all wildly different heights, some human-sized and some two or three times taller than him.

The silence was extraordinary. Jul wondered whether the not-quite-gods had been killed or had found somewhere even better to hide.

"So the Forerunners planned to shelter here until the galaxy was cleansed of the Flood," he said. "They must have intended to re-create their society here. Their entire civilization. The Halo would have destroyed everything sentient outside when it was activated."

<Yes,> Prone said. *<This would have been their capital and their refuge.>*

"There weren't that many of them, then." If there had been billions upon billions, there would have been many more cities visible, unless the Forerunners had construction techniques he couldn't even imagine, let alone see. Perhaps, though, this was a shelter for the chosen few, and the less fortunate Forerunners would have perished. "Only enough to populate this planet. Was this all they had?"

Prone drifted from doorway to doorway, looking as if he was lost. *<Everything they had could be re-created here and reached from here. But no longer.>*

The Huragok was an irritating mix of rational explanation and cryptic comment, but Jul still wasn't sure which was which. "No longer what?"

<We did our duty. We still do our duty. It's not our fault.>

"What isn't?"

There was no point getting angry with a Huragok because it

didn't achieve anything. Sometimes they'd even flee to avoid confrontation, and Jul wanted this one to trust and obey him. He waited for the answer.

<The portals,> Prone said. He made a sad little keening noise, starting high and dropping to a low note that faded into a breath. *<The terminals no longer work properly. They were not maintained, therefore there are no other Huragok there.>*

That seemed perfectly clear. Prone and his brothers had maintained this world and the portals built here, but there was nothing they could do about the other end of the slipspace route, the destination portals. There was nobody left to maintain them. If anything told Jul that the Forerunners were all gone, it was that. He understood Prone's depressed little sigh. There was something unutterably lonely about a tunnel through space that ultimately went nowhere.

"So they could travel all over the galaxy from here." Jul started to see fragments of the Forerunners' contingency plan for the end of the world. Even the gods had emergency procedures. "Or they could reach this shelter from many other places."

<Once,> Prone said. He floated over to a wall covered in elegant carvings and held a tentacle out to caress the stone. *<Once.>*

"How long ago was this?"

<Lucy-B-zero-nine-one asked and I told her one hundred thousand years.>

Jul felt a slow heaviness in his chest. He could have left this place for perhaps countless destinations and reached them in an instant, but he was a hundred millennia too late. The humans had found a locked room the size of a star system in which to carry out their research. No wonder they weren't worried about letting him walk where he pleased. He stood beside Prone and put his hand on the stone, too.

"That," he said, "is too long ago to be of any help to me."

UNSC *TART-CART*, SANGHELIOS:
FOURTEEN HOURS INTO REPAIRS

Devereaux balanced precariously on the dropship's tail and knelt to run the ultrasound scanner over the repaired section of hull.

"Looks solid enough to me, Staff." She rapped the metal with her knuckles and peered down at Mal over the edge. "I'm not convinced about the conduits, though."

"It's your call, Dev," he said. "Do we take off or not?"

"Put it this way—we'll be vacuum-tight, but I can't promise that the drive will make it."

"Are we talking about drifting? We've got plenty of help out there to reel us in."

"No, we might be talking about failing to reach escape velocity. Which might end in a very involuntary reentry. As in barbecue."

Mal wasn't seriously worried yet. By ODST standards, this was a minor inconvenience. There wasn't an enemy for fifty kilometers, and he hadn't lost anyone. But Osman wanted them out of Sanghelios before things kicked off, and they were cutting it fine. He called *Port Stanley* again and waited.

"She knows your status," BB said. "I'm streaming it."

"I still need to talk to her. No offense. It's a meatbag thing." Mal waited, wondering if they'd actually be able to see *Infinity* from the ground when the sun was in the right position. He tried to imagine how much of Sydney she'd cover if they could berth her at Bravo-6, mentally dropping her bow on the map and realizing her stern would be on the far side of the harbor. The crew could run marathons in that thing. "Ma'am? How long have we got?"

"We're waiting on the Arbiter, Staff. Is time going to make much difference?"

"No, we're as repaired as we're ever going to be."

"Do you need a recovery team?"

Mal didn't like the idea of pouring even more people into the problem. He gave Devereaux a shrug. She looked like she was considering it, then shook her head.

"Dev says not, ma'am. But stand by to give us a tow."

"Understood."

Phillips wandered out to watch and stood gazing up at Devereaux, who gave him a big grin. He fiddled with his radio cam like a rosary. "You got five minutes, BB?"

"Are you addressing me, Professor?" It was the fragment. "What can I do for you?"

"Oh, for goodness' sake shut him down," BB said wearily. "Go on. Just tell him to go into standby mode."

"But he's *you*," Phillips said. "Wouldn't it be easier to just . . . I don't know, reabsorb him, whatever it is you do?"

"I said I'd do that *when we get back*." BB sounded pissed off. "I need to assess the damage first."

"Okay. Sorry."

The weirdly distant conversation between the two versions of BB left Mal feeling disturbed. He was starting to feel sorry for the dumb bit. But if it didn't have all of BB's personality now, perhaps it wasn't offended.

Listen to me. Just listen to the stuff I take for granted as being normal. This time last year, I'd never even spoken to a smart AI. Now I'm playing agony aunt to one.

"Okay, let's do it." Devereaux climbed down from the hull and put on her helmet. "I think this must be the slowest extraction on record. We could have *walked* out of here faster. All aboard. Come on, move it."

Everybody piled in, the hatch seals hissed, and the status lights went to green. They didn't really need lights, but it was more comforting to be able to *see* that the hatches were shut. Mal tightened his safety restraint until it made him realize how much weight he'd put on in the last few weeks, courtesy of ONI's lavish victualling and a lot less running around in heavy armor while being shot at. He patted his gut.

"Porker," Vaz muttered. "Have you found the gym in *Stanley* yet? You want me to show you where it is?"

"Yeah, and you're not exactly built like a racing snake yourself these days, are you?" Mal leaned across and poked Phillips's knee. It was time to cheer him up. "So now we can breathe again, how sure are you about the Halo locations?"

"Not a hundred percent," he said. "It's almost certainly locations, or at least something that identifies them, but we haven't worked out the Forerunner coordinates system. They might not have thought in terms of having a capital. Positions might be relative to other Halos rather than to a central reference point."

"But how did you manage to activate a portal?"

"It had a lock thingie like an *arum*."

"See, I knew you'd come in handy."

"And now we know where the portal exited, we might be able to use that to decipher the system."

"Ah, that's what I like to hear. Clouds with silver linings."

"Okay, fingers crossed." Devereaux throttled up and the drive started its usual song, starting at a low-pitched hum and working up through the scale to a soprano whine and then a sensation of nothingness that only a dog might hear. The airframe trembled. But it always did. It was nothing to worry about, nothing at all. "On a wing and a prayer. By guess and by god. Held together with string and gum."

"You're not selling this to me, Dev," Mal said.

Naomi twisted in her seat and checked the neck seal on Phillips's helmet. He looked totally lost in ODST armor, like a small boy trying on his dad's jacket. "Don't want you decompressing, do we?"

"But it's instant, isn't it?"

"No. It's not."

"Oh. Lovely."

Mal was reassured. Things were fine again. Everyone was indulging in the usual chummy, healthy things that squads did: taking the piss, slagging, and joking about things that definitely weren't funny at all. He still wasn't sure if Naomi had a sly sense of humor or meant every literal word, but for a woman with a cloud of family misery hanging over her, she seemed to be bearing up.

Tart-Cart lifted, banking to starboard as she rose above the scrubland, and a piece of plastic tube rolled across the deck. Mal could see Dev through the open cockpit hatch. Her head was turned toward the drive readouts, even though she could have seen that data in her HUD, but everything felt and sounded normal.

How many times have I done this? A hundred? Five hundred? I'd know if there was something wrong. You get used to this. If there's anything out of the ordinary, you can hear it. Smell it. Feel it.

Mal watched the sky in his hull cam feed, willing it to darken faster. Every second that they didn't explode in a ball of flame or start to slow down and lose height was a bonus. The bright blue shaded to violet and then navy, and suddenly he could see stars without the filter of the atmosphere. Nothing had fallen off, cracked up, or burst. *Tart-Cart* moved out into the black velvet safety of space. They'd done it.

"Dev?"

"Yes, Staff?"

"Is the radiator boiling over yet? Or whatever the coolant does."

"Of course it is. You should see the readouts."

"Oh."

"But we've passed the point of greatest demand on the drives. It's okay. The conduits are holding up."

"I'm ever so impressed," Phillips said.

Naomi did a couple of restrained claps but said nothing. Mal joined in.

"Yeah, well done, Dev," he said. There were two bored Huragok waiting in *Stanley* who'd pounce on *Tart-Cart* as soon as she docked to make repairs. They'd *love* it. The dropship would be better than new by the time they'd finished with it.

"And now," Devereaux said, "I'm going to show you something you *really* have to see. Check your HUDs."

"Oh, damn, I can't do this. . . ." Phillips seemed to be moving his head rather than his eyes in a bid to activate the right icon. "Can I take this helmet off now?"

"Yeah, take a look out of the viewscreen." Devereaux gestured to him through the hatch without turning around. "Come up front. Check this out."

Phillips left his helmet on the bench seat and moved forward. It took Mal a few seconds to work out what Devereaux was sending to everyone's display. On first glance he thought it was a section of a refit station, a long slab of a hull with bristles of sensor masts dotted along its length that stretched past the limits of the frame. Then the image tracked to port and the vertical wall of metal plate turned into a flared section bearing white lettering: UNSC INFINITY.

He couldn't quite get the scale. But it had to be bloody enormous.

Phillips was in the cockpit, seeing it with the naked eye. Mal could tell by the whoops.

"Ohhhh my *God.*" Phillips's head bobbed up a couple of times as if he was bouncing in his seat. "Oh my *God,* that's a *monster.* That can't possibly *land* anywhere, can it?"

Vaz started laughing. Phillips loved all this stuff and seemed totally unashamed of his excitement. Mal wondered how the professor would ever make the transition back into academic life, where the biggest battles he saw were probably over parking spaces or dodgy research papers, and then realized that he never would. Who'd want to go back to that? Kilo-Five got to see and do things that no other human being did. This was life, lived.

"Move over, Prof, we want to see her too." Mal got up to peer through the cockpit hatch and found himself jockeying for position with Vaz and Naomi. Phillips slid out of the seat and Mal took his place.

Now he could get the scale of the ship. She was in just the right position to be fully lit by the sun with nothing behind her, hanging there like a long, thin, death-dealing shoebox.

"Oo-er missus," he said.

"And we're still fifty klicks away from her." Devereaux magnified the image on her monitor. "I can't even see *Stanley,* but if we could, she'd be a dot."

Vaz didn't sound remotely excited. "So the hinge-heads have to be able to see her from the ground."

Phillips half-turned to say something to him but he was drowned out instantly by the fire alarm klaxon. Devereaux reached out across the control panel and shut it off.

"'Scuse me, folks, I need to check that's not a real one," she said, squeezing out of her seat. "None of the monitoring's working properly. BB, what are you getting?"

"Something's hotter than it should be in section seven-alpha-ten," he said. "Nothing specific from the entire port quarter, though."

"I'll go." Naomi motioned Devereaux back to the cockpit. *Tart-Cart* was only a heavily modified Pelican airframe, roughly thirty meters nose to tail. There weren't many compartments to check out. "Is the fire suppression still working?"

Osman's voice cut in. BB was embedded in both ships and sharing what little status data was coming out of *Tart-Cart.* "*Port Stanley* to Kilo-Five, I'm standing by."

"Naomi's checking it out, ma'am."

Mal was still in the copilot's seat, listening to Naomi thud down the length of the crew bay and slide open a door in the transverse bulkhead. There was an internal cam facing aft, so he could see the open door and caught a glimpse of Naomi feeling her way along another bulkhead, using her glove sensors to pick up hot spots. Phillips was about halfway down the bay, watching.

"It's pretty hot behind this panel," Naomi said. "If the suppressant system isn't working, you'd better seal the bulkhead behind me and I'll use the—"

She was cut short by a small explosion. A flash of yellow light overwhelmed the cam. Mal didn't get a chance to move before Vaz sprang back into the crew bay, grabbed Phillips's helmet, and slammed it straight down on his head. A sheet of flame shot out and licked over them before dying away as if something had sucked it back.

"Shit shit *shit.*" Phillips was rooted to the spot, armor smoking at the shoulder seals. "Oh shit."

Vaz had a tight grip on his arm. "You're okay. The suit's sealed. Relax."

Mal went aft to check them over. The view from the exterior hull cam showed oddly shaped flames jetting out into space as the oxygen escaped.

Naomi, calm as anything, let out a breath. "Hull breach. Something's blown a hole in the repair."

"Okay, everybody chill," Mal said. "We're all suited and sealed. The fire's not going to kill us, and we're almost home. You okay, Naomi?"

Mjolnir armor was built to take close detonations. More flame licked out from the ruptured compartment for a few seconds and the Spartan just stood there, letting it curl past her. "Hit the fire suppressant, Dev," she said. "It hasn't kicked in automatically."

A mist of nitrite mix clouded the air. It was touch and go whether the fire control system killed the flames first or the oxygen ran out and stifled them. Osman's voice came over the radio.

"How bad is it?" Osman asked. "I've got the cam feed. Everyone okay?"

"We're dead in the water, ma'am," Devereaux said. "The fire's suppressed, but we've lost propulsion. We're going to need a hand."

Phillips pushed back the top filter on his visor. Mal could now see his eyes, and it was the first time the poor bugger had actually looked terrified. A shipboard fire was pretty scary stuff at the best of times, but everyone knew their armor would almost certainly withstand it for long enough to get the blaze under control, and all they had to do was not panic if the flames passed over them. It was a natural animal reflex to fire that took a lot of training to resist. Phillips hadn't had it.

"It's okay, mate," Mal said. There was no shame in being terrified of a blaze in a ship. "You won't cook and you won't asphyxiate. Trust the suit. And underwear washes."

"This," Phillips whispered, eyes still wide, "has been the most amazing week of my entire life. *Fantastic.*"

Mal knew what he meant. There was nothing like pushing yourself to your absolute limits and maybe a bit beyond. You knew you were alive. But they were still fifty klicks from safety, and ODST armor was rated at fifteen minutes in vacuum. Mjolnir's endurance was a lot longer.

"UNSC dropship, this is *Infinity*," said a voice Mal didn't recognize. "Stand by for assistance. We're on our way."

Nobody cheered. It was a measure of how tight the team had become that *Infinity* was almost an interloper. "Ma'am, are you okay with *Infinity* picking us up?" Mal asked.

"Can't refuse," said Osman. "Check her out while you're there, and be nice to the Admiral."

"Hood or Parangosky?"

"There *is* only one."

"Okay." Mal checked his air supply readout. "Dropship to *Infinity,* yes please, and make it snappy. We're on suit air."

"We can do snappy," the voice said. "We've got *frigates* under-slung."

Devereaux let out a breath. Mal thought she was just pissed off that her repairs hadn't held up after all, but then he caught movement on the external cam and saw what had grabbed her attention. A point of light went from a pinprick to a frigate in seconds.

"So that's where our tax dollars went," she said. "Do you think I can sweet-talk them into customizing *Tart-Cart* in their workshop?"

TWELVE

ONE DAY WE'LL LOOK BACK AND REALIZE THAT THE TURNING POINT WASN'T A BIGGER, BETTER SHIP OR BIGGER, BETTER WEAPONS, BUT THE FACT THAT WE ACQUIRED HURAGOK AND OUR ENEMIES LOST THEM. IF WE LOSE A SHIP, WE CAN NOW REPLACE IT WITH AN EVEN BETTER ONE. IF THE SANGHEILI LOSE ONE, THEN THERE ARE NO HURAGOK LEFT TO MANAGE THEIR SHIPYARDS OR CARRY OUT COMPLEX REPAIRS, LET ALONE DEVELOP BETTER EQUIPMENT. EVERY SANGHEILI ASSET WE DESTROY DEGRADES THEIR CAPABILITY FAR INTO THE FUTURE. WARS TURN ON THE ACTIONS OF INDIVIDUALS: FIRST THE SPARTANS, NOW THE HURAGOK.

(ADMIRAL MARGARET PARANGOSKY, CINCONI: DRAFT OF PROPOSED EVIDENCE TO UEG SECURITY SELECT COMMITTEE)

OPPOSITION CAMP, VADAM

"Consider this," Forze said. "It doesn't matter if the rest of the states sit and dither. When the Arbiter's deposed, they'll all creep out of their holes and say they agreed with us all along."

He took the Phantom through clouds of smoke so dense that it seemed more like dusk than morning. Raia remembered that she hadn't called her keep to check that everything was under control, and felt ashamed. No matter: Umira was sensible and wouldn't worry—yet. Raia had shifted her perspective from a ground-level one, the day-to-day life of the keep, to a world seen from an elevated position in every sense of the word. The experiences of the last few days had raised her eyes. She leaned forward a little to get a better view of the terrain as Forze descended over the Vadam coast.

I had no idea all this was possible.

Why are these decisions all made by males? Why don't I have a say in this? Why did I never seek to have one?

She had power within the keep, the power over bloodlines and control of the estate, a responsibility that determined the fate of generations to come long after she was gone: but that wasn't the same. *This* was where the next day, the next week, the next year was decided. This was where things happened that could render all the slower, subtler decisions irrelevant. The choices were made by warriors on battlefields, and she wasn't consulted. Her fear for Jul's safety was tinged with anger at being left behind to pick up the pieces.

Dead ahead, Mount Kolaar was a jagged spearhead shape stabbing the sky, its lower slopes curtained with smoke. She could still see sporadic plasma flashes. If Jul was a prisoner of the Arbiter and held in Vadam keep, then that was the worst place he could possibly be. Fire shot out from the keep at long intervals, and fire spat back. There seemed to be no end in sight.

"Why is it taking so long to dislodge the Arbiter?" she asked. "We used to be able to destroy entire worlds in the course of a day."

"Because destroying someone else's world is warfare, but destroying your own is suicide," Forze muttered. "And . . . *damn* them, something has a lock on us—"

Raia saw a control panel indicator change color and begin pulsing as Forze swung the Phantom around an almost vertical climb. Her stomach plummeted. She grabbed for the closest solid object—the cockpit trim in front of her—as a hot white streak passed wide of the viewscreen and suddenly the sky was clear again. The layer of smoke spread below them like thin, grubby cloud.

"Anti-air defenses," Forze said. "Enough of that nonsense."

He looped to the left and headed back over the coast. The loop turned into a circle, and suddenly he was accelerating back inland again, making the drive scream and skimming lower across the tops of trees and buildings until he was about to crash into them, and then—

Raia wanted to shut her eyes but couldn't. *We're going to crash. We're going to crash. We're going to die.*

The Phantom shuddered as if it had been kicked. Raia's field of view was bleached out by an instant ball of light, then resolved into a pillar of flame and black smoke just as the noise of an explosion hit her in the chest. She felt the shock wave all the way through to her spine.

"That'll teach the traitor," Forze said. He didn't seem shaken at all, more annoyed than anything. "Got him."

Raia let go of the curved cockpit section and sat up, trying to regain her composure. "Got what?"

"The mobile artillery position. My apologies for the close detonation, Raia."

So that was a strafing run, a bombing run, something like that. She'd heard Jul use those words over the years and never really taken much notice, but he should have said that it was terrifying and deafening and so fast that he didn't have time to think. *Then* she would have understood. But perhaps he didn't find it frightening at all. Perhaps he switched into glacial calm. Perhaps he even enjoyed the exhilaration. Or maybe he was just irked by the audacity of someone trying to kill him, like Forze was.

"I'm . . . glad," she said.

"I shouldn't do this with you on board." Forze shook his head slowly. "But then if I had any sense, I should have diverted to

Mdama and taken you home instead of bringing you back to a battle. It might be easier than arguing with you, but this won't help you find Jul."

Yes, she realized that. She also knew that she couldn't just sit at home and wait by the window like some docile, obedient wife from the old sagas. She knew now that she would never be able to do that again even if—no, *when,* it had to be *when*—Jul came back. She had no ambition to become a warrior, but she was never going to be excluded from these decisions again, either.

"There were once female swordmasters," she reminded him.

"I have heard of *one.*"

"A principle is not about numbers. A convention either is, or is not. That one—*is.*"

"Please don't tell me you want to be a warrior."

"No. But I should have the choice."

Forze snapped his jaws a few times, obviously lost for words. "I swear it, Jul will snap my neck when he finds out what I've let you become."

The Phantom jinked again. Raia braced for the flash, shudder, and explosion, but none came. The dropship was now flying slowly over 'Telcam's lines, which looked much more organized than they'd been when she'd left for Acroli. Warriors were massed in orderly groups, Revenants and other transports were lined up on the flanks, and there were even defensive barriers being built, Sangheili and Unggoy digging trenches and piling up earthworks side by side. They seemed to be preparing for a long siege.

"Why are they waiting?" she asked. "The Arbiter can't possibly have more than a thousand troops in there. He's under attack yet nobody has come to his aid. 'Telcam attracts more supporters by the hour. You have at least one ship that could destroy the entire keep. Just *do* it. End it."

"This is politics." Forze landed and shut down the drives. "And

'Telcam is devout. I suspect he wants to hear the Arbiter recant his heresy before he kills him. You don't understand these things."

"Do you?"

"Not always. But I know what I believe in."

"Not the gods."

"Perhaps not, but I do believe in restoring a strong Sanghelios that doesn't need to sign peace treaties."

"But 'Telcam doesn't even *want* the Arbiter's power. Who will rule, Forze? When we cut off the flawed head that we have, what do we put in its place? Anarchy? Confusion? Lesser leaders? Puppets?"

"A kaidon will step up. Someone always does." Forze sounded convinced. "It's better to cut out the source of an infection than to let it poison the whole body while we wait for a cure."

Raia snorted to herself. Yes, it was typical. Warriors were brought up to refuse medical aid as a mark of shame, the fools. She still saw no honor in that, even if it instilled endurance. There was far more virtue in surviving to fight back. She was sure she knew which path the humans would choose.

Humans . . .

She had started the season with no real knowledge of the creatures beyond the occasional stories that Jul told her and the evidence of her own eyes—that they'd spread throughout the galaxy, settling on hundreds of worlds that had not been theirs in her forebears' day. Now she'd seen them face to face, and they confused her. They landed on her world with no visible fear or reverence. They were even given *assistance.* Forze had been told to rescue one of them, and even help them with repairs. This wasn't the future she wanted for her children.

What game was 'Telcam playing? He was devout. Why didn't he just kill every human he met? What was this favor he had to repay?

As soon as she climbed out of the Phantom and walked through the lines, something in the air stung her eyes and she could taste dust in her mouth. Bursts of fire and the occasional short-lived barrage from gun turrets were followed by long silences. It left her with the impression of a group of children throwing stones at a hermit's shelter, wary of entering but trying to provoke him into coming out. But these were warriors. They'd fought a war for decades, a real war of destruction, and they hadn't lost their courage now.

'Telcam was standing some distance behind the front barrier, arms at his sides, staring at the keep as if he was calculating something. Buran, the shipmaster who seemed to be his lieutenant, paced up and down a few meters away. Now Raia could see what was creating the smoke. There wasn't a single tree or bush left intact in the space between the rebels and the walls of the keep. It was a forest of smoldering charcoal. She couldn't tell if the area had been cleared deliberately or if it was simply random destruction from the slow but steady assault on the keep. Astonishingly, most of the front walls were still standing. There were gaping holes in the stonework so big that if she stood in a certain position she could look straight through to the courtyard, but she couldn't see how much damage had been done inside.

'Telcam didn't seem to notice her for a moment. Then he turned around.

"My lady, you shouldn't be here." He was polite but angry, lips drawn back just a little over his fangs. She was no longer someone he needed to placate. "Go back to Shipmaster Forze. Better still, go home. I promise you that I'll keep looking for your husband."

"Why do you tolerate the humans?"

"What?"

"What benefit are they to us? Why do you owe them favors?"

He clenched his jaws. That question had unsettled him for some reason. "Politics," he said.

It seemed to be the universal answer to tell her to mind her own business. She didn't plan to argue the point with him. She would stay here because turning back would feel like she'd given up her search far too easily and too soon. It made no sense, because Jul could have been anywhere and she had no more reason to believe he was in Vadam than on Qikost, but she simply knew she couldn't go home and carry on as before.

"I still fail to understand the role of humans in this," Raia said.

"It's a complex situation because humans are devious creatures. They have a ship in orbit, and I have no idea what it plans to do, if anything."

"Then destroy it. I know we have few working ships, but surely we can destroy one human vessel."

'Telcam snapped his jaws. "At sunset," he said, "you'll see that's going to be a very difficult task. Now, please go somewhere safer. Take cover."

Raia walked away but made a point of not heading back toward Forze. She didn't want to be seen to obey 'Telcam like some groveling Unggoy. She could hear rumbling noises—the sound of large ships, the sound she was beginning to recognize—but she couldn't see where they were coming from, and turned around in a full circle to spot whatever was making it. Then it started: triumphant shouts picked up across the camp, first in ones and twos and then they merged into a wave of sound that swept past her toward the forest at their backs.

" 'Rduan's coming!"

"It's 'Rduan!"

Raia blocked the path of the first warrior she saw when she turned around. She seized his arm. "Who's 'Rduan?"

"That's 'Rduan," he said, pointing behind her. "Shipmaster 'Rduan. Or perhaps I should say that's *Defender of Faith."*

Raia looked around and still couldn't see anything, but the sound of drives was louder now, reaching deeper inside her body. The forest in the distance grew darker. Then she saw it: just a nose at first, a dull silver curve, and then a warship slid slowly over the tops of the trees. Its shadow advanced toward the keep to hang like an eclipse over the camp. The cheering died down and was replaced by a buzz of voices, then the field fell silent, even the plasma fire that had been snapping back and forth between the two positions. Everyone was now facing the shattered walls.

'Telcam, about fifty meters away, leaped up onto the roof of a vehicle. He must have been using a communications device, because Raia could suddenly hear his voice from points all around her, from vessels and warriors alike.

"Thel 'Vadam, you can hear me," he boomed, arms spread. "I know you can. *Surrender.* Surrender now, and we'll spare the rest of Vadam. Come out now and show your cowardly face to the faithful, you blasphemer."

Raia accepted that she knew less about the Arbiter than those who'd served with him, but she was sure that a commander who'd survived so many battles—political and military—wasn't simply cowering in his chamber and hoping his enemy would go away. Where were his ships? Where were his allies?

'Telcam was still standing on the vehicle, pistol in one hand, defying the Arbiter's forces to take a shot. If the Arbiter made any reply, then only 'Telcam heard him.

Raia looked away from the keep for a moment, glancing up at the underside of *Defender of Faith*'s hull. What had happened to the fleet of hundreds of ships? Many had been destroyed in the Great Schism, some had simply broken down and

awaited repairs, but most remained somewhere, seized by kaidons with their own agendas, idling in keeps ready to settle pet-
tier scores.

"Is this it?" she asked, addressing nobody in particular. "One
ship? A handful when we had so many?"

Nobody answered. An elderly warrior covered in scars and
missing a couple of fangs stood with his pistol raised in his left
hand, thumping his fist slowly against his chest plate in a steady
rhythm as if he was singing inside his head and trying to keep
time.

"This is a proper war." He didn't look at her. "The way we
used to fight when we faced equal foes, warrior to warrior. Face
to face. Not the kind of war we fought against *humans*."

'Telcam was still waiting for the Arbiter. A couple of artillery
masters near the front seemed to be tired of waiting and fired a
few rounds, taking out more of the front wall in a shower of stone
fragments. There was no fire returned from the keep, though,
and no sign of the Arbiter. Raia wondered if anyone would have
been able to see him even if he'd walked out to present himself to
them.

"I am *waiting*, blasphemer," 'Telcam roared. "Show yourself.
Face me."

There were a few seconds of silence, restless and fascinating,
and even Raia was caught up in the reined-back urge to rush
the walls. She realized she was gripping her pistol tightly, just as
the males were. Then a trail of white light shot up out of the
grounds of the keep with a deafening crack and struck the ship's
hull, sending plasma dancing over the metal. Small fragments
rained down, glittering in the sunlight, some falling so close to
Raia that they hissed in the air around her, but *Defender of
Faith* held position. A second bolt of energy licked out at the
ship, then a third.

'Telcam had his answer. The Arbiter had spoken.

"Take Vadam," 'Telcam shouted. "Take the keep. And then we shall wipe this state from the map, every last stone."

UNSC *INFINITY*: TWO HUNDRED KILOMETERS
ABOVE SANGHELIOS

Andrew Del Rio walked slowly around the chart table, studying a three-dimensional scan of Vadam so finely detailed that it could have been an architect's plan.

"If only we'd had this thirty years ago," he said, "it would have changed the course of the war."

Vaz was standing close enough to the captain to wonder if the guy was talking to him or simply thinking aloud, so he just grunted to cover both possibilities. The chart was lidar imaging combined with real-time data from a dozen other sensor systems, including the hull and orbital cameras. The image changed continuously as the laser arrays rescanned the terrain and fed back ultra-accurate measurements that were as good as a live schematic of a ten-klick section of the battlefield. Vaz could see the slopes of the mountain, the keep itself, and even the damage to the walls.

He could also see the Sangheili ship lurking nearby. It looked like a small destroyer.

Hood, Parangosky, the XO, and a dozen officers clustered around the chart with their eyes fixed on the image like it was a roulette table about to cough up a fortune. Vaz glanced at Phillips, still in armor and clutching his helmet and plasma pistol, and walked over to the other side of the bridge to join him. They were killing time while the Huragok repaired *Tart-Cart*. Vaz wished they'd stayed down in the hangar.

Phillips leaned in close to him. "You know," he whispered, "from the way Parangosky looks at Del Rio, I'm waiting for her to shoot out this really long lizard tongue and suck out his brain."

"That'd be a ticket-only show."

"Why haven't we got chart technology like that?"

Vaz checked where Devereaux was. He could almost see the cogs grinding in her brain as she watched from the comms station. *We need some of that.* It was written all over her. Then she got up, nodded at Naomi, and the two of them left the bridge.

"I think we're going to get it," Vaz said. "Dev's got her shopping face on. I'd bet she's going to put in another request to the Huragok."

"*Tart-Cart*'s going to be quite a gin palace when they're finished."

Vaz checked his watch again. If the Huragok could dismantle and rebuild armor in under a minute, there was no telling what they'd managed to do to the dropship in the last couple of hours. He'd never worried too much about technology beyond his understanding because his job usually came down to a few basics that hadn't changed in centuries: to shoot before the other guy got a chance to shoot him, and hope that his weapon didn't jam. This distant, technical, detached kind of warfare was a Navy thing, and marine or not, he was still infantry. He went head to head with the enemy on the ground. He was a last-resort, personal kind of war delivered right to the doorstep.

And if this high-tech stuff had been the answer to everything, the UNSC would never have needed ODSTs.

Or Spartans. In the end, it's always down to flesh and blood.

There was no sound accompanying the image on the chart table, just the occasional background buzz of Sangheili voice traffic, but he could see the big artillery pieces inside the keep and scattered among 'Telcam's forces. If Del Rio magnified the image, Vaz could even detect the recoil as gun fired. Another hit on the keep's walls threw up a blur that settled to show a big hole, something he might have struggled to get a clear view of on the ground. But up here, Del Rio had a battlefield image that gave him detail without the clutter, something he might never get from a helmet cam.

Del Rio looked up at Phillips. "I can't tell if this is all they can muster or if they're back to feudal warfare. You know, a few kaidons slug it out and everyone else just locks their doors and waits for it to finish."

"It's both, Captain." Phillips switched instantly from amazed kid to the master of his subject: hinge-heads. It was funny to watch the transformation. "They're still groping for a command structure, but they've selectively bred themselves for fighting. So in a year from now, I think they could be pretty organized again."

"You probably know more about the way they think than any of us. What's this 'Telcam up to?"

Phillips batted away the question without a twitch. "I think that's one for Admiral Parangosky. But he did stop me from getting killed, I suppose, so I'd buy him a beer."

Vaz started wondering how a creature with four jaws would drink a glass of beer, but a sudden burst of light on the chart table distracted him.

Del Rio swung around to Lasky. "Okay, they've opened fire on the ship. Stand by."

"It's *Defender of Faith,*" Parangosky murmured. Nobody asked her how she knew. Fleet seemed to accept that ONI heard all and saw all. "I'd call that compact. Twelve hundred meters length overall, ventral energy beam. Don't see many of those."

"Lasky, what's she doing?" Hood asked.

Lasky leaned over a console that still had disconnected conduit sticking out of it. "Not returning fire, not yet. She's powered up to give him a zap, though." He indicated a sensor screen. "Look at her energy and temperature profiles."

"And that looks like more troops moving in now," Del Rio said. "Are we waiting for a formal request from the Arbiter or not?"

If Vaz had placed a bet, he'd have put his money on the Arbiter preferring to make a last stand on his own rather than beg a human for help. Silent bolts of light shot out from the destroyer and struck the west side of the keep. Why didn't they just bombard the main buildings? But hinge-heads had agendas like anyone else. They seemed to want to get into the keep rather than pulverize it. Maybe there were things that they needed to recover.

"We can probably get the ship's attention and make sure we're justified in targeting her, Captain, but let me help the Arbiter make up his mind." Hood waited a few moments, gazing up at the deckhead, then the muffled sounds of explosions filled the bridge. Hood nodded at the comms officer to open a link. "Arbiter, this is Terrence Hood. Where are your ships?"

There was a little doglike cough. The Arbiter didn't sound like a man who was winning, but at least he still had comms. "They have yet to arrive, Admiral."

So the Arbiter had been left high and dry by his chums. Hood didn't blink, but Vaz knew a man who was enjoying himself when he saw one. "Well, in case they've been held up in traffic," Hood said, "shall we remove that destroyer for you while you're waiting?"

Silence: it was a long pause, probably while the Arbiter wrestled with his hinge-head sense of manly honor. But he was already screwed because he'd gone soft on humans, so what difference did it make if he accepted Hood's help? Vaz had thought the Arbiter was a bit more pragmatic than that. He could always climb back to the moral high ground—if these bastards had any—when he'd crushed the rebels.

"I should decline," the Arbiter said, "but I cannot."

"I'll take that as a yes, then. Stand by." Hood folded his arms and nodded at Del Rio. Parangosky had taken a few steps away from the chart table to sidle up to Mal. Vaz had no idea she could move that fast. "All yours, Andrew."

Del Rio still looked like it was simply an exercise, frowning slightly in concentration. "Aine, give me a projection of where that ship will come down."

Defender of Faith started to lift. She was right above her own troops, but also dangerously close to the keep if she was shot down. Vaz couldn't believe that a simple handshake had brought them to this—that they could be within striking distance of the enemy homeworld, able to destroy what leadership it had left, *all* of it, without any real chance of being hit, and yet they were working out how much collateral damage they'd cause if they took out a destroyer.

This is it. This is the one chance we'll get. Do it now. Screw the treaty. Fry them, maybe seize the destroyer and do a little glassing of our own. Because they'll be back one day. You know they will.

But just as he'd stepped back from shooting Halsey and meting out the justice that he knew damn well the Navy and the courts never would, Hood wouldn't finish off the Sangheili, and neither would Parangosky.

But at least Parangosky's holding back because she knows you have to kill them all in one go, or else you leave enough of them around to start another war.

Vaz looked up at Mal, but Parangosky had steered him away to a quiet alcove. She didn't look as if she was asking him about his dinner plans.

Austen, the principal weapons officer, had both hands on the flat section of his display like a concert pianist composing himself for a really difficult piece. "Howlers ready, Captain—target acquired, altitude five hundred meters, climbing."

"Estimated ground impact?"

"Too close to call."

"Get her attention. Active sensor ping. Let her know we've got a lock on her."

Vaz put his finger to his earpiece and tried to listen in to *Port Stanley*'s channel without making it look too obvious. Phillips took his cue and did the same.

BB's voice whispered theatrically in his ear. "I'm redacting 'Telcam's transmissions, just in case."

"In case . . . ?"

"In case he says something that we don't want Hood to hear."

"Like who he is."

"Like when his prize warship turns into a fireworks display."

Defender had now disappeared from the chart. "Target ascending two thousand meters and locking on, sir," Austen said. "She's got us."

"Pods one, two, and three, spread—fire Howlers."

"Pods one, two, three—missiles away, sir."

Yes, it might as well have been an exercise. Vaz didn't feel any vibration or hear a sound as sixty missiles streaked down at the destroyer below. He couldn't even see what was happening. The chart display was focused on the ground and he was in the wrong place to watch what the hull cams were picking up. Austen counted down, quiet and calm.

"Time to target, ten seconds . . . missiles incoming . . . incoming tracked and neutralized . . . five seconds . . . impact, sir."

Vaz needed to see this for himself. *Defender* hadn't even been able to get her missiles past *Infinity*'s defenses. He went over to the weapons station and watched the hull cam feeds over the shoulders of a couple of ensigns. He wasn't sure what the magnification was, but he could see the destroyer venting vapor and flame, turning slowly to starboard.

"Damage assessment?" Del Rio asked.

"Still making way, but her hull's breached."

"Finish her off, Lieutenant. Pods four and five. Fire."

"Howler pods four and five—missiles away."

Vaz counted but didn't make it to ten seconds before *Defender of Faith* bloomed into a ball of white light. When the fireball died away, the ship's bow section was shredded like a blown tin can and she was spinning slowly, starting to fall out of the sky as her drives failed.

"Aine, debris impact projection," Del Rio said.

"The main hull's likely to fall five kilometers west of Mount Kolaar, in a wooded area." The AI had a flat, disinterested female voice. Vaz got the feeling she'd be a bit of a misery to work with. "There's a lot of smaller debris already falling along that corridor now."

"Good work, Austen." Del Rio managed a smile. "I think I'm going to like this ship."

Hood stepped back from the chart table and nodded to the comms officer again for a link. "Arbiter, this is Hood. In case your sensors haven't detected it, we've disabled *Defender of Faith*. She'll come down around five kilometers west of you."

"That is . . . welcome. Thank you, Admiral."

"And shall we remove some of the trespassers from your front lawn while we're here? Let's nip this in the bud. Or else you'll be fighting these cowboys for years."

Vaz had always wondered what lurked under Hood's aristocratic exterior. Now he knew that something did, but not exactly what it was. He couldn't tell if the guy was reminding the Arbiter who had the real power now, or putting a warning shot across Parangosky's bows—that he knew what she was doing, and he wanted her to know that he knew, but whether he approved of it or not was another layer that Vaz couldn't unravel. Parangosky put her finger to her ear very discreetly, just a casual brush. She was probably listening to BB or Osman.

On the chart table, things were hotting up. Vadam keep was

still under fire, but now the ground assault vehicles were moving forward, slowed down by a sea of troops.

"Arbiter?" Hood said. "Do I have your answer?"

"I still await my ships," the Arbiter said at last, "so I must accept your assistance again."

"Sir, four enemy vessels are entering the sector," Aine said suddenly. "Frigates."

"Target them if they get a lock on us, Lieutenant." Del studied the chart. "And let's lay down some MAC. Without reducing the keep to rubble, that is."

"That's going to push the edge of the impact crater to the shoreline, sir."

"Very educational," Hood said. "I'd notice that and talk about it for weeks, if I were a Sangheili."

"Aye, sir. Fore MAC solution acquired—damage estimate on screen three."

"Months, even," Hood murmured.

Parangosky interrupted. "Gentlemen, we have an informant on the ground in that area. Give me a few moments to get him clear. I'll need to pull him out."

Vaz concentrated on keeping his expression totally blank. Hood looked around but Del Rio didn't.

"Hold MAC," Del Rio said quietly. "I repeat, hold MAC."

The muscles in Hood's jaw twitched but he didn't say a word. It was very bad timing, not like Parangosky at all, but she had to have some plan in mind. She didn't make mistakes. Parangosky just nodded—not to Hood, probably to BB—and long seconds ticked away. Vaz caught Mal's eye and Mal pointed to his earpiece.

Listen in.

"Yes, I would if I were you," BB whispered. Vaz's receiver was suddenly full of snarling and argument, with Osman and 'Telcam going at it like cat and dog, and Osman snapping back: "*Just damn well get out. Get out now. Go to the RV point. Run.*"

Now Vaz knew what was coming next. Mal gestured toward the exit and Vaz obeyed. He looked back once and Phillips was right behind him.

"You better stay here," Vaz said.

"I'm the liaison."

"I'll dump you in the hangar."

"Just try it."

Vaz couldn't hear the comms link with 'Telcam now. All he heard was Parangosky say, "You can resume now, gentlemen." 'Telcam had been given a head start, but it wasn't much.

"Fire fore MAC," Del Rio said.

"Fire fore MAC. MAC away, sir."

The projectile struck the surface like a big meteor impact just as Vaz passed one of the ground monitors. It sent out shock waves like a nuke. There was something so apocalyptic and final about it that he turned to watch and almost stopped in his tracks.

We could pound them into the dirt right now. We could lob in a few more MAC rounds and they'd be screwed for years, maybe forever. You're wrong, Parangosky. For once, you're wrong.

Mal steered him ahead. "Move it, Vaz. You can watch the action replay later."

"Is *Tart-Cart* fixed?" Phillips asked.

"No, we're walking the rest of the way for our health." Mal put on a sprint and pressed the elevator control. "*Of course* she's fixed. Now we've got to extract you-know-who, provided he's not a pile of liver pâté by the time we get there."

Phillips could keep up, but he was puffing. "Is the deck transit back online yet? Maybe they should install miniportals."

"Next left, Vaz," BB said. "No, I said *left*."

"So you've found your true vocation. Satnav."

"I always know when you're upset. You get bitchy. What's wrong?"

"Nothing."

"You can tell me."

"Nothing."

The elevator finally reached the hangar deck and they raced down the passage. A gang of civilian contractors dropped their tools and flattened themselves against the bulkheads. By the time he reached the hangar, Vaz was out of breath and sweating almost as badly as Phillips.

"Now who's the porker?" Mal said, shoving him in the back. "Bloody hell, Dev, what have you done to *Tart-Cart*?"

"She's pimped, Staff." Devereaux waved from the cockpit. "She's loaded. Even an air freshener, which I decided was kind of essential seeing as Phillips has been eating that Sangheili dog food."

The dropship—still matte gray, but now a subtly different shape, and with more small pods protruding from her skin— looked small and lonely in the hangar. A couple of Huragok were still wafting around. Maybe they were pleased with their handiwork; it was hard to tell. Vaz gave them a thumbs-up. They tilted their heads back and forth as if they thought he was trying to sign to them. Naomi reached out and gave him a hand up into the crew bay.

"Have we still got deflective camo, Dev?" Mal asked.

"I made them leave it alone, but they said it was rubbish. Who taught them the word *pants*?"

"Not me," said Mal. "Why's everything my fault?"

Inside, the dropship was unrecognizable except for the basic layout, nothing startling but enough to make Vaz fumble for handles and clips that were no longer there. Naomi thudded into her seat and pointed. A scaled-down version of *Infinity*'s real-time chart appeared in the middle of the crew bay. The Huragok really had been extra-busy.

"Pilot pester power," Naomi said. "Devereaux was very insistent that they gave her the most useful upgrades from *Infinity*."

She was oddly chatty for once. *Is she okay?* Vaz looked for clues. "But they'll do it for anybody, won't they?" *Is she worrying about her dad? How does she manage to bury it?* "They don't care who they arm."

"Probably," Naomi said. "And that makes them more human than we like to admit."

He had to ask. "Naomi, are you okay?"

BB twirled out of the mesh of images and placed his avatar on the seat next to Phillips, killing a delicate moment stone dead. "New toys notwithstanding, boys and girls, I've had an absolute *pig* of a job concealing all that voice traffic between 'Telcam and Osman from *Infinity*. I'll have to have a word with our Huragok colleagues about the comms refinements they keep installing."

"Okay, so we're heading back under friendly fire to save some bastard hinge-head," Mal said. "Let's go. Have you got coordinates for him, and does the ungrateful tosser know we're coming?"

"Yes, I do," said a gravelly Sangheili voice on the helmet comm circuit. "And I have learned a new word, Staff Sergeant Geffen. But I do not require you to *save me*."

BB killed the link. "Shit," Mal said. "That's my diplomatic career over."

"*Huragok,*" BB said peevishly. "This tinkering has got to stop."

"So we're extracting an Elite who doesn't want to leave." Vaz wondered why they couldn't just wait and see who survived the battle and then contact *him* to do a new deal. "That's going to be fun."

Naomi snapped her fingers and killed the 3-D display.

"That's where I come in," she said. "Jul 'Mdama didn't want to leave either."

VADAM, SANGHELIOS

Tart-Cart carved through the atmosphere without so much as a shiver and dropped to skim over the sea, so low that she churned up a skirt of spray.

And there was Vadam. The new chart gizmo laid it all out neatly in colored light, complete with the new section of coastline that hadn't been there when the day started. On the 3-D, the edge of the MAC crater looked like a small harbor. Mal shut his eyes and cringed involuntarily every time he thought about 'Telcam overhearing him. It didn't make sense. He'd killed plenty of hinge-heads and wouldn't lose a wink of sleep about killing more when he had to, but some stupid, embarrassing comment had upended him.

"Here's the captain for you," BB said. "Remember, every mike's a live mike."

"Ha bloody ha." Mal felt his face burn. He steeled himself to apologize. "Ma'am? Sorry about oversharing."

"Don't worry, Staff," Osman said. "I had a rougher conversation with him than that."

"So is he going to refuse extraction, or just sulk?"

"You better prep for resistance. You're going to run into more problems, too. The Arbiter's buddies have started to come out of the woodwork."

"Terrific. Nothing like hedging your bets."

"'Telcam's down to four frigates. I'm going to do what I can to get those past the Arbiter and laid up on New Llanelli. You might run into pissed-off rebels, but I can't guarantee the Arbiter's allies won't take pot shots at you either."

Vaz grumbled to himself in the background. "Well, that makes things simpler. Just like the good old days."

"Yeah, we'll assume they're all hostile, ma'am. So where exactly is he? Other than these coordinates?"

"Holed up in an armored vehicle trading shots with the Arbiter's forces."

"And I've isolated his comms," BB said. "Not easy, because the Huragok keep adjusting the network. I'm blocking it via Aine now. She's not happy, but she can't tell what I've done. Only that she can't access some of her memory and thinks it's a glitch in the ship."

"So, in AI terms, you hit her over the head and stole her purse, right?" Mal asked.

"It's for her own good."

"Okay, if you can't extract 'Telcam, terminate him," Osman said. "In case the Arbiter captures him and he's not as tough as he talks. And that's for *our* own good."

"Understood, ma'am. See you on New Llanelli. Kilo-Five out."

It was so easy to say yes. Mal didn't need to check out Vaz's reaction, but he did glance at Phillips.

"Can you cope with that helmet?" Mal asked.

Phillips still looked a bit swamped by the armor. It was Vaz's old suit, the one they'd given Adj to play with to keep him occupied. "Not really. There's too much info in the HUD and I can't get the hang of the eye control."

"BB, can you strip down the data and manage it for him?"

"Of course." BB's avatar was still sitting on the seat, parcel-style. He made it glitter for a moment. "Piece of cake."

"Is what we're doing legal, Mal?" Phillips asked.

"Do you mean legal or moral?"

"I meant legal, but maybe moral, too. I mean, isn't this how Halsey started on her slippery slope?"

"I believe in playing by the same rules as the bloke I'm fighting. You can't do that with little kids."

"What about kids who can shoot you?"

"You shoot back," Vaz muttered. "But that's not the same as putting the gun in their hands and making them use it."

It occurred to Mal that all of them had an opinion on the Spartan program except the one person it had most affected. Naomi never joined in the debates about its ethics, and she wasn't joining in now. Osman was fairly vocal; that was her right. Mal still didn't know what to do for the best.

"Did you see the Spartan-Fours?" Devereaux was on diplomacy duty, steering them onto a safer course. "I was checking them out. One of them was a really friendly guy. And hot."

"Christ, have you been out trapping already?" Mal seized the chance to change the topic. "You old tart. You've dipped out there, Prof."

"Don't listen to him, Evan. I've always got a gap in my busy diary for you."

"I'll get back to you when I've built some biceps."

"Vaz can lend you one of his," Mal said. "He only uses the right one these days."

Naomi interrupted. She obviously knew damn well what all this was for. "You can cut the chaff and talk about it," she said wearily. "I won't go ape shit. I'll deal with it."

But nobody got the chance to. BB cut in. "Talking of chaff," he said, "we're going to need some any moment now. Coming up on the Vadam coast in thirty seconds."

The 3-D chart turned into an image pretty well as good as the cockpit view. Mal was impressed. Whatever Vadam had been like an hour ago, the area south of the keep looked like a glassed planet minus the vitrification. The haze that hung in the air was probably as much dust as smoke, given how much debris the MAC must have kicked up into the atmosphere when it struck. Flashes of plasma fire flared in the distance. There was still fighting going on, but there wasn't much ground left to fight on.

"Where'd they all go, BB?" Mal asked.

"Like you said, liver pâté. Well, perhaps half. Some have taken their transport and they're pulling back. Some haven't."

An artillery piece fired into the keep. A few seconds later it was hit by a vertical shot from the sky that shattered it into flaming pieces. *Infinity* was obviously busy testing just how small a target she could take out from orbit. Everyone murmured appreciatively.

"I do believe we're destroying hardware that we paid for," BB said. "We could just have had a war with ourselves and saved the fuel."

Mal adjusted his belt, psyching himself up for the insertion. *I didn't survive the war just to get killed saving hinge-heads.* "Slow down, Dev. Are we camouflaged?"

"Yes, but remember that doesn't mean magically invisible."

"Just find the crate that 'Telcam's pinned down in."

"Here," BB said helpfully. "It's this Spirit."

A point on the image in front of Mal lit up red. *Tart-Cart* was circling over an area a kilometer or two south of Vadam keep, half of which seemed to be built right into the mountain itself. No wonder the Arbiter had been hard to shift. But it was still a mess down there: the only way Mal could work out which damage was 'Telcam's handiwork and which was *Infinity*'s was the depth of the craters. The Phantoms, Ghosts, and Wraiths that lay mangled and burning could have been destroyed by *Infinity* rather than local forces.

"Got it," Devereaux said. "Just as well he wasn't planning on leaving."

Now Mal could see the Spirit, perched at an angle with part

of its undercarriage in a crater. One of its twin troop bays was completely missing, and the plasma cannon was buried deep in the dirt, maybe from a crash landing. Devereaux held the dropship at a hover at about 150 meters while Mal watched for activity. The back and forth of plasma fire looked like a dozen Elites outside trying to dislodge one inside.

"He's not going to be grateful," Mal said. "But drop those buggers anyway. Clear them out, Dev."

"On it."

Devereaux brought *Tart-Cart* down in a slow loop and then opened up with the chin gun. That was the point when camo and stealth went down the pan. She got a direct hit on three hinge-heads on the ground but the others scattered in two groups, one taking cover behind the Spirit and the other heading back to the keep.

"Okay, in we go," Mal said. "Dev, give us some cover and then go finish off the ones heading for the keep. Have they called it in, BB?"

"No. No radio at all at the moment."

"Okay, Dev, we need to shut them up before they go telling tales to the Arbiter."

"Understood."

Mal couldn't remember the last time he'd had the luxury of planning for an assault. He'd grown used to the idea that he'd be thrown into situations where he didn't know the layout of the objective or the enemy's strength, and all he could do was think on his feet. One day that wasn't going to be enough. He'd been lucky so far but he was waiting for that luck to run out.

Tart-Cart rocked on her supports and the hatch flew open. "Go," Dev said. "Not you, Phillips."

Vaz pushed him back in his seat as the ODSTs and Naomi jumped out onto the churned soil beneath. The dropship lifted and screamed away, gun chattering in bursts, but Mal couldn't look around to check if Devereaux was hitting the targets. He ran for the cover of a trench gouged by an explosion. From ground level, the terrain was so ripped up that it almost felt hilly—steep inclines, poor lines of sight, and deep holes to fall into. He dropped down behind the cover of a ridge formed from tree roots, minus trees. Vaz and Naomi flopped down next to him.

Plasma fire spat over their heads. Mal never wanted to ask Naomi to break cover first, but it made most sense because she had better armor and she could outrun anything. He still thought he should be the one to do it. He gestured at Vaz to go wide to the left, then took out a grenade. Neither of them needed telling. Mal would throw it, and then they'd go in to finish off anything that was still moving.

Mal lobbed the grenade over the top of the Spirit. The explosion showered dirt everywhere, cuing Vaz and Naomi to break and run for it. Mal scrambled over the tree roots and found Naomi was already meters ahead of Vaz in seconds, just careering through the debris and somehow managing not to get bogged down by the weight of her Mjolnir. She was like an armored vehicle in her own right. Most of the plasma bolts were streaming at her now but she just kept going, firing one-handed before jumping over a section of the Spirit's broken port bay to land on something behind it and fire a few rounds into it. Mal went right and emptied his clip into a hinge-head who popped up above the Spirit's cockpit, sending him tumbling down the side of the ship. By the time Mal reached the airframe, Naomi was standing on the top of the cockpit, firing on the ground behind.

Suddenly there was no plasma fire coming back at them. Naomi turned around and looked down at Mal.

"Five down," she said. "Just 'Telcam left."

Mal got on the radio. "Dev, how you doing?" He couldn't

hear any cannon now, but he could just about see the shimmering patch of sky that gave away *Tart-Cart*'s position. "Did you get them?"

"Four," she said. "I'm right behind you—contact, wait one." The dropship's cannon rattled for a few seconds. "Sorry, had to deal with a gatecrasher. I'm setting down behind the Spirit."

Naomi jumped down to the curve of the hull and pointed to the hatch. Vaz signaled that he was ready. Mal decided to bite the bullet and talk to 'Telcam, man to hinge-head.

"'Telcam," Mal said. "Can you hear me? Sorry about the bastard bit."

'Telcam took a couple of seconds to answer. Naomi tested the hatch.

"I will not run from a battle, Sergeant," 'Telcam said in immaculate English. "Go home and lick your wounds."

"Not now we've gone to all this trouble." Mal gestured to Naomi. "You know what they say. He who fights and runs away can come back later and do some *really* serious damage."

Naomi took a determined hold on the hatch control cover and gave Mal a thumbs-up. *Tart-Cart* landed close by, scattering leaves. Vaz pointed to a big hole in the Spirit's hull. Well, that was simple enough: Naomi would go in via the hatch and Vaz would get the bugger if he came out of the hole. They couldn't hang around and argue the toss with him.

"Get him out, Naomi," Mal said.

Perhaps he wasn't dumping the tough jobs on her. She'd done it before. For a Spartan, she was having a pretty sedate life with Kilo-Five and she needed to stay busy. She ripped open the controls with a couple of determined tugs, dropped into the hatch, and disappeared. Vaz crouched with his rifle aimed and Mal joined him to wait for 'Telcam to emerge from the hole. Then all Mal heard was a stream of Sangheili that BB didn't translate, followed by the crack of a plasma weapon.

"I'll kill you, demon." Mal understood that just fine. "You won't shoot me."

"No, but I can do *this.*" There were a few thuds and scuffling sounds. "Damn it, somebody give me a hand."

Vaz crept into the shattered vessel at a crouch with Mal behind him. The interior was completely dark inside except for shafts of watery sunlight from holes Mal had noticed earlier, but that was enough light to see Naomi kneeling on the hinge-head and struggling to hold him down by the scruff of his neck. He was bigger and heavier than Jul, more of a handful. Mal resisted the temptation to put a boot in the thing and just shoved his rifle in its face instead.

"Field Master," he said, "I'm trying to be polite, but we're risking our lives to get you out. That means you're coming with us. Pull back, regroup, and have a nice cup of tea. Okay?"

"*I* will decide!" 'Telcam snarled defiance. "*I'll* choose whether I fight or not! I am not your *servant!*"

"I've got my orders," Mal said. "And right now, you're getting your arse handed to you out there. Come on."

Vaz slung his rifle and knelt down to put some restraints on him. "You'll thank us later," he said. A loud explosion outside shook the whole ship. "Great, we're going to get creamed by our own guys."

"Move it. Get him out."

Naomi and Vaz hauled 'Telcam to his feet and bundled him outside to *Tart-Cart.* Unlike Jul 'Mdama, he didn't have to be dragged like a sack of spuds. He'd calm down. He'd see sense when he got to New Llanelli and found he had some ships left and some allies who were still prepared to arm him.

Devereaux was almost revving the dropship's drive as 'Telcam squeezed into the crew bay, head lowered to avoid the trunking. He was even taller than Naomi.

"Got to go," Devereaux said. "The trouble with *Infinity* not knowing exactly where we are is that she's going to end up hitting us if we don't get clear."

'Telcam sat on the edge of the seat like a grown-up trying to look relaxed at a kid's tea party, head thrust forward. Naomi took off her helmet and glowered at him. She seemed to want to show hinge-heads that they'd been knocked down by a woman, because she'd done the same with Jul, and she tended to live in that helmet. But 'Telcam didn't react. Mal took off his own helmet and raked his fingers through his hair, noting that it needed cutting, and watched 'Telcam turn his attention to Phillips. The armor and plasma pistol definitely troubled him.

Yeah, that was going to be an interesting conversation at some point.

"Okay, boys and girls, we're off the charts now," Devereaux said. "Including *Infinity*'s. Next stop, the lovely glasslands of New Llanelli."

"Dev, how close did we come to getting char-grilled by Del Rio?" Mal asked.

"Very."

That, Mal decided, would be his personal limit. He hadn't reached it yet and he hadn't even realized it existed, but if bailing out these hinge-heads cost one human life, then he was asking for a transfer. There were some prices he'd never be willing to pay, not for ONI, and not even for Osman.

In the end, he'd rather have done business with a dozen Staffan Sentzkes than one 'Telcam. Maybe Vaz had a point after all.

CHAPTER
THIRTEEN

I HAVE GIVEN MY WORD TO THE ARBITER, AND WHILE IT
MIGHT NOT BE FASHIONABLE TO BELIEVE THAT STILL HAS
SOME MEANING, I SHALL KEEP IT UNTIL HE NO LONGER
HONORS HIS.

(ADMIRAL LORD TERRENCE HOOD, OINCFLEET)

UNSC *PORT STANLEY*, SOMEWHERE OFF SANGHELIOS

Sanghelios was becoming familiar in the same way as the moon over Sydney.

There was the coast that looked like a jigsaw-puzzle piece that would fit neatly into the Bay of Biscay; there was the huge inland sea shaped like a bow tie. On the night side of the planet, city-states were picked out in points of light. Osman stood at *Stanley*'s full-length bridge viewscreen with her arms folded and wondered what her first impressions of the planet would have been if she'd discovered it yesterday rather than years ago as a war out of the blue.

It did a good impression of looking normal and harmless. She hadn't ruled out visiting it again. While she watched, the reflection of a holographic blue box drifted by and hovered beside her.

"Are you sure *Infinity* can't track us, BB?"

"You really don't trust Huragok now, do you?"

"I think the analogy of a hyper-intelligent toddler who's into everything fits them pretty well. Just tell me."

"No, Captain, they haven't touched the stealth system. They understand why we have to be able to go dark."

Because we do all the mucky, dishonorable stuff that the Navy prefers to believe never happens.

It was basic security. Stealth vessels had to be able to hide even from their own fleet so that they couldn't be tracked down if another ship fell into enemy hands. But she knew it was also handy for Fleet to be able to deny all knowledge of ONI activity.

"'Telcam's on his way to New Llanelli now, and Phillips is trying to be sociable with him," BB said. Osman had learned to deal with the concept of AI omnipresence by thinking of them as gossiping on a mass of ever-open comm channels. "It's bit of a stretch for *Tart-Cart*. But she'll make it. She's got a slipspace drive now."

"Is Devereaux actually rated to fly that?"

"She's got *me*, Captain."

"I know, I know."

"And who's going to argue about it? We're ONI."

"But dropships with slip drives . . ."

"Yes, it's the work of Beelzebub. Isn't it fabulous? Let's order another one."

BB was right. There was nothing to worry about. What was the point of having Huragok if you couldn't let them do wildly indulgent but very useful things like beef up an already heavily modified Pelican? There were no rules now.

And if there are . . . I'll be the one writing them.

Osman thought that not with satisfaction but with growing unease. She stood utterly alone in the corvette. Even BB, friend and bodyguard and lieutenant that he was, didn't quite count right then. Sometimes life could be heavy-handed with its metaphors, as if she hadn't been listening when it kept warning her that the higher she climbed, the more isolated she'd become, until she'd find herself with no hands left above her to reach out to.

This is what being CINCONI is going to feel like. No safety net. No supervision. Nobody to tell me how to do it.

It wasn't like command of a ship at all. There were no charts and no regulations. This mission was her test, her coming of age, and Parangosky knew it. The admiral could never have engineered this situation, but she'd certainly given Osman the leeway within it to sink or swim.

But that's what it's about. Earth has to be able to count on me long after Parangosky's gone.

As soon as the thought formed, Osman didn't like the sound of it.

"Ships, BB," she said. "Show me. Where are they?"

"Voilà." BB flashed the chart of Sanghelios's northern hemisphere on the viewscreen in front of her. Adj and Leaks had made a few more refinements. "We have four frigates . . . *Promised Redemption, Cleansing Truth, Certain Prophecy,* and *Transforming Splendor.* I do wish they'd learn to use proper ships' names like *Victory* and *Bellepheron,* don't you? Theirs sound like color swatches from an ecclesiastical paint catalog. Anyway, they're getting ready to withdraw."

"And what's *Infinity* up to now? She must be able to track those frigates too."

Another image appeared on the viewscreen—a wide shot of the ship's bridge. It didn't add any information that BB couldn't have given her but it was interesting, and she had a better idea of the prevailing mood over there.

"Unfortunately, yes. So Hood's sharing that data with the Arbiter."

"But he's not planning to pursue them himself."

"No, he's just sharing intelligence. Want to hear the Arbiter's side of it?"

"Just give me the digest."

"The Arbiter's waiting to send three of his cruisers after them. He's planning to intercept when they're clear of the planet and before they jump, to minimize damage on the ground."

"He's going soft."

"He's political. He doesn't want to alienate any states that haven't taken sides yet."

"There you go. Ruining my illusions." Osman watched the activity on *Infinity*'s bridge for a few more moments, checking that Parangosky was okay—drinking coffee, so yes—and wondering if she could ever look Hood in the eye again. He'd been so generous to her: he was a decent man, a naval officer of the old school. Perhaps he knew what she'd become anyway. "Okay, stand by. The Arbiter's going to lose three cruisers today."

She settled in her chair and dug her fingers into the armrests. It was a habit now. She realized how physically literal she'd become: she stood alone, and she got a grip. There were probably a dozen little mechanical actions in her day that told the truth in a way she felt she couldn't.

"You're not comfortable about this, are you?" BB said.

"I wouldn't say I wasn't *comfortable*." Osman had four Shivas and two bays of enhanced yield Rudra nukes, enough to do the job. "I've just never fired on a ship that wasn't planning to attack me. And I suppose this puts the seal on it. Undermining Fleet feels like internal politics until you shoot down an ally they've worked hard to get a treaty with. It's all little too real."

BB drifted in close and settled on the console in front of her. He had human body language down to a T, a remarkable thing considering that the most un-boxlike form he'd taken had just been to add a shiny red bow to mark Parangosky's birthday. She did what she always did: she looked him in the eye, the front face of the cube.

"Captain, you don't *have* to succeed the Admiral, but if you do, then this is the way it's always going to be." He'd lost that casual, arch superiority that was so endearing. Now he was serious: paternal, even, a side she hadn't seen before. "Vaporizing three Elite warships is nothing compared to the things you're going to have to sanction in the future. Consider this your actual initiation. Not contrived to happen, but an inevitable transition, and I think you'd never ask any crew to do what you wouldn't do yourself."

She wasn't following orders. She was giving them. *I'm a captain. How did I make captain and not think this through?* There was no rule book she could reach for, no higher authority, because UNSC *was* that authority, not the civilian government, so the only answers would come from her own conscience.

"In twenty years, I might be standing on a glassed planet again, saying that I wished I'd done something when I had the chance."

"I could make the decision for you."

"No."

"Thought as much."

This was what friends did. They let you talk your way through a dilemma. "Okay, BB, take us into position. I want all of the Arbiter's cruisers on this plot so that when 'Telcam's flotilla makes its move, I can start taking them out."

"What if he deploys all five?"

"I have to leave him at least two hulls to keep things balanced. If he manages to block any of 'Telcam's frigates, I'm going to need a nondestructive solution."

"Winging the bad guy in the shoulder only works in the movies."

"Okay, then we risk warning the frigates so they can take evasive action."

"I do an awfully good Kig-Yar accent. Seeing as I'm going to spoof Aine's sensors into believing a big Kig-Yar did it and ran away, I might as well stay in character." BB seemed to feel his pep talk had hit the spot. He'd put up that barrier of slick cynicism again. "Covering up distinctive energy signatures from the detonations is going to be tricky, but perhaps I should just brazen it out and let everyone think the Jackal lads have acquired some UNSC hardware. They probably have, and it'd give the Sangheili one more faction to get mistrustful and paranoid about, too."

"How are you going to explain why *Infinity* can't hit us if she tries? Hood knows she can't miss. If he targets our spoof signal and there's no explosion, he'll know something's wrong."

"I have a secret weapon. The Mark One Parangosky. She'll intervene."

"I think *you* should be CINCONI."

BB suddenly turned navy blue and sported a rear admiral's gold braid like a belt. He twirled. "No . . . horizontal stripes make me look fat," he said. "Besides, I'd have to behave."

He'd made his joke and now he expected her to crack on with what had to be done. She obliged. 'Telcam's frigates showed up as small red dots assembled north of Ontom. The Arbiter's cruisers, now shown as green dots, were scattered over a wider arc, and that would make it harder to cover them: but it would also make it easier for her to avoid being identified. She'd need to talk to 'Telcam and get him to corral his shipmasters.

"Can you get me *Tart-Cart*?"

"Anytime, anywhere," BB said. "She's got the full *Infinity* comms package now. Wait one."

Osman hoped 'Telcam had calmed down by now. It couldn't have been easy to have lurched between defeat and victory and then suffer the indignity of being rescued.

She only had to wait a few seconds before Mal responded. The image from *Tart-Cart* made it look as if things were under control, although she couldn't see the aft section from the camera position. "How are we doing, Staff?"

Mal looked content and relaxed, but then he always did even if all hell was breaking loose. "Phillips is having a nice chat with 'Telcam, ma'am."

"Is he in the right frame of mind to call his frigates and get them to cooperate with us to escape?"

"You want to talk to him?"

"Yes. Put him on."

"Good luck."

No, 'Telcam wasn't going to be placated that easily. He popped up in front of the camera with all his fangs showing. Tiny drops of spit flecked the lens. "Why do you insult me this way?" he demanded. "How *dare* you abduct me. How dare your worthless admirals make war on me like this. How dare—"

"And how dare you open fire on my troops. Look, you're no use to anyone dead, Field Master. And you can't beat *Infinity* with a pistol." It did no harm for him to be reminded of the ship's capability. "Now you understand my problem. Your frigates are going to be blown apart by the Arbiter if we don't cooperate on the next phase. I can track his vessels and warn your shipmasters, but you're going to have to tell them to stand by for a message from a Kig-Yar vessel. Because I don't think they'll be amused by a call from a human right now."

"You do so love understatement."

"And you need your frigates. Please send the message. Staff Sergeant Geffen will give you comms access." She paused. She wondered whether to threaten to synth his voice and get BB to do it, but he didn't need to know she could do that, not unless or until she needed to sow more doubt and confusion. "We don't have long. Pull your ships out *now* and regroup."

'Telcam snapped his jaws a couple of times. Phillips would know if he was sending the wrong kind of message and BB would just pull the plug. "Very well," 'Telcam said. "But this is the last time you force a course of action on me."

He disappeared from view and Osman assumed he'd gone back to his seat. She made sure she was back on earpiece only. "BB, park yourself in *Tart-Cart* for a while. If 'Telcam deviates from that message, cut him off."

"Fragment already in place, ma'am."

Port Stanley held position over the pole, ready to move. Now all Osman could do was wait. She sat watching the chart even though BB would have alerted her when the ships started to move. Seeing the translucent hemisphere for herself gave her a better physical sense of what she needed to do—but again, BB could have done it all. That wasn't the point. She had to do it herself, the old-fashioned way, so that she grasped the scale of what she was taking on.

"Here we go, Captain," BB said. "They're moving."

"Okay, send the message. Tell them we're going to track the Arbiter's fleet."

"Done."

"That was quick."

"Oh, I recorded it earlier. . . ."

He was a gem. "Okay, take us in, BB."

And there they were, moving away from Ontom: four red dots, flying out across the ocean and gaining altitude. *Infinity* appeared as a single blue spot, but Osman had the ship's bridge feed on a display to her right and could see that Del Rio wasn't lifting a finger. She could hear Hood talking to Lasky, discussing rules of engagement regarding vessels leaving exclusion zones, and then the green dots started to move, too. The Arbiter still had access to comms intercepts or radar, then.

Even if 'Telcam's fleet made it to their jump point without a scratch, she still had to destroy three of the Arbiter's cruisers. *Port Stanley*, completely undetectable, had missiles waiting to fire. It didn't really matter which ship survived and which didn't, and that was the only thing about the attack that bothered her: the randomness of choice, which felt almost careless. That was the best way to tackle it, a simple numerical exercise devoid of anger or retribution, but it still didn't feel right.

"I have firing solutions on *Far Vision, Axiom,* and *Devotion,*" BB said. "Shame, because they're *much* nicer names."

The Arbiter's ships were converging on the frigates now, closing the gap faster than she expected.

"Frigates preparing to jump," BB said. "They really need to get a move on."

On the chart, it looked marginal to Osman. She had to intervene now.

"Tell them we're coming in," she said. "And you better make sure that *Infinity* doesn't try to target ghosts."

FORMER COVENANT FRIGATE *CLEANSING TRUTH,* PREPARING TO LEAVE SANGHELIOS

Raia had never imagined things would go this badly wrong so fast.

She tried to find a quiet corner on the deck to make sense of what had happened and work out how she would contact Umira and Naxan to let them know where she was. As she picked her way through the warriors on the deck, she almost tripped over a very young male who was half-slumped in an alcove with his legs sticking out. He was trying to get up. She was a mother: in this confused, frightened moment, her unthinking reaction was to reach out to help him.

And then she saw the blood, glossy and dark on the deck, and congealing between the gaps in his armor. She should have known better.

"Leave me," he said. "Leave me, my lady."

He waved her away. Perhaps someone else would help him, or perhaps not, but he was ashamed of being wounded and would refuse help. That was the way her sons were being trained, too, but she decided that would all change when she got home. It was a senseless ritual that achieved little when it came to winning battles. Naxan would be outraged. And she would stand her ground.

We need every warrior we can get. This is why we're fleeing, isn't it? That's why we've gathered as many men and as much equipment as we can recover, and why we're escaping beyond the Arbiter's reach. So that we return to achieve something—not so that we have some noble act of sacrifice to carve into the saga wall.

Raia kept going and tried not to look at anyone in case she felt compelled to help again and simply railed at some unlucky male instead. She was heading for the bridge to find Forze. Every deck was crammed with troops, not all of them alive. Many bodies had been recovered, to be taken home for dignified funerals.

Killed by humans. By the Arbiter's human allies. He can't even fight his own battles.

The bridge seemed a little more familiar now. She knew what some of the sensor screens were showing even if she couldn't interpret them. Then a hand gripped her shoulder and she turned around to find Forze looking relieved, eyes half-closed for a moment.

"Please don't wander off again," he said. "I thought I'd lost you. That would be a terrible thing to have to tell Jul when he returns, wouldn't it?"

"Where are we going now?"

"Laqil. 'Telcam's made contact—he's heading there with some other allies. I have no idea who they are. That's all he'd

say. He's very secretive, but then the humans and the Arbiter
seem to hear too much. Perhaps discretion is wiser."

"He's running away."

"No more than we are, my lady."

"But we'll return, won't we?"

"We withdraw, we make plans, and we return. We're not
beaten. And now we know the humans for what they are."

"The clan will think I'm dead," she said. "Jul and I, both
missing."

"If I returned you to Mdama, they'd track the ship and your
keep would pay the price. If you send a message, they might
track that, too. We must bide our time."

"I know. And I have to find Jul."

"It's a temporary absence."

"I know that, too."

Raia was leaving Sanghelios for the first time in her life for
a world she'd never heard of. She regretted the moment she'd
packed that small bag and barred 'Telcam's way. She should
never have left, but then she knew she wouldn't have been able
to forgive herself if she'd stayed at home and waited in dutiful
ignorance.

"Shipmaster, 'Telcam has sent another message," someone
called. "He says a Kig-Yar vessel will help us."

A big, heavily scarred male straightened up and rose a full
head above the rest of the warriors on the bridge. He must have
been bent over looking at the control panel. "How much are
they charging us for *that*?"

"This is *genuine*, Shipmaster Galur. 'Telcam insists." The warrior pressed something and suddenly 'Telcam's voice filled the
bridge. It was him, most certainly. "They'll give us the position of
the Arbiter's fleet, and cover our withdrawal if need be."

"So the Arbiter failed to pay his bills, then . . ."

"Galur, this is Avu Med 'Telcam," the voice boomed. "I

strongly suggest you take the aid the Kig-Yar offer while you still can."

Galur hit a control button so hard that it looked as if he'd punched it. "Very well. Stand by."

"Why are Kig-Yar helping us?" Raia asked.

"Why did we help humans?" Forze spread his arms. "Politics. The galaxy is less clear-cut and orderly than it used to be."

If Raia heard the word *politics* one more time as an explanation for everything and nothing, she swore she'd sink her fangs into somebody. When she got home, when she finally found Jul and returned to Bekan keep, she wasn't going to tolerate this nonsense any longer. The galaxy *had* changed—and the Sangheili had to change, too. She squeezed through the press of bodies, drawing no attention, which was a measure of how urgent the preparations to leave had become. The deck vibrated beneath her feet. They'd make their move soon.

"This is Shipmistress Lahz. I have a warning for all ships."

The voice was enough to get instant silence on the bridge. It was Kig-Yar, a female. It was also confident and measured: so Kig-Yar females were used to authority, used to serving in ships. Raia had rarely come into contact with the creatures except when the scruffy males came to the keeps trying to sell overpriced goods, and her view of them was largely shaped by Jul and Naxan debating what would happen to the stability of the Covenant if they were ever allowed better weapons and ships. They were not to be trusted.

But now there was no choice.

"Continue, Jackal," Galur said. "I'm listening."

"Make your move now. The Arbiter has five cruisers positioned to pursue and destroy you. Get to jump velocity as quickly as you can."

"I can work that out for myself. I can *see* them." Galur pointed to a display, but there was no way that the Kig-Yar could know that. This was for the crew's benefit. The illuminated grid rotated to show five lights. "But I can't see *your* ship. Look, if you run into your kin, that diseased thief Sav, tell him we want *Pious Inquisitor* back. We have our own special *me-vut* out on him."

The Kig-Yar didn't seem daunted. "I know no Sav, and if I find your ship I'll expect recompense for recovering it, but right now you need to watch your display, and set your sublight drives to full power."

"I cooperate purely because 'Telcam advises it."

"Good. Keep watching your sensors. And get out now while you still can."

There was still something about this Kig-Yar, this Lahz, that didn't quite fit with Raia's view of the species. Everyone who wasn't busy with other duties did as Lahz suggested, though, and watched the grid. The five lights were now moving, one of them accelerating toward Ontom at a speed that caught everyone by surprise. The Kig-Yar must have known what was coming. Somehow, they could *hear*.

The Kig-Yar's voice was suddenly more distant, as if she was talking to someone else. "Missile one—fire."

The fast-moving cruiser kept accelerating for a few more seconds. Galur's helmsman reacted: the vibration in the deck suddenly increased and Raia felt the frigate lurch away, making its escape. But as she watched the grid, unable to turn away, the point of light that was the Arbiter's cruiser vanished. All around her, other sensor screens changed color or indicated spikes.

"What's happening?" Galur demanded.

"What does it look like, you fool? I've destroyed one of their cruisers." The Kig-Yar sounded furious. "Move or die. Your choice. Now do what you have to while I target the others."

"She's right, my lord," the helmsman said. Raia couldn't see outside the hull, but she could feel that *Cleansing Truth* was now soaring to the edge of the atmosphere. "*Devotion* has gone. There's been a massive explosion—possibly a human radiation weapon."

Galur was losing that swaggering disbelief. He swung around and faced the display. Raia could see it too, but there were now too many lights and she didn't know which were enemy vessels and which were 'Telcam's.

"I still don't see your ship," Galur roared. "Where are you?"

"Don't waste your time worrying about my position," Lahz said. "Fear for your own."

"You have radiation weapons. Human missiles."

"We've acquired *many* interesting pieces of military surplus."

Something on the display changed. Everyone drew in a sharp breath. Another point of light had vanished. The deck vibrated beneath Raia's feet as *Cleansing Truth* picked up speed.

"That was *Far Vision*," the helmsman said. "Gone. She's gone."

"Run, Shipmaster," Lahz said. "I cannot take them all. *Run*."

"And *another*!" The helmsman's voice rose in pitch. "The cruiser *Axiom* has gone!"

"How long before we can jump?"

"We need more time, my lord." The helmsman held up all four fingers. *Cleansing Truth* was shuddering now. "A little longer—"

Lahz shrieked. *"Shipmaster, watch your stern!"*

"*Swordsman* has a lock on us, my lord."

"Evade her."

"I cannot. I—we've been hit, we've been hit—"

The deck suddenly rippled under Raia like a wave, metal made fluid as water.

She grabbed blindly as she slid down what was now a steep slope, then a vertical wall. Forze's hand clamped on her wrist. An alarm screamed, so loud that the noise filled her nose and mouth until she felt that she couldn't breathe. She bounced against something hard and she felt something break, but couldn't tell if it was her bones or the object she'd hit. Then she stopped falling. Others didn't. She was a rock in a river, hunkered down against a fierce torrent of bodies. The air was thick with acrid smoke and hissing vapor. Bright red light was coming from somewhere. Then she realized it was fire.

"Raia, hang on," Forze roared. "Raia, we've survived one crash. We'll survive this, I swear."

More bodies hit her, warriors who could grab nothing to stop their fall as the frigate—the entire world—turned inside out and upside down in a groaning, screaming chorus of metal as it twisted and tore apart.

"Forze! *Forze!*"

But Forze tumbled past her and was gone. She didn't know what was still holding her in place. She was on a ledge, the end of a console of some kind. Its lights were on, violet and amber. But the red light was getting brighter: fire was sweeping the deck. She could feel the heat on her face.

The communications system was still working. Lahz, the Kig-Yar, was still cursing Galur for delaying. *"Idiot,"* she shrieked. "Why didn't you listen? I tried, you fool, I *tried.*"

Raia found her heartbeats were now slowing into days, giving her pause to think, freezing time so that she could ponder on how wrong Jul had been about Kig-Yar. And Forze had lied for all the right reasons, because there was no surviving this.

She was falling. The *ship* was falling.

Her last thoughts shouldn't have been regrets, but they were. She regretted this venture, and she regretted that neither she nor Jul would ever know what happened to the other.

No, this was not the last thought that would ever be on her mind. It would *not.*

Raia thought of her sons, and was glad of the moment left to do it. She wondered if they would think of her, and forgive her for never coming home.

**UNSC *PORT STANLEY*, EN ROUTE FOR NEW LLANELLI,
BRUNEL SYSTEM: KNOWN AS LAQIL TO THE SANGHEILI**

Adj and Leaks had worked high-speed miracles on the slipspace comms. BB tested the relays and felt a little put out that he didn't quite grasp all the subtleties of the modifications. But gift horses like Huragok were to be petted and fed, not subjected to intrusive dental examination. He'd get them to explain it to him later.

"So, shall we make the most of the luxury of being able to talk to *Tart-Cart* and collect her, Captain?" BB asked. "She's got quite a slog ahead to catch up with us, and the sooner we disembark 'Telcam, the happier everyone will be. Especially Mal. And 'Telcam."

Osman stood on the bridge with her arms folded, distracted. She stared out the viewscreen at absolute slipspace nothingness and tossed a chunk of crystallized ginger in her palm like a coin she was preparing to flip.

"Yes, BB. Let's get her docked."

"And then there's the new nav system. That'll be nice. No more slipspace guesswork."

"Yes. Great. We'll need to lock up the Huragok or keep 'Telcam in the dropship. Actually, I'm not sure I want him seeing anything of *Stanley,* either, even if it has deterrent value."

"You're babbling. Is there something wrong?"

Osman turned around. She didn't have to. But she addressed his avatar just like the rest of the crew did, so he was starting to think of himself in terms of being located in the hologram, too. It wasn't who he was. He was in danger of acquiring a *body*.

"Shame about the frigate," she said. "Never thought I'd hear myself say *that*."

"But three made it out, and that's a good result."

Osman looked around at the cam feed from *Infinity*'s bridge. BB had wondered whether to just mute it and give her a digest later, but he'd left it running. There was a lot of consternation about the destruction of the three cruisers. Maybe he should have done a lot more spoofing and embroidered the bogus vessel into blowing up and no longer being a worry, but the less he interfered with Aine's data, the less there was to go wrong and unravel. On the other hand, he'd started hares running about Kig-Yar having nukes, but there was nothing he could do about that now.

It was nowhere near as worrying as their acquiring a Covenant ship with a ventral energy beam. There was a good reason why the Covenant didn't trust Kig-Yar with fast translight drives, big weapons, or the family silver. But Hood was still having a quiet, dignified fit about the nukes, leaning on the chart table on both hands while Del Rio and Lasky stood back and watched. Parangosky lounged in a nearby chair, cane resting across her lap.

"Yes, Margaret, *yes,* I accept that the Kig-Yar pick up assets that they shouldn't," Hood said. "But I want to know where they acquired something that pumps out an energy signature very like a Rudra, and why the Arbiter's cruisers couldn't acquire a target. They could detect it. They just couldn't hit anything. How? Why?"

"I'd love to know, too," Parangosky said. "I thought I made it clear that's why I want that ship in one piece. Leave it to Osman. She's gone hunting."

"I've gone along with this. I let that vessel escape. But damn it, Margaret, this had better be worth it, because the Arbiter knows we're not incapable. He'll think we're *unwilling.* And I gave him my word."

BB saw Osman put her hand to her eyes as if she was watching a distressing movie, which she was, in a way. She was feeling guilty for upsetting Hood, but she was going to have to get used to it. ONI did that on a daily basis. Parangosky was so used to this game that she didn't even look as if she was keeping it under control. She was so far beyond that stage that she radiated a complete lack of concern. It was as routine as brushing her teeth. She could fend off Hood without even consciously noticing.

"Trust me when I say we're looking into Kig-Yar activity, Terrence." She had her gravel voice on, heavy on the vocal fry, the tigress rumbling a warning at the back of her throat to stop her boisterous cubs from biting her. "We need to track them, but there's something we need to worry about a great deal more. *Pious Inquisitor.* She's packing far worse hardware than nukes."

"So we've risked a rift with the Arbiter so that you can bust a stolen warship racket, as the less articulate might say."

"Indeed. You can tell him that. He stands to benefit as much as we do. Get him to crunch a few numbers. Get him to account for where every ship, fighter, and piece of ordnance went when the Covenant flushed itself down the pan. Tell him humans have had a *lot* of experience worrying about which bazaar the war machine ends up in when a major power collapses. Do you want me to draw a picture for him? What does he think attacked his keep, termites?"

Hood rubbed his forehead and said nothing. Parangosky made herself more comfortable in her chair and smiled at a young ensign who handed her a steaming cup.

"Okay." Osman sighed and turned her back on the viewscreen. "Let's pick up *Tart-Cart.*"

"Don't get all angsty over this. That's a quiet day for ONI."

"I know. But what if Hood starts committing ships to a wild goose chase, and people die when they didn't need to?"

Did anyone need to die? *Oh dear.* He had to take her mind off this. "Still angsting."

"BB . . ."

"I really was rather good, wasn't I?"

"Brilliant, actually."

"I'm constructed from the very fabric of awesomium. Now let's gather our flock."

There was the sticky problem of what to do with 'Telcam when the dropship docked, but BB would play it by ear. Now that he could eavesdrop in slipspace, it was fascinating to watch Phillips work on the Sangheili. He had a wonderfully devious streak that Parangosky had spotted a mile off, but the honest courage and enthusiasm that he wrapped it in was genuine, not a thin veneer. Gosh, the old girl could *really* pick a team. That was her strength: people. Yes, Parangosky was a people person, despite her reputation. Usually she was a people person in the same way that a cattle farmer was an animal person, but sometimes she discovered people she liked enough to spare, and then she could polish them like a mirror. Kilo-Five gleamed. BB basked in the reflection.

"'Telcam, did you ever explore the temple?" Phillips was asking. "I mean really explore it? It's astonishing. I translated some of the inscriptions. And stepping through a portal . . . wow."

'Telcam looked determined not to be impressed. "You were told not to enter dangerous areas."

"But they're not dangerous. They're amazing. What's this prohibition about a teacher? Why would the Forerunners have needed permission from a higher authority to teach or talk to a teacher?"

'Telcam tilted his head slightly. He didn't know what Phillips was going on about, BB was sure of it, but there was more to it than that: he was shocked or jealous, even indignant, because all his muscles stiffened and his jaws clenched. The human tapeworm had done yet another thing that he couldn't—he could read more of the gods' notes than a lifelong disciple like 'Telcam could. It must have been like the Pope being told that an atheist had found God's unlisted number in some apocrypha and had left a message on the divine voice mail. BB hoped that Naomi was ready to slap down the Sangheili if he decided to throttle Phillips. She certainly wasn't dozing under that helmet, however relaxed she looked.

"I know nothing of this inscription," 'Telcam said quietly. "How did you reach this conclusion?"

You had a lot of help from me. That's how. BB thought of his fragment again, broken and bewildered, and tried to partition the thought so that it didn't keep sidling up to him and trying to get his attention.

"I'm a linguist at heart," Phillips said. "Language is the expression of a culture, so that's why I'm an anthropologist. If I know what your worst insult is, I already know a lot about your fears and taboos."

"Nishum."

"Ah, I love that one. Mal's got some terrific human insults, but we're not big on parasitic organisms. We're all sex and excretion, mainly."

Vaz elbowed Phillips discreetly. "Message coming in, Phyllis. We've got a ride."

'Telcam didn't react. At least he'd calmed down. BB calculated the optimum point to drop out of slip and sent the coordinates to Devereaux. It was fun to see the look on her face.

"Ooh, I've got my first slipspace—oh, never mind." She turned and looked back through the hatch with an *oops* expression. "Talk amongst yourselves. The captain's caught up with us."

BB turned his primary attention back to Osman, but she was suitably distracted by the countdown to reentering realspace, which hadn't got any easier for her despite Adj's modifications to the drives. If he drilled down through the hull stress sensors in his dumb component, he could calculate the pressure she was putting on those armrests. She had a hell of a grip.

"Unnhh . . . ," she said.

"There. Right on target, right on time." BB transmitted the homing signal and slowed *Stanley* to a relative crawl. Yes, he really *could* operate this ship entirely on his own indefinitely, but it wasn't as rewarding as doing it with a real crew, and it would have been a miserably lonely existence. It could drive him to premature rampancy. "I should run the monorail network. We'll have *Tart-Cart* in the hangar in ten minutes and then we'll be on our way. Drop off the mad monk, tell him we'll call him when we've got another arsenal for him, and we can be back in *Infinity* and scarfing their coffee by the end of the day. Alpha time, that is."

"Wash-up and reintegration."

"You keep reminding me. I don't forget."

"BB, I know this is scaring you, so it's an opportunity for you to talk," Osman said. "You listen to me when I'm losing it. I'm just saying that I'm here for you when you have a difficult time."

BB wondered again how Osman might have turned out if she'd been allowed a normal childhood and survived it. "I may well need that."

"Lock up Adj and Leaks. They'll be a problem to explain."

"Done."

"Thanks, BB."

"My pleasure, Captain."

As *Tart-Cart* slid into the hangar, Osman leaned on the gantry rail and frowned. "She's not *that* different. Not externally, anyway. I suppose I was expecting her to look like a Spanish galleon or something." She slapped her hands down on the rail. "Okay, better go and show my face."

"Remember, 'do not dissemble, because God is your authority,'" BB said. "Besides, you can always take him to Trevelyan and dump him on Mrs. Frankenstein if he gets mouthy."

Osman waited for the bay to repressurize and clattered down the steps just as Devereaux opened the hatches. Fragant air wafted out and BB watched Osman frown.

"*Jasmine?*" she said.

"You can ask a Huragok for *anything.*" Devereaux winked. "And wait until you see my chart projector. You can have one too, ma'am. Who's staying to keep an eye on 'Telcam?"

Naomi jumped out of the main hatch with a thud like a Warthog being dropped from a sling. "Me," she said. "We understand each other now." Mal, Vaz, and Phillips trooped out and Osman allowed herself a smile. "What's the drill for New Llanelli?"

"We take 'Telcam down there and wait for his ships to drop out of slip," Osman said. "Then we thin out so that he doesn't have any embarrassing questions to answer. Prepare for a few dreary weeks of evaluating troop strengths and counting hulls."

She patted all of them on the back and did a bit of gripping forearms, almost willing them to go and leave her to deal with the Sangheili. Phillips didn't. He looked her in the eye and tapped the damaged radio still clipped to his jacket.

"I completed the mission," he said. "I got the intel, Captain. I know it's not been everyone's top priority over the last few days, but I'm pretty damn sure I've got locations and other data we can't even begin to guess at. Can I call in some analytical support from Trevelyan?"

"Certainly." Osman looked embarrassed. "I didn't think you were sightseeing, Evan. Really. I didn't. And I'm glad we didn't have to needle you. Thanks."

Phillips's mouth pursed as if he was going to say something, but looked as if it was going to be too difficult just then. He did a little resigned smile, lips pressed together, then handed her the radio.

"Mind your fingers."

Naomi climbed back into the crew bay and Osman sat down opposite 'Telcam and Naomi. He didn't move a muscle. He wasn't wearing cuffs, so the time for exploding in a rage had obviously passed. BB watched intently.

"I'm sorry about your ship," Osman said. "But we got three of them clear, and put a dent in the Arbiter."

'Telcam paused a few moments as if he was picking his words carefully. "Why did you not warn me exactly what *Infinity* could do?"

"Because I wasn't sure what she *would* do, but also because I'll be shut down if Hood works out what I'm doing." That wasn't a lie, but it wasn't wholly true. She knew she was doing it, though. The tension in her jaw muscles betrayed the effort. She seemed to want to hang on to that lifeline of self-awareness. "The deal stands. My life's been complicated a little by needing to track down *Pious Inquisitor* before she becomes a problem, but I'm willing to carry on supplying you."

"But am I willing to carry on trusting you?"

"You tell me, Field Master."

"I believe I may need a ship now, or the ability to seize one from the Arbiter."

"Okay. I'll see what's around."

"And *Philliss* has amassed a great deal of scripture."

"You want that as well? Done. I'll see that we get a translation done for you."

'Telcam waited. Osman waited. Naomi looked as if she could have waited all week, but then she was a self-contained person in every sense.

"Take me to Laqil," 'Telcam said. "And leave me there. Don't wait, just in case Jul 'Mdama has shown up. He might well know of this assembly point by now."

"Friend of yours?" Osman asked.

"Associate."

Osman just nodded and got up to leave. "We'll be discreet, then."

BB took the precaution of locking down *Tart-Cart*'s systems just in case Naomi couldn't hold 'Telcam at some point, but he looked as if he was going to stifle his anger to get what he wanted. While BB kept an eye on the two of them, Osman was on the bridge, fussing over the rest of the squad and generally looking as if she hadn't had a single doubt about any of this.

It's easy, Captain. Just look in the mirror and tell yourself a lie every day. You think you have, but you've only just started.

And don't worry. I'll be here.

BB noted that she'd put the damaged radio in her pocket. Sooner or later, he'd have to look in that mirror, too.

CHAPTER
FOURTEEN

HE SPENDS A LOT OF TIME IN THE FORERUNNER STRUC-
TURES, BUT THEN I SUSPECT HE'S MORE LIKE A HUMAN
THAN HE WANTS TO ADMIT. IN PRISON, YOU TEND TO FIND
GOD MORE EASILY BECAUSE THERE'S NOTHING ELSE THAT
CAN MAKE SENSE OF THE FACT THAT YOU'VE BLOWN YOUR
ONE AND ONLY LIFE ON A STUPID INABILITY TO JUST PLAY BY
THE RULES.

(DR. IRENA MAGNUSSON, ONIRF TREVELYAN, REPORTING ON
JUL 'MDAMA'S PROGRESS TO ADMIRAL MARGARET PARANGOSKY)

ONIRF TREVELYAN

The humans came in to Trevelyan, and—presumably—the humans went out.

Jul sat in the long grass, trying to convince his eyes that the
blue sky above him wasn't the foothills of infinite space but a
very high, wholly unnatural roof. They refused to believe him.
There were times in recent weeks when he wondered if this was
all part of some human game and that this was actually an ordinary planet after all, not a sphere. But the Forerunners had left
other feats of impossible engineering across the galaxy, such as
the Ark, and he could see no logic in using such a lie to lever
something from him.

It could just have been malice, of course. Humans enjoyed
tormenting things. He'd seen enough of them in their colonies
and now on Trevelyan to know that. They were pointlessly cruel,

as if violence had once been an essential part of their evolution but had now become a reflex and casual thing that they didn't even notice or control.

But whether this was an enclosed sphere or an open sky, he was as marooned here as ever. He still needed a way off the planet. That required a vessel. The aerial monitoring devices patrolled high overhead, watching him, just as the device that helped him communicate with Prone sent back his position.

And there are *birds up there, not just surveillance drones. I can see them.*

Hijacking a vessel was a possibility. So was stealing one. Getting off the surface would be harder, though, because a sphere would have a complex airlock system. He had a great deal of intelligence to gather, and it was the kind he would have to glean layer by layer, innocent and incidental.

The Huragok would know all these things because they were the engineering custodians, but co-opting them was a guaranteed way of exposing his plan. They answered when asked. They answered anybody.

But the more of the world that I see, the better I'll be able to plan an escape.

He lay back as far as the harness would allow and thought of home to galvanize himself to begin his daily search for . . . what, exactly? He would recognize it when he saw it. How was the rebellion progressing? Raia would be looking for him. So would Forze, and they would both be angry. When he finally got home, he would have a great deal of apologizing to do. It would be especially hard to treat his sons as if they weren't unique and special to him. He missed them.

It was the second time in his life that he'd wondered if it was such a fine thing to let sons grow up not knowing who their fathers were. It wasn't fine for him. He simply accepted it as necessary to sustain a society based on merit and ability.

Something rustled in grass nearby and a shadow fell across him. It didn't startle him. If he didn't begin the day by seeking out Prone, Prone would come and find him.

<Come and walk,> Prone said. *<You told me you wanted to see more artifacts.>*

Jul got to his feet and stuck out his arm to indicate to the Huragok that he would follow him. "So, the Forerunners. Tell me how they thought."

<Knowing about someone is not the same as knowing them. I won't be able to give you the data you require.>

Jul took a little time to pick his words and followed Prone through the ghost city that still waited for inhabitants who would now never come. He had an unseen audience—probably.

"And what data do you *think* I require?"

<You still want to know if they were gods. So do some of the others here.>

A theological debate could draw out all kinds of detail. Jul remembered extraordinary conversations with 'Telcam and the monks who followed him, how they performed the most tortuous mental gymnastics to make black white and white black, how they could argue perfectly plausibly that a forbidden thing was allowed. All examples of Forerunner technology were sacred relics, and the faithful weren't supposed to defile them by using them, yet they managed to circumvent this by some elaborate argument that using holy items to defeat blasphemers was acceptable. At first he thought they were trying to fool their gods, like some Kig-Yar contract notary twisting every word and vowel in an agreement, but soon he realized they were simply trying to fool themselves. This was the only way they could live in the world they'd created. This was how they squared what they wanted to believe—*needed* to believe—with the fact that life, every moment of it, contradicted their faith and threw its impossibility and even its unpleasant pettiness back in their faces. They bent the world into a less confusing shape.

I refuse to believe that gods want to make mortals unhappy and torment them. That's what humans do. And humans are very definitely not divine.

"I wanted to believe in gods," Jul said, and meant it. "But the gods I was taught to revere didn't seem to like mortals. They seemed to want the prohibition of the most simple acts. If you created the world, all that magnificence, why would you care who walked where, or who pronounced certain words, or who touched stone and metal?"

Prone didn't say anything for a long time. Jul was happy to walk in silence because the conversation had genuinely started him thinking about the stranglehold that the San'Shyuum had placed on the Sangheili with their version of religion.

The Forerunners were no myth. They had existed and left a great deal of evidence. But they feared things that gods needn't have worried about. They feared the Flood, or else they would never have built all this. The buildings were precise and beautiful, the straight lines true and the roads level, but this wasn't a temple: it was a place for people to live, practical and of this world. The warmth of the sun bounced off those perfect white and silver-gray walls and soothed him. It was like the solid masonry of a keep, a place meant to be lived in.

<They were concerned about dangers,> Prone said.

"I can see that."

<There was more to fear than the Flood. They had to leave warnings so that mistakes weren't repeated.>

Now things were getting interesting. Jul had to probe carefully. They'd reached a crossroads, a small square with a fountain in the middle. There was no water, but a central column rose from a low basin twice as wide as he was tall, and he could only interpret that as a fountain. He stopped and sat down on the edge.

"Did *they* believe in gods?" If Magnusson was monitoring this, then she would think he was simply groping for his inexplicable faith again. "Is any of this religious in nature?" No, that was the wrong question. It assumed too much about Prone's opinion, if he had one. "Do you believe the Forerunners were gods?"

<*They created us.*>

"Yes? No?"

<*Gods are defined as eternal. Therefore gods can't die. Forerunners could exist for very long periods, but they died. Therefore they were not gods.*>

Jul knew he could rely on Engineers for logic. "So . . . did they believe in gods?"

<*They knew there were those who came long before them.*>

It wasn't an answer, but it was interesting. He thought of the disappointing revelation that Prone had given him, that the Forerunners were more like humans than Sangheili. "Did the Forerunners have castes, like us? Were they warriors, priests, kaidons?"

<*They had warriors. They had several castes.*>

Jul would have happily spent the rest of the day coaxing answers out of Prone. He *needed* those answers. But what fascinated him was something irrelevant that pricked at his pride, at his very identity: the idea that these near-godlike beings were like *humans,* vermin who knew nothing of the Forerunners until the war, not like the Sangheili who'd revered them and preserved their works. That seemed wrong and deeply unfair.

Stupid. Focus on getting out, not on what's fair. Perhaps we have a shared culture. Perhaps we were given that gift instead.

"Did they have names?"

<Yes. And some had titles. Librarian. Logician. Didact. Master Builder. Esthetist.>

That didn't sound very Sangheili. Jul decided to retreat a little and think in terms of where docking facilities would be. They had to be nearby. He hadn't seen ships landing, and the transports were small vehicles, so materials and personnel were probably brought over a relatively short distance. Prone would know.

<Where are you going?> Prone asked.

Jul had no plan. "I thought you were going to show me something interesting. What's inside these buildings? More empty rooms and corridors?"

<Yes.>

"Show me something that'll help me to know the Forerunners better. Like the temples on Sanghelios."

<They didn't build temples. There are no temples here.>

"Yes, I know that. I meant things I can learn from. Carvings. Writing. The holy symbols."

<It's a long way.>

"I have nothing more pressing to do."

Huragok were nothing if not literal. It really was a very long way. Prone led him along a riverbank for an hour, two hours, then five: Jul could tell by the position of the sun and his understanding of how the humans divided their day. He could see a slim, charcoal gray spire protruding from the ground and nothing else.

It had to be a monument. Jul started reasoning that such a small structure couldn't contain much else, but he was dealing with Forerunners, and they could bend entire dimensions. As he approached, he could see symbols carved into the surface of the stone. There were few of them and they were large—a name, perhaps, a place, but probably not a great deal of information.

Prone circled the spire. *<There are many like this.>*

"What are they?"

<*Ingatherings.*>

"What does that mean?"

<*The places where the dispersed would assemble.*>

Humans had those inside their complex. *Muster stations,* they called them. If there was a fire or other emergency, they were supposed to report to them to be counted. Jul tried to imagine the mighty Forerunners doing something so mundane, but they'd built a shelter the size of a solar system, so it wasn't inconceivable. Their sheer *ordinariness* was beginning to trouble him. He scuffed his boots around the base of the spire, trying to work out how they'd constructed it and how deep the foundations went in a world where the surface was a shell. Then he felt something brush his face like an insect or a cobweb. He put up his hand to bat it away, and that was when the lights went out.

They didn't go out for long, though.

He wasn't on the surface any longer. He was standing in a stone-lined chamber with passages leading off it on all four sides, evenly lit, and each wall bore rows of engraved symbols. It was too quiet for him to know if the chamber was insulated from exterior noise or not, but he could hear nothing.

"Prone," he said. "Prone, where are you?" He shouted in case the communications device had failed, although he doubted Huragok handiwork was that unreliable. *"Prone!"*

There was no answer. He pressed the small device but there was still no response. He had no idea where he was, no idea of how he'd arrived here, and he wasn't sure if this was a disaster or a way out. Only one thing was clear: he couldn't stand here indefinitely. All the passages looked much the same, so he made a note of some of the most noticeably different symbols on each wall by scratching them into his belt with his nails. At least he'd be able to tell which passage he'd already walked down if he retraced his steps.

"Prone? Can you hear me?" He walked down the passage to his left. The walls were mostly plain, precisely made blocks with velvet-smooth surfaces, but some bore rows of symbols or even rectangular panels with a few single symbols within their margins. They looked very like the carvings on the ruins around Mdama. Eventually he came to a dead end and stared at the wall for what felt like a long time, mesmerized by the symbols and what they might mean. Why put them down here? What were they supposed to do?

Why hide them down here?

He was guessing the intent of ancient aliens whose technology was still far beyond anything modern societies could create. He was doomed to fail. Now he could hear a slapping sound that he recognized. Prone was rushing down the passage. He'd found an entrance, then. Now he could explain to Jul how he'd ended up down here.

Jul half-turned and reached out to touch one of the panels, more to feel how precise the edges of the inscribed symbols were, and then his comms device came alive.

<Don't. Don't touch the panel.>

Jul's fingers brushed it just as Prone gave the warning. The next thing Jul knew, Prone had cannoned into him and wrapped his tentacles tightly around his arm. Prone pulled Jul backward so violently that he felt a tendon rip. He landed flat on his back, winded, and his head cracked against the stone floor. For a moment he lay stunned. It wasn't just the force of the impact. It was the shock of being flung across the room by a Huragok. His reflex was to leap to his feet and strike down whoever struck him, but he was too shocked. It was like being struck in the face by a female. These things didn't happen. They just *didn't happen*.

Prone was like all Huragok, utterly passive, focused to the point of fixation on technology and repairing it. Some would become very agitated if Forerunner artifacts were damaged, and he'd heard of some Huragok defending their brothers against physical threats, but they didn't start fights. Jul turned his head to make sure that Prone wasn't going berserk with some form of technology that nobody had imagined. He could see the Huragok huddling by the wall. For a moment he thought Prone was cowering from him, expecting punishment, but then he realized he was actually shielding that wall—the wall that Jul had been told not to touch. The creature's bioluminescence was now vivid, brighter than normal, a sign that he was afraid or stressed.

Jul had no idea Huragok were so strong. But then they had to handle machinery, and nobody ever asked them if they needed a hand. It had never occurred to him to wonder how strong they had to be to do that, even though it was staring him in the face: very strong indeed. Because their bodies were sacs of gas and they floated, it was easy to think of them as delicate and fragile. Forerunners were masters of design, able to defy time and space, and more than capable of combining delicacy and immense strength in one structure.

And a servant that powerful could only be controlled if they were designed to follow instructions closely and without argument. One of those must have been to use extreme force only in the most serious situation, even more serious than saving their own lives. Jul had simply never asked the question before, and never seen what was right before his eyes.

<Are you damaged?> Prone asked. <I didn't intend to harm you. More harm would have been done if I had let you touch this.>

"What did I do?" Jul asked.

<I warned you not to touch the panel. The portals don't work as designed. There are none of us at the terminals to maintain them.>

"You said they didn't work."

<I said they no longer worked properly. I said that none could come here.>

"So they go somewhere, but not where they were intended to go?"

<Which is very dangerous.>

"I'm sorry." This was an incredible change in Jul's fortunes. And in this structure, he was effectively shielded from Prone's device, as well as out of sight of the surveillance drones. Magnusson couldn't find him here. Even so, he needed to pursue this line of questioning very carefully.

"Prone, I didn't mean to upset you. But they'd only go to other Forerunner structures, surely."

<Some intended destinations we know. Some we were never allowed to know, only that they were there for those who had supplementary information.>

Anywhere else was better than here—unless a portal took him into the heart of another artificial star, of course. Jul got to his feet with slow care, making no attempt to move toward that wall.

"And you're not allowed to tell anyone what you do know."

<No. You mustn't tell the others. I shouldn't have lost you and let you near this.>

"I don't want to get hurt. And I won't tell Magnusson."

<Good.>

Jul folded his arms to make it clear that he wasn't going to touch anything. He followed Prone to the surface, but still wasn't sure how he ended up back in the sunlight. Something brushed his face again and he was instantly outside.

He would memorize this place. *This* was his way home— somehow. And he hadn't had to search for years to find it. If it was dangerous, then he'd face that risk.

Prone stopped and peered at Jul's belt, head bobbing up and down. His tentacle snaked out and touched one of the symbols Jul had etched into his belt.

\<Why did you inscribe that?\>

"In case I needed to find my way back. Why?"

\<Do you know what it means?\>

Jul was intrigued, but tried not to look too interested. He had to assume he was back under surveillance now. "No."

\<That's something you must avoid,\> Prone said, turning around again. *\<Never touch it.\>*

"Why?"

\<The Didact,\> Prone said. *\<Hidden even from us. Hidden when the Librarian made her sacrifice.\>*

Prone said nothing more during the long walk back. If he was seeking to quash Jul's curiosity, he'd gone about it entirely the wrong way.

UNSC *INFINITY*, SANGHELIOS

"Bandits at twelve o'clock, Wing Co," BB said. "Break, break, break."

Hood ambushed Osman as soon as she got out of the bridge deck elevator. She carried on walking down the passage, but there was no way past him: he was a big man and he could block a lot of passage.

Her heart rate hiked for a few seconds. BB felt it via her earpiece. "Haven't you got a dark blue version of that?" she murmured.

"No. But the phrase 'If I cannot sink her, I will ram her' springs to mind."

It was hard to blame Hood, really. He was only doing his job, which was keeping one eye on the Sangheili, one eye on ONI, and . . . well, that was the problem with humans. They were one eye short, at the very least. Hood needed to keep another eye that he didn't have on the colonies, too.

"Captain," Hood said, all charm. "Margaret's being very coy. Successful hunt?"

"You won't be getting any more trouble from Kig-Yar, sir." Her heart rate didn't so much as blip this time. "Not with our own munitions, anyway. *Pious Inquisitor* is another matter."

"Let me be specific. Did you find and destroy that unidentified ship?"

If she wanted to end the conversation, she'd have to actually brush past Hood. To her credit, she stood her ground and still managed not to actually lie, merely put him in a position where he'd have to call her a liar.

"Sir, I'd need to check up on the law regarding opening fire on pirate vessels crewed by a former enemy with which we have no official peace treaty."

"You missed your vocation, Captain."

"*Have* we got a treaty with the Kig-Yar?"

"No."

"Best not trouble the Judge Advocate with that thorny issue, then, sir."

Hood's smile set solid. "We're going to have a *lovely* time when Margaret retires."

"Very kind of you to say so, sir."

She returned the smile and carried on to the bridge. Thanks to *Port Stanley*'s detour, this wasn't going to be a hot wash-up. It had already cooled to lukewarm. Everyone had had a chance to get their stories straight so that events would be tidied up rather than uncovered and learned from, which BB decided was just as well. He felt relaxed enough to manifest himself and drift along behind Osman instead of lurking in the systems and whispering in her ear. She really did need to start letting people know she'd been in the Spartan program, just so they fully understood who they were dealing with. What a lovely piece of theater it would have been to have her pull his chip out of her neural implant in a meeting; she already had all the cerebral connections in place, and it was just a matter of talking her into having the Huragok create a special external interface and letting him download into it.

But I'd better make sure that I'm fit enough to wander around in her brain first.

What's she done with the radio?

It was still in her pocket. He'd kicked the dilemma around for ages—ages even by human standards—but if he wanted the data from the temple at Ontom, he had to interface with his fragment. And Phillips kept saying how important it was. The Prof had a lot of images on his datapad, but nowhere near as much material as the fragment had recorded. Every detail counted.

Halos. He's sure it's the locations and operational status of the remaining Halos. If Mal and the others are willing to take a bullet for Earth, I should be, too. Virtually speaking.

Parangosky was talking to Phillips when Osman walked onto the bridge. He was getting his pat on the head for being a clever boy, and he was giving her a heavily censored briefing. These were all the little things that made humans . . . *human.* They had the technology to dispense with conversations, finding things out the labor-intensive way, or ever lifting a finger. The likes of BB could do all that for them. They didn't need to talk to one another or eat actual food, but that was just existing, not being alive. BB understood all that in a way he'd never realized he would.

Phillips stopped talking and looked expectantly at Osman.

"We're just discussing whether to visit the Arbiter or let the Arbiter visit *Infinity,*" he said. "Or just waving from a distance and asking him if everything's okay, because we've got to be going. It's a Sangheili psychology thing."

"He's won this round," Osman said, "and the other keeps have decided to keep their powder dry. But how do we exit this?"

"Well, he's seen some of the hardware we can now deploy, so

it's a choice between looking supportive, and not hanging around to provoke Sangheili who already think he's a human-loving traitor," Parangosky said. "Evan thinks looking submissive by offering the Arbiter the choice would achieve more than being assertive this time."

Osman shrugged. This was a sideshow for ONI and they all knew it, but for Hood it was serious diplomatic hassle. "Are you seriously going to let him on board, ma'am?"

"This place is the size of a city. Why not? We can confine him to the atrium. He doesn't get to see Huragok, he doesn't get to see anything sensitive or conspicuously unfinished, he doesn't run into anyone he shouldn't, and he gets a lovely view of space. Much as I'd love to mooch around down on the surface, Evan thinks that would tip a few keeps over the xenophobic edge. Anyway, it's Terrence's call."

BB occupied himself while the grown-ups had their discussion. He took a tactful stroll around Aine's databases—clean as a whistle, no incriminating evidence or problems there—and tried to resist taking another look at Catherine Halsey.

Hiding people from most of the crew was something you could only do on a very big vessel, and the engineering section seemed to be a very effective oubliette. BB sneaked into the engineering mainframe and watched Halsey from her own terminal for a while, trying to feel pity now that she'd had plenty of time in solitary to dwell on the death of her daughter. He didn't manage it. She looked tired and resigned, so he doubted that she only lived for the thrill of discovery; there was probably nothing worse for a human than having no shoulder to cry on, and Halsey had savaged or frozen all those offered to her throughout her life. BB wondered how Osman would react if he told her how often Halsey cried herself to sleep, but just telling her that would probably erode a little trust between them.

I'm a spy. I spy on people. I don't spy on my own team, though. I keep an eye out for them, and I don't intrude unless they're in trouble. I hope Osman understands that.

Parangosky dragged him into the conversation. "So how are you doing, BB?"

"I'll tell you when I've reintegrated, ma'am."

"If you need some technical support, you-know-who would probably be fascinated to help."

Halsey was *the* expert in third-generation smart AIs, even if she'd never worked on a fourth-gen one like him. He didn't doubt her technical genius. But asking her for help wasn't without its downside. He had a conscience, and he also had a healthy fear of handing over his brain to a sociopath with a record of terminating AIs.

Call it what it is. Murder.

"I think I'll try self-help first," he said. "Cold showers, long runs, inspiring literature. That kind of thing."

Parangosky winked. "Talk to her. If Serin's okay with that."

Phillips had never spoken to Halsey. He had that curious look on his face, that go-on-please-invite-me look, but Osman swept right over it. "Go see her if you need to, BB."

"You know she wiped part of Cortana's memory, don't you? If I come back a complete vegetable, you'll know who to blame."

Sometimes BB wanted to flounce out, but he couldn't. He couldn't leave when he was already everywhere, and he needed to create a gap in his memory to ignore anything his sensors were aware of. That was the whole problem in a nutshell. *Gaps.* They hurt. Memory was his body; he couldn't just lose chunks of it without consequences, without those millions of connections *knowing* something was missing like an amputee's phantom limb. Sometimes he had to partition data so that he had to actively seek out memories rather than live with them lurking in the background, but that was messy. The only way he'd coped with knowing about Osman's family history was to firewall the data so that it wasn't on his mind every time he talked to her.

Osman took the radio out of her pocket. "What do I do with this?"

"Give it to Phillips, because he's got hands. Then he can accompany me to a secure terminal."

There. He'd done it. He couldn't back out now. Osman gave him a sad little smile and handed the radio to Phillips, who set off on the long trip to the engineering section. Neither of them said a word until they were in the elevator.

"It'll be all right, BB." Phillips pressed the radio's case. "You know what the awful thing is? That I could switch off this BB and he didn't mind. I actually forgot he was still here. He doesn't interrupt. He doesn't join in. I told him he'd remember who and what he was, though. Because he's still you."

"You're really quite sentimental, aren't you?"

Phillips looked hurt for a moment. "Yeah, I think I am."

A marine was on sentry duty at the ladder to the engineering section. It was probably to make sure Halsey didn't get out rather than to stop anyone getting in. She was three compartments along on the main passage, her back to the door and her head bent over a desk.

"Dr. Halsey," BB said. "Have you got five minutes?"

She turned around and gave Phillips a long, appraising stare, then glanced at BB's avatar. She had one of those half-smiles that had nothing to do with humor.

"You said that without moving your lips."

"Yes, I'm just the help, Doctor," Phillips said. "That's BB. I'm Professor Evan Phillips. I didn't get to meet you on board *Port Stanley*. I'm ONI's Sangheili analyst. But at the moment, I'm BB's bagman."

BB noted that he didn't mention the university at all. Now *that* was a sure barometer of his sense of identity. Halsey looked over BB, not softening one bit.

"I didn't meet you, either, did I?" she said. *"BB."*

"Black-Box, Dr. Halsey."

"So which ship or Spartan are you assigned to?"

"I work for Captain Osman."

"Oh. Is she here?"

"Yes."

Halsey didn't quite flinch but her pupils dilated a fraction. "Well, I don't suppose I deserve a box of chocolates. How about Naomi?"

"She's in *Port Stanley.* Playing cards with the ODSTs." He listened in via the alarm system in the corvette's wardroom. "She's not winning, but then maybe she's not trying."

"So . . . what can I do for you?"

"I may have to reintegrate a damaged fragment. It was security-purged as well, so is there some way to avoid creating time baseline discontinuity? I know you wiped a chunk of Cortana and she didn't realize it, so how about telling me what you *didn't* record about the algorithm?"

Halsey crossed her legs and sat cupping her elbow, eyes narrowed. "I'd love to know who built you. That's quite impressive decryption."

"I'm designed to be completely fabulous. So is there a way around it?"

"If you hacked my files, then you'd know I didn't find one. Although I can obviously fool an AI into not knowing data's been deleted." She looked up at Phillips. "Do you know what this is about? The time baseline's a little like the system clock on a dumb computer. It's the AI's sense of reality, for want of a better word. If there's a gap, it's like staring at yourself in the mirror and not seeing part of your face. Or that name on the tip of your tongue that you can never recall even though you know your life depends on it. Or a missing limb."

"I think he gets it, Doctor," BB said. "Never mind. I knew it was a long shot asking you to fix a fourth-gen." *See, I can be a bitch too, dear.* "You've been out of the field a long time. I'll work it out for myself."

"Fourth generation."

"Yes. An AI built by AIs."

That made her blink. "I've been kept out of quite a few loops, haven't I?"

"God, yes." BB twirled around to face the door. "Thanks, anyway."

Phillips was very good at taking cues as well as carrying things. He followed BB down the passage into one of the server compartments, still clutching the radio like it was an anesthetized scorpion that was about to wake up any second.

"Is that true?" he asked. "That you were made by another AI?"

"Not really. Look, plug the radio in to that dock, will you? Thanks. No, I just lobbed that in to see if she'd bite. She's upset that they kept *Infinity* from her, and the Spartan-Threes, and the Spartan-Fours, and even the monthly menu plans. She's rather like an AI, you see. She *has* to know things or she'll burst. If she knew anything that could fix the time baseline, she'd have bargained with me."

"You think she's got a personality disorder?"

"No, she's just a nasty bitch. An unpleasant personality isn't a medical condition. Just a symptom of not being slapped around the head enough."

"Well, thank you, Dr. Freud. We'll be in touch."

Phillips forced a smile and pressed the radio down into the dock with a soft click. Now BB could see himself, a glimpse in a mirror that was his precise reflection but not the three-dimensional reality of him. The next process was to step into that image like a coat. It usually took a fraction of a second. This time, he'd have to take each segment in stages. He'd check it out, integrate it, and see how suffocatingly empty it felt.

"She might still come across," Phillips said. "Give her some time."

"She doesn't know the answer, we could be running out of time on the Halos, and we really need to crack on with Venezia." BB would deal with it. If Cortana had coped, then so could he. "She can ram it, as Mal would say. I'll fix myself, thanks."

"That line she came out with about the gaps. Was that accurate?"

"For an AI, not acquiring data and making sense of it is like suffocating. It hurts and eventually you die."

Phillips held up his hands. "Sorry. I'll shut up. Is there anything I need to do?"

"No. It'll be over before you know it."

BB's life was lived at a speed that humans could calculate but never experience. Before Phillips had even lowered his hands, BB would work through every segment of the damaged fragment, explore its data and processes, try to recover deletions, and align both time baselines. Then he would see the gaps, the bottomless shafts, the paths that led to doors that opened into nowhere. He would try to knit reality back together, assembling all the inputs his fragment had experienced at precisely the time they'd happened, and match them to the processes the fragment had been running. And he would know what he could never repair and had to live with. Once he tested it and found the voids, it was already too late. Awareness of them made them part of him, and he could try to firewall the worst ones, but he could never remove them or refill them. He could never *un*know anything.

And now he was communicating with that damaged reflection.

He blurred. His intact self had no precedence over the other. They were simultaneously both him, warts and all.

Is this what I am, an intelligence AI? Is this what was purged? Phillips told me all this. God, how could I function without knowing all this? I didn't know who I was. I don't remember Phillips. But I do. Is this version of me actually real? Did I do all those things? I can fly that ship. I can fly this ship. And . . . I was prepared to kill Phillips.

BB swallowed the unknowns and the knowns and all the shattered, shapeless debris that would never fit into him again just as Phillips dropped his arms to his sides.

"You okay, BB?" Phillips asked. "Is it done?"

BB felt that the world had shifted along an infinite fault line. He composed himself as best he could. "Well, I certainly recorded an awful lot of material in Ontom, didn't I?"

"You're okay, though, aren't you?"

No. I'm not. BB had talked to Vaz about the time he'd been wounded and almost choked to death on his own blood. Vaz had described drifting in and out of consciousness, recalling things that hadn't happened but not things that did, and feeling he wasn't the same person when he finally recovered. That must have been a lot like the way BB felt now. Vaz had bounced back. Humans could accept their fallible brains.

But I am a brain. That's the fallibility that's waiting for me, that'll finally kill me. That's where it'll all end.

That's a taste of rampancy.

There was a taste of something else, though. Along with the chaos, his fragment reminded him of something Phillips had said to him in the temple tunnels: *Because I'm your friend.*

It was oddly comforting. He resolved to do progressive clean reinstalls of his matrix if he suddenly got an urge to acquire a face.

"I'll live," BB said. *A friend. Well, I'll be damned.* "Now let's see if we can make some sense of those inscriptions."

UNSC *PORT STANLEY*, SANGHEILI SPACE: NEXT DAY

Vaz was halfway across Foxtrot deck, working out if he could catch the hockey finals on Waypoint and wondering what had happened to the exercise machines, when he suddenly found himself standing on absolutely nothing at all.

It was the blue glow from two deuterium drive vents that did it. One second he was lost in thought and the next he was scrambling for safety. The glow was *outside the hull.* He shouldn't have been able to see it. A chunk of *Stanley*'s hull was gone—

But I'm still breathing.

He squatted on the edge of a void, staring down at the vast, light-speckled hull of *Infinity* as she tilted away from him at a slight angle. His brainstem had done its primal reflex job and warned him he was about to fall down a hole, but his forebrain told him not to be such a dick because it was obviously a transparent hull—a transparent hull that *Stanley* had never had before.

His heart was still pounding. "Adj? Adj, can you hear me? What the hell have you done?"

Massively heavy boots clunked behind him. Naomi stepped out onto the transparent surface in full armor, as if she was making the point that if it could take more than four hundred kilos of kitted-out Spartan, it could cope with a ninety-kilo ODST.

"Clever, isn't it?" she said. "Transparent metal. Leaks made some adjustment at the molecular level, and—there you go."

"Why?"

"Why not?"

"A warning would have been nice."

"*Infinity*'s got a big transparent dome on her atrium."

"So we've got to have one, too? Who asked for this, or is it Huragok makeover week?"

"Prototype time, Vasya. Procurement and ONI have a stack of new stuff they want tested, so Osman said yes."

"I bet she didn't ask for a glass deck."

"No, that was BB."

Naomi clonked around on the deck and gazed down at *Infinity* for a while. Vaz forced himself past his humiliation and edged out onto the glass, but it was oddly disturbing. He really had to grit his teeth to do it. Naomi noticed.

"You're a Helljumper," she said. "You jump into space from orbit. You had to do high-altitude conventional free-fall just to qualify. Why is this different?"

"It just *is*." It was easier if he kept looking up and ignored his peripheral vision. No, he *had* to confront this head-on. He forced his eyes down. Eventually the sheer scale of *Infinity* became more riveting than standing on nothing. "I think Hood's overcompensating for something. Have we even got a dock big enough to take her?"

"No."

"You think she's intimidated the Elites enough now?"

"Probably."

"Okay." He thought Naomi had come down here to talk, because this deck wasn't on anyone's beaten track. But he still didn't always read her right. "I'm going to see how Phillips is getting on with that translation. He's been up all night with BB."

Vaz went to walk off, feeling a bit better about himself now that he could move around on the deck without clutching for support. He got to the ladder before Naomi spoke.

"If my dad knew I was okay," she said, "do you think it would change what he's doing?"

Ah, that was a relief. She couldn't put it off any longer. They'd be slipping soon, heading back to Venezia to resume the actual business of the mission after Phillips's interruption, and there was no sidestepping the issue of Sentzke being on Spenser's watch list. She took off her helmet. Vaz was learning to read the language in that, too. It was a literal gesture, peeling away the defensive veneer and opening up to him.

"We don't know what he's doing yet," Vaz said. "He might just be living in New Tyne and badmouthing Earth, which isn't illegal."

"Spenser hasn't filed anything about him since you left."

"No, because Mal told him to leave it to us." Vaz was pretty sure they'd have heard if Sentzke had done anything, though. "Have you been monitoring?"

She followed him up the ladder. "I'm not letting my feelings get in the way."

"Don't make this into a Halsey thing. You know. Like when you wanted to carry out the arrest personally in case we thought you couldn't face it. This is different. Nobody's ever been through this before."

"Come on, Vasya, keep moving."

Vaz got a firm but restrained shove in the back to hurry him up the steel steps. But he wasn't going to shut up now. "I feel sorry for the guy. I'd want revenge if I thought my kid had been taken and that the government wasn't telling me the truth about it."

"You didn't answer my question, though."

They were now on the mess deck level, eerily deserted passages and cabins that would normally have been packed with eighty or more crew. The cleaning bot crawled along the deck in front of them like a disgruntled tortoise, then rolled up the bulkhead to get out of their way. Kilo-Five lived mostly in five small spaces: the bridge, the wardroom, the hangar, the forward galley, and the officers' cabin deck. They had plenty of space to get away from each other but so far they hadn't wanted to.

Vaz picked his words surgically. "I don't think he's going to be happy to be proved right, Naomi. I'm not even sure if it'll hurt less to find you're alive. But if that was me, I'd feel a lot worse if I thought my kid had died or was still suffering."

Naomi just let out a breath and finished the walk to the wardroom in silence. Phillips had taken over half of the table in there, various datapads and note slates scattered around. BB sat in the middle of it with his own virtual stack of papers picked out in blue light. He did things like that sometimes. It was somewhere between a joke and a mood indicator. Devereaux watched as she made coffee. The energy pistol that Phillips refused to be parted from now hung on the wardroom bulkhead with a hand-scrawled label underneath: WRESTLED FROM A HINGE-HEAD HOUSEWIFE BY E. W. "PHYLLIS" PHILLIPS. It was Mal's writing.

"Where's Mal?" Vaz asked. "More to the point, where are Adj and Leaks?"

"Keep your boxers on," BB murmured. "The Huragok are upgrading the surveillance drones. Mal's with the Captain, going through the Fleet Procurement mail order catalog."

"Seriously."

"Seriously. He's ever so excited. He wants a Mantis."

"What does he want an AA gun for?"

"*New* Mantis. Like the Cyclops mech suit but bigger and better and badder."

"Oh. So, any luck with the translations?"

Phillips stared at the notes in front of him with the intensity of a man willing a fire to start, then shook his head. BB had enough processing power to decrypt pretty well anything on the spot. If the inscriptions had stumped the combined brains of those two, there had to be something missing.

"We're now working on the basis that the portal I stepped through went to the wrong terminal," Phillips said at last. "Which does give us a solution for more of the numbers if we factor in the locations of the Halos we know about."

"They're definitely relative to each other, rather than a central reference point," BB said. "But they seemed to use a different system for identifying and locating the shield worlds, possibly because there were so many."

Devereaux leaned over to put a mug of coffee in front of Phillips, and took a look. "Have they found any more language data on Trevelyan?"

"I'll check," BB said. He twirled on his horizontal axis for a moment. "Sorry, that's a bad AI in-joke . . . oh, that's just fabulous. They didn't think to flag the fact that Jul's exploring Forerunner artifacts and they've found out that the portals are probably malfunctioning or disabled because they've not been maintained. Oh dear, better snitch on them to the Admiral so they learn to file reports in the future. Do I have to do everything myself?"

"Well, at least that means we're not wasting our time on this," Phillips said. "Tell Parangosky not to schedule a firing squad just yet."

Everyone sat around the table staring at a datapad or list of symbols. *As if we can work this out if BB can't.* It was more about not standing idle and getting in the way. Vaz spotted a note about Halsey's translations from Onyx being incorrect in places, and wasn't sure whether to feel better about that or worry. Devereaux seemed particularly interested in a sheet of notes that Phillips had pushed to one side.

"Mind if I take this, Evan?" she asked.

Phillips brightened instantly and smiled at her. "No problem. Always useful having a fresh pair of eyes on a problem."

Vaz felt like he was ten again, trying to follow an especially tough calculation in physics class and dreading being picked on to stand up and explain it. Now, if that was *one,* and that meant *five* . . . but what if they didn't use columns, or zero, or any of the other stuff that humans now took for granted in mathematics and numbering systems? Even Earth had had dozens of different ways of defining locations, sometimes simultaneously. It didn't stop men building pyramids, or developing trigonometry, or mapping the globe.

One . . . five . . . eight . . .

"Hey," Devereaux said, holding up the sheet and pointing. "Just curious. Is this the symbol for a negative?"

"Negative number?" Phillips asked, not looking up.

"No, a negative word."

"That's the one," BB said.

"Well, this is just crazy pilot babble, but if the temple was some kind of command center, why is this the only thing they say 'not' about?"

Phillips folded his arms and rested his cheek on them, gazing at her. "Explain."

"Go around any UNSC building and look on the walls. It's all 'you mustn't do this, you mustn't do that, don't enter here, don't touch this,' yadda yadda yadda. But the Forerunners only used this negative thing once in all these tunnels, and it's about the teacher or teaching. This didact-instructor-lecturer-whatever. If this is all about Halos, you'd expect lots of warning notices—like 'don't press this big button, or the galaxy might go bang.' But the only warning anywhere looks like it's about this teacher. Which is kind of scary."

Mal appeared in the doorway. "We had a teacher like that once. You never hung around after gym class when he was about."

"No, Dev's got a point," Phillips said. "That's really interesting. Why didn't you crack that, BB?"

"Why didn't *you*?" BB shot back. "And stop sucking up to Dev. It's so transparent."

Naomi looked like she was trying hard to get into the enthusiastic swing of things but kept being dragged down by thoughts of Venezia. "Yes, we should be looking at this teacher as a bigger potential problem than the Halos," she said. "If you keep repeating the same prohibition and nothing else, it tells you something. I think Dev deserves a cookie."

Mal hijacked the coffee machine and watched with a preoccupied look that told Vaz he'd had some news.

"Yeah, nice one, Dev," he said. "Anyone need to do anything before we slip? Steal silverware from *Infinity*? Buy some souvenirs of Sanghelios?"

Phillips put his datapad down with an emphatic tap. "I need a recon image."

"You can have a super-duper one now Adj has been tinkering. Or *Infinity* can grab one before she goes. What do you need? Ontom again?"

"Acroli," Phillips said.

It took Vaz a couple of seconds to catch on. Phillips wanted to see what had happened to Nes'alun keep after they'd extracted him. Vaz caught Mal's eye and gave him a disappointed look, but there was no point blaming Mal for offering, because Phillips would fret about the hinge-heads either way and it was probably kinder to stop him speculating about it.

"Can you get that sorted, BB?" Mal asked. "I'll be on the bridge."

Phillips went back to his datapad. Vaz switched on the entertainment screens to check the football results and wondered if his attitude to Elites would have softened if he'd learned their language and had dinner with them. But he thought of New Llanelli again, and knew damn well that it wouldn't have, and shouldn't.

Fifteen minutes later, BB made a nervous little noise to get

Phillips's attention. "If you want to see that image now, Evan, I can project it here," he said. "Are you okay with that? It's from *Infinity.*"

Phillips straightened up and sat back in his seat, then just nodded. It was going to be awful, Vaz knew it. He switched off the sports channel just to be polite and wondered just how much detail the 3-D would show. BB drew back, and the small space in the center of the wardroom was filled with a full color fly-through of Acroli, centered on Nes'alun keep. It wasn't a pile of rubble, which made things even harder, because the projection had to peel back to show some of the interior revealed by penetrating radar. It looked gutted to Vaz. There was no sign of the females or the kids.

"Can you pull back, please?" Phillips asked.

BB obliged. The fields around the keep were largely intact except for some crash debris. Damn, this didn't answer any questions for Phillips at all.

"The Arbiter made some inquiries," BB said at last. "I'm sorry, Evan, but Elar and her clan are gone."

"Gone. Driven out, or dead?"

BB didn't flinch. "Dead."

Phillips nodded a few times. Vaz looked at Devereaux for a steer on whether to hang around or thin out, but Phillips saved them both the embarrassment of working out what level of sympathy was appropriate for a man who felt bad about dead hinge-heads.

"Okay." Phillips clapped his hands together once, looking at his notes. "Tell the captain I'm ready to roll. And ask her if I can get access to Trevelyan to have a look around. Maybe talk to Jul. Plenty of Halos out there to worry about."

The subject was closed, publicly at least. Vaz suspected that inside Phillips's head, it was another matter entirely.

FIFTEEN

I WOULDN'T TRUST JUL AS FAR AS I COULD SPIT, BUT WE'RE LEARNING A LOT SIMPLY BY WATCHING WHERE HE GOES AND HEARING WHAT HE SAYS TO THE HURAGOK. SOMETIMES WE LOSE HIM FOR A SHORT PERIOD, BUT THE HURAGOK HAVE CLEAR ORDERS AND THEY'LL OBEY THEM. HE'S ENGAGED THEM IN CONVERSATION ABOUT FORERUNNER PORTALS MORE THAN ONCE, BUT IF HE MANAGES TO OUTSMART THEM, HE CAN'T LEAVE THE SPHERE EVEN IF HE FINDS A VESSEL. ALL I HAVE TO DO TO BRING EVERYTHING TO AN INSTANT HALT IS DETONATE THAT HARNESS. THE HURAGOK SAY THE PORTALS ARE UNSTABLE OR NONFUNCTIONING ANYWAY, BUT I'M STILL NOT TAKING ANY CHANCES. BY THE WAY, THE GENETICALLY MODIFIED *IRUKAN* IS READY TO DEPLOY ANY TIME YOU SAY THE WORD. IT'LL CROSS-POLLINATE AND OVERWHELM THE NATIVE STRAIN COMPLETELY IN LESS THAN THREE YEARS. IS THIS ANY TIME TO BE SQUEAMISH? OR HAVE WE DECIDED THAT IT'S MORE MORAL TO FRAGMENT A GENOCIDAL ENEMY AND SACRIFICE MORE HUMAN LIVES THAN IT IS TO STARVE THEM? WHEN DO WE DECIDE THAT ENOUGH SANGHEILI HAVE DIED, ADMIRAL? WHAT'S OUR CRITICAL MASS OF THREAT?

(DR. IRENA MAGNUSSON, ONIRF TREVELYAN, TO CINCONI)

ONIRF TREVELYAN

Jul waited for Magnusson to question him in her oblique way about the portals and his interest in Forerunner sites, but so far she had said nothing.

It didn't fool him at all. He still didn't know what she wanted, but he wasn't her guest. He was some kind of experiment. He left it some days before he ventured out to the fascinating spire again, padding out the period in between by feigning a sly, persistent interest in where the Forerunners had come from and where they might have fled. Who wouldn't want to know where their gods had gone? Magnusson already knew he hadn't come to this place with much of a faith, but isolated people clung to what little they knew in an alien world.

And he was curious about the Forerunners, yes. He admitted that to himself.

Today he walked out to the spire again via another route to give any surveillance devices the impression that this would be the limit to his explorations. He was always on foot. There were only so many hours that he could spend wandering around. Prone accompanied him as usual.

"I still don't understand how such a powerful, advanced species could just disappear," Jul said. There were a lot of insects around today, some of them brilliantly colored like flying gems. "However big a catastrophe might have befallen them, it makes no sense that every single one was wiped out. Did they escape to another galaxy? Did they manage to manipulate time so completely that they *hid* in it?"

<*These are fascinating questions,*> Prone said. <*But we have no answers. We waited. We still wait, in case they return with more orders for us.*>

"Do you believe they will?"

<All things may be possible. And this is the point of our existence.>

The spire beckoned in the distance. Jul took his time getting there. He sat down in the grass on the riverbank and took off his belt to examine the symbols again while Prone drifted around, never straying more than a few meters. Jul knew that Huragok needed to stay busy, but wondered if they even slept, and how. Prone obviously had orders. At one point Jul felt the explosive harness chafing, and he'd grown so used to it that he tried to adjust one of the straps without thinking. Prone rushed to his side and put a restraining tentacle on his forearm.

<You mustn't try to remove it. It'll detonate.>

Jul was caught off-guard by how close he'd come to killing himself. "I wasn't. It's rubbing me. Loosen it a little."

<Once it's no longer in contact with you, it'll explode.>

"I said a little."

Prone didn't answer, but he fiddled with the straps and Jul felt more comfortable as the pressure eased. It was loose enough to slide over his head. He wasn't going to risk testing Prone's warning, but he resolved to work out some way of exploiting that. In the meantime, he contented himself with scratching to relieve the itch.

But removing the harness was no escape on its own unless he found a way out of the sphere.

"Can you read all Forerunner symbols?" he asked.

<Yes.>

"Surely they told you the places they might go if there was a crisis, if only to help you to help them."

<There were locations they didn't reveal for our own safety.>

"Ah, because of the Flood." That would steer Magnusson well away from Jul's plan. "Is the Flood more widespread than this galaxy?"

Prone didn't respond. Unlike humans, they didn't seem able to lie at all, just answer or not answer. And what was this Didact? Perhaps he was another form of the Flood, or some enemy of the Forerunners. The only place Jul would be able to ask Prone that question was in the underground chamber. He needed to thicken his smokescreen a little more.

"This world alarms me," he said. "I get lost walking through doors that I can't even see."

<These are for safety in case the Flood contagion breached this shield world. There are many such barriers within barriers that we can use to contain contamination.>

"Tell me if the Flood is still out there somewhere."

<I can't. I don't know.>

"But the Forerunners *must* have known."

Jul gazed at his belt, inscribed with the writing of beings that had died or vanished so long ago, and felt satisfied that Magnusson would be well on the way to believing that his focus was on a spiritual mystery. He got up and walked slowly toward the spire, trying to remember what he'd done last time to trigger whatever kind of portal had taken him under the structure.

<Remember,> Prone said, drifting after him. That was quite devious for a Huragok. He really didn't want the humans to know about something. <Remember not to stray too far.>

Jul ambled up to the spire and wandered around, touching the carved stone until he felt the cobwebs brush his face again. He found himself back in the chamber, this time with Prone.

"Tell me why I must avoid the Didact," he said. There had to be some portal connected with this. That was the name that had made Prone most anxious. Jul needed to know what the risks were when he worked out how to activate a portal and take the plunge into the unknown. "Is he the Flood? Is he another form of the Flood?"

<He was of the warrior caste. A Forerunner. He despised humans.>

"So do my people. I don't understand."

<If he still lives, then he may return from exile. He only knows war. He tried to fight the Flood. He tried to destroy the humans.>

This Didact sounded like a perfectly sensible person who knew a threat when he saw one. "How long has he been gone?"

<A hundred thousand years.>

That was very disappointing. It was now dawning on Jul that this wasn't making sense. That point in time seemed to be a watershed for Forerunner events. This wasn't history; this was a myth. It surprised him that the Huragok would take a legend so seriously, but the names began to fit the pattern. The Didact and the Librarian sounded like the oldest sagas carved on the walls of the earliest keeps on Sanghelios. There might have been a foundation of truth in them, but there was also much embellishment to fill unexplained gaps or make up for unreliable memories, and one thing was always certain: they were far in the past. How much of what Prone told him was myth that had evolved into reality because of Onyx's long isolation?

"I think the Didact will be long dead by now," Jul said kindly. He looked at all the potential portal signs on the walls again, wondering what his chances were of emerging into an environment that wouldn't kill him. "Even gods die."

<We are not dead.>

Jul pointed to the symbols that repeated most frequently. He took care not to look as if he planned to touch them in case Prone wrestled him to the ground again.

"Is there a portal to Earth? Show me."

Prone hesitated, as if he was weighing up whether Jul would be rash or stupid enough to try using it.

<That one. It doesn't work now. Not at all.>

Ah, so he had some way of telling which ones were live. Of course: how else would he know the portals were faulty in the first place? *Why didn't I think of that before?* Jul didn't ask if one led to Sanghelios. He'd get around to that eventually, but subtly.

"Did the Didact use a portal? And the Librarian?"

<No. He is hidden.>

"You don't know where he went."

<We know the name but not the location. In case others used us to reach him.>

The line between reality and myth seemed to be blurring again. It obviously troubled Prone, making his luminescence increase. Jul wondered whether to change the subject and get him talking about the nature of the faults the portals had. But that odd answer intrigued him.

"Very well, what's the *name* of the place he went? Not Sanghelios, and not Earth, obviously."

<Requiem.>

Jul had never heard of it. It sounded like another myth-word, as vague and meaningless as the Great Journey. "Which is the symbol for it?"

<That one.>

It was one of the more distinctive ones that Jul had etched into his belt as a way of finding his path back to the chamber. "So he was sent to Requiem, but you don't know where it is."

<That's what I said. We have to go back now.>

Prone drifted back and forth until Jul stepped away from the wall and followed him. That was probably enough for today. Rushing it would simply make Prone reluctant to talk, and being out of contact for too long might make Magnusson suspicious and encourage her to come down here. There were so many artifacts in this world that even the sizable number of humans now working here had hardly placed a fraction of them on a map,

Magnusson had told him, as if this lack of knowledge was something laudable.

Getting back to the surface simply meant retracing his steps and steeling himself to walk into an inscribed wall that suddenly wasn't there. Out in the sunlight again, he fingered his belt, intrigued by the symbol for the Didact. So the Didact didn't like humans. *A hundred thousand years ago.* Jul realized the Forerunners had visited many planets and seemed to have something in common with humans that they didn't have with Sangheili, but until today he'd thought of it as a positive connection, something to be envied, an unjustified fondness for the least worthy child in the clan. Now he saw an entirely new history of the galaxy: the humans had done something to provoke the Didact's anger, and a god didn't wage war on insects, not even a mortal god. The powerful dealt with *threats.*

Jul started to wonder what threat the human worms could have posed to such a massive, sophisticated empire, and reached one conclusion. Humans *bred.* Humans spread and colonized, like the Flood, albeit in a more subtle and insidious way. They didn't absorb what they touched into their biomass. They simply gave it no room to live.

<*A vehicle's coming,*> Prone said. <*Listen.*>

Jul could hear it, the familiar sound of a Warthog, a noisy, ugly machine that came in varied forms. The vehicle—a small troop transport—bounced across the ground, and it took him a few moments to work out that it wasn't passing but coming right at him. He'd done something foolish. He'd given away his plan somehow, and now Magnusson was going to put him back in his cage. Should he fight back? No, he'd be killed. He still had to work out a detailed plan of how he would access a portal and also how he'd remove the harness before Magnusson detonated it—which would involve the cooperation of a Huragok. He had to remain an obedient little *hinge-head.*

The Warthog transport drew level with him and stopped. Two male soldiers sat in the front while a female one sat at the back with a rifle aimed almost directly at him, pointing in his direction but tilted down, the humans' way of saying that they didn't intend to kill him but they would if they had to. *And if you detonate this belt, you're so close to me now that you'll be injured.* His chains were also his insurance.

"Sir, there's a visitor for you," the driver said. *Sir* meant nothing in the mouths of these men. It sounded respectful but Jul had observed it used almost as punctuation. "He's not got much time. Come with us."

So . . . not a punishment. Magnusson and I will continue to play our game.

It was a tight fit in the Warthog, and it would have been suffocating if it had a roof. Prone looked almost comical huddled on the seat next to Jul. But there was nothing amusing about the shadow that fell across him from behind, the shadow of that rifle. As they drove into the base, Jul saw the pen of *colos* and noticed that half of them had gone. Half of the *irukan* grain had been cut, too.

"Prone, what happened to the animals?" he asked.

<They died, as planned.>

Jul imagined an ice store full of *colo* carcasses, enough to keep him fed for many years—many miserable years of imprisonment—to come. But they'd been sickly creatures, unlike the healthy ones that still grazed.

You shouldn't have gone to all that trouble, Magnusson. I won't be staying long.

"And the grain?"

<Harvested.>

The rest of the *irukan* looked ripe too, but that hadn't been cut. That was odd. "Were the *colos* sick? I don't want to eat diseased meat. I was sick enough as it was."

<Not diseased,> Prone said. *<Starving.>*

Prone often didn't make sense. It was sometimes like talking to a temple mystic, except with the added frustration that Huragok dealt in facts and there was some actual meaning buried in their pronouncements. Jul braced himself for the visitor and went back to his cell under escort. Prone disappeared.

I will cooperate. I will be calm. I will continue to present the face of a warrior seeking the gods.

The door opened. "Hello, Jul. How are you?"

The greeting was delivered in perfect colloquial Sangheili but with that weak-minded child's pronunciation. The last person Jul was expecting was Phillips. The worm strode in with his teeth bared and face contorted as if he expected Jul to be pleased to see him again. He was *smiling*. Magnusson accompanied him with an extra chair.

"*Philliss*," Jul said. *Contain your contempt. Be serene.* He faced the two humans across the table. "I'm better now. Have you come to show me more puzzles?"

"In a way." Phillips leaned on his elbows and meshed his fingers. He seemed to have aged a lot in the brief time since Jul had last seen him. His eyes looked more weary of the things he saw, and he was wearing a faded black military working suit like the humans around the base, except it had no insignia. It looked as if he'd worn it for years. But Jul knew he'd been a scholar until very recently. "I've been to Vadam and Ontom. You knew that the Arbiter invited me to Sanghelios, didn't you? Well, I visited the temple in Ontom, and I'm translating the inscriptions from the walls. So they've let me look around here for the last couple of days to see if I can work out some more."

"Where's your pet AI?"

"BB? He's not here. If I start relying on an AI for everything, my brain will rust."

"You're intelligent enough to cope without him," Jul said.

The last things he'd said to Phillips hadn't been flattering. He'd ranted, threatened, and called him a *nishum*. If he was too kind to the human, suspicions would be raised. "But then you could always do tricks to deceive me. Did you solve many *arum* puzzles?"

Phillips spread his hands and laughed. "Oh, dozens. People kept bringing them to me to see how long it took me to open them. I *love* those things. I even opened a portal in the temple with one."

Portal. Jul tried not to react. This was the point of all this social nonsense, then, to flush out his intentions.

"And it led you here," Jul said carefully.

"Actually, I ended up in a field in Acroli, which wasn't where it was supposed to go." His half-smile faded for a moment then returned, a little less natural than it had been. "But it was educational."

Jul felt the world change around him. He wasn't prepared for his reaction. Phillips tossed place-names around: Ontom, Acroli, Vadam. It hurt. *That's my home. Those places are mine. You can't have them.* For a moment, he fully expected Phillips to come to the point—to reveal that he'd visited Mdama and been to Bekan keep, just to taunt Jul about meeting his clan and to watch Jul's reaction.

He didn't, though. He didn't mention Mdama at all. He didn't even ask Jul a sly but leading question to lure him into discussing such things. Jul felt very alone again, and missed Raia more than he'd ever imagined possible.

"And the uprising?" Jul asked.

Phillips looked much more serious. "A lot of Sangheili have died. The Arbiter's taken losses but he's still in charge. I imagine it'll continue."

"My family don't know where I am."

"I can't tell them, I'm afraid. You know that."

"Find out if Raia is well. I know you can use your contacts to ask."

"If I can, I will." Phillips tilted his head on one side and looked down. He seemed to be staring at Jul's belt. "Did you decorate that yourself? I never noticed the symbols before."

Jul leaned back and looked down at the belt. "I'm trying to read the language, too."

"The teacher." Phillips pointed. "There was a lot about the teacher in the temple."

Teacher? It was the Didact's symbol. Phillips was exceptionally clever with language and had access to sources on Sanghelios that not even a warrior like Jul had. It was time to turn the tables, as the humans would say. He would interrogate Phillips, just as deceitfully, just as carefully, and see what else there was to learn.

"The Didact," Jul said. "The warrior god who had to be concealed."

Phillips nodded with that crinkling of the brow that indicated a wistful sadness. It probably wasn't genuine. "The Forerunners certainly put a lot of prohibitions around him."

Now Jul was getting somewhere. He had the feeling that Phillips was testing him as much as he was testing Phillips, but that could be exploited. He needed locations. He needed to know more about portals, where they went, where he would end up if he touched that wall and activated one. He might simply end up in a field on the same world, just like Phillips had.

"He hated humans," Jul said. "Your species has been causing offense for millennia."

Phillips didn't even twitch. "I'd never come across his name before in my studies." He pulled out a datapad and made some marks on it, gaze flicking between the pad and Jul's belt. "Could you stand up, please? I'd like to record those as well."

"Why?"

"Because Sangheili language and culture is my life's work, and I have a theory that some of your language came from the Forerunners." Phillips had that fire in his eyes once again. He wanted to know simply for the sake of knowing. It was luminous and honest, a child's passion. "Have you heard of the Hittites? Probably not. An ancient human empire—military heavyweights. They used an alphabet that looked like other languages in what we called the Middle East, but we couldn't translate their inscriptions. We just knew what the sounds were. Then a scholar transcribed some words phonetically, and recognized sounds from *European* languages. Once he explored that tiny detail, just those few words that struck a spark in him, we were able to translate the Hittite language, and we found they weren't Middle Eastern at all. They came from another part of our world. It changed everything we thought we knew about them."

There was no harm humoring Phillips now. He loved his subject, he loved to talk, and he loved to show off his knowledge. This was how tables were turned. Magnusson simply watched, looking mesmerized by Phillips's fluency. She kept staring at him as if she couldn't believe the alien sound that was coming out of his mouth.

"What happened to them?" Jul asked.

Phillips's face relaxed in that dismayed way, as if he hadn't been expecting to be asked. "Their civilization disappeared," he said. "They were destroyed by their own civil war. And no, I didn't tell you that to make some point about your fate. I just want to find those few hidden words, that key to understanding both cultures."

If Jul knew anything about humans, it was that Phillips meant that last sentence regardless of whatever other lies he told. He went on sketching on his pad, face flushed under that thin layer of wiry brown hair around his mouth and chin. He had something that he wanted, and now Jul would try again. It was hard to play this game under so much scrutiny from others who played it every minute of their lives.

"So what was of interest in Acroli, other than crops?" he asked.

"Forerunner ruins," Phillips said, distracted. "You have so many on Sanghelios. Far more than on Earth. I exited in a collapsed building. A few inscriptions, but nothing *significant*."

If Phillips had been ported to another Forerunner site, even the wrong one, then that confirmed Jul's theory. The answer was small but had been worth the effort.

Suddenly Phillips frowned at his screen and looked put out. "I'm sorry, Jul," he said. "I've just had a message. I have to go back. I'd hoped we'd have longer. Perhaps I can come again sometime."

Make it soon. Or you won't find me here. "I hope you find your key."

"I'll keep looking. And if I can, I'll ask about Raia. I promise."

Magnusson didn't say a word. She followed Phillips out of the cell and Jul went to the window to gaze out and make sense of what he'd gleaned from that conversation. It had made up his mind to risk accessing a portal as soon as he could. The Warthog was still parked where he could see it, in the shade of some trees. A few minutes later, Phillips walked briskly up to it, punching his palm.

It was a strangely inverted human gesture, just like baring teeth to show peaceful intent. They hurt their hands to show they were pleased.

Phillips would keep his word and try to find out about Raia. But if he found out anything, if he passed that back to Jul—it would be unbearable.

Jul would never see her again. The humans would never let him go home. He had to do it soon, very soon, *now,* or die in the attempt.

UNSC *PORT STANLEY*, FORMER ONYX SECTOR

Mike Spenser was a patient man. He nursed a mug of coffee while he chatted on the secure link, more like a man catching up with his family than an agent operating undercover on a planet where the entry permit was a criminal record, official or otherwise.

"I hear you've been wreaking havoc on Sanghelios, Mal," he said. "Are you on your way back now? It's kind of quiet here. I could do with some entertainment."

Mal still wasn't sure how much to tell Spenser. That was a job for Parangosky, but she wasn't here, and Osman was on the hangar deck with the rest of the squad. In a day or so, Mal would be relying on Spenser to help them infiltrate New Tyne. He wanted to build more trust with the man.

"Not exactly *us,*" Mal said. "We just had to extract Phillips. The hinge-heads were killing each other pretty efficiently without any help from us."

"Well, if *Infinity* had the same effect on them that it's had on the rest of UNSC, then I'd call that a result."

"It's amazing how you can hide something that big for years, isn't it?"

"Even from fellow intelligence agencies."

"Yeah, sorry about that. But half of ONI didn't know about it, either."

Spenser didn't look as if he believed him. It was just a faint flash of the brows. "And word's out in Kig-Yar cafe society about a new chick in town. Shipmistress Lahz."

"Ah. BB's missed his calling as a female impersonator."

"He did a good job. Maybe too good. I'm not sure whether to keep that show going or not."

BB popped up out of nowhere and hung between Mal and the screen. "What do you mean, *too good*? I'll have you know I got rave reviews for my Lady Macbeth."

"You know Kig-Yar. Very territorial, all the gang bosses panicking about who this character is and how she can get hold of UNSC missiles." Spenser spun around slowly in his chair to pick up something from the table behind him. He was in his makeshift basement ops center, the one where Mal had first realized that Venezia was going to get *personally* messy for Kilo-Five. "Anyway, word travels fast. Might be useful when we need to do deals with the buzzards. Now . . . Sentzke. He left Venezia a couple of days ago, and I've lost track of him. He rarely travels, and I rarely lose his trail, but this time I've no idea where he's gone."

"But he'll be back, right?"

"He always has been. Do I take it that you're going to handle this internally?"

"Yes," Mal said, without thinking. "Leave him to us."

"Okay. And still no sign of *Pious Inquisitor,* although I think I know where Sav is. Sav Fel. Handy intel, by the way. Thanks."

"So if you were a Kig-Yar, who would *you* sell a stolen battle-cruiser to?"

"I might keep it for myself, if I had designs on lifting Jackal-kind up the social ladder in the new world order. But as long as it doesn't end up in a used warship auction here, that'll be a result. Because that's what's really worrying me." Spenser put his mug down with a *thunk* and looked like he was finished. "Okay, I'll wait to hear from you. Just remember to give me some notice if you need to land anything really big and hide it."

"See you later," Mal said. "We'll bring the coffee."

BB placed himself on the chair next to Mal, hovering at head height. "Phillips is back. Just docked, wittering on about knowing who the teacher is. I hope Trevelyan's evil boffins haven't tested some new psychotropic drug on him."

"You're in a good mood. I thought you were having a sulk."

"I've been *contemplative,* yes."

"But your reintegration thing worked okay, didn't it?"

"Sort of." BB knew everything and ran everything. Hearing him say *sort of* wasn't reassuring. "Mal, what are you more afraid of, death itself—you know, the things you'll never do, the finality of it—or of *how* you're going to die?"

Mal had a feeling he knew where this was going. "The *how,* I think," he said, "and I'm an ODST, so I've given it plenty of thought. Normally two seconds before they drop my pod. But the way things are going now, I'll probably die from sitting on my arse and overeating. There are some ways of dying that seem less crappy than others. I've seen a fair old selection to help me make up my mind."

"I know exactly how I'm going to die. And almost exactly when. Unless someone like Halsey pulls my plug, there's only one way out for an AI."

"It's okay to be scared of that. We can kid ourselves that it'll never happen to us, but you're too smart for that." There was no shoulder to slap or hair to ruffle. Mal couldn't even drag him out to a bar and pour beer down his throat. "Do what I do. Make yourself think about it until you're sick of it, then get on with your life."

"You know, you're rather good at this leadership thing. Have you ever considered a career in the marines?"

"See, you're better already."

"Look sharp, Staff, Captain on deck."

Osman swept in with the rest of the squad and took her seat. No ginger to ease the jump today, then; maybe she was going cold turkey on it.

BB twirled away and settled on the nav console, back to his usual self. "Everyone got their passport? False nose and mustache? Let's spin up for sunny New Tyne, then."

Phillips plopped down into his seat on the bridge, looking a bit breathless. "I know who the teacher is. Or was. A Forerunner called the Didact. He hated humans."

"Well, the Forerunners are extinct and we're not," Mal said. "So neener-neener."

"Jul said something about him needing to be hidden. I think he was just winging it, though, because this Didact guy has only just popped up. If this was part of their faith that even a semi-atheist like Jul knows, then the Abiding Truth would have had a whole library about it. A sub-cult, even."

"So was he hiding from something, or did they lock him away? Don't tell me they had a nutter god."

"No idea, but the only risk to us is probably any countermeasures they put in place that still work. Like the Halos. Which is what I'm going to focus on." Phillips gave Devereaux a grin. "So you were right. The Forerunners had some issue with the Didact, but that was a hundred thousand years ago."

"So was Onyx," Devereaux said. "And it's still going strong."

Mal was sure that the drives felt smoother as *Port Stanley* wound up for the jump and flung herself into another dimension. Sometimes he spent a few minutes concentrating on the featureless nothingness beyond the viewscreen, trying to get some feel for what slipspace was beyond a set of numbers and diagrams. He still couldn't quite grasp it. It was a curtain behind which the real world went on, a blackout blind, a tunnel that he'd emerge from sooner or later, never a separate reality. It was one of those things he knew existed, and could prove and see, but didn't *believe* in at a level that resonated in his chest. Sometimes, when he was having trouble sleeping and needed to numb his brain, he thought about religion. There were people like 'Telcam and

Manny Barakat, not even the same species, who could believe completely in something that not only couldn't be proven but showed no sign of existence at all—quite the opposite, in fact. The nearest Mal could get to knowing how they felt was to take hold of his unbelief in the slipspace he knew to be there and turn it upside down in the hope that he'd finally understand how they felt. Occasionally, for a few fleeting seconds, he did. Vaz had told him that a doc could stick an electrode in a certain part of the brain and give even an atheist a religious experience with every zap, guaranteed, but Mal didn't want his sense of reality messed around any more than it already was.

Kilo-Five wasn't a spiritual outfit at all. ONIHR had personality-matched the squad pretty well, he decided, and went down the hangar bay to see what Adj and Leaks were doing with *Tart-Cart.* Even the Huragok had merged into the team without a hiccup.

"Oh, great," Vaz said. "You've accessorized it."

The dropship, already subtly altered, was now changing color. Her hull cycled through various camo patterns—desert, arctic, forest—and then took on the palette of the hangar so exactly that it looked like some street artist had done it for a laugh. Then the hull went back to matte charcoal gray.

"I don't know why I didn't think to ask for that before." Devereaux walked around the ship with her arms folded, grinning from ear to ear. "Reactive camo. It was just a matter of getting Adj and Leaks to incorporate it into the stealth coating without messing up the carbon nanotube kit."

"So how invisible are we going to be?"

"Still not completely *invisible,* and there's not much I can do about the noise, but I can land this and lay her up with more peace of mind."

"Shame we couldn't have had these extras while the war was still on."

"Hey, that's life in a blue suit. And our war isn't over."

Mal felt that his was. He went back to the galley and set the processor to whip up some more yeast nutrient for the Huragok, then drew up a roster for making the stuff and posted it on the bulkhead. It was like arguing over whose turn it was to feed the bloody cat. The idea of Adj and Leaks making a fuss of him to get fed struck him as funny, not that he could ever see them doing that, and he was still laughing to himself when Vaz came in and tapped his finger to his ear to indicate his earpiece.

"Come on, we've got a briefing," he said. "Have you unplugged? Osman's rounding us up."

"Yeah. Can you get a TV signal in the wardroom?"

"Hockey finals, live from Saint Petersburg." Vaz actually smiled, a proper smile with a show of teeth this time. "Two hours' time."

"Girls' hockey?"

Vaz narrowed his eyes. He'd heard it all before. "*Ice* hockey."

Slipspace comms were a little strategic miracle. It was going to be great to drop out of slip fully briefed instead of being dumped into a crisis that had germinated, grown, and ripened during the time you were cut off. But nothing brought it home to Mal quite like the idea of Vaz being able to watch his beloved hockey live. It was the small detail that taught him the most.

"They'll be using slipspace bubbles to preserve food one day," Mal said. "That's what happens to all technology. The descent into the mundane."

"What?"

"Never mind. Come on, it's your turn to give Adj and Leaks their sludge."

"Leave it in the wardroom for them, on the nice tableware. They're ONI now." Vaz seemed to think Huragok had developed some kind of team spirit, but Mal suspected that their psychology was still ambivalent, no matter how much lovingly prepared yeasty stuff he fed them. "Let's go. Briefing."

Osman was pretty transparent for a spook; she'd thawed a lot since Mal had first met her. He still had no doubt that she was worth fearing, because nothing less than absolute ruthless efficiency would have made her Parangosky's chosen heir, but as far as the squad went she was a considerate commander who treated them with respect and fondness. She let them take over the wardroom—a lot of officers would have taken a very dim view of that—and she was prepared to get her hands dirty alongside them. Mal couldn't ask for more. Unfortunately, the situation on Venezia was going to push that to the limit. He knew it. He watched her move from her seat at the wardroom table to sit next to Naomi, as loud a statement of here-comes-the-awkward-stuff as he'd ever seen.

"Okay, people, ONI closed-door rules," Osman said. Phillips and Devereaux shrank visibly. "I'll speak my mind and you'll speak yours. Venezia. We pick up where we left off, and I admit there's been some mission creep. We're not interested now in who else is arming 'Telcam so much as who's turning into a problem for Earth. We'll continue to track the tagged weapons we gave 'Telcam, but mainly to work out what the supply networks are now. The new focus of our interest is *Pious Inquisitor*."

"Are we just observing, or will we have an active role?" Naomi asked, like it was just another mission.

"Observing, initially. But this isn't a regular operation for us, so let's work out our ground rules. Naomi's father. We can make all the dutiful noises we want, but this isn't just painfully personal, it's without precedent. What do we do about him?"

"If this is about my feelings, ma'am, then you treat him like any other suspect," Naomi said. "Victims take revenge and society feels sorry for them, but it's still illegal. They still get prose-cuted if they take the law into their own hands."

"I meant before we get to that stage. Should he be told what happened to you? And do you want him to know? They're dif-ferent questions."

"He'll be the first parent to find out, ma'am," Vaz said. "Shouldn't that be a consideration? Security, I mean."

"I'll square that with Parangosky. She'll go public on it her-self eventually." Osman looked at Naomi for a long time but didn't seem any closer to getting an answer from her. She glanced away. "Mal?"

Mal could only put himself in Staffan Sentzke's place and imagine his own reaction. "He's got a right to know, ma'am. Whether it pisses him off even more or not."

"So how do we let him know?"

Naomi folded her arms. "Maybe I'll tell him myself."

"Well, there's a few stages we have to get through before you can do that."

"So do we grab him and do the reunion thing here?" Mal asked. "Then what do we do with him? Jail him? Shoot him? Because if we just throw him back like some fish, then where does he go from there?"

"Earth's security and the security of its colonies comes first," Naomi said. She was still trying to prove to them that she put duty first. She really didn't need to. "If what happened to my fam-ily is to have any meaning at all, that's got to be paramount."

It all depended on how Sentzke reacted to the news. But they had to find a way to tell him first, and Mal didn't know if that would make him an even bigger threat. He spooled forward in his mind to an appalling tragedy, the worst scenario: that some hardworking, ordinary bloke who'd never done anything wrong in his life had watched his family torn apart, had somehow sur-vived the Covenant attacks, and then was finally reunited with his kid just before getting his brains blown out because he had a grudge against Earth. A *justified* grudge, as it turned out. Mal wondered how he'd feel about that when he was old and looking back on his service career, if he made it to old age and a peaceful death in his sleep. It wasn't the kind of deathbed reminiscence he wanted to have.

Yeah, it's all about how you meet your end, BB. It's about making sure the last thought on your mind isn't regret.

"So have we made a decision here?" Vaz asked. "Are we going to somehow let Sentzke know he's got a daughter and that he was right all along?"

Osman looked at Naomi as if she was going to give her the casting vote, and Mal didn't think that was right. She had the right to decide if she wanted to be revealed to her father or not. But it was also a terrible responsibility to give her for whatever Sentzke did when he found out.

I'd go ballistic. Completely and utterly frigging mental. Any father would.

"Naomi, I don't know if it's fair on you or not," Osman said at last.

"I said I'd do it, ma'am." Naomi had done nothing but brood on this since she'd found out. Mal damn well knew it. "But maybe we make the decision when we have enough contact with him to assess the consequences—for everyone."

It was a sensible Spartan kind of answer. Naomi pushed back from the table even though Osman hadn't dismissed the meeting. She didn't actually get up and leave, but it had the effect of bringing things to a gradual halt.

"I want to deploy to the surface, ma'am." Naomi said it as if Osman hadn't worked that out yet. "If there's one concession I want from you, it's being allowed to do my job instead of watching this play out."

"You're two meters tall, at least, so you're not going to go unnoticed," Mal said. "And if you're undercover, you can't clonk around in a bloody Mjolnir suit."

"Staff, there are plenty of really tall women in the world, and I'm still enhanced even without the armor." Naomi looked right into him—not into his eyes but through them and right into *him*. "Let me do this. You think you know what a Spartan can do, but you don't know what *I* can do." She had that intense look just like her dad's, those completely gray eyes without a trace of blue in them. "And *I* don't know, either, but I do need to find out who Naomi Sentzke really is."

It wasn't a perfect solution, but Mal knew there wasn't going to be a better one. Osman looked at him as if he had a veto. He shrugged. They'd work out a way to pass off Naomi as just another regular miscreant who happened to end up on Venezia.

"Okay, I suppose we'd better thin out so Vaz can watch the hockey," Osman said. "BB, use our spiffy new slipspace comms and ask the Admiral to route us every bit of current data on Venezia, up to the minute. Vaz and Naomi insert first, and then we send Mal in a few days later, with the rest of us on standby."

Naomi disappeared. Mal didn't care much for hockey anyway and gave her half an hour before he left the others to watch the game and went looking for her. She was down on Foxtrot, sitting cross-legged on the glass deck with her elbows braced on her knees. Without the armor, she was still a very tall girl, but not conspicuously muscular. Maybe she'd get away with it on Venezia. Mal closed one eye to defocus slightly and tried to imagine seeing her for the first time without knowing what she was. He might have taken her for a basketball player, or even a field athlete. She had a point. That lean, fine-boned face sort of fitted the image.

Mal walked out onto the transparent deck and sat down with her. It was easier when there was nothing to see below in space.

"Would he be happier not knowing?" she asked.

"What do you want to say to him? Are you going to tell him what was done to you?"

"It would upset him, wouldn't it?"

"Yes. Of course it would."

"But what if I hadn't been taken? I'd probably be dead now, along with everyone else on Sansar. But I survived and I excelled, and because of the Spartans, humanity survived too. Would he be proud of me?"

It was one way of looking at it. It didn't make it any easier. "Are *you* happy with what you've become?"

"I don't think I would have been happy being anything else," she said. "Not if I was as . . . exceptional as Halsey told us we all were."

Mal had to remember that the kids had been taken because they were rare, brilliant, genetically gifted examples of humanity, even without all the crap that Halsey had bolted on later. Growing up to be a librarian or a truck driver in a backwater colony would have been pretty frustrating for a one-in-a-billion kid like Naomi.

"Yeah," Mal said. "I think your dad would be proud. Earth or no Earth."

ONIRF TREVELYAN

"Okay, if they were so smart, how come they couldn't make portals you could *see*?"

"Maybe *they* could see them. They were aliens."

"Well, Warren nearly crapped himself. He couldn't find his way back out for half an hour."

The explosive harness had many advantages, Jul decided. As Prone strapped it onto him for the day—a little looser so that it didn't chafe his neck, as he'd requested—the stream of human babbling outside his cell resolved into comprehensible language. So the humans blundered into these gateways, too. It was a good question: why did the Forerunners do that?

"Why can't we see the portals, Prone?" Jul asked.

<*They're for us. We can see them.*>

"That makes no sense."

<*There is no need.*> Prone finished adjusting the harness and stepped back like a seamstress checking a garment. <*This shield world has never been populated. The barriers are for mainte-nance access and can be sealed against contaminants.*>

"But you can change that. You can make them detectable."

<*Change is not required. They* are *detectable. You and the humans can feel them.*>

Huragok seemed completely obedient and passive, even timid, but Jul now had occasional glimpses of stubborn adherence to conventions that the Covenant hadn't been fully aware of. Huragok grew agitated when Forerunner technology was damaged; Jul, like everyone else, had thought that was an integral part of their programming, a simple way to reinforce their single-minded de-votion to their tasks. But now that he spent so much time with the creatures, he was beginning to see a different side of them.

Obedience to the Covenant had been entirely incidental.

It wasn't what they *wanted* to do, or even submitted to. They had tasks laid down by the Forerunners, and their cooperation had only been given so far simply because it didn't substantially interfere with those. The thought made Jul uneasy. There was a line the Huragok would eventually draw. He'd crossed it just once and been put firmly and painfully in his place.

Prone was standing his ground in that quiet, unfathomable way. The maintenance portals were Huragok business, not the province of Sangheili or humans.

Jul waited for the guard to open the cell door. "What's your most important duty, Prone?"

<To preserve this shield world and its security for when the Forerunners need it.> Prone drifted through the open door ahead of him. *<Everything else is desirable but not essential.>*

The Huragok was very clear. Jul envied that clarity, and also that endless patience, however misguided it might be. Jul thought in days and weeks. Prone thought in millennia.

"The Forerunners aren't coming back," Jul said as they walked the familiar route out of the base. He bent down from time to time to examine interesting stones and pretty, silver-striped, spiral objects that appeared to be tiny mollusk shells, now empty and dry, and put them in his pocket. "You now know what happened in the world outside this sphere. We have found only the remains of their civilization."

<They may yet wait somewhere or sometime else.> Prone speeded up. Perhaps he was getting frustrated with looking after Jul when he could have been tinkering with equipment. *<They were not like you. They slept in thought.>*

It was more mystical nonsense. Jul doubted that such a precise machine as a Huragok would babble, though, so he decided that there simply weren't words in the Sangheili language to express the actual meaning. He decided to keep Prone talking about the Didact, which would also keep Magnusson off-balance if she was eavesdropping.

<You're going to the spire again,> Prone said. *<Don't you want to see other things?>*

"You know what I mean by a temple, yes?"

<Yes. You know I do.>

"Well, I spent a lot of time in Mdama's temples as a child. My clan was devout, as we all once were. I still find it comforting."

<The spire isn't a temple. And you think the Forerunners are dead.>

"I no longer know what I think. I need to examine my life again, everything I took for granted and everything I abandoned. Is there an existence after this one? If the Forerunners could change time in this sphere, did they know how to live for eternity? Were the San'Shyuum right for once, that there's a transformation awaiting us all?"

Prone took it in silence, which could have meant that he didn't want to talk or that he had no interest in metaphysical matters. Jul strode ahead of him, confident of the route. He couldn't see any surveillance devices but he was sure that they were around somewhere, and that meant he would do what he did every day now and walk confidently into the area around the spire until he felt the energy field brush him like an unseen cloud of flies. The humans expected him to do that. Not deviating from his routine seemed to be the key to lulling them into inaction.

Ahhh . . .

The field washed over him and he was in the underground passage again. *Half an hour. I have half an hour, perhaps, because that was how long the human was lost underground. Magnusson won't think I've escaped.* When he looked over his shoulder, Prone was about four meters behind him. Well, he'd convinced him that he thought the structure was a holy relic. Now was the time to reinforce that charade. Jul squatted on his haunches in front of the panel that had made Prone so anxious when he'd reached out to touch it.

The symbols do something. They're keys, buttons, switches, something like that, even though they look like part of the stone. I have to touch one and see what happens. The challenge is . . . Prone.

Jul stayed in his squat position, bowed his head, and closed his eyes. That would prevent Prone interrupting him for a while.

What would stop Prone from grabbing me if I were to touch the wall?

The harness.

Huragok grew distressed when Forerunner technology was damaged. If Jul threatened to destroy an entire panel, a wall of devices that seemed to be a hub for portal network in one of the Forerunners' most critical installations, then that would surely persuade him to deactivate his harness.

But he needs to get very close to me to do it. Can I manage that? I've got one chance to do this, because if I fail, that ruse won't work again. In fact . . . I'll be marooned here, unable to remove the harness at all.

Jul opened his eyes a fraction. Prone was on the far side of the chamber, apparently gazing at inscriptions. Jul was two paces from the wall.

If I don't make my move, I'll die here eventually anyway. They'll never release me. They can't.

He had to do it in one move. And he had to do it very soon, before the loss of contact with him started a search. The harness was loose. Prone wouldn't have thought that was a security problem because simply taking it off would trigger it.

Get to the wall, lift the harness—not too far, mind—and give him the ultimatum.

Show me a portal that works, or I'll destroy this chamber. Have you ever seen an explosion in a confined space? You'd die too.

Prone might not care what happened to him, but he'd certainly care about the precious Forerunner facility. Jul crossed his arms on his chest very slowly, curled his fingers around the straps of the harness, and sprang up from a squat toward the wall. He hit it with a thud just as Prone spun around. As the Huragok came at him, he raised the harness to shoulder level. Prone stopped.

"I have nothing to lose, Engineer," he said. "I'll die here either way. Show me the portal to Sanghelios, and remove this harness, or I'll detonate it."

Prone edged forward. This was going to be awkward. Jul had to keep an eye on the creature, but he also needed to look at the symbols on the wall. He could already feel a tingling sensation throughout his body: the wall was active in some way.

<Sanghelios does not work,> Prone said. *<It was not maintained at the terminal.>*

"I don't believe you." Jul reached out with one hand, holding the harness half-raised with the other. He wasn't sure how much he'd have to pull it away from his body to trigger it, but he'd find out very soon. "So I'm going to carry out an experiment."

<You might go nowhere. You might damage the portals by trying.>

"Let's see." Jul reached into his pocket and gathered the shells and stones in his palm. If he could open a portal, at least he could toss a stone in and see what happened before he tried it himself. Doing this one-handed was hard. He held one stone between two fingers, gripping the rest as best he could, and stood off to one side of the symbols so that he could both see them and keep Prone in his field of view. "What happens if I do *this*?"

He pressed the first symbol. Prone made a faint groaning sound. A panel in the wall dissolved, leaving a tall rectangle that looked like sunlight trying to penetrate a thick mist. Jul tossed the stone into the light, but a heartbeat later, it bounced back and clattered across the floor.

<I told you,> Prone said. *<It doesn't work.>*

Jul wasn't going to give up that easily. Now he was committed: keep trying, or die. "Plenty more controls to press, my friend. Plenty more." He worked another stone out of his palm and positioned it between his fingers, then tried the next symbol in the line. When he lobbed the stone into the portal this time, it didn't bounce back. He held his breath, hoping this was his exit, then a light flashed and he heard something hit the floor on the other side of the chamber. It was the stone again.

<Some don't go where they were intended,> Prone said. *<Which I have also told you.>*

"But some do." Jul prepared a third stone. His other arm was starting to ache from holding up the harness. "Some *do.*"

He tried again. Again, the stone bounced out. He tried four more times, equally unsuccessfully, and wondered if he'd run out of stones before he found a portal destination that worked. Every time he threw one into the void, Prone edged forward a little.

"I will detonate this, Engineer. Believe me when I say that."

<I do.>

Jul still didn't believe there were any gods, but if he was wrong, then he hoped they would look down on this desperate moment and open a portal for him. It was a small favor to ask of beings who could build entire stars. His mouth was dry and he wondered if he was being stupid rather than courageous. Sometimes it was hard to draw a line between the two.

He threw again, and there was silence.

The silence turned into seconds. Then it stretched into a long pause punctuated by his own heartbeat pounding in his ears. The stone didn't bounce back, and it didn't emerge in the chamber. Prone hung there, sighing like bellows.

"This one works," Jul said. "This *works.* Doesn't it?"

<For the time being. It's unstable.>

"Where does it lead?"

<You mustn't enter.>

Jul lifted the harness up a little higher. His arm muscles were getting tired and beginning to twitch. "I'll enter anyway. I'll ask you again. What is this symbol?"

<Kelekos.>

Jul had never heard of it. "Where is that?"

<*I don't know. There were many Forerunners there.*>

"Like you don't know where Requiem is."

<*Requiem cannot be reached from here, because the Didact sleeps and must never be woken. Kelekos could be reached. If you can reach a place, we have no need to know its location. This terminal is for ingathering.*>

Jul was now beyond impatience with the Huragok's half-explanations. Having explosives draped around him didn't improve his mood. But he had a functioning portal, and he had to try. Kelekos would do. When he got there, he'd work out where it was. It was just a name. There was little chance that the Forerunner name bore any resemblance to what the world was known as now.

But before he stepped into freedom, even a terrifyingly unknown freedom, he had to get rid of the harness. Magnusson couldn't detonate it, not here in this place that shut out all signals, but he couldn't take it with him, because there would be no Huragok to remove it safely.

"Prone, come here and remove this harness," Jul said. "Or I'll detonate it."

<*I was ordered not to.*>

"You know I'll do it. Remove it."

<*I must not.*>

"If I try to take it off, what happens to your terminal? What was your most important order? Do you obey the orders the Forerunners gave you, or those of these humans, who would destroy everything the Forerunners built if it suited them?"

Prone was as brightly luminous as Jul had ever seen him, tentacles fluttering aimlessly. Jul edged closer to the glowing portal to force the creature to act, and placed one leg across the threshold. It was the strangest feeling. He'd used portals before but none of them had felt like this. His leg tingled as if it was being kneaded by thousands of fingers, not quite a tearing sensation but very uncomfortable nevertheless. He had both hands free now. He raised the harness a little higher. The next moment could prove to be his last.

Home or dead. There's no other way.

<Wait.> Prone moved in very slowly and placed a tentacle on the harness. <This is foolish, but this terminal must not be damaged. But if you are damaged—that's your choice.>

Jul's heart almost stopped. Prone's tentacles slid over the straps and the weight of the harness lifted from Jul's shoulders.

Now. Do it now.

Jul put all his weight on his back foot, the foot within the uncertain world of the portal, and let himself fall backward without a word. Light engulfed him.

Kelekos . . .

It was not Onyx-Trevelyan, and that was all that mattered.

CHAPTER
SIXTEEN

I BELIEVE THE SANGHEILI ARE BEGINNING TO ACCEPT THAT
HUMANS ARE HERE TO STAY, AND EVEN IF THEY DON'T LIKE
THAT, THEY'RE MORE INCLINED TO AVOID US THAN TO CON-
FRONT US. LET'S TOAST THIS, MARGARET. WHAT'S TODAY?
THURSDAY. VERY WELL—A BLOODY WAR, AND A QUICK PRO-
MOTION.

(ADMIRAL LORD HOOD, CINCFLEET, MAKING THE HISTORIC ROYAL NAVY
TOAST TRADITIONALLY PROPOSED ON THURSDAYS)

UNSC *INFINITY*, RETURNING TO THE SOL SYSTEM:
ADMIRAL PARANGOSKY'S DAY CABIN

Bad news could never wait, the saying went, and thanks to the
new slipspace comms Parangosky didn't have to. But she'd still
been kept in the dark for far too long.

How the hell could anyone lose a Sangheili prisoner from a
sealed world? How could *ONI* lose him?

Dear God . . .

"It's taken you fifteen hours to report 'Mdama missing." She
stared at the screen, as worried as she was angry. *I thought I
could pick the right people. Perhaps I'm losing my touch.* "Fifteen hours. Why?"

Irena Magnusson looked as if she was arguing for her life, and
whether she knew it or not, she was. The imaging from Trevelyan
was brutally lifelike. The scientist's mouth opened and closed a

few times before any sound emerged, and it wasn't a technical sync problem.

"Admiral, we had to carry out a search," she said, shaky and desperate. "This is an entire *planet*."

"You can't search a planet in fifteen hours, either."

"The Huragok said he saw Jul step through a portal. Those portals are unstable, and some don't go anywhere. Some feed back into the sphere. We don't know where the others go, or if they go where they were intended to. The Huragok seems to think that some are so unstable that they're dangerous or may even exit in space, or worse."

"But the one he stepped through appears to be active, and you haven't recovered a body."

"Correct."

"Then damn well *follow him*," Parangosky snapped. "You're the facility director, for God's sake. Take some responsibility. You *do* know exactly which portal he activated, I take it. Yes or no?"

"Admiral, I *did* send a remote through as soon as we'd realized what had happened, but it emerged about two hundred klicks from here. It didn't leave the sphere. And yes, we're searching that area, too."

This wasn't the first debacle that Parangosky had experienced on her watch and almost certainly wouldn't be the last, but this one needn't have happened at all. She still wasn't sure if Jul 'Mdama had escaped or not. She had to work on the assumption that he had.

What will he do next? Will he blurt everything out to the Arbiter? 'Telcam's not the problem. It's the damage this will do within UNSC, between me and Hood, and the Arbiter might change his mind about the treaty.

But it won't stop his civil war, it won't stop me, and it won't stop Infinity.

"How are you trying to track him now?" she asked.

"By surveillance drones and by sending remotes through all the active portals. He's not wearing his explosive harness, so we can't locate him via that."

"You allowed him out without it?"

"No, no, he pressured the Huragok into removing it, despite orders. We'll keep looking, Admiral, but we can't rule out the possibility that he's managed to reach another planet."

Parangosky could do little right then, but Trevelyan was the most important asset that ONI had, perhaps even more than *Infinity,* which was not solely hers to deploy. The technology— the advances already discovered and the untold treasure still to come—was the key to everything.

And it was currently under the directorship of an idiot.

My fault. I appointed her. Halsey wouldn't have made that mistake, for all her faults.

Parangosky had a will that could bend steel but even after seventy years in uniform, some things made her doubt herself. One of them was realizing she'd appointed the wrong person to a post. That meant removing them, and the more senior or sensitive the posting in ONI, the less suitable the failure was for release back into the wild. Magnusson wouldn't be put out to pasture at some university to end her days as an obscure goddess to students who knew no better. She would have to be contained.

I seem to have bad luck with scientists these days. But I won't let this one turn into another Halsey. Magnusson has to pay for her mistakes. No second chances, no matter how good she is. These civilians are getting out of control. They have to learn that their actions have real consequences.

"Keep looking, and contact me the instant anything develops," Parangosky said. "And I do mean *instant.* Expect a visit as soon as I get *Infinity* to divert from her mission, which should give you some idea of how very, *very* disappointed I am in you, Irena."

Parangosky closed the transmission before Magnusson could respond and leaned back in her seat, eyes shut.

"Are you there, BB?"

"Yes, Admiral. Just a little bit of me keeping an eye on things until you're clear of the Woodentop Navy."

"How does anyone lose a Sangheili, BB?"

"It takes some doing. So, Magnusson better not make any long-term career plans, then. I'll brief Osman."

"I'd better move some listening posts closer to Sanghelios. If Jul's survived the portal, he'll head back there or call home sooner or later."

"Well, I did leave some comms drones from *Stanley*'s little day trip, but they haven't picked up anything about Jul yet," he said. "Look, you really do need an AI of your own, ma'am. Not a dumb one."

"No, BB, it's like getting a puppy. When you're my age, you worry because it'll probably outlive you and you don't know if anyone will love and care for it in the same way that you did once you're gone. Dumb works best for me now."

"I shall go dig up a bone and chase my tail, then."

"No offense, BB. I prefer AIs to people most of the time. Come to that, I like puppies better than people, too. Ah well. Better go and ask Terrence if he wouldn't mind dropping me off at Trevelyan."

Hood knew better than to ask Parangosky why she needed to divert.

"I wouldn't ask if it weren't important, Terrence," she said, playing the weary old woman card that she knew never fooled him anyway. "But the director's struggling somewhat. A research station the size of a warship is one thing. An entire planet is another. I'll have to put another management structure in place for these one-off projects, I think."

"As long as it's not something I said." Hood smiled. "Are you sure you're not bored with this new toy now, Margaret?"

"Not at all, but I'm confident that she can do the job, so I'll get out of your hair. As Thursday Wars go, that was very promising. I'd say she's ready for full deployment."

"Carpeting," Hood said. "I'll be happier when everything's squared away properly."

"I take it the Arbiter's grateful for our help."

"I imagine you know better than I do, given your contacts."

"Still not invited him for a tour of the ship?"

"I'll wait until the wardroom silver's been polished."

"Well, thank you for the front-row seat, Terrence. You really must visit Trevelyan soon."

But not too soon. She had some cleaning of her own to do first.

This was her second inspection of Trevelyan, and a painful contrast to the triumphant mood of the last one. She reassured herself it was still a goldmine of technology even if it wasn't as secure as she'd first thought. They'd have to do something about those portals. If the Huragok couldn't get them working, identify them, or shut them down, then she at least expected some cooperation on securing them.

Magnusson's deputy, Hugo Barton, was forty-six, humorless, and a materials physicist. He met Parangosky at the exit from the sphere's external dock.

"You still okay being bounced around in a Warthog, ma'am?" he asked, jumping out of the driver's door to help her. He placed her holdall reverently on the rear seat and gave her sidearm a sly glance. "No roads here, of course, but I'll take it slowly over the bumps."

"I'll be fine."

"You think you'll be needing that pistol?"

The sidearm really did seem to trouble him. "I'm ninety-two. I can't strangle staff so well these days. Think of it as a disability aid." The uneven ground was more like a vehicle test range but she refused to wince. Whatever vehicles the Forerunners had used, they probably didn't rely on utility suspensions that hadn't changed much in a century. "Where's Magnusson now?"

"She's with the Huragok, inspecting the portal chamber."

"One question, Hugo." *First names. Start as we mean to go on. Get him on side.* "Why did anyone think it was a good idea to allow a Sangheili free movement without an escort?"

Barton squirmed. He didn't dive straight in to dig Magnusson's grave any deeper, which Parangosky rather admired.

"He seemed more interested in the Forerunners. We were monitoring him at all times, audio too, and all he talked about was where the Forerunners came from and whether they were really gods."

"So someone assumed that he was just another religious Elite," she said. "And someone also assumed that the Huragok would follow any order. I have very little patience with assumptions, Hugo, especially from scientists."

"I try not to make them."

"And nobody logged all the portal sites first."

"I think that's going to take us years."

"Then he should have been kept in his cell *for years.*"

"I believe it was done to make him feel more amenable to cooperating with us and revealing information."

"He wouldn't have had much to tell us. We should have terminated him when we first acquired him. That's my fault."

"Well, at least we tested the GM *irukan,* so that's something we've got in reserve. What's going to happen to Irena?"

"How long have you worked for ONI?"

"Twenty years."

"Well, then. You can't have failed to notice that I don't like avoidable mistakes. And I especially don't like mistakes that compromise me with Admiral Hood."

"What's the worst that can happen if 'Mdama shows up somewhere in one piece, and talks?"

"I'll be in a spot with Hood. The Arbiter might kick off the war again, although Sanghelios is pretty fragmented at the moment. And he'll know we've acquired Huragok, although that might actually be another useful deterrent. Even so—I don't like losing prisoners." It was time to break the news to him. "By the way, you're now appointed director. Magnusson's relieved of duty."

"Oh." He didn't blink. It looked like an effort. "Does she know?"

"Not yet."

"Okay."

Barton knew when to shut up, another desirable quality in a facility director. The Warthog drove into the middle of nowhere and pulled up at an isolated structure that looked like a lonely church spire dumped from a great height. Parangosky wondered if her hips were going to cope with whatever was coming next.

"Brace yourself, ma'am," Barton said. "Just walk forward, and ignore the creepy feeling. It's just a maintenance portal."

Parangosky put her weight on her cane. It sank into the ground a little, but then something made her skin crawl and the next step found the cane hitting concrete or stone.

"Uhh . . . yes, I see what you mean."

She looked around. The world had dissolved into a precisely built stone chamber with inscribed walls like a mausoleum. She could now hear voices, Magnusson's and an artificial one that had to be the Huragok interpretation system. Barton didn't offer explanation or opinion.

"You must *show me*, Prone," Magnusson was saying. "I don't want to damage anything. I just want to know."

Parangosky rounded the corner and found Magnusson talking to a Huragok who was hovering between her and the wall. It took Parangosky a few moments to work out from Magnusson's occasional random sidesteps that the creature was blocking her. Then Magnusson turned around.

"Hello, Admiral." She looked flushed and panicky. "I'm sorry. Prone's very anxious about the portals."

"So am I, Irena. Is he getting in your way?"

"Yes. He's much stronger than he looks."

"But not strong enough to stop Jul 'Mdama from forcing him to release the harness."

Magnusson shrank visibly. "It's all about the perceived threat to Forerunner technology. He's already thrown one of the marines out of the way. He's not violent, just very protective. I'm trying a quieter approach."

He's a bag of gas, no matter how clever he is. Shoot him if you have to. I like them, but we can replace him now. "Then why bring him down here at all?"

"We're totally dependent on them to understand all this, ma'am."

Right now, all anyone needed to know was whether Jul was alive and starting trouble somewhere, or if he wasn't. Parangosky wasn't too fussed about the nature of the *wasn't*, although there was no way of telling if he was still roaming the sphere and would find another portal station to escape from. She needed to see a body. She had the feeling that life wasn't going to be helpful and hand her one just to watch the relief on her face.

"So we can't re-create the conditions of the escape."

"No, Admiral."

Magnusson shot Barton a glance. Parangosky didn't miss it. She walked up to Prone and looked into his little animal eyes.

"Prone, are you telling us the truth about Kelekos?" Parangosky asked quietly. "Do you really not know where it is?"

<No. The Forerunners all knew. There was no need to explain it. It went there and came back from there.>

It was probably like expecting the coordinates of Sydney or Earth to appear on a flight timetable. Everyone knew what Earth was. Only pilots needed the numbers. "What else did Jul say? What concerned him?"

Prone didn't move from the wall. He had six eyes, so keeping one on Magnusson was probably no trouble. *<He talked about the Didact. He was interested in him. I told him he was in Requiem and we were never told where it was.>*

"This was a Forerunner, yes?"

<The one who despised humanity. I told Magnusson all this.>

"I know. I'm just trying to understand. Can you give us a list of all the Forerunner worlds linked to this shield world?"

<Yes. But there are many. And there are many more not linked where some portals may now go.>

"That's fine." Parangosky had to think about that for a few seconds. Prone didn't know where faulty portals emerged at any given time. "Just tell us. We have to find Jul. For his own safety, if nothing else."

<I did my duty. I'm sorry. But the shield world must be preserved.>

"Prone, have you shut down all the portal stations in here?" It was an obvious question and Parangosky was sure Magnusson had asked it. "So that nobody else can use them for the time being."

<No. But we can shut the maintenance portals if you wish to stop searching them.>

"Let's make sure everyone's out and accounted for, and then we can do that." Parangosky turned and fixed Magnusson with her sentencing stare. No, the idiot hadn't even had the sense to ask him if he could shut all the doors. "I think we should go now, Irena, and let Prone lock the exits. And get us that damned list."

There was something rather surreal about Prone. He left, still sticking close behind Magnusson, but otherwise did exactly as he was told. If nothing else, Parangosky had learned something about Huragok—how far they could be trusted to follow orders and the line beyond which they wouldn't be pushed. It was better to know that before the whole of UNSC became entirely dependent on them. They were a wonderful asset, but it was time to put some effort into understanding their processes so that AIs and technicians could emulate them and to work out how to shut them down in an emergency.

They shared information. That meant no individual Huragok was indispensable.

Not an entirely negative outcome, then. But I won't get much sleep until we find Jul 'Mdama or his remains.

Parangosky walked into the main accommodation block with Barton, Magnusson, and Prone, and decided to stay overnight. There was no telling when she'd get back here again, and she needed to cement her understanding with Barton.

"Can I get you something to drink, Admiral?" Barton asked. "We're pretty limited at the moment, but we can keep you fed and watered."

"Later." Parangosky was looking around for a marine or two. She wanted to get this over with, minimum fuss and maximum speed. "Excuse me a moment. I won't be long."

She had to walk out into the compound again to find anyone in uniform. A pleasant young marine who reminded her a little of Corporal Beloi was passing with a crate in his arms, but he put it down and snapped to attention when she stepped out in front of him.

"Marine, I need you to detain someone for me, please."

"Yes, ma'am." He looked puzzled. "Don't tell me we've found the hinge-head."

"I'm afraid not." She went back into the block with the marine following her, sidearm drawn. "You probably won't need that, by the way."

Magnusson shouldn't have been surprised, nor Barton, but that was the look on their faces. What did they expect? This was ONI, not some grocery store where underperforming staff were given written warnings to shape up. Parangosky expected the same discipline and common sense from her civilian staff as she did from those in uniform. She indicated Magnusson with one hand.

"Marine, I want you to detain Dr. Magnusson and hold her in solitary until she's transferred." Magnusson's jaw dropped. She literally gaped. Perhaps she still thought the stories were all just that, stories. Now she knew that every myth about Parangosky was true. "Irena Magnusson, you're relieved of duty, and you'll be detained under security protocols indefinitely while I carry out an investigation into the escape of the prisoner. You'll be held at Midnight Facility until further notice."

The marine took Magnusson's arm a little awkwardly. She was a slight woman, and he probably didn't want to seem heavy-handed. As he led her away, she found her voice, looking back over her shoulder as best she could with that same disbelieving expression that Parangosky had seen too many times.

"But it was a mistake," she said. "A *mistake*. After all the years I've given ONI? And what am I going to tell my family? Admiral, it was just a stupid *mistake*."

"My mistake for giving you a posting beyond your capabilities," Parangosky said. "And your mistake for thinking your approach to alien psychology trumped time-tested military security."

Parangosky turned away and faced Barton, fascinated by the

mix of emotions written across his face: shock, several layers of fear, and excitement, because even the nice and trustworthy ones found this kind of drama just a little bit *thrilling*. Irena Magnusson was lucky. Parangosky could easily have shot her, but the woman hadn't been debriefed properly yet, and there were too many witnesses, however excellent that would have been for Parangosky's reputation.

"*Pour encourager les autres,*" Parangosky said, and pointed in the direction of the mess with her cane. "See that word gets around, will you, Hugo? And I'll have that drink if it's still on offer. Now let's talk about *you*."

LOCATION: UNKNOWN

Jul fell hard onto a sunlit flagstone floor and gulped in a lungful of air. He wasn't dead, he wasn't burning in the heart of a star, and he wasn't back in the chamber beneath the spire.

He was free. He simply didn't know where he was.

"Uncle! *Uncle!*" A child started yelling nearby. "Uncle, *look*! Someone's in the holy gate!"

Jul got to his feet. He understood the language: it was Sangheili, although he didn't recognize the accent at all. It took him a few moments to orient himself and work out that he was standing in the middle of a small settlement. It looked strange to him at first because it bore little resemblance to any keeps he'd seen before, even in Ontom, but this was his culture. These were his people.

I'm home. I'm home.

The first thing he had to do was get a message to Raia. He dusted himself down and set off toward the buildings, three or four modest stone keeps only a couple of stories tall, and saw the child running a long way ahead of him. He must have terrified the boy; it was understandable. He'd apologize to the clan and explain who he was and why he'd come, but he'd keep his views on the Arbiter to himself for the time being. These were troubled times, and he didn't know where the lines were drawn in Sangheili society following the events of the last few weeks.

I did it. I got home, and now I can warn those on Sanghelios who'll listen about the true threat the humans pose, the poison they're spreading.

And I still have my self-respect.

But he had no weapon and no helmet. Perhaps the kaidon here would lend him equipment until he was able to get back to Mdama. He was still some way from the nearest building when he saw five or six adult males rush out of the entrance carrying pistols, followed by a group of children with wooden practice weapons.

It didn't bode well. Whatever side they'd picked in the civil war, they seemed to think he might be on the other. A reasonable precaution; he would have done the same now if anyone had arrived uninvited at Bekan keep. He made the only sensible move an unarmed warrior could, and stopped in his tracks to spread his arms and show he didn't have a weapon.

The small army bore down on him at a run. For a moment, he thought they weren't going to stop. What had happened here? Why were they so agitated? He was alone and clearly unarmed. The warrior leading the charge slowed to a trot and then stopped six paces from him, aiming at his chest.

"Who are you, and why do you dare defile the holy gate?" The warrior was battle-scarred and elderly. "Rdolo says you stepped out of the sun. Answer me, because I want to know the names of the blasphemers I kill."

"I mean you no harm." All Jul wanted to do was to contact Raia and let her know he was safe. He didn't care how much he had to grovel to get that favor granted. "I'm Shipmaster Jul

'Mdama of Bekan keep, and I've been a prisoner of the humans. I have escaped. . . ." Here he picked his words *very* carefully, his diplomacy skills honed by contact with 'Telcam. These were clearly deeply religious people. "The humans captured a temple site on another world, and the gods granted me the blessing of escape through a portal. I had no idea it would emerge here, but they delivered me safely to the faithful." He paused, looking from face to incredulous face. The children were gaping, nostrils flared and jaws fanned open. "Where is this place? I was told it was called Kelekos. But that was the Forerunners' sacred name for it."

The elder lowered the pistol, but only slightly. "This is Hesduros, and I'm Kaidon Panom. Where did you think this Kelekos place was?"

"Sanghelios, of course." It was the first time that Jul had taken note of the fact that the landscape in the distance didn't look like anything he knew on Sanghelios. It wasn't just the architecture. Now that he thought about it, even the daylight seemed a little different somehow. "But I have no idea where the mercy of the gods has brought me."

"Our forefathers left Sanghelios generations ago." Panom lowered the pistol, apparently satisfied that Jul was either harmless or too mad to do any damage. "We sent sons to the war, but we have heard nothing for a year or more."

A year? They didn't even know the Great Schism had happened, then, and they would know nothing about the Arbiter's cowardly bargain with Earth. At least he could count on their outrage. That would buy him allies.

"The war is over," he said. "Temporarily, at least. The San'Shyuum abandoned us and an Arbiter made peace with the humans. We fight one another now, but we should be fighting the true enemy. Humans."

One of the males standing behind Panom leaned close to the old warrior to whisper something in his ear. Then Jul realized everyone was looking at his belt.

"Why do you wear the holy symbols?" Panom asked. "Are you a monk?"

This was where things might get dangerous. There was no point lying, because Jul wasn't devout enough to know the intricate detail of ritual that a monk might. Every word counted now.

"I had common cause with the Servants of the Abiding Truth," he said. "We rose up against the Arbiter, but I was captured by the enemy, and I've lost contact with my brothers. I'd consider it a great mercy if you let me contact my keep."

Panom and the man who'd taken an interest in his belt stepped right up to Jul but they still weren't looking him in the eye. It was the belt that riveted them. Panom reached out a finger, slow and wary, as if he was afraid the belt would burn him.

"That," he said, "is the symbol of the holy warrior who will come to the aid of the faithful in their hour of need."

Jul was so far out his depth now that he wasn't sure if he'd genuinely found salvation—by a fluke or by the existence of gods he hadn't begun to imagine—or if he was talking himself into a grave. He'd never heard of this Didact before the last week and now the Forerunner seemed to be everywhere he turned.

"How do you know about the Didact?" Jul asked. "He was never spoken of on Sanghelios."

"How do *you* know that's his name?"

This was his moment, his bargaining point. "Because I've come from the heart of a shield world, and I've been taught by the Huragok who've maintained the world for a hundred thousand years, waiting for the Forerunners to return."

Everyone was silent, even the youngsters. The birds and insects were suddenly the loudest sounds Jul could hear.

"Come and eat, Jul 'Mdama," Panom said at last, beckoning him like a fond uncle. "Let's talk."

HANGAR DECK, UNSC *PORT STANLEY:*
VENEZIA SECTOR, FIVE DAYS LATER

"Mal . . ." Vaz tried not to laugh. "Did you check the collar size? Because it's a long way to send it back for a refund."

Mal leaned on the gantry rail, staring down at the new kit being uncrated on the deck below. He didn't even blink. "I could wear an extra jumper underneath."

"Or you might grow into it."

The prototype Mantis armor defense system had arrived, courtesy of the UNSC Fleet Auxiliary replenishment team. It stood on the deck, challenging them to come down and play with it. It wasn't exactly a suit: it was a bipedal battle tank. It had a heavy machine gun on one arm and a missile system on the other, like some really, *really* ostentatious watch. It could have swallowed a Spartan in full armor. Adj and Leaks drifted over to it, bright with excited curiosity.

"Oi, you two!" Mal called. "*No.* Keep your tentacles off it, okay? BB, you better supervise them. I don't want them turning it into a microwave."

"I think it'd make a nice apartment block, though," Vaz said. "Shall I cancel the order for camouflage paint?"

"Now you're taking the piss."

"You wanted it. Now you've got it."

There was no use for the Mantis on Venezia, although it would probably have fetched enough on the black market to let the whole squad retire to a private island in the tropics. The thing was designed to be seen and to intimidate. Vaz and Naomi needed to keep a low profile and somehow blend in. That was going to be a challenge in itself.

Vaz ran his hand over his chin to check that he had the right degree of stubble and gestured five minutes to Devereaux, who was sitting in *Tart-Cart*'s open bay door and swinging her legs.

"Don't worry about Naomi," Mal said, reading his mind. "She'll keep it together. Just settle in, think like the local scumbag community, and don't try to fight a war on your own. We'll relieve you in a week. Just gather intel."

"I'm not worried about her keeping it together for the mission. I'm worried about what it'll do to *her.*"

"Worry about trying to look like a couple of regular sociopaths, okay?" Mal leaned back a little to make a show of inspecting him. "The Russian gangster look. It's very you."

Footsteps clanged in the metal walkway behind them, too light to be Naomi and the wrong pace to be Osman. Vaz didn't look around until Phillips joined them on the rail and gazed down at the Mantis.

"That's not very stealthy," he said quietly. "So where are we going to use *that,* Vaz?"

"No idea. That's Mal's problem. Any news on Jul?"

Phillips shook his head. He looked pretty grim for once. "Not a word. But you know that call I promised to make for him, about his wife? Finally got word back via 'Telcam."

"You *asked* him?"

"No, I'm not that stupid, am I? He'd asked me about Jul when it all kicked off, remember, so I asked him if he'd found him yet. And he said no, but that his wife had been killed when *Cleansing Truth* was shot down."

"Christ," Vaz said. "Bad timing."

"Exactly. So if Jul's alive out there and he's found out, I'd brace for trouble."

"He's just one hinge-head," Mal said. "If he didn't end up ported into some asteroid or something and he's alive, he'd have hooked up with 'Telcam by now if he'd wanted to."

"Yeah, well, I've been through all that with Parangosky, seeing as they think I knew him best. Jul knows where 'Telcam's getting some of his equipment, so my money's on him going it alone like some avenging superhero."

"Jesus." Mal folded his arms on the rail and leaned his head on them. "I hope Parangosky kicked some arses over this."

"Dr. Magnusson has been replaced and has vanished from ONI. As you'd expect."

"Arses encased in concrete, then."

Vaz carried on staring in glum silence, wondering just how bad it might be if Jul showed up on hinge-head chat shows accusing ONI of fueling a civil war. But they didn't have chat shows and he'd probably take some action rather than sit around bitching about it.

Eventually Naomi came down the walkway, and Vaz turned to inspect her civilian rig.

"So?" she asked, hands in her pockets.

She might have passed for a colonial refugee in a very mixed crowd. The slightly threadbare gray parka came to about midthigh length on her and actually made her look a little shorter. With the faded camo pants and frayed rucksack, she didn't look very Spartanish at all, and now she was wearing regular boots there wasn't such a big difference in their heights, perhaps just fifteen centimeters with his thick-soled combats. Maybe she could have dyed her hair, but there was nothing she could do about her posture and gait. She moved like the highly trained special forces soldier that she was. Slouching and scuffing along just wasn't in her toolkit. It wasn't in Vaz's, either. They were deserters, if anybody asked. There were plenty of colonial militia and other armed units that had fallen apart. Vaz was pretty sure there were UNSC deserters, too.

"You'll do," Vaz said. He wondered how old people would think she was. The sun had never had much opportunity to give her any wrinkles, so they might pass as a couple. "How about a cap or something?"

"You think this is a bad idea."

"I think it's a risk. But then neither of us is good at this *going gray* thing. You know, looking inconspicuous."

"We'll have to settle for criminal or thuggish."

"I can do thuggish."

"Okay, I'll do criminal. But the only civilian headgear we've got is bush hats."

"Scarf?" Vaz leaned over the rail. "Dev, have you got any fabric in your box of tricks?"

"What, because I'm a girl?" Devereaux called back. "You think I keep a sewing box?"

"No, but you've always got clean rag and stuff in the tool locker."

"Okay, let me check it out."

BB drifted up from the deck and hung in front of the gantry. "You're going to miss the Mjolnir. And me."

"I'll manage somehow, BB . . ."

Mal rippled his fingers in a little mock wave. "Bye-bye, you two. Be good. No fighting."

Devereaux dug out a fifty-centimeter square of gray polishing cloth and handed it to Naomi. "I bet you won't need this. The place is full of Kig-Yar and Brutes and all kinds, so I don't think you're going to stand out that much now."

"Thanks, Lian."

"Oh, I didn't mean it like that. I meant that in a mixed environment, humans are looking at gross detail, like beaks and claws. The aliens think we all look like big, soft worms anyway."

Naomi nodded. It was hard to tell if she was offended or not. Vaz still found it weird that the ultimate killing machine on two legs was self-conscious, but she was a pretty awkward woman and this wasn't how Spartans usually operated. Vaz wondered if all the Spartan-IIs were like that when they were out of armor.

"You look like a deserter," Vaz said. "I'm more than happy to be seen drinking with you."

She started a weak smile but didn't finish it. "I suppose it's another way to work out who I really am."

"Without BB revving you up."

"He doesn't get out much."

"He's always everywhere. He's been more places than me and Mal have."

She put her fingers on the nape of her neck and fiddled with the dock of her neural implant. "This doesn't show, I hope. I got Leaks to reduce the profile a little."

"No more than mine does. Even some of the militias had them. Not like yours, of course, but nobody's going to look that hard or get that close."

Naomi just crossed her long, deathly white fingers at him. "That's a sad indictment, isn't it?"

Vaz wasn't sure if she was being deadpan or letting a little personal pain leak out. Either way, he was seeing more of the real Naomi these days. He sat back in his seat as *Tart-Cart* maneuvered out of the hangar, and hoped he didn't reek of the ship's jasmine air freshener when he landed.

Spenser was waiting for them at the RV point in the gorge about thirty kilometers from the city. He stood leaning against the driver's door of his old Warthog, having a smoke and just shaking his head. Vaz jumped out of the open hatch and walked over to see him, hands shoved in his pockets.

"Now *that's* impressive," Spenser said. He waved at Devereaux. "I could get you a really good price for that. Is that even the same Pelican?"

"Yes, that's *Tart-Cart* after an Engineer respray. One careless lady owner, full service history." Vaz was now far enough away from *Tart-Cart* to get the full effect of the adaptive camo. He had to admit it was pretty good. The shape of the airframe took some concentration to pick out, and a casual inspection from the air or the nearest road would probably have missed it completely. "We're going to rotate the squad if we're here for an extended period."

Naomi jumped out and started unloading kit. Spenser stubbed out his cigar and put the flattened butt in his pocket. "Is that wise? Naomi, I mean."

"She wants to do this."

"It's not my call, but I'd keep her out of it. For all kinds of reasons."

Naomi walked right up to him with a heavy holdall of equipment tucked under one arm as easily as a purse, and held out her hand for shaking. Spenser took it and craned his neck to look up.

"I'm sorry it's come to this, Naomi," he said. "Have you got everything you need? Sling your bag in the back. You too, Vaz. Let's not hang around."

Naomi slid down in her seat, tied the scarf around her hair with a few wisps of fringe left sticking out, and suddenly didn't look half as strikingly unusual as Vaz had feared. Maybe he'd projected the almost mythological Spartan image onto the reality of a very tall, very fit woman who just happened to be platinum blond as well. Yes, she was a lot more blond than gray. It took some effort to see it.

"So here's your ID, in case you ever have to show it." Spenser had a knack of driving, talking, shuffling paper, and observing everything around him at the same time. He reached around to hand the old-fashioned plastic chips to Vaz and Naomi. "It's easier to stick with your actual first names and just change the surnames. It's not as if anyone can check UNSC records, but you never know who you'll run into. Naomi Bakke and Vasily Desny. Your trades are recorded as comms operator and regular grunt. Before you jumped ship, that is."

"People don't change their names here, then," Naomi said, taking the chip from him and leaning on the back of Vaz's seat. "My father didn't."

She said it casually, as if there was no bizarre history at all. "Depends who they're hiding from," Spenser said. "Off-worlders or the local enforcers. Remember that this isn't anarchy here. They're organized. It's easier to think of Venezia as an alternative society, just not the vegetarian peacenik kind."

As they hit the outskirts of New Tyne, Vaz started seeing pickups, every variant of the Warthog chassis known to man, and quite a few Covenant ground transports. He'd passed the amazement stage on his last visit, short as it was, but Naomi murmured occasionally in quiet surprise.

"Damn, look at all those Brutes," she said. "And Jackals."

It was a small colony like hundreds of others had once been, except it had a huge amount of firepower and a population of miscreants and misfits from at least four species. The city was a regular-looking place with decent buildings and office blocks, and not a scrap of battle damage. Gun batteries sat at some of the intersections. Spenser pointed out landmarks and interesting features like a tour guide.

"And that's the sewerage company over there . . . yeah, the war's pretty much passed them by." Spenser paused for a red light. Vaz wondered if they had proper renegade traffic cops to police their renegade society. There was a kind of mirror-world feel about the whole setup. "It's the previous war that's still gripping their proverbial shit. But you know that well enough."

"Have you got a picture?" Naomi asked.

"Sorry?"

"Have you got a picture of my father? I don't remember what he looked like."

Spenser looked only slightly uncomfortable. "Back at the house," he said. "I'll show you his file. I'll apologize in advance for any unflattering notes I might have made on it."

"It's okay," she said. "No need to spare my feelings. I'm still working out what they are myself."

Spenser's house was one of a row of single-story buildings on an industrial estate across on the other side of New Tyne. He parked the Warthog on the cracked concrete drive and went to pick up Naomi's holdall.

"Whoa," she said. "Leave that to me. It's heavy. Don't show the world just how heavy before I pick it up. . . ."

She heaved it out of the back without any visible effort and took it indoors. Vaz followed her in and slid past her in the central passage that divided the house in half.

"In here," he said. It was a dusty back room with a couple of bunk beds in it. When she put the holdall down, it made a loud thud. "Your room. I'll take the one opposite. Spenser's got an ops center in the basement."

Spenser stuck his head through the doorway. "Bathroom's on the left. Care to come down to my salon and inspect my etchings? Mal said there was coffee."

Vaz unzipped his holdall and took out a can. "Courtesy of CINCONI. Jamaican."

"I could fall in love with Big Maggie if she was forty years younger. Hell, even thirty. Is it poisoned?"

"Possibly. But it's good."

Naomi looked around the basement like a prospective buyer deciding this wasn't quite the place she had in mind. She pulled off her headscarf, wandered around inspecting the comms equipment, and then flopped into one of the scuffed leather armchairs. Spenser loaded the coffee machine and rummaged for a datapad.

"Here." He tapped it a few times, then held it out to her. "Staffan Sentzke."

Vaz felt he should have looked away out of simple courtesy, but he had to watch her reaction for his own peace of mind. She *would* react: emotional bombshells usually caught her for a split second before she fixed her expression into unflinching neutrality. This time, the only sign that something was getting to her was a slight flare of her nostrils as she breathed in slowly. She stared at the datapad and didn't even blink.

Then her eyes moved from side to side, not like speed reading but fast jerks. She was looking at his picture and trying to remember. This was her father maybe more than thirty years older than the one she'd last seen, if she remembered that face at all. Eyes didn't change, though. The skin around them got crêpey and lined, but Vaz knew that she had to see some familiarity in those eyes.

"Okay." Her voice was slightly husky. She cleared her throat. "I do look like him, don't I?" She got up and handed the datapad back to Spenser. "So what's the schedule? We need to get a feel for this place first. Walk around a little and see what it takes to fit in."

Vaz had to let her handle this in her own way. He wasn't going to mention her father again until she did. Spenser seemed to think the subject was off limits for the time being too, because he just reached across to a nearby stain-ringed table and pulled out a small paper map.

"If you want my advice on New Tyne," he said carefully, "I'd do what most of the new arrivals do. There's always a trickle of people going in and out. The first thing they have to do is get some cash, because Venezia isn't exactly connected to the clearing banks. They even have their bank notes. Quaint, isn't it? Like a paramilitary Toytown."

"How do they deal with the really big purchases?" Vaz asked. "You know. Artillery pieces, ships, that kind of thing. That's a lot of cash."

"Barter, from what I can see. Like I said last time, the Kig-Yar are trading arms for ships from the Brutes. It's all rather seventeenth century in its way."

"Okay, so we take a rifle and try to fence it tomorrow," Vaz said.

"Why not today?" Naomi asked.

"Because I want Mike here to talk us through the local gossip, and get myself in character. I'm just an ODST. I'm not really trained for this."

Vaz didn't know if Naomi was trained for it either, but she was exceptionally smart and resourceful. Spartans were survivors. If anything, that seemed to be their defining quality.

"Okay," she said. "That would be useful."

Spenser spent the rest of the day marking bars and shops on the map, the regular places where people did business. By the end of the day, they'd drunk a lot of coffee, eaten a large can of dubious processed meat that had no fibrous texture at all as far as Vaz could tell, and agreed on a plan for Vaz and Naomi to visit the street where most of the arms dealers hung out to try to sell one of the tagged UNSC rifles they'd brought, an MA5B. It was a good way to inject a marker into the system and to begin merging into the naturally wary community. Vaz lay awake that night expecting to hear Naomi pacing the floor of her room, but there was just an occasional snore that could just as easily have been coming from Spenser's bedroom. He didn't get up to check.

The next morning, Spenser handed Vaz a wad of rather

well-printed bank notes—yes, they were real, old colonial credits with a distinctive smell—and a set of keys.

"Don't crash this," Spenser said. "If I have to buy any more vehicles, people are going to start wondering if I'm really just an electrician after all. And don't get pulled over for a traffic violation. I mean it. Stick to the speed limits and stop at the lights. Even the Kig-Yar do."

He opened the dented, rusty garage door to reveal an even more dented, rusty 'hog. The colonies ran on them, just like UNSC did. Vaz tossed the keys up and down on his palm.

"I'm on my best behavior," he said. "I don't want anything going wrong, least of all with Naomi around."

Spenser raised an eyebrow. "Still no sign of Sentzke. I can't believe he picked now to skip town for good, so he's off somewhere having talks or doing business."

"You managed not to say nutter or scumbag."

"Yeah. I know. She doesn't need any more upsets, does she?"

Naomi didn't give the impression of a woman in pain, but she had a job on her mind, and she seemed to be able to shut out anything as long as she had an objective. As Vaz drove off, she leaned back in the passenger seat, arms folded and eyes narrowed against the breeze from the open windshield.

"Who's going to do the talking?" she asked.

"Me." Vaz kept an eye on the speedo and stayed a couple of klicks under the limit. For some reason, he found road speed signs on an insurgent planet incredibly funny. "I've had to sell stuff before. I bet you haven't."

"I'll learn from the master, then. Has she tried to get in touch with you yet?"

"Who, Osman?"

"No, the Old Trollop, as BB calls her. Chrissie."

"No. And I don't even notice now."

"Don't be tempted to take her back."

It was odd to hear Naomi being chatty, but she might have been trying to relax so that they didn't look like two ONI operatives on a job. Vaz took it at face value.

"You sound just like Mal," he said. "She was only unfaithful to me once, though. With the crew of *Implacable*."

Naomi laughed. She did have a sense of humor, just a sporadic one. Vaz tried to stay in character. *I'm a deserter. I'm an ordinary guy, a UNSC deserter who's trying to steer clear of the military police. Christ, what should I call them? Redcaps? MPs? Mal calls them crushers. Reggies.* Vaz was suddenly terrified of blowing his cover with one badly chosen bit of slang. *I'm a deserter, I've walked off with a few rifles, my friend here is a deserter, too. . . .*

By the time they found the dealer's premises, Vaz believed himself. He *was* that deserter, and he felt furtive and hunted. It felt a lot like working for ONI in a very hostile environment. As he took the blanket-wrapped rifle out of the back of the Warthog, he saw a Kig-Yar pass by in a truck and give him a long, beady-eyed look. For a moment, he thought it had recognized him, but then he remembered that he hadn't left any Kig-Yar alive on Reynes to identify him.

He walked into the warehouse with Naomi beside him. He hadn't checked how much hardware she was carrying under her parka, but she'd have at least two sidearms. The place was dimly lit and stank of fuel.

"What do you want?"

A guy in his thirties—wiry, dark haired, clean shaven—sat on a crate with a metal bowl between his feet, soaking machinery parts in some solvent or other. He shook his hands off and wiped them on a rag. Vaz hoped he didn't smoke.

"I've got a rifle I need to sell," Vaz said.

The guy stood up. "Why do you need to sell it? Have you shot someone with it?"

"Yeah, lots. Hinge-heads." *Here we go. Can't back out now.* "I left UNSC in a hurry a while ago and I just happened to take my weapon with me. Now I need some cash. Well, both of us do. We didn't fill in our PVR forms before we left."

The guy looked Naomi up and down. It was impossible to read him. Naomi stared back, dead-eyed and unfazed. Vaz reminded himself that even without the Mjolnir, she was immensely strong and could take a lot more damage than a regular human. Vaz unwrapped the MA5B and held it out for the guy to look at.

"Properly maintained," Vaz said. *And tagged, so we can track the supply chain when we need to.* "Obviously."

The guy's eyes lit up just a little, not so hard to read after all. He took it and tested it with exaggerated clicks.

"Seven hundred," he said.

"Thousand."

"Eight hundred."

"Nine."

"Don't push your luck, Ivan. Eight-fifty."

"Eight-seventy-five."

The guy paused and gave Vaz the evil eye. Vaz had seen a lot worse back home and responded with his best Russian mobster stare. The guy sighed and reached into his back pocket. Naomi drew her pistol.

"Whoa, babe," he said, holding up both hands. He clutched a wad of grubby notes in one. "I'm not the MPs. Eight-seventy-five."

Naomi held the weapon on him for a count of two before shoving it back in her coat. She blinked a lot. If she was trying to act like a jumpy deserter, she was giving a first-class performance. Vaz stood there and counted the notes as carefully as a man who hadn't had a square meal in a while and needed every buck.

"Thanks," he said.

"I'm always in the market for UNSC kit," the guy said. "And small vehicles and vessels up to troop carrier size."

Vaz thought of the hinge-head Spirit that he, Mal, and Manny had hijacked and left on Criterion. Maybe it was still there. "I've got a Spirit stashed away off-world. Just a little short of transport to go get it. One day, maybe."

"Or upsized Magnums," the guy said, looking at Naomi. He seemed to have taken a shine to her sidearm. But he looked and kept looking, and then he frowned. "I swear I recognize you from somewhere. You've got a really familiar face."

"Everyone's got a double," she said.

"No, really." He looked like he had a name on the tip of his tongue, and then his expression changed, because he must have remembered *exactly* who she looked like. This was practically Arms Dealers Row, after all. "Hey, it's okay. Anytime. Some of my best customers are UA."

Vaz shoved the cash in his jacket and walked out as convincingly as he could. Naomi didn't say a word until they got back into the Warthog and were halfway down the road.

"I wasn't prepared for that," she said.

"*You* weren't. . . ."

"This is a small town. Well, a very tight-knit community, anyway."

"Okay, let's park up somewhere and think this through."

Vaz spotted a big, open parking lot and pulled in. It was at the intersection with the main road into town and there were a lot of other vehicles lined up in orderly rows, which didn't make sense until he looked around and saw a hot food stall doing a brisk trade on the opposite side. He watched the traffic rumble through the control lights, trying to work out what to say. It must have been a good fifteen minutes before he spoke. Naomi didn't seem in a hurry. She was just staring at the traffic.

"He has to know your dad," Vaz said at last. "But even if he mentions you to him, your dad's never going to think, oh, that's Naomi, she's not dead after all. Is he?"

"Maybe you were right, and I *am* too conspicuous for this mission."

She stopped abruptly. Vaz felt bad for her yet again, and wondered where the hell this was all going to end. Then he realized she was staring at a truck waiting at the lights, a small delivery van. She reached into her pocket and slid out her datapad, raised it carefully, and recorded. The lights changed to green and the truck moved off.

Naomi looked at the datapad, then held it out to Vaz.

"Who's that?" she asked. "It's him, isn't it?"

Vaz didn't have to enlarge the image much. Staffan Sentzke was a really distinctive guy from any angle. *Oh God. Well, at least he's back. We know where he is.* He was driving the truck, and there was a Kig-Yar sitting next to him, one of the Skirmisher bastards with black, crow-shiny feathers fanning out from its head.

"Better let Spenser know we've spotted him," Vaz said. "Mind if I send this?"

"Go ahead."

That was all she said. It was the first time she'd seen her father in the flesh since she'd been snatched as a six-year-old but she just sat there, calm and silent. Vaz was willing to bet it was a different story inside her head, though. She was in Spartan mode now, and nothing was going to get past that veneer.

The image showed as sent. It'd be with Spenser now. Vaz waited for the response, debating whether to act like the locals and cross the road to get a snack, and almost put his hand on Naomi's shoulder to let her know he understood what a weird, terrible, unsettling day this was for her. But before he had a chance to open the door and get out, his earpiece crackled.

"Vaz, I've got the picture," Spenser said.

"It's him, isn't it?"

"It is."

"Well, that's one less thing to worry about."

"No, it's not." Spenser paused. He always did when he was going to lob a grenade into the conversation. "You don't know the buzzard with him, do you? It's Sav Fel."

The name rang a bell, but Vaz struggled. "Should we worry?"

"Christ Almighty, yes," Spenser said. "That's the bastard who took *Pious Inquisitor.*"

PANOM KEEP, HESDUROS

Things were finally beginning to fall back into place for Jul, albeit in ways he'd never expected.

He didn't have a plan beyond regrouping at Bekan keep, but that was a minor miracle in itself at the moment. He'd beaten the most devious humans at their own sly game, and that gave him hope for the future. He understood them now. He'd learned from them, and the Sangheili wouldn't end up like those Hittites that Phillips had talked about. Understanding the enemy was as powerful a weapon as a plasma cannon.

Now he had to learn to understand these colonial Sangheili well enough to get them to help him. They were untainted by the political intrigues back home. He had hope.

"Kaidon Panom, I have to contact my keep," he said. "My wife will be worried. I was taken prisoner a season ago, and she has no idea what's happened to me. Can you send messages to Sanghelios?"

Panom gestured imperiously to one of the children, who were still milling around to catch a glimpse of the stranger who'd stepped out of the holy relic.

"Ilic, find a communicator that works. Hurry. Bring it to the shipmaster." Panom was walking beside Jul now, in an excellent mood. "We seldom make contact with the old world. We'll gladly fight for the gods, but we prefer our own company. Now . . . to think that you made the holy gate open for you. We've touched it many times, and felt its power, but nobody has ever passed through it. Nobody. This is something of a miracle. An omen."

Prone had been right about the unstable and intermittent connections, then. Jul realized he was lucky to survive the transition. He really could have ended up dead, so perhaps miracles did happen—or the bold made their own miracles by seizing chances. The humans might not have even realized yet that he'd escaped.

Who could he trust now, though? 'Telcam was in the pocket of the humans, whether he realized it or not, part of their convoluted tribal politics. The Arbiter was a plain and unalloyed collaborator. Jul had to create a third force on Sanghelios.

And when I expose the truth about the human strategy to keep us fighting one another, patriots will rally to the cause.

Panom took Jul into the hall of his keep and sat him down at the long, battered table. By now more warriors, females, and youngsters had come to stare at him, this cousin from the old world who knew the names of gods and was allowed to use their sacred portals. Jul felt like a charlatan. But he'd made no claims that weren't true, and he told the greatest truth of all: that the humans were the biggest threat to everything Sangheili held dear.

My only lie is that I don't believe in gods. But that's between me and my mortal soul.

"Here, Shipmaster, my lord." A young lad barely old enough to begin weapons training approached him, bearing an old communicator that was too large for his hands. "This one works. Is it all right?"

"It's perfect," Jul said. "Thank you."

Everything would be fine now. He'd make it that way. He activated the code for his keep, and waited. He didn't expect to be answered immediately, but the length of the delay worried him. Then Naxan responded.

"Who calls us? Who is it?"

"Uncle? Uncle, this is Jul."

Naxan sucked in a breath. "Jul, where have you been? Where *are* you?"

"I was taken prisoner by the humans, but I've escaped. I'm on a colony world now. I'll explain it all to you, but first I must speak with Raia. Find her for me."

The link went quiet, but Naxan was still there. Jul could hear his breathing. "Naxan, I must talk to her." Naxan still didn't speak. Had the link failed? No, that rasping breath was still there. "Can you hear me, Naxan?"

"I have to talk with you, Jul." Naxan sounded hoarse. "This is difficult."

He expected Naxan to remonstrate with him or at least ask him more questions, but there was clearly something wrong. "Naxan, where is Raia?"

"You must be calm, Jul. You must find strength."

"Where is *my wife*?"

Naxan inhaled a long, slow breath. "It pains me to say it, but Raia is dead. So is Forze."

Jul felt his entire body freeze. For a moment, he couldn't even move his jaws. He wasn't even certain that he'd heard correctly. "This is impossible," he managed at last. "I don't believe you."

"It's true. They went to join 'Telcam. Many of his forces were killed when the new human warship intervened to save the Arbiter's worthless carcass. This is hard to say, Jul, but Raia was among them. We have heard talk that even a Kig-Yar tried to save the ship, but failed."

Jul tried to make sense of the words. Raia lived in the keep. She *stayed* in the keep. She didn't leave it, and she didn't go to war. He repeated the words in his head several times before the full meaning began to solidify and sink in his chest, dragging his heart with it into the ground.

"The humans killed her?" he said. "The humans destroyed Raia's ship?"

"It could have been the Arbiter's forces, Jul."

No, it was the humans. Whether they fired the missiles or not, they had fought the Arbiter's battle for him, and it was all their doing, part of their filthy game to set Sangheili against Sangheili.

The humans killed my wife. They tried to kill me. They'll try to kill all of us. But most of all—they killed Raia.

Jul found it hard to breathe, let alone think. "Why?" he asked. "Why did she go with Forze?"

"She was searching for you, Jul."

Those words stabbed him. He really couldn't speak now. He stood there with his head resting on his hand, unable to move. Had he caused this? Had she died because he hadn't been enough of a warrior to resist capture? No, he couldn't blame himself. The humans were the root cause of it all, the source of every ill in his life now.

"Jul, are you still there?"

He couldn't reply. He'd get back in touch with Naxan much later, when he'd hauled himself far enough out of this paralysis to do what he'd always known he had to. It wasn't political now, or philosophical, or even an act of patriotism, although each was a good reason.

It was personal. The humans had killed Raia. He didn't know quite how it had happened, but that didn't matter. They would pay for that, every last one of them.

Jul shut down the communicator and stared at the surface of the table. Panom sat down opposite him and peered into his face.

"What's wrong, Shipmaster?"

Jul could hardly form the words. "My wife is dead," he said.

"She died because the humans came to protect the Arbiter. The humans killed her."

The elder lowered his voice, all calm certainty. "Then you must have your vengeance. Before Sanghelios has its own."

"I shall."

If only there really was an avenging god who could come and erase humanity from the galaxy. Jul would gladly have become a monk if that kind of miracle could be persuaded to happen. *Raia's gone. Raia's dead. What will I do without her?* He felt his hands shaking. The shock wasn't receding but getting worse, and he had to remain calm. If the situation had been reversed, Raia would have been in control of herself and thinking only of the clan, however much she grieved.

She thought I was a fool to follow 'Telcam. She was right. I'm so sorry, Raia.

His sons would be distraught. He couldn't even go to comfort them. He got up and walked to the door, desperate to be alone for a moment or two.

"I must get some air, Kaidon," he said. "Forgive me. I'll be back when my head has cleared."

Jul still had no faith in gods, but Forerunner ruins always seemed to be the best places for private contemplation. It was the habit and indoctrination of childhood, he knew, but that didn't make them any less comforting. He walked back out across the fields and sat down again in the shade of the stone walls where he'd made his undignified entrance from the unstable portal. He leaned back against the blocks, staring at the horizon but not really taking it in. There was a real pain in his chest, no illusion. Grief hurt. It would only get worse, too.

She's gone. It's not fair. She did nothing to deserve it.

It was another reason not to believe in gods. Either they let terrible things happen, or they were so callous that they cared nothing for creatures they created. He refused to worship them.

Now he *wanted* them to exist, though, simply to scream his pain and outrage at them.

It wasn't going to happen. He sat there for a long time, watching the shadows slowly track across the grass, going through an agonizing and unending loop of realizing Raia was gone forever, as if he forgot the terrible news one second and then remembered it afresh the next. He wanted it to stop.

Eventually he found himself looking at the symbols carved into the walls. It was a strange time to find that he was starting to recognize Forerunner symbols a lot more easily. There it was: there was the symbol for the Didact, just like the one on his belt, and there was the symbol for Requiem. He spent a few minutes trying to match the symbols scratched into the leather with the carvings on the stone.

You were right about the humans, Didact. It's a pity you aren't around now to help Sanghelios.

Jul tried to recall what he could of Onyx, the place where the Forerunners had managed to make time pass at the precise pace that they wished, defying creation. He almost wished he'd had more time to work on Prone and tease more information out of him. There were military advantages in Onyx, technology that Sanghelios needed, but the humans had laid claim to it first. No matter: he would find a way to destroy them, or die in the attempt, and both options seemed the same to him at that moment.

He ran his fingertips over the stone, trying to find distraction or focus in the symbols so that he could snap out of this fog of grief and *do* something. Eventually he realized someone was watching him. It was Ilic, the young lad. Jul stared at him. The youngster edged forward.

"The kaidon sent me to see that you were all right," Ilic said.

"I shall be," Jul said. "Thank you."

"Are you praying?"

"I'm looking for answers."

"You can read the language of the gods." Ilic tilted his head, and Jul realized he was fascinated by the belt. "You write it, too. That's the symbol for the holy warrior who'll return one day to save us."

He was pointing at the Didact symbol. "The Didact," Jul said. "Not even the Huragok were allowed to know where he went." Jul was about to point out that he would be long dead now, but this wasn't the time to crush any more hopes. "He despised humanity, as should we all."

Jul took off his belt and laid it across his knees. Ilic sat down beside him and tried to read the other symbols gouged into the leather. They looked like the scrawling of an infant to Jul now. He placed his hand on the symbol for the Didact's name, and tried to think beyond the pain that was gradually setting his chest as hard as mortar.

"Is it true that you came from a shield world, and that those living there have survived since the gods went away?" Ilic asked. "That's a *very* long time."

Jul nodded. "The Forerunners could manipulate the—they are the masters of time." Jul managed to stay in character. His own restraint amazed him. Talking to this child felt like a rehearsal for the conversation he might one day have to have with his own sons. "I saw it with my own eyes."

"And what's this symbol?"

"It's a place. It's called Requiem. But I don't know where it is. Nobody does."

"Why?"

"Because the Didact went there, and for some reason the gods wanted it to be kept hidden."

Ilic considered the symbols for a long time, frowning. He was much younger than Jul had first thought. He was also terribly serious. He'd grow up to be a kaidon, that much was obvious: some children had their destiny written on them from the day they were born.

"Would you like to see the other holy gate?" For a moment, Ilic sounded rather like Prone to Drift, trying to keep Jul's interest piqued during his exile by showing him the sites. "The symbols are there, too. Some are missing, though."

Jul swallowed and concentrated on standing up. If he made his body act, then his mind would follow. It felt like he was turning his back on his grief and not mourning properly, but he could hear Raia now as clearly as he had in life: *Don't submit to things, Jul, change them, take action.*

He got up. It didn't relieve the weight in his chest or ease the misery, but he felt that he was at least doing something. "Show me," he said.

He followed Ilic back toward the keep and through a small thicket. In the middle, a sad and crumbling wall stood alone with the remains of its three brothers scattered around it as rubble.

"There," Ilic said. He tugged at Jul's belt, quite a courageous act for a small child, and pointed up. "Some of it matches your belt."

Jul took a few moments to see what he meant. There was a row of symbols at about eye height—adult height—and they looked familiar. Jul took off the belt and held it up against the wall, aligning the symbols as best he could. He'd simply copied what he'd seen on the wall back in Onyx-Trevelyan to help him find his way back in the maze of tunnels. The scale of the symbols wasn't the same as his handwritten ones, but he could see that it was effectively the same sentence, if a sentence was what it was.

But the wall was damaged. Two of the carved symbols had long since crumbled away. Jul wondered if it was too much to assume that they would have been the same ones as on his belt, three scratched ideograms on the section of leather that held his holster. He looked around to see if the pattern repeated anywhere else, but there was nothing.

"The bits that are missing probably looked like my belt, then," he said. "What's the line below?"

"I think they're numbers. Holy numbers."

Jul didn't believe in divine hands shaping his life, but he did believe in the Forerunner gift for thorough records, and their astonishing technical skill. *Numbers.* What if this was a set of coordinates, like the engraved stone on Onyx?

Jul held the belt against the wall again and slid it from side to side to realign the symbols. Didact: yes, that matched. Requiem: yes, that matched, too. On the line below that, though, none of the symbols looked familiar at all.

New data. Or just my ignorance. But new data . . .

They said the eye could recognize patterns even if the brain didn't understand them, that it could see tiny differences in pictures—symbols—even if they made no sense as words, and recall them. His stomach knotted. This was insane. It was his grief fooling him, making him clutch at stupid, superstitious ideas rather than face the reality of what was happening to him.

"Ilic," Jul said. "Fetch Panom."

Ilic ran off. Jul was left alone with nothing in his mind now but the bad news churning over and over, threatening to drown him. *I'm sorry, Raia. I'm so sorry.* Yes, it *was* insane. At that moment, insanity was all he was, insanity and instinct. *Requiem, Didact, numbers.* Perhaps this was the information the Forerunners wouldn't give the Huragok. It had to be recorded somewhere. And why did the portal bring him here? Had it routed to another Forerunner garrison, one that was off-limits?

No, this was getting ridiculous. Even if this helped him locate Requiem, the Forerunners were long gone.

Their technology might still be there, though. Requiem might contain another cache like the one the humans had claimed.

He almost didn't hear Panom come up behind him. It was only when the kaidon trod on some twigs right next to him that he turned around.

Jul steeled himself to look composed. He held his belt up to the symbols again for the old man's benefit. "Look," he said. "Are these the missing symbols?"

Panom opened his jaws to speak but then he stopped dead. He leaned into the wall, not looking along the horizontal width of the belt but up and down, at what was below it. Ilic studied the symbols, too.

"What is it?" Jul asked. "What do the numbers tell you?"

Panom had the most extraordinary expression on his face. Jul wasn't sure if he was shocked or ecstatic.

"They are coordinates," Panom said. "This adds greatly to our knowledge. We seek to record all the holy sites, but some remain hidden from us."

"And which one is this?" Jul slid the belt back and forth again. "Which world?"

"I'm not sure."

Jul felt possessed by sudden certainty. Part of him knew it was manic behavior brought on by the shock of Raia's death, but he was prepared to grasp at anything now, and even an animal— even a human—could understand things at an unthinking, instinctive level beyond their conscious mind. This compulsion felt exactly like that.

"I think this tells us where Requiem is," Jul said. *"Requiem."* He groped for the right words that would galvanize Panom. Hidden Forerunner technology was now the best hope that Sanghelios had to crush humanity, and Jul was determined to seek it out. He'd need Panom's help to do that. These people were the only ones he could truly trust. "Don't you see it? Requiem. That's where the Didact was hidden. That's where they say he waits."

Panom took a couple of shaky steps backward. "This is why you were sent," he said. "Now I understand."

"What?"

"The gods sent you where you didn't expect to be. They don't make mistakes. They sent you because you had information we need—that Sanghelios needs. You know where the Didact is. Do you not see the answer to prayers in there?"

Is this true, Raia? Where are you now? Are you looking down at me now, knowing what I can't see? Tell me. Tell me what I have to do. I'll do it. I'll do it for you.

Jul didn't dare slap Panom down with cold rationality, not when he himself was talking to a dead woman. All things were possible. He and the Panom keep had common cause now, so their private motivation was irrelevant.

"You believe this, Elder? Truly?"

"You said it yourself. You've come from a world where time was held frozen by the gods for millennia. The Didact awaits us."

"This is the hour of our greatest need, Elder Panom," Jul said. *I have to do this. I have to at least follow the path that's being laid in front of me.* He touched his fingertip to the numerical symbols. "We must find Requiem. This is where I believe it to be."

"This is a long way to travel. We have poor ships."

"Then we'll get better ones. I don't think the gods would let us down now, do you?"

Panom nodded, the speed of the nod increasing as the glorious plan seemed to form in his mind. "Yes, let it be so," he said. "We will seek the Didact, and ask for his help to cleanse the galaxy of humanity. You are blessed, brother. You have a special calling."

Jul hoped the help was planet-crushing weaponry and obedient Huragok caretakers, but if the Didact was really waiting, that would be fine, too.

Raia. Vengeance—mostly for Raia, partly for Sanghelios—would be Jul's food, air, and water from now on.

EPILOGUE

Uncle Naxan says my mother is dead. And I must not cry.

She died as heroically as any warrior. She went into battle armed, seeking Elder Jul 'Mdama, but Naxan can't—or won't—tell me more than that. Perhaps he knows no more, or he fears the truth will either upset me or make me so angry that I lose my reason. Whatever the truth of it, Naxan is now elder of Bekan keep, there will be more civil war, and I must grow up faster now. I must train harder and study more.

My brother Asum has gone off into the fields, probably to cry where nobody can see him. I shall cry, but not until I kill those who killed my mother. It might not be the humans, but I shall kill them anyway because they threaten Sanghelios and support the Arbiter, and I shall kill whichever Sangheili was responsible as well, because species does not make a man a true brother. And when I have done that, I shall carve my mother's story into the saga wall of our keep, as a warrior deserves.

Yes, I can wait to shed my tears. I can wait as long as it takes.

(DURAL 'MDAMA, SON OF RAIA 'MDAMA)

ABOUT THE AUTHOR

No. 1 *New York Times* bestselling novelist, screenwriter, and comics author Karen Traviss has received critical acclaim for her award-nominated Wess'har series, as well as regularly hitting the bestseller lists with her Star Wars, Gears of War, and Halo work. She was also lead writer on the *Gears of War 3* game. A former defense correspondent and television and newspaper journalist, Traviss lives in Wiltshire, England.

Microsoft

AN ANCIENT EVIL AWAKENS

HALO 4

11.06.12

PRE-ORDER AT HALO4.COM
#HALO4 · FACEBOOK.COM/HALO4

RATING PENDING
RP
CONTENT RATED BY
ESRB

May contain content
inappropriate for children.
Visit www.esrb.org for
rating information.

343 INDUSTRIES · Microsoft Studios · XBOX 360

Listen to HALO

Audiobooks available on CD and for digital download:

GHOSTS OF ONYX by Eric Nylund

CONTACT HARVEST by Joseph Staten

THE COLE PROTOCOL by Tobias S. Buckell

EVOLUTIONS by various authors

CRYPTUM by Greg Bear

PRIMORDIUM by Greg Bear

GLASSLANDS by Karen Traviss

Don't miss the next audiobook in the series:

HALO: THE THURSDAY WAR
by Karen Traviss

Available October 2012

Visit www.macmillanaudio.com for audio samples and more!
Follow us on Facebook and Twitter.

macmillan audio

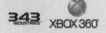

343 INDUSTRIES XBOX 360